"You shou ⊲ in my room."

"I can't very well do this in front of your father." He slid his arms around her, pulling her to his chest, letting his lips claim hers in a soft, tempting kiss. Michaela yielded as soon as he touched her. He tilted her head back and her hair fell from her shoulders to slither down her back.

She wasn't supposed to allow this. Michaela knew she should run or call for help but all she could do was enjoy his embrace, his kiss. Without her corset and big skirts to interfere, Michaela was sure she felt every muscle in his body. She felt strength in his arms, passion in his lips, tenderness in his kiss. A sweet thrill trembled through her. Being close to him like this was so different from being held while wearing so many clothes. It was more desirable, more enticing. It was what she wanted. And it was wrong.

With that realization, she twisted her face away from his lips, although she remained locked in his arms, fitted firmly against his hard maleness. "You shouldn't be in here. I'm not properly dressed." Her voice was husky, undemanding.

"I know."

Samuel was ardently pursuing her, and she loved it!

★

PASSION'S CHOICE

Gloria Dale Skinner

POPULAR LIBRARY

An Imprint of Warner Books, Inc.

A Time Warner Company

POPULAR LIBRARY EDITION

Copyright © 1990 by Gloria Dale Skinner
All rights reserved.

Cover illustration by Don Case

Popular Library books are published by
Warner Books, Inc.
666 Fifth Avenue
New York, N.Y. 10103

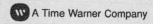 A Time Warner Company

Printed in the United States of America

First Printing: October, 1990

10 9 8 7 6 5 4 3 2 1

In Memory of My Friend
Betty Brennen Fuller

VERMONT
1863

Prologue

MICHAELA dropped the empty pail and ran as fast as her trembling legs would carry her. Her long braid of auburn hair swung from one shoulder to the other, while fear mounted in her chest and spurred her booted feet forward. Early morning sun had not yet warmed the chilly air, and dampness nipped at her flushed cheeks. Her tattered wool coat lost its last button when she stumbled and fell, hitting the earth with a jolting force that left her breathless. With a slight groan she lifted herself and was on the run again, faster.

As she neared the small cave where she had spent the night, she started screaming, "Papa! Papa! Come quickly, Papa!"

When she saw her father crawling out of the small cave's opening, she let the tears held inside tumble from her eyes. She fell into his warm, protective arms. At last, she was safe. Safe from the memory of the past and from the man down by the stream. Her cheek rubbed against a cold button on his waistcoat, and her hands slid around his thick waist.

"Dear, dear child! What's happened? Heavens, you were screaming as if some devil were after you."

Michaela squeezed her eyes shut and pressed her face deeper into the scratchy wool of her father's coat and wept.

Padraic Brennen tried to dislodge his young daughter, but she clung to him desperately. Had she been a bit stronger, she would have squeezed the breath from his lungs. When she wouldn't budge, he realized he was going to have to let her cry for a few moments, so he soothed her with comforting words.

"There, now, Kayla. See? You're safe. Nothing's going to harm you." He held her close with one arm and brushed a loose strand of hair away from her face with the other.

When the sobs subsided, he gently eased her arms from around his waist and lifted her chin. He smiled. The tears had cleaned the dirt from her face, and what a lovely face it was. So like her mother's with a little rosebud mouth, straight nose, and eyes as green as an Irish hillside in spring. He brushed his thumb across her clean cheek, smudging it with residue that clung to his hands from gathering wood for the fire.

"Now tell me what frightened you."

Michaela hiccuped, and her teeth chattered. "There's—a man down by the stream. He—has—blood all over his shirt just like Mama—when she was shot." The memory of her mother lying on the ground with an Englishman's bullet in her chest flashed across her mind.

Padraic drew his daughter to him again. This time he

was the one afraid to let go. While he held still and listened for any sound of approaching danger, his eyes scanned the wooded area for intruders. A gust of cold wind made the fall leaves rustle, but nothing appeared out of place. The pale blue sky was tranquil. There wasn't even the chirp or whistle of a morning bird to be heard.

He had been foolish to send Michaela for water alone while he started a fire. She was fourteen, and she seemed so capable, so reliable, but he should have known better. He wasn't familiar with this area of Vermont at all, and in the last town, he had heard that Confederate soldiers were hiding in the hills. Was there safety anywhere on this earth? Had he taken Michaela away from the fighting in Ireland only to subject her to more of the same in America? A cold shiver shook him when he thought of what could have happened to his beloved daughter.

He had to act fast. Padraic took hold of Michaela's slim shoulders and lightly pushed her away from him. "Listen, child, I have to go down and see this man for myself. He may be alive. And if he is, he needs our help."

"I don't—think so, Papa. He was still and pale." She sniffed and hiccuped again. Her clear emerald eyes sparkled from the wash of tears.

"Even so, I must go."

"No, Papa, please!" She held on to the worn sleeve of his brown coat with a tightly clenched fist.

"You've got to be strong, Michaela," he said, giving her a little shake. "Now listen carefully. I want you to go into the cave and warm yourself. If I don't come back within the hour, you head for the town we were in two days ago. It's about six miles in that direction." He pointed south. "When you get there, go directly to the sheriff's office and tell him what happened. Do *not* come after me. Do you understand? Do not go back to the stream under any circumstances.''

"Yes, Papa."

"Good." He pulled the lapels of her black coat together, looking for a button but finding none. He patted her cheek affectionately. "Don't worry about me. I'll be careful. Now go—off to the cave with you."

Michaela was shaking again when she stopped to enter the cave. Thick smoke stung her eyes and filled her lungs. She was exhausted and ashamed that she had broken down when she had been trying so hard to be mature and helpful. It was warm near the fire, but fear kept her cold. Facing the opening of the cave, she moved closer to the small fire, taking what little comfort it offered. Light from the low-burning flames cast shivering, distorted shadows on the hard walls of stone, and she fought back the terror that turned them into imaginary beings.

She had made a promise to her father that she knew she wouldn't keep. If he didn't come back, she would go looking for him. He was the only family she had. How could she leave this place without knowing what had happened to him?

With a trembling hand, she made the sign of the cross. "Oh, Holy Mary," she murmured, beginning the prayer of safety for her father.

As the fire burned low, a depressing chill settled over her. Time passed so slowly as she waited, listening for sounds from outside. Finally, she could endure her vigil no longer; she had to find out what was happening.

As she crawled toward the opening, the shuffling sound of a horse picking his way carefully over the stone-covered ground reached her ears. Fearfully, Michaela edged backward as the sound came closer. It couldn't be her father coming. He had no horse. Fear as thick as the smoke enveloped her; and when she saw her father's face loom in the doorway of the cave and peer anxiously inside, she went limp with relief.

"Michaela, up quickly!" Padraic's voice was excited, and he pulled on her arm with unintentional roughness. "We have to leave as fast as we possibly can."

"Why? Is someone after you?" she asked in a high-pitched voice. "And what's that you have in your hand?"

Padraic leaned close to the dying embers of the fire to capture what little light it afforded and said, "Look!" He opened the leather pouch he carried so she could see inside. It was filled with gold coins and paper money. Her green eyes rounded in shock.

"Whose is it?"

"For now, it's ours." He closed the pouch quickly, then stuffed a crinkled piece of paper into the pocket of his jacket. "The man was dead, Michaela. When I checked to see if he had anything to identify him, this was all I found. We must leave here now. Whoever shot that man may still be after him." With his booted foot, Padraic shoveled dirt and rock over what was left of the fire, then knelt in front of his daughter. He held her upper arms firmly, his round puffy eyes staring into hers.

"This money is a gift from heaven we can use to restore what the English took from us. I found that man's horse, and we're going to get on him and ride away from here. When I feel it's safe, we'll stop and make plans. I don't guess it would hurt to use some of the money for new clothes and decent food. But enough for now. We must hurry!''

Three days later, Michaela grasped her father's hand tightly as they walked into a bank. They were several towns beyond the one nearest the dead man. The money her father had found was carefully hidden between wads of cotton in the pockets of Michaela's new petticoat. She had spent most of the night cutting and sewing so that all the coins and paper money would fit. In his pocket, Padraic carried two 50 dollar notes he planned to change into small bills for the train fare to Boston.

He had used some of the paper money from the pouch to rent a room in an old boarding house in town. While Michaela bathed and rested, he had gone out and purchased some decent but ill-fitting clothes. There would be time for proper fittings and better clothing once they were out of Vermont.

For Michaela, Padraic had bought a dark-blue-and-white plaid dress that was now covered by a plain wool coat. Her bonnet was the same shade of dark blue and trimmed with white lace. He had put together an undistinguished brown outfit for himself. He didn't want to present a figure people would notice and remember.

"Ah—we arrived at the perfect time," Padraic whispered to Michaela. "Only a couple of people are in line. Remember now, Michaela, don't say anything. I'll get change, and we'll be on our way to Boston and a new life."

"Are we going to keep all the money, Papa?"

"Indeed we are. I told you it was a gift from the saints above. We must use it wisely and prove ourselves worthy of this blessing."

"We don't have much time before the train," she said, anxiously checking the clock that stood in a corner.

"We have more time than we need. Now let's get in line. And don't worry. Just look calm, as though we walk in and out of banks every day."

Michaela moved behind her father as he stepped up to the cashier's counter. No telltale jingling came from the coins snuggled deep in the folds of Michaela's clothing; she had done a good job of arranging them. And her father could rely on her. She would guard the money with her life.

The woman in front of the cashier walked away, and the man in front of Padraic took her place. Michaela watched the beautiful woman with envy. She had on the loveliest bonnet Michaela had ever seen. The color of the sky on a spring day, it was decorated with satin roses and feathers. Someday she would have a bonnet just like that one.

Suddenly the door burst open, and the elegant woman was cruelly pushed to the floor by a man with a kerchief over his face. Michaela's eyes widened with sudden fear.

Two other men rushed in behind him and ran to each side of the room, pointing their guns at the tellers behind the counter. Then two more men stormed in, and one kicked the door shut.

"This is a holdup! Don't anyone move!"

A holdup? Michaela's eyes darted back to the door to see who had spoken. They were going to rob the bank. They had guns! Were these men going to kill her just as her mother had been killed that day in the park? *No!* her mind screamed. Padraic pushed her firmly against the wall and stood in front of her, hiding her with his bulk.

She closed her eyes tightly. If they shot her, she didn't want to see the blood on her dress.

"Everyone keep quiet and stay still. No one will be hurt. We only want the money."

Padraic had successfully blocked Michaela's view of what was going on by pinning her against the wall, then covering her with his arms. Determined to know what was happening, she squeezed and twisted against her father's pressing weight until she managed to turn her face and see the room from beneath his arm.

The bank patron who had stood in front of her just moments before now stood on the other side of the room with the woman who had been pushed to the floor. Two of the robbers had jumped over the counter and were pointing their pistols at the cashier, demanding he open the vault. Another blocked the door; one held his gun on the man and woman Michaela had been watching, while the fifth man pointed his pistol at Michaela and her father. She watched the gunman closely. The red kerchief that covered his mouth fanned in and out with each breath, and his eyes kept blinking.

"Don't let them know you have the money even if they ask for it," she heard her father whisper hoarsely.

Michaela's eyes darted back to the man at the door. His dusty gray hat was pushed low over his eyes, but she knew he was watching her. Was there something about her skirts that looked suspicious to him? If that man guessed she had the money, there would be no safety for her or her father.

The two robbers were out of the vault now with their grain sacks bulging. They shoved the cashier and another man who was behind the counter into the vault before slamming it shut. Michaela's eyes froze. One of the men had started toward her and her father. The kerchief tied around his head covered everything but his squinting blue eyes. Those narrowed, dangerous slits were all she saw clearly. She smelled stale sweat, horse, and tobacco when he stopped in front of them.

"Believe me, sir," her father protested, "I have nothing to donate to your cause."

With the back of the hand that held his gun, the man hit Padraic squarely across the face. Padraic grunted, and Michaela bit her bottom lip to hold in her scream. She had to stay quiet for her father's sake.

"You wouldn't be in a bank if you didn't have money," he yelled into Padraic's trembling face.

Padraic fumbled in his pockets and brought out the two 50-dollar bills he was going to change. "Here." He shoved the money at the man. "This is all we have."

Suddenly the bank robber gathered Padraic's shirt front and stuck his gun under Padraic's chin. Michaela's breath caught in her throat. She was too frightened to scream. Any moment now she feared she would see blood all over her father's shirt. She squeezed her eyes shut again, trying hard to dispel the image of her mother's white blouse stained with blood.

"Be brave. Be strong." Her father's words came back to reassure her. No! She wouldn't let this smelly man kill her father. The money would have to be surrendered.

"Now you don't expect me to believe that, do you? Not with that gold watch chain showing from underneath your waistband." The man pushed the gun, and Padraic's head tilted back farther.

"No, sir, I beg you to let it be. It's not a watch, only a locket with my dear wife's picture in it."

"Sure, and it's gold," the robber said, mocking Padraic's accent.

A cold chill engulfed Michaela. All thought of the money vanished from her mind as she realized the man might take her mother's locket. Never! It was all she had left of her mother except memories, and those were fading.

The man's dirty hand reached for the chain and jerked it out of Padraic's pocket. When she saw the chain slip from Padraic's waistcoat, Michaela squirmed from behind her father and grabbed hold of the chain.

"What do we have here?" The man chuckled menacingly.

Michaela's fearful eyes met his with all the defiance she could muster. Yes, she would fight him for the locket.

"Give it to him, Michaela," Padraic said, taking hold of her wrist.

"No, Papa. It belonged to Mama. I won't give it to him." Michaela was surprised at how strong her voice sounded. She didn't take her eyes off the robber, and her father didn't take his hand off her wrist.

"Let her have it!" someone yelled, and Michaela recognized the voice of the man who had stood by the door and issued the orders.

The robber turned his head and glanced at the man who'd spoken. When he looked back at Michaela, his eyes were gleaming with anger. "You little—"

"Leave her alone, and let's get the hell out of here while the streets are clear."

Although Michaela's eyes were glued on the man who threatened her, she heard the shuffle of feet running and knew the other robbers were leaving the bank. She didn't know what to do. If he pulled the chain hard enough, it would break— and he held the half with the locket. The only picture of her mother that she possessed was tucked safely inside.

The man's eyes glittered as they roamed over her face. "I can't let you keep the locket, honey." With a swift jerk the chain tore through Michaela's hand, cutting into the tender flesh.

"No!" she screamed once before her father's hand covered her mouth and held her against him firmly.

Seconds later she heard shots in the street and angry voices shouting orders. For now she was safe, folded in the protective arms of her father. The money was safe, too, but she'd lost something far more valuable than the gold coins in her petticoats.

Padraic bent toward his daughter and whispered, "It's more important than ever that we be on that train to Boston. We don't want anyone asking us too many questions. Come, let's go while everyone is still excited."

As they passed the man and woman, Michaela heard his excited voice. "Did you hear those Southern accents? Did you see those gray pants? They're the same band of Confederate soldiers who have been robbing banks all over the state."

ATLANTA
1867

One

"WHERE'S Kate?" Padraic Brennen asked as his daughter walked into the bank lobby. "I can't believe she let you out of her sight."

"I fired her." Michaela's deep green eyes shone.

"What? You fired Kate?" Padraic dropped the papers he was holding. "What kind of nonsense . . . ?"

A smile started at the edges of Michaela's lips, moved up to her eyes, and ended in a soft, lilting laugh. "Of course not. I was only teasing you. I'm almost nineteen now. Perfectly capable of walking from the milliner's to your bank without Kate. You've told me this section of Atlanta is very safe. Besides, I don't think chaperons are needed after a girl turns eighteen."

Michaela straightened the ribbons of her dark brown bonnet. The late February wind had almost taken it off her head.

"That's Kate's job, Michaela, and will be until you marry," Padraic reminded her.

"I know, Papa. She's a very nice lady. I'm sorry I teased you."

Padraic smiled indulgently and picked up the scattered papers that lay on the counter in front of him. "So," he asked, "did you have a question for me, or did you come simply to get away from Kate?"

"Simply to get away from Kate for a few moments," she answered honestly.

There were times when she longed for the freedom she had had when they'd first come to America. It hadn't been an easy life. They had had no money, and her father couldn't find steady work because of the war; but during that year she'd learned how to take care of herself and now found it difficult to rely on others. Everything had changed when her father found that bag of money. He'd enrolled her in a boarding school in Boston and come south to make his fortune in banking.

"Papa, do you remember—" Michaela began her campaign for greater freedom, then stopped when a tall, handsome man stepped into the bank. For a moment he stood assessing the room, alert to everything. Michaela's heartbeat quickened. There was something vaguely familiar about the way he stared at her face through slitted eyes.

When he approached them, however, she saw he was a stranger. The skin of her cheeks colored when his dark eyes brushed across her face and down the velvet fabric of her dress. The steel stays in her corset and hoop seemed to be weighing her down so that she could hardly move. Not until his gaze shifted to Padraic did she turn her back on him and join her father behind the counter.

"May I help you?" Padraic asked.

"I'm looking for Padraic Brennen."

"Well, sir, you've found him. What can I do for you?"

"I want to talk about a loan."

Padraic rubbed at his nose before asking, "And who might you be?"

"Samuel Lawrence."

A gasp escaped Michaela's lips. Both Samuel and her father turned quickly to look at her. With a gloved hand, she pulled a small handkerchief from the sleeve of her dress and patted daintily at her mouth. Samuel Lawrence was the owner of Twin Willows. And according to gossip, at least five women wanted to marry him. No wonder she had been so attracted to him. Apparently he had the same effect on other women.

She turned slightly so she could see him again. He was clean-shaven, with a straight nose and a well-defined mouth, just as handsome as the ladies in her embroidery circle had described him. His suit was expensive, but, she noticed, not the latest style. The sunlight filtering through the window briefly reflected the luster of thick light brown hair combed neatly away from his forehead— or was that light shade now considered blond? She wasn't sure, but it was obvious, even under layers of freshly pressed clothes, that his body was in good physical condition. She hid a smile behind her handkerchief. How had she missed seeing this man before?

Trying to cloak her interest in him by picking up some

papers, Michaela edged closer to her father so she could hear what they were saying.

"Ah—yes. I've heard about your Twin Willows. One of the biggest plantations around."

Michaela listened to her father while she watched Samuel's dark eyes. What was it one of the ladies in her sewing circle had said about Twin Willows? "It's the grandest house this side of the Mason-Dixon line, and what's more, the poor man is in danger of losing it."

Samuel's eyes drifted to Michaela and caught her stare. Unconsciously her mouth parted slightly as she inhaled. The color in her cheeks heightened.

"That's my daughter you're looking at. Michaela."

"I'm sorry for staring. You have every reason to be protective. She's lovely."

Michaela's heart raced at his compliment, but she wouldn't let him see that. Outwardly she merely acknowledged his words with a quick nod of her head. His eyes lingered on her face for a moment before he turned his attention back to her father.

"That she is," Padraic said approvingly, expanding his chest. "Let's go into my office where we can talk in private. Michaela, dear, will you watch the front until Mr. Richards returns?"

Michaela looked away from Samuel. "Of course. If anyone comes in, I'll call you."

"Thank you, lass." Padraic patted her arm affectionately as he passed her. "This way, Mr. Lawrence."

Samuel followed Padraic Brennen into the small office and closed the heavy wooden door behind him. A chilling wind from the half-opened window had overpowered the warmth emanating from the fire in the wood stove. As

Padraic lowered the sash, Samuel studied him carefully. For a few moments when he'd first come in, he thought he'd recognized Padraic as someone he had met before, but no name had come to mind, so he'd dismissed the feeling.

"Don't stand, my man. Have a seat, please." Padraic pointed to one of the rosewood chairs while he settled himself behind a large mahogany desk.

"Well now, Mr. Lawrence, you say you're in need of a loan. Why don't you tell me what you have in mind?" Padraic picked up a pen and dipped it in the small jar of ink.

Samuel suspected Padraic had already heard he'd been turned down by every bank in Atlanta and others in outlying towns because he wouldn't put a mortgage on Twin Willows. It was logical that if he had heard about Padraic, then Padraic had heard about him.

Samuel needed a loan if he were going to make the plantation prosperous again. Without it, he would be forced to turn his inheritance to tenant farming or sharecropping as most of the plantation owners had already done.

From several different people, Samuel had heard that Padraic was the man to see only when every other alternative had been exhausted. He had the money, but his interest was high and he never gave extensions. He had foreclosed on more than one home, including the one he presently occupied on Peachtree Street. The only good thing anyone had said about him was that he didn't try to alter the figures. No one had caught him cheating or trying to charge more than his due.

Asking a Yankee for a loan was the last thing Samuel

wanted to do. At first he had tried explaining everything to the men in all the banks he had approached in the last few weeks. More than half a dozen had listened to him, nodded in all the right places, then said no. Well, he was tired of explaining. He needed money, and that was all anyone needed to know—especially some Northerner making money from the South.

Samuel spoke bluntly. "I want to borrow ten thousand dollars, and I want three years to pay it back."

Padraic stared at him for a moment, then laughed. "I'm a clever man, Mr. Lawrence. Don't mistake me for a fool."

"I'm no fool, either, Mr. Brennen. I'll make it worth your wait. I'll give you double the money I've borrowed by the end of three years."

Padraic sighed with an apparent lack of interest. "I'm not concerned about three years down the road, Mr. Lawrence. I don't even know what's going to happen a year from now. No, all my loans are for six months. Take it or leave it."

Samuel moved to the edge of his seat. "I can't pay you back in six months. I need time to plant, harvest, and replant. I need time to rebuild the mill and make it productive." He paused. Padraic was his last shot. If he didn't strike a deal with this man, he would have to mortgage Twin Willows. What could he offer that would make Padraic reconsider?

"I'll triple your return, Mr. Brennen. In three years I'll pay you thirty thousand dollars." Samuel knew the risk if Padraic took his offer. But at this point his options were running out.

That kind of money sounded enticing to Padraic, but

he didn't want to wait three years to get it. He could get far more than that for the plantation if Lawrence defaulted on the loan. And in only six months, too. In fact, he knew of a man in New York who was looking for a big place like the Lawrence planation. It was time to be firm and stop playing around.

"Let me tell you what I'll do, Mr. Lawrence." Padraic laid the pen down and pushed back his chair. "I'll give you three thousand at twenty-five percent for six months."

"That's not enough, and I need longer to pay it back. I need at least a year to build Twin Willows back up again."

"I'm sorry. That's the best I can do."

Samuel rose from his chair. "Then I'll have to go elsewhere."

"Where else is there to go?"

Padraic's words stung. He was right, but Samuel wasn't ready to admit it.

"We've already agreed we're not fools, so why act like one?" Padraic's eyes glistened. "My dear sir, I'm not a planter, but even I know that next month is planting time. Your harvest will be in by late summer. That's six months from now. That's when I would have to be paid."

Samuel felt every one of his twenty-eight years. "If I agreed to your terms, I'd have to borrow from you again next spring and the next. I need time to put Twin Willows back together again. I can't do that under your terms."

"Of course, I can't force you to take my money." Padraic stood. "Are you sure you won't change your mind?"

Samuel studied the man. Brennen wanted his land just as a lot of other banks did. But it wasn't planting season yet. He still had a few weeks. "Thanks for your time," was his only answer.

With a tug at his tight shirt collar, Samuel opened the door of the office and walked out. Anxiously, he mulled over his situation again. The taxes were paid on the land, and right now he had enough money to put food on the table for his mother and sister. But where was he going to get the money for seed or wages for workers? And if he couldn't get cotton or corn in the ground by the end of March, there wouldn't be money for next year.

Samuel glanced at Padraic's daughter as he walked by. What had he said her name was—Michaela? An unusual name, but it suited her. She was busy talking to a man—a Yankee, who, no doubt, was putting his money into Padraic's bulging bank.

When he reached the door, Samuel turned around to look at Michaela once more and found her staring at him. Their eyes met; he felt his blood stir and warmth rush up his neck. Damn, she looked good to him, but it was futile to be attracted to her. No Southern gentleman with any pride left should look twice at a Yankee woman. Still, she was so lovely. Her eyes were as green as late summer's grass, and her skin looked soft as goose down. The light pink shades of his mother's azaleas were nothing to compare to the soft pink in her cheeks. A brown hat covered most of her hair, but he saw enough to know it had a touch of auburn. Embarrassed that she had caught him staring, Samuel nodded and walked out.

From the doorway of his office, Padraic watched the prolonged glances between Michaela and the plantation owner. He then looked at the man Michaela was talking to, and a plan started forming in his mind.

"So you see, my sweet Michaela, all we have to do is enlighten the South, replace baneful anachronisms, and enforce freedom for everyone," Cabot Peabody declared.

Michaela looked into the man's pale blue eyes. He wasn't more than a couple of inches taller than she. He didn't overpower her as her father did. Until today she had thought Cabot the handsomest man she'd ever seen, but that was before she'd met Samuel Lawrence. She now knew why the ladies made such a fuss over him. It was surprising that none of them had staked a claim on him by now.

"Do you agree?" Cabot asked.

"To what?" Michaela responded. "Oh, yes . . ." She recalled his pronouncement with difficulty, "That's a very noble attitude, I'm sure."

Michaela had met Cabot a few months earlier when her father had invited him to dinner. Cabot wanted Padraic to contribute to his campaign for the United States Senate in the next election. As far as Michaela knew, Padraic had not given any money to the Republican's cause, but he had succeeded in establishing a relationship between Cabot and his daughter, which Michaela assumed was her father's primary reason for inviting the man to dinner in the first place.

Cabot's thin lips widened into a smile. "Ah—my sweet, you do know how to make a man feel understood." He reached out and took her hand. "I'm told that I would have a much better chance at the Senate seat if I were a married man."

Michaela wasn't surprised to hear Cabot mention marriage. He had kissed her good night a few times, and gentlemen didn't usually kiss a woman they weren't planning on marrying. Somehow, the idea didn't excite her very much.

Cabot came from a good family, which was something her father would insist upon for any man she chose. He was nice, intelligent, and eligible, yet she didn't tingle all over at the idea of being his wife.

"Have you ever thought about getting married, Michaela?" Cabot's voice was soft, and his hand squeezed hers possessively. He looked into her eyes while he waited for an answer.

"Well, yes, the possibility has crossed my mind."

She supposed, if she were going to marry, it should be to someone like Cabot. Unless she could meet someone who made her feel warm and desirable, who could make her feel special even if she was the only woman in the room. Someone who looked at her the way Samuel Lawrence had.

"Good." Cabot smiled. "May I take you and your father to dinner at the Mayflower Hotel tomorrow night so we can discuss the matter?"

"I have a better idea. Why don't you come to our house for dinner. We have a new cook, and I know you'd enjoy her peach cobbler."

"That's a splendid idea. What time should I come?" His eyes danced with excitement.

"Seven o'clock will be fine."

"I can hardly wait." He carried her hand to his lips and kissed it.

From the doorway of his office where he had been watching, catching a word now and then, Padraic cleared his throat with a hearty sound.

Michaela saw disapproval written on her father's face

and withdrew her hand. "I think Papa wants to speak with me. I'll see you tomorrow night."

Cabot said his good-byes to her father and left.

"Fancy your meeting Cabot in here," Padraic said when Cabot had closed the door. His tone held a mild accusation.

Michaela lifted her chin and said, "Papa, our meeting was purely accidental. He was walking by and happened to look in the window and see me."

"And hastened to take advantage of your being alone."

The light that crept into her father's eyes let her know he wasn't really angry. "Correct." She laughed and hugged him briefly, her arms barely reaching around him. "Oh, Papa why are we bound by so many rules? Now that I'm out of that stuffy old boarding school, can't I have a little more freedom?"

Padraic shrugged as he walked over to the front door and lifted his wool coat from the brass-tipped clothes rack. "Only as much as society considers proper."

How true. And how boring! Michaela pushed her lace handkerchief back into her sleeve with a sigh. "You needn't worry about my being alone with Cabot. He's a very nice man, Papa, and he has good ideas for helping both the Negro people and the white. He wants all of us to live in peace. He wants to stamp out ignorance, intolerance, economic inefficiency, and violence and replace it with freedom and prosperity for everyone."

Padraic patted his daughter's cheek with an indulgent hand. "There's nothing so inspiring as a politician's ramblings. You're beginning to sound like him."

"That's because what he says is worth quoting, Papa, and you know it," she declared with a hint of defiance.

"Listen, Kayla. I'll talk with you about Cabot later. Right now I've got to run out for a few minutes. There's an errand I must attend to immediately, and that fool Mr. Richards still hasn't returned from lunch. I'm not happy with the liberties that man takes. I'll have to have a word with him. Would you stay until he returns?"

Michaela's eyes flashed to her father's round face. He was going to leave her alone in the bank. She was immediately fuzzy with fear. "I don't think you should leave me here by myself." Her voice was husky, and her lashes blinked quickly.

"Certainly you can handle it, Michaela. You know, you sound as if you're afraid."

She was. Nothing frightened her more than the thought of being alone in the bank. In the first year they were in America, Michaela had found herself confident and undaunted in many places that would raise fear in the breast of more faint-hearted women, but being in the bank alone summoned up the terror she had felt when the men with kerchiefs over their faces had threatened her with guns.

"I'm not afraid, Papa," Michaela lied. She didn't want Padraic to know how the bank robbery haunted her. "It's just that I wouldn't know what to do if anyone came in. Besides, Kate is expecting me to join her at the milliner's."

Her father chuckled. "If you don't join Kate right on time, I have no doubt she'll come looking for you. Should anyone come in, ask him to wait for Mr. Richards to return. If he doesn't soon, he'll be fired. Though how I'd replace him I don't know. I've yet to find a competent man in this town." Padraic took out his pocket watch and looked at the time. "I'll see you at dinner," he called back to her as he walked out the door.

Samuel stood at the far end of the bar and stared at the amber liquid in the shot glass. He had downed the first drink too quickly. His throat and eyes still burned from the eighty-proof whiskey. One thing could be said about O'Brian: He didn't water down his good stuff. Samuel leaned heavily on the bar. It had been months since he'd had a strong drink, and it had gone straight to his head.

What was he going to do? Padraic Brennen had been his last hope of getting money from a bank without a mortgage. Now he had three options: take Padraic's offer, do as the rest of the plantation owners had and go into tenant farming, or marry Corrine Johnson.

Corrine was a young widow who owned Merrywood, a plantation fifteen miles south of Twin Willows. She had made it quite clear to Samuel the last time they'd met that she needed a man to take care of her land. What Corrine didn't realize was that if Samuel married her, he intended to sell her land and use the money to rebuild Twin Willows. Right now that idea seemed mighty tempting, but nothing about Corrine appealed to him. Her eyes and hair were the same shade of dull, lifeless brown, and her cheeks and lips never had a hint of color to them. And although she wasn't exactly fat, there was a little more of her than he wanted.

Samuel stared at his reflection in the dulled mirror above the bar and remembered Michaela Brennen. She must be the most beautiful creature God had put on this earth. Those green eyes of hers sparkled like no others he had ever seen. Everything about her was beautiful. She'd moved with a quiet grace he found very appealing. Thinking of her made him feel warm, and he wiped at his forehead with a stiff white cuff.

He took a deep breath and emptied the shot glass. This time it didn't burn. Why couldn't Corrine Johnson look like Michaela? Why couldn't Corrine make him feel as Michaela did? It wasn't right, what he felt for a Yankee woman, but his body didn't care.

Samuel grimaced as the bartender poured another ounce of whiskey into the glass. He had to get Michaela off his mind and find an answer to his problem. A thought that he had suppressed a long time came suddenly to the fore. He knew damn well where he could get the money. A cold sweat chilled him as he recalled with distaste the last job he had pulled with the Confederate rough riders.

In the beginning there had been seven of them, the South's best, hand-picked by President Davis to slip through enemy lines and bring back money to help the Confederacy. Samuel was told he had been chosen because he was the best shot of all Atlanta's gentry. A lot of good that did. He had never killed a man the whole time he was with the gang, and he sure wasn't proud of the ones he'd killed when he was made colonel and put in charge of his own battalion. The scarlet battalion!

After the rough riders had robbed three banks, two of the men were given the money they had stolen and sent back to the Confederate Capitol in Montgomery, Alabama. Samuel never heard whether or not they'd made it.

The remaining five robbed two more banks before they were chased into the hills by a band of Union soldiers. After a day of hard riding along the Canadian border, when it was clear they couldn't shake the soldiers, they decided to bury the money and split up in five different directions. Samuel was the one elected to draw a map so they would know where to find the money at a later date. The map was torn in half and given to the two ranking officers. As far as Samuel knew, no one had ever gone back after the money.

Samuel rubbed his chin. He had a pretty good memory, and since he was the one who had drawn the map, there was a good chance he could find the gold. There must have been over fifty thousand dollars in those bags. Now that the Confederacy had been wiped out, he sure as hell wasn't going to give the money back to the Union. Why not use it to restore Twin Willows?

Samuel finished off the last of the whiskey, and the bartender was right there to fill it again. This time Samuel covered the glass with his hand. If he drank any more, he'd have to spend the night at Belle's place, and Belle didn't like a man to stay the night if he wasn't going to spend a little money on one of her girls. Samuel sure wasn't in the mood for a woman tonight. Unless she was Michaela Brennen.

He pushed back from the bar, stood straight, and stretched his arms over his head. It seemed he couldn't hold even a little liquor without feeling the effects. During the war he could down five or six shots before his head felt fuzzy. But he'd been a struggling colonel at the time, and he'd drunk a lot more often then. He'd had to in order to survive. Damn, what a stupid way to settle differences, going to war and leaving scores of dead men scattered across burned-out fields!

Thank God the war was over, and he could return to the life of a Southern gentleman. A man of principle and honor. From infancy he had been taught to be tolerant, hospitable, and courteous. How quickly war had made him forget those things.

Because of his scruples, he knew he couldn't justify going after that money in order to save Twin Willows. He couldn't marry Corrine Johnson, either. Corrine would have to find someone else, and the gold would have to stay buried. The money didn't belong to him, the Confederacy, or the Union. It belonged to all those faceless men and women the rough riders had robbed.

"Let me buy you a drink, my man."

At the sound of the man's voice, Samuel glanced up into the hazy mirror and saw Padraic Brennen. Samuel turned slowly until he looked straight into round, green eyes. The two men were equal in height, but Padraic's frame was fuller, thicker. Samuel would just as soon tangle with a bear as this man.

"No, I've had enough."

Padraic motioned for the bartender to fill it anyway, and when Samuel gave him a questioning look, Padraic said, "I think you're going to need it when you hear what I have to say."

Two

S AMUEL shifted uncomfortably. He was interested, but it wouldn't do to let Padraic know he had been hoping for a second chance. Maybe now Padraic was ready to strike a deal. This was more like the man he had heard about.

"What have you got to say that will make me pick up that drink?" Samuel kept his eyes hard and his hands steady on the bar so he wouldn't give away his relief at Padraic's approach.

"I want you to marry my daughter."

"What the devil?" Samuel's dark eyes narrowed, and his brows crinkled together. What kind of man said a thing like that?

"Maybe now you'll have that drink." Padraic motioned to the shot glass.

Maybe not. Samuel's head was already fuzzy enough.

This man wanted to talk serious business, and he needed all his wits about him.

The bar was getting crowded as the end of a workday drew more people to the saloon and when Padraic was jostled by a whiskery old man who'd lost all of his teeth, he took Samuel by the arm. "Let's go over to that table for a bit of privacy." He nodded in the direction of an empty card table in the far corner of the square room.

Squinting, Samuel studied the man standing before him. The lamps had been turned all the way up as dusk gathered and he had no difficulty seeing Padraic. He had green eyes like Michaela, but they weren't clear and innocent like hers. Samuel didn't know what Padraic was up to, but he sure had piqued his interest. It wasn't every day a man walked up to you and told you he wanted you to marry his daughter. Especially one as lovely as Michaela. She must have had at least a dozen marriage proposals by now.

Leaving the whiskey where it sat, Samuel followed Padraic to the table. When they were seated, Padraic began immediately.

"I'll try to be as brief as possible. Details would only cloud the real issue anyway. I have something you want: money. And you, Mr. Lawrence, have something I want: a respectable name for my daughter."

That said a lot, but not enough. "Isn't Brennen a respectable name?" Samuel wanted to make sure he wasn't misreading the older man.

Padraic smiled, his cheeks rounding jovially. "In some places. That's not my concern. It's the name she might take in marriage that has me worried." He downed his drink in one gulp, then continued. "You see, Mr. Lawrence, except for the few pleasures I afford myself from time to time'' —he paused to clear his throat—''I live only to see my daughter happy. There have been times in the past when she's had to . . . Well, if I go into that, I'm getting into the details I wish to avoid.''

''How is marrying me going to make your daughter happy?''

Samuel leaned back, keeping only the two back legs of the chair on the floor. He faced the dingy wall with peeling paint. A poster depicting a carnival that had come to town last fall still hung on the wall above his left shoulder.

''In the long run, you'll have more to offer her. Right now, I have reason to believe she fancies herself in love with a man who rode into town last year with nothing more to recommend him than a string of fancy words. I don't want to see my daughter marry a man more interested in what he can do to redeem the South than what he can do for her. On the other hand, I don't particularly want her to marry a man like you, either.''

Samuel's eyebrows shot up, but Padraic apologized gracefully with a wave of his hand and continued. ''I only meant to imply that a father will never think any man is good enough for his only daughter.'' He sipped his drink, then wiped his mouth with a large white handkerchief.

''What you're saying is that you think I'm the lesser of two evils,'' Samuel commented dryly.

''That's an unpleasant way to put it and not totally accurate,'' Padraic replied. ''I know very little about the family of this other man aside from what he tells me, but your family has been in this area many years. Your name is well respected among the people of Atlanta. I've no doubt that with your integrity and the land holdings of Twin Willows to back you, you'll find a way to restore your wealth. You can give Michaela a name and a home she can be proud of. I'm afraid the only thing the other man will give her is empty platitudes concerning social reform and unkept promises. If I had wanted that kind of life for my daughter, I'd have stayed in Ireland."

Samuel wiped his mouth with his hand. "Who is the other man?"

"Cabot Peabody."

Yes, Samuel recognized the name, although he didn't know him personally. Samuel stayed as far away from politics as he could get, but like everyone else, he'd heard talk. Peabody was a relatively young upstart who was trying to force an unrepentant South to its knees.

Padraic placed both hands on the table and leaned closer to Samuel. "What I want to offer is the money you asked for in exchange for your courting my daughter with the intention of marrying her."

His voice was a whisper, but Samuel heard every word. It seemed odd to get such an offer just when he had been thinking about marrying Corrine in order to get his hands on some money and had decided he was too much of a gentleman for that. Well, maybe this was different. Michaela was certainly desirable. And her father was obviously sanctioning this liaison.

"She's a Yankee," he said aloud as the thought struck him with more force than expected.

Padraic blinked rapidly; his eyes bulged with indignation. "I beg your pardon, sir. Michaela is Irish. We had loyalty to no one save ourselves in the war."

Samuel digested that bit of information. He had recognized the brogue in Padraic's speech, but that didn't mean anything. Lots of Yankees had come from Ireland originally; however, that put his proposal in a different light. Except for the fact that Padraic was still, in a way, trying to sell his daughter's hand in marriage.

"What makes you think I can change her mind if she's in love with someone else?" Samuel questioned.

"I don't know that you can, but to me it's worth a few thousand dollars for you to try. Neither of us can force Michaela to marry against her will. She's much too determined and independent for that."

Samuel rocked the chair on its two back legs. "Let me get this straight. You'll lend me the money I need for Twin Willows if I'll court Michaela? Whether we marry or not?"

"No." Padraic shook his head. "I'll give you the money."

"Wouldn't that be taking a big chance? What would prevent me from taking the money and never seeing Michaela again?"

Padraic smiled knowingly. "A noble Southern gentleman like you? I don't think I need worry."

Samuel was beginning to have a certain respect for this man. "If I'm so noble, why would I even consider your offer?"

"Because you want to protect your home. And I saw the way you looked at Michaela. Don't make a decision right now. Come to dinner tomorrow evening. Spend some time with Michaela, then decide whether or not you're interested."

Samuel rubbed his chafed neck. His mother had used too much starch on his collar. It was wrong that his mother, so gently reared, must be doing her own ironing. He needed that money for her as well as himself. "Have you made this offer to anyone else?"

"Indeed I have not!" Padraic said righteously. "I've only this day been made aware that Michaela might have an interest in Cabot Peabody. By St. Brigid, do you think I'd put a proposition of this sort to others? I thought this through clearly before I approached you." He pointed a warning finger at Samuel. "And should Michaela ever get wind of this, she'll never speak to either of us again."

Samuel considered his offer. He did want to see Michaela again. "I'll come to dinner, but I'm not making any promises."

"Excellent. Now why don't we have a drink." Padraic motioned for the bartender.

"You go ahead. I've got a long ride ahead of me." Samuel pushed back his chair and stood, holding out his hand.

Padraic took it and smiled. "Until tomorrow at seven."

Michaela sat on a high-back rocker in front of the fireplace waiting for her father to come home for dinner. Flames leaped from the burning wood, hissing and crackling, sometimes popping sparks onto the Oriental rug. Light from the fire cast her shadow on the wall. Although she held embroidery hoops in her lap, her hands had been still for some time.

At last, with a sigh, she laid the work aside and stood, trying to rub her aching back through stiff stays. The fire wasn't low, but she added another log to the irons and stared thoughtfully at the glowing red embers.

Now that she was home and safe, she was glad her father had left her alone in the bank today. She'd handled that dreadful fear of being robbed without letting anyone know, and she was pleased with herself.

In time, she was sure those turbulent feelings would go away. Since accepting and dealing with the anxiety of losing her mother, she had ably coped with every fear that presented itself, but this one had persisted.

Michaela closed her eyes briefly, and Samuel Lawrence leapt into her mind. He was a proud-looking man—by all appearances accustomed to exerting control. His hair was a shade or two darker than cornsilk just before the corn was ripe. His eyes had a nice shape, too, and were like the color of bark on a pine tree, brown with a little gray mixed in.

Just thinking about him sent a rush of heat up her cheeks. She'd liked the easy way he'd looked at her. Rather than leering at her as some men did, he seemed to, well, appreciate her. Cabot always said she was beautiful, but he didn't send a message right to her heart as Samuel had.

There was something else about the man that intrigued her. Maybe it was that gentle tone in his voice. What little she had heard had been nice. Soothing. Perhaps it was his courage. It couldn't have been easy for the owner of Twin Willows to ask her father for a loan. Many Southerners believed her father was a Yankee and in with the Republican party, although that couldn't be farther from the truth. Padraic had never taken sides with any particular group for fear of losing his station in life again. And he'd rather have an arm cut off than donate a single dollar to their cause.

"Michaela, I'm home," she heard her father call from the front of the house. She smiled when the door shut with its usual resounding bang. Padraic never took the time to close it properly, preferring to give it a shove with his foot.

"What took you so long?" she asked, half scolding

him as she walked into the hallway and kissed his cool, ruddy check.

"Can't a man stop for a drink without his daughter checking on him?" He pouted a little, like a small boy. Her heart went out to him. For all his gruffness, he could be so sweet, and she loved him very much.

"I'm not checking on you, Papa." She helped pull his wool coat over his shoulders and off his arms. "But Kate had to ask the new cook to hold dinner for almost an hour."

"Heaven's sake! Since when do I have to answer to Kate for my coming and going? A greater nuisance of a woman I've never met." His hands flew into the air in impatience. "There was a time when I was master of my own house. Now it seems I'm at the mercy of a scullery maid."

"Papa, keep your voice down. She'll hear you," Michaela admonished him. Even though he sometimes said dreadful things about Kate, Michaela was sure he had fond feelings for the gentle woman. No one could dislike Kate. Michaela had to hide her smile, though. The thought of the elegant Kate being called a scullery maid was incongruous.

"Go tell the cook to put supper on the table. I'll wash and be right in. By the saints in heaven, I'll never understand why I put up with women," he muttered to himself.

Michaela decided it was best to change the subject. "Papa, I asked Cabot to join us for dinner tomorrow night. I hope it's all right?"

Padraic grunted. "You'd do well to ask me before you make so many plans. It just so happens that I've invited someone else to dinner as well."

"Oh, that shouldn't be a problem," she hastened to say. "Whom did you invite?"

"Mr. Samuel Lawrence."

"Papa, no!" she cried. "We can't have the two of them here together. You know how strong Cabot's political views are. And Mr. Lawrence is probably a Democrat since he's a Southerner."

Padraic lifted his thick eyebrows, and for a brief moment Michaela thought she saw a hint of deviltry in his eyes. It wasn't like her father to enjoy someone's discomfort.

"Then you'll have to speak to Cabot," he said. "I don't intend to ride out to Twin Willows tomorrow and withdraw my invitation."

"Oh, Papa, I can't disinvite Cabot. What are we going to do now?"

"I suggest you ask Kate to help you with this one. That's what I hired her for. She will know how to handle this." Padraic patted Michaela's cheek and strode into the dimly lit hallway.

Michaela turned swiftly and headed for the stairs. Lifting her heavy skirts, she raced up the steps as quickly as she could. As she made it to the top, Kate was just coming out of her bedroom.

"Did I hear Mr. Brennen come home, Michaela?" she asked in her unhurried voice.

"Yes, Kate, and I'm afraid we have a problem." Michaela stopped in front of the small woman dressed in dark blue velvet that made her appear taller than she actually was.

"I invited Cabot for dinner tomorrow night, and Papa invited Mr. Samuel Lawrence, the owner of Twin Willows. They'll never get along. What are we going to do?"

Kate pondered the question for a moment before saying,

"We're going to make the evening a pleasant one for both our guests."

"How? They'll hate each other."

Michaela clutched at the folds of her skirts in frustration. It seemed she was the only one upset about this, the only one who saw how awkward the dinner might be.

"That's not our problem, Michaela. Come now. Take that stricken look off your face." Kate touched her shoulder tenderly, and they started down the stairs. "Cabot is a nice man. He wouldn't be rude in your father's house, and as for Mr. Lawrence, I've never met him, but I've heard of him and know he's a gentleman."

Michaela sighed heavily. She supposed Kate was right. They'd all have to make the best of the situation. Still, she would have enjoyed an evening alone with Samuel Lawrence.

A knock at the door disturbed Samuel's sleep. He tried to ignore the light but persistent noise. It must be Henry with his morning wash water, and he wasn't ready to get up. The ride to Twin Willows had been long, cold, and dark. Because of a late afternoon thunderstorm, the moon had been covered by clouds, making it difficult to travel with any speed. He covered his head with the pillow and groaned.

"Are you awake, Sam?" his sister, Davia, called from behind the oak door.

Samuel threw his pillow to the foot of the bed and pulled the covers over his naked chest as he sat up. "I am now, Muffin, come on in."

Samuel smiled at her as she entered the room with a bounce. She wasn't tall for thirteen, but she was going to be a beauty someday. Her honey-colored hair and big brown eyes would turn men's heads soon.

Davia Lawrence giggled and pointed a slender finger at her brother. "Your hair looks as if rats had slept in it."

Flashing his sister a teasing smile, he answered, "I'm sure that long mane of yours looks the same way each morning, so who are you to talk? Besides, I had a rough night." He patted the bed.

Davia jumped up on the quilt, her faded blue dress a contrast to the dark colors in the rose of Sharon pattern. "What time did you get home last night?"

"Actually, it was the wee hours of this morning. Not that it's any of your business, Miss Muffin," he teased. Samuel brushed at his wayward hair with his hand.

"Will you take me riding today?"

Samuel leaned against the spooled headboard as he considered his sister's request. The wood was cold to his bare back. He knew his mother wouldn't let Davia ride alone.

"Of course, but for an hour only. Then I have to dress to go back into town."

"Why?"

"Inquisitive little thing, aren't you?" He reached out and playfully rubbed the top of her head.

Since he'd come home, Davia was always anxious about where he was going and what time he was returning. He guessed it was because she missed their father. Davia had been spoiled by David Lawrence. When Samuel was born, the doctor had told David and Evelyn, his wife, that she wouldn't have any more children, and for fifteen years she hadn't.

Then came Davia as a welcome surprise, and David had pampered his little girl by allowing her to do things with him that most men wouldn't dream of permitting their daughters to do. On the other hand, Evelyn had tried to raise Davia in the tradition of a true Southern belle. But from the beginning, David's namesake was more comfortable being a tomboy. Now Davia expected Samuel to pick up where her father had left off.

"What's Mama doing?" he asked. He wasn't ready to tell Evelyn that he still didn't have the money for seed corn. Losing her husband and way of life had been difficult for her. She looked at Samuel to bring back a part of the life she used to know, and he couldn't bear the thought of letting her down.

"She's starching your shirts. She says you'll never get a loan if you're not properly dressed," Davia said, imitating her mother's tone of voice.

Samuel rubbed his neck; it was still sore from yesterday's shirt, and he could almost feel the stiffness of the collar she was readying for him today. Henry used to take care of the laundry, until the family found out he could cook better than Evelyn. Samuel smiled to himself. His mother tried hard, but she didn't know very much about cooking, or washing and ironing.

Even though David Lawrence had freed most of his slaves before the first shot was fired, Henry was the only Negro who had stayed around after the war started.

"What time is it?" Samuel asked.

"Almost noon."

"I don't have much time, Muffin. You run along downstairs and tell Henry to put water on to boil while I stoke the fire. It's cold as Christmas in here."

Davia smiled and jumped off the four-poster bed. "I told him to put it on before I came up. I'm sure it's ready now."

"Then get going, and send him up."

When Davia had closed the door, Samuel swung his feet off the bed and hit the cold wood floor. Damn. The room was like ice. He threw his flannel robe over his nude body and went to light the fire.

Then he stood with his back to the warmth and looked around the room. Twin Willows didn't even have decent rugs on the floors anymore. The hand-flocked wallpaper was smoked and peeling. His eyes drifted over to the walnut highboy. It needed polishing. The yellow silk had faded and worn thin on the armchair, and the cotton stuffing showed through.

It wasn't just his room that had been neglected since the war. The whole house had deteriorated. Rebuilding and refurnishing was going to take a lot of time and money, and right now time was the only thing he had.

He thought about Padraic Brennen's offer. Marry Michaela? Uncertainty twisted inside him. She was beautiful, but what kind of wife would she be? Her lips were tempting, but would they kiss him with passion?

He did need to marry soon. He was twenty-eight. He would have been married by now if that blasted war hadn't taken five years out of his life.

Michaela dressed with care that evening, wearing a gown she had been saving for a special occasion. It was made of green silk as delicate as spring needles on a Georgia pine. As soon as the hoop and petticoats were in place and the dress buttoned, she sent her maid away, wanting to finish her toilette alone.

When she had first tried on the dress, she'd thought it was too low cut, but the seamstress insisted it was fashionable. This was the first time she'd worn a gown that showed so much bosom, and she felt a little older, a little prettier, and maybe a little wicked. She *did* want to impress Samuel.

Michaela went over to the full-length mirror. Behind her reflection, she saw her bed, covered in a white satin spread. Five eyelet-trimmed pillows lay scattered on top. Sometimes it was still hard to believe that four years ago she had been wearing rags and sleeping in caves and barns. Now she dressed in silk and slept on a feather bed in a beautiful house.

Michaela pushed from her mind the memory of the dead man whose money had made all this possible. Sitting down at her dresser, she picked up her brush, swept the sides of her long hair up and away from her face, and pinned it at the back of her head so that the length fell down her back in shimmering curls. Her brown hair had just enough auburn to give it highlights. Then she tied a piece of green ribbon into a bow and pinned it to the back of her hair.

The parlor was still empty so she made her way to the dining room to make sure the new cook had prepared everything properly. She opened the double French doors and stepped onto the Venetian rug. In the chandelier all twenty-six brass candlesticks were burning, causing the Waterford crystal to glitter and sparkle. A low burning fire added its light and warmth to the room.

She wiped her forehead with the back of her hand and continued her inspection. The double pedestal table was covered in a linen cloth so fine it looked like silk. A loaf of fresh-baked bread had been placed on one end of the table, filling the room with its appetizing aroma. Two crystal dishes of sweet butter sat on each side of the loaf. The wine and water goblets were banded with gold, adding an extra touch of elegance to the table. On the Regency sideboard a copper wine cooler was chilling a bottle.

There would be no fancy French dishes gracing the plates tonight. Padraic refused to eat them. As far as he was concerned, meat and potatoes couldn't be improved upon.

Michaela heard her father call from the parlor and knew that one of their guests had arrived. She took one last look at the room before hurrying into the kitchen.

After last-minute instructions to the cook, she returned to the parlor, hoping to see the handsome Samuel Lawrence. Instead, she saw Cabot Peabody standing in front of her father.

"Oh, Cabot." She smiled, hiding a slight twinge of disappointment. "How good to see you again."

"I don't think I've ever seen you look lovelier." He took her hand in his and placed his lips softly to the back of her hand.

"Thank you, Cabot, and you look dashing as . . ." She stopped when a loud knocking sounded from the front of the house. Michaela took a deep breath. She hoped Kate was right, that Samuel was a gentleman. Maybe she was making too much of this. The two men could surprise her; it had happened before. Surely somewhere in Atlanta there was a Republican and a Democrat, a Northerner and a Southerner, who liked each other.

"Are you expecting someone else?" Cabot asked.

"Yes," Padraic answered for Michaela, who was glad he had finally seen fit to speak.

"Oh," Cabot said. "I thought we were . . ." Then his

good manners returned. "Excellent," he declared, almost as if he meant it.

Michaela turned away from Cabot's blue eyes when Bessie showed Samuel into the fire-warmed room.

"Ah—here's our other guest now. Michaela, you remember Samuel Lawrence, the owner of Twin Willows," her father said.

"Yes, of course I remember Mr. Lawrence." Stepping away from Cabot, Michaela walked toward Samuel with outstretched hand. "It's a pleasure to see you again."

She avoided his eyes as he took her hand very firmly in his and carried it to his lips. Michaela gasped and drew her hand away and looked into Samuel's teasing brown eyes. Then she cleared her throat quickly to cover her gasp. While kissing her hand, Samuel had run his tongue lightly over her skin. His forwardness shocked her but, at the same time, sent delicious tremors up her spine. She was glad Kate hadn't joined them yet. She would surely have caught Samuel's indiscretion and Michaela's blush.

Samuel had disturbed her so deeply that all she could do was stare at her father while he introduced the two men.

"Samuel, this is Mr. Cabot Peabody from Massachusetts. He's running for the Republican seat in the United States Senate. Cabot, this is Samuel Lawrence, decorated colonel and distinguished owner of Twin Willows."

Cabot was the first to extend a greeting, shaking Samuel's reluctant hand vigorously. "It is indeed a pleasure to meet you, Mr. Lawrence. Of course I've heard of Twin Willows."

"And I've heard about you," was Samuel's terse comment.

Michaela noticed that Samuel barely looked at Cabot before returning his attention to her. He seemed to be looking to her for an answer as to why he'd been invited on the same evening as Cabot. A lengthening hush fell over the room. He must hear her heart pounding rapidly against her ribs. The trouble was that she didn't know if it was because of the way Samuel had kissed her hand or because the animosity between the Blue and the Grey would cast a pall over her dinner table.

Samuel's expression softened, and suddenly Michaela felt warm inside. His eyes scanned her features briefly, then lingered on the faint swell of her breasts that showed above the neckline of her dress. The desire in his eyes made her breath grow short. The intimacy of his gaze alarmed yet excited her. What was there about this man? All he had to do was look at her and her heartbeat increased, her skin prickled, and she felt light-headed.

When everyone remained silent, Cabot spoke again. "I've done a great deal of study on your kind, Mr. Lawrence, and I would be most delighted to talk with you about my findings."

Samuel's gaze drifted to Cabot. His dark eyes were brooding. "If you have studied my *kind*, then you know I don't like your *kind*. So save us both a lot of insults."

"Oh, my goodness! Look how late I am." Kate Spencer flowed into the room with the grace of an angel. "I'm simply appalled at myself for not arriving before our guests. Gentlemen, Michaela, do forgive me."

Kate flew by Michaela in a puff of amethyst silk, the scent of roses trailing behind her. Her dark hair with its faint trace of silver was in a perfect chignon at the back of her neck. "Cabot, delighted to see you again," she said, extending her hand.

No one had perfected the Southern accent as well as Kate. Each word was pronounced slowly with dramatic ease. She turned sparkling hazel eyes on Samuel. "Mr. Lawrence, I'm Kate Spencer, and I can't tell you what an honor it is to make your acquaintance. Your daddy was once received at my home in Savannah, and I recall my mama saying he was a joy to have as a guest."

Samuel kissed Kate's hand properly and said, "I've had the pleasure of being in Savannah a few times. Had I known you were there, I'd have certainly stopped in to see you."

Michaela smiled. Kate had the ability to make everyone feel special, and she could see Samuel wouldn't be an exception.

She also noticed that her father wasn't at all happy about Kate's making a fuss over their new dinner guest. Michaela could sense his jealousy and didn't know why he couldn't admit how much he liked Kate. She was beautiful, charming, and intelligent. She would be the perfect woman to run Padraic's house and keep him in line.

"Well, now," Padraic interjected when Kate took a breath. "I do believe dinner is getting cold. Shall we go in?" And with that statement he called a halt to Kate's conversation with the handsome young Samuel.

Cabot held out his arm to Michaela. She caught Samuel's icy stare before he extended his arm to Kate. Ceremoniously, Cabot led Michaela into the dining room, followed by Kate and Samuel, with Padraic bringing up the rear.

While the soup was being served, Michaela tried to keep her eyes off Samuel, who sat at her right. Unlike

Cabot, he was being quiet, and she wondered if it was his nature.

"So tell me, Cabot," Padraic said. "What are your chances for the Republican nomination?"

Cabot put down his spoon. "Oh, very good, sir. My opponent is a Radical Republican, and I don't think the Radicals have a chance this term. It's not wise to be against President Johnson's reconstruction plan, and, truthfully, I don't think the South is ready for black suffrage. In fact, the Joint Committee on Reconstruction is meeting this very month to reconcile conflicting opinions."

"Hmm," was Padraic's only reply.

When her father didn't pick up the conversation, Michaela did. "But the Democrats are still very strong in the South. Isn't that true, Mr. Lawrence?" She tried to keep her eyes on his while she waited for an answer, but they drifted to his lips.

Samuel took his time answering Michaela. He was watching her watch him. "Yes. For all the good it's going to do. I don't think politics is the answer to the South's current problems."

"Secession and rebellion are still too rampant in the Democratic party, weakening it considerably," Cabot added, although no one asked for his opinion. "Reconstruction should lead to loyalty to the Union, guarantee freedom to the Negroes, and destroy noblesse oblige."

"It sounds like your plan for reconstruction is merely an extension of the war," Samuel remarked in a low tone.

Michaela wanted to hear more from Samuel. His distance intrigued her. He obviously wasn't as vocal as Cabot, so she prompted him to answer again. "What do you think the answer is?"

He searched her face, his eyes dark and troubled. "I'm not certain what the answer is. I think there has to be some healing before unity can take place."

Michaela started to speak, but Kate's soft voice intervened.

"Was that thunder I heard just now? Dear me. You don't suppose we're in for a storm this time of year, do you, Mr. Brennen?"

Padraic looked up from his soup. "I'm sure I'm not as familiar with the weather in the South as you are. Perhaps you should direct your question to Samuel."

Kate turned to Samuel, Padraic and Cabot returned to their soup, and Michaela smiled. Yes, she liked the handsome Mr. Samuel Lawrence. If only she could have a few minutes alone with him. It would be heaven!

All through the meal, Samuel couldn't keep his eyes off Michaela. She was so beautiful, with her flashing green eyes and flawless white skin. He had never seen a woman with a more beautiful neck. It looked so creamy that he wanted to run his tongue down the length of it.

He hadn't intended to be so bold when he'd kissed her hand, but when he'd gotten close to her, she'd smelled so good that he had to know what she tasted like. And now he knew he had to find out if her pretty red lips tasted as fresh as peppermint.

As he continued to watch her, he decided he liked the way she chewed. What had happened to him? How had he become so enamored of this woman that he watched her lips? He liked her voice, too. Her brogue wasn't as heavy as her father's; it was as gentle and pleasing as a feather caressing his bare skin.

No wonder Padraic didn't want his daughter marrying that carpetbagger. He'd drive the man crazy with his incessant talking, not to mention what he'd do to Michaela. Only a politician would keep running on when no one was listening.

Ever since he had walked through the door and seen Peabody standing with Michaela, Samuel had been of the same mind as Padraic. He didn't want her marrying this prig. In fact, he didn't want Peabody to touch her, talk to her, or even look at her.

Forcing his eyes away from Michaela, Samuel glanced at the woman they called Kate. A nice-looking older woman with vibrant hazel eyes, she had referred to herself as Michaela's chaperone. Now that dinner was finished, she allowed her delicate hand to rest gracefully on the snow white tablecloth. She was a charming and likable woman who reminded him of his own mother—as she had been before the war.

He looked again at Michaela, trying desperately to understand Peabody's double talk. Padraic, he noticed, was interested only in his food. Through the parted draperies at the far end of the room, Samuel saw lightning streak across the darkened sky. His long ride back to Twin Willows would be difficult in the impending storm.

"Do you agree with that, Mr. Lawrence?"

Samuel turned toward Peabody. He hadn't heard a word the man had said; but if anyone had asked, he would have made a bet that Peabody was talking about improving the South. It seemed to be his favorite subject.

Samuel laid the cutwork lace napkin on the table. "I wasn't listening, I'm afraid. What did you say?" Just to provoke Cabot, Samuel let his gaze wander freely over

Michaela's features, down her neck and lingering on her breast. She didn't blush. He liked that.

Cabot cleared his throat. "Education is the answer to the prejudices that still exist in Southern society today."

"I don't know that education could change what's in a man's heart." Samuel purposefully kept his voice low so Padraic wouldn't look up and see the way he was coveting his daughter. The man might change his mind.

"I'm not talking about his heart. I'm talking about his mind," Cabot shot back quickly as if he were dealing the finishing blow in a long, heated debate. "Once the ill-conceived pseudoaristocracy of the South has been eradicated and the Negroes have been educated, the North and South will once again be a progressive commonwealth that can move into the next century with the political goals the war achieved."

"Who gives a damn about the political goals of the war? It's the economic results we should be worrying about. All the livestock or food that was not requisitioned by the Confederate forces was confiscated by the Union. We haven't recovered from that." Samuel's voice rose. For the moment, Michaela was forgotten. Words burned on his tongue. "Food production has declined to almost nothing because the plantations have been broken into thirty- or forty-acre lots for tenant farming or sharecropping. These farmers are planting only enough food to survive on, then putting the rest of their acreage in more profitable market crops like cotton. Have you ever tried to eat cotton?"

"Economics isn't the issue we were discussing," Cabot said, trying hard to erase the truth of Samuel's words.

Samuel held his temper in check, but raw anger was

eating away at him. He'd heard enough from this pompous carpetbagging Yankee. "Oh, pardon me. We were talking about education. Well, try educating a white or Negro man whose stomach is empty and see how much he learns."

Padraic pushed back his chair and grunted loudly enough to draw attention to himself. When he was sure all eyes were on him, he spoke. "Kate, would you please tell the cook that dinner was delightful." He gave a slight bow in her direction, then turned to Cabot. "Will you join me on the porch for a smoke? Unfortunately, Samuel doesn't enjoy tobacco."

"I'd consider it an honor, sir." Cabot rose, giving Samuel a smug look. "Perhaps we could continue this discussion later, Mr. Lawrence."

Samuel looked at Cabot for a moment. Obviously the man didn't know when to let well enough alone. "Any time," he replied in a voice that was punctuated with deadly calm.

Cabot touched Michaela's arm. "I won't be long. Just a quick smoke with your father."

"Take your time. Enjoy yourself."

Kate was the next to rise, and Samuel quickly stood and helped her with her chair.

"Thank you, Mr. Lawrence."

"Samuel." He smiled down into her eyes. "Call me Samuel."

"My pleasure, and you must call me Kate. Michaela, if you'll show Samuel into the parlor, I'll speak to the cook, then bring in coffee."

"Thank you, Kate. That would be nice." Michaela

looked into Samuel's dark brown eyes. "Will you join me?"

As Samuel held Michaela's chair, a loud clap of thunder rattled the windows. "Looks like we're in for a bad storm."

Michaela looked out the window into the darkness. "Yes, storms can be quite violent here in the South."

"Do thunder and lightning frighten you?" he asked.

She faced him with clear eyes. "No, not at all."

As they walked through the doorway, Samuel put his hand to the small of Michaela's back. Her shoulders lifted and she stiffened. She wasn't indifferent to his touch. That was a good sign.

Samuel smiled. She was going to be his. With Padraic's help, fate had sealed their destiny. He didn't care whether or not Peabody redeemed the South or won the election. Cabot Peabody had just lost Michaela.

Three

WHEN Samuel's hand touched Michaela's back, she took a deep breath and held it for a long time. The heat of his hand burned through her clothing. Silently they walked through the shadowy hallway into the warmth of the parlor.

The fire had burned down to embers and Michaela went to the fireplace to add more wood before the room became chilled. It was a relief to move away from Samuel's scorching touch. She could breathe more easily again. Yet she could feel his gaze upon her, making her conscious of every movement.

Over dinner Samuel had proven himself able to hold his own against Cabot's endless assault of words. She liked that. It was also obvious that he wasn't impressed with Cabot's intelligence as she had been. Of course, she reminded herself, they both had passionate feelings about the subject they were discussing, which enhanced their argument. For now, she would add caring and wit to the growing list of adjectives she could use to describe Samuel Lawrence.

"Let me do that," Samuel said, taking the wood from her hands.

He was so close to her that his words sounded like a whisper in her ear. His voice was slow and easy. She caught the faint fresh scent of shaving soap and found it a pleasant change from Cabot's spicy cologne. The dark suit he wore was superbly cut. His muscles strained the fabric when he stooped to place the log between the brass-tipped andirons. In the back, his hair was longer than that of most men, but Michaela liked the way it fell in neat waves just below his collar.

It was unlike Kate to leave her alone with a guest, especially a gentleman. Now that she thought about it, Kate had also been late for dinner. The possibility that she could be ill worried Michaela for a moment.

"Thank you, Mr. Lawrence," she said softly when he faced her again, brushing his hands together to remove the shavings that clung to them.

For a long moment his dark eyes lingered on her face. He was staring at her silently, the slightest hint of a smile playing at the edges of his lips. Michaela found herself returning his gaze with more daring than she thought she possessed.

"My name is Samuel. I'd like you to call me Samuel, Michaela."

"All right, Samuel," she agreed, still unable to break away from his gaze. The thrill she felt in her breast when she looked into his eyes was completely foreign to her.

There was no doubt about it. She liked the way he looked at her, the way he made her heart flutter in her chest.

"Are you engaged to Cabot?" he asked at last as they stood before the fire.

"No," she answered truthfully.

"He seems rather possessive."

His words were intended to challenge her, and they did. "Cabot has been courting me for some time now."

The log caught fire with a *swoosh*, and Michaela's eyes were drawn to the flame. The smell of burning wood hung heavily in the air. Thunder rumbled in the distance.

"And he hasn't asked you to marry him yet?"

Puzzled, Michaela looked back at Samuel. She couldn't tell if he was making fun of Cabot or questioning his motives. Neither idea appealed to her. She lifted her shoulders a little higher.

"No, not exactly. And who gave you the authority to question me about Cabot?"

He ignored her question. "What does 'not exactly' mean? He has either asked you to marry him, or he hasn't." The merest hint of amusement lurked in his expression.

This time there was no doubt that he was making fun of her suitor, or at least her attempts to defend him. And now that she thought about it, she hadn't quite forgiven him for his forwardness when he'd kissed her hand. She took a deep breath, eager to put this man in his place. The problem was, she really wasn't angered by his questions. She was more . . . intrigued.

"I don't intend to discuss my personal life with you, Mr. Lawrence," she said as she moved to the rose-colored settee, away from his disturbing presence. Her green silk dress fanned gracefully over the velvet cushion of the small sofa.

Samuel pushed her dress aside and sat down beside her, leaving only a tiny space between them. His hard-muscled thigh pressed against hers lightly. There was a faint heat from his touch.

He looked deeply into her eyes and asked, "Do you want to marry him?"

Light from the fire and the burning lamps cast shadows on his face, giving him a mysterious look. He was too close. Her stomach quivered, and her breath grew shorter. No man had ever made her feel this nervous. Why was he asking so many questions about Cabot? "That's none of your concern." Her answer was weak.

"It is if I want to court you, too," he said in a low, compelling voice. His breathing had thickened.

Michaela's head snapped up. Her heart beat rapidly in her chest. With each shallow breath, she caught the scent of his clean fresh soap. He smiled at her, and the quivering in her stomach increased and spread to her breast and limbs. His fingers caressed her soft cheek before gliding down her neck. Michaela went rigid under his touch. No man had ever been so bold. His hand stopped just short of the top of her dress. Now she wasn't breathing at all. A flare of excited panic held her in its grip.

With the gentleness of a butterfly, his hand cupped and slid around the nape of her neck, under her hair. Michaela shivered, although she had never felt warmer in her life. His hand kneaded the muscles gently, and a sweet, soft thrill eased through her. Had she ever felt this good?

"Is that all right, Michaela? May I court you, too?"

He was trying to seduce her with his eyes, his words, his touch—and she could feel herself yielding. His face moved closer while the strong line of his mouth made its descent toward hers. There was a huskiness to his breathing as his lips parted ever so lightly and touched hers. Stunned, she kept her eyes open, watching him, although his were closed. His lips were warm, soft, moist. A tingle started at the back of her neck, eased down her spine, and continued all the way to her toes.

"Kiss me back, Michaela. You won't feel anything if you don't join me," he whispered against her closed lips.

But she did! His lips were soft and wonderful, flooding her with delicious, anticipating shivers of desire. She wanted him to kiss her again. Did that mean she was in love with Samuel? She didn't even know him.

Samuel's lips seemed to answer her question silently as he gathered her into his arms and pressed his lips to hers, moving them gently back and forth.

A moan of protest caught in her throat. This wasn't the sort of thing you did with a man you didn't know. But it was all so new, so sweet, so wild, enticing her beyond caring. Michaela didn't want to give him up or the sensations. She folded herself into his circling arms, giving in to the discovery of her new feelings.

Her eyes closed, her lips opened, and she accepted the wondrous pleasures that flooded through her. Her arms slipped around his neck, and her hands clutched at the light wool of his jacket. A quivering attacked her insides, and a roar filled her ears.

His lips tasted of wine, and that was so exciting that she flicked out her tongue and with a light gossamer movement caressed his lips, hoping to taste the sweet wine once again. Samuel groaned softly and pressed her to him as he slid his own tongue into her mouth. Michaela gasped, pushed away from him, and stood.

"Why did you do that?" she demanded; her eyes glared outrage.

Samuel remained unperturbed on the sofa. "I kissed you because I wanted to. Your lips are about the prettiest I've ever seen, and I had to see if they tasted as good as they looked."

The casual intimacy of his gaze was disturbing. "I'm not talking about the kiss. Why did you put your tongue in my mouth?" she asked without the least bit of reservation.

A curious look formed on his face. "If I'm not mistaken, Michaela, you started it."

"I did no such thing," she answered with all the indignation she could muster. Just who did he think he was to put the blame on her? She wouldn't have it.

A pair of burning eyes stared at her. "Michaela, when I felt your tongue on my lips, I assumed you wanted to kiss me in that way."

"I liked the taste of wine on your lips," she declared. "That's all." Her breath came thickly.

"That's all?" he queried doubtfully.

"Of course. What else could it be?"

Suddenly he smiled. "Well, it could have been passion." She gasped. He went on. "But I'm sure it wasn't." He was teasing her now. "There are other ways to taste wine, you know."

His smile was so charming, Michaela wanted to smile, too. But she didn't. She couldn't forgive him so easily for taking liberties, then making fun of her. Maybe she shouldn't have admitted the truth.

"You shouldn't have kissed me. I hardly know you." Even as she said the words, she knew she didn't mean them. Right now, she wanted nothing more than to be kissed like that again, to be held close to his warmth one more time. "What would Kate have said if she'd seen us?"

Samuel leaned against the scalloped back of the sofa, stretching his long legs out in front of him with unconstrained naturalness. "Oh, I think she would probably have insisted we get married."

The ease with which he made the statement astonished Michaela; but when she looked down at him, trying to be angry or appalled, she liked what she saw. His smile was genuine, and his eyes danced with humor.

"Why did you kiss me?" she asked.

"Because I wanted to. I told you, I had to find out if your lips were as sweet as they looked."

"And were they?" she asked.

Samuel stood and looked deeply into her eyes. He laid gentle hands on her shoulders and with a husky voice said, "Oh yes. They are very sweet."

His words sent fireworks splintering through her. Was it lightning and thundering outside, or was the clash of the elements coming from inside her? She tried to control the feelings, but excitement danced through her senses.

"Shall I pour the coffee, Michaela?" Kate asked as she came into the room carrying a silver tray covered with a white linen cloth.

Michaela spun away from Samuel. She had completely forgotten about Kate. Now those new, wonderful feelings evaporated with her appearance. "Uh—no, I will, Kate. Thank you for bringing the coffee. You will stay and have a cup with us?"

Her voice was shaky. Tension coiled inside her at the thought of Kate witnessing the kiss or overhearing their conversation. She wasn't used to being in a compromising position. If she weren't careful, Samuel Lawrence was going to get her into trouble.

Kate smiled graciously and looked from Michaela to Samuel. "I was going to, but I must speak with Bessie about something first. The rain has started, and it looks like we're in for a major storm. Don't wait for me. Go ahead and enjoy the coffee while it's hot. And I think Samuel might like a little brandy in his, dear."

Kate's voice grew softer and more eloquent when she spoke of Samuel. It made Michaela's skin bristle. Why was a forty-year-old woman making such a fuss over a much younger man? Especially the woman who was supposed to be an example to Michaela on the proper way to behave. Michaela had always thought Kate to be the epitome of decorum.

"Thank you, Kate, brandy would be very nice." Samuel made his words sound like a glowing compliment. Michaela felt the sting of jealousy when he looked at Kate with appreciation in his eyes.

When Kate left the room, Michaela went over to the mahogany Sheraton sideboard and looked at all the liquor bottles arranged on the marbled top. She didn't know anything about spirits, except for the fact that her father had a drink from time to time. Kate had said Samuel would like brandy. Michaela didn't know which bottle it was in. Some of the liquors, she noticed, were in unattractive bottles with labels, while others were in beautiful crystal containers. She scanned the labels quickly, looking for the right one.

"This is the decanter you're looking for, I believe."

Michaela jumped. She hadn't heard Samuel come up behind her. Clearing her throat, she stepped back slowly and asked, "How do you know that's brandy?" He had picked up one of the crystal decanters.

He looked down at her with a heavy-lidded gaze. There was a faint trace of humor still lingering in the depth of his eyes, an appealing grin on his lips. "The good stuff is always in the fancy bottles."

She watched as he lifted the top and poured a generous amount into one of the china cups; he looked back at her and asked, "You've never had brandy in your coffee?"

"No."

Samuel watched her for a moment longer before pouring a small amount into another cup. "I know some people don't think it proper for ladies to partake of strong drink, but I have a feeling you've always wanted to. How old are you, Michaela?"

"Nineteen—almost."

"Well, I think that's old enough to have your first drink. My father gave me my first drink on my sixteenth birthday. Unfortunately, what he gave me wasn't the good stuff. As I recall, it was bitter as wormwood. I thought it was supposed to taste bad. Anyway, I drank too much, which he planned. I was sick for several hours."

He picked up the meticulously polished silver pot and added coffee to both cups. "With the brandy we don't need sugar, but a little cream makes it very smooth."

Michaela watched him stir thick white cream into the

coffee. The motion of his large hand going round and round was mesmerizing. She didn't know why she was letting him take over. She should be the one lacing the coffee with brandy and cream.

With a steady hand and observant eyes, Michaela took the fragile cup from Samuel and sipped the coffee just as he did. The smooth liquid flowed across her tongue and coated the roof of her mouth, leaving in its wake a little bit of a sting. But the drink did indeed have a light sweet taste. The aroma was also pleasant. She inhaled it deeply.

"Well, what do you think?" he asked.

She took another sip, savoring the warm liquid a bit longer this time. "It's actually very nice," she admitted.

"Yes, this is. Some of it is as foul as kerosene."

She took another sip, then returned to the settee. "The smell is strong, but I like it. Why do you suppose it's not ladylike to drink it?"

Samuel chuckled and sat beside her. "Because if you drink too much of it, you'll get drunk, and getting drunk is definitely unladylike."

Michaela nodded slowly. Already the lingering warmth of the liquor spread through her. Although her father had a drink most evenings, she had only seen him drunk on two occasions. He had acted very differently each time.

The first time was long ago, the night her mother had died. He was so depressed that it was weeks before he finally pulled himself out of the slump; and by that time he had decided they were going to America. The other time was a couple of weeks after he'd found the leather bag filled with gold coins. Then, instead of becoming depressed, he was happy to the point of being careless with the money he had found. Thank goodness that his fondness for money overshadowed his taste for liquor and that he hadn't stayed drunk more than a couple of days that time.

"Have you ever been drunk?" she asked Samuel.

She felt him tense. Frustration clouded his features, and he looked away from her and into the depths of the fire for a few moments before answering.

"I think most of the men who went through the war got drunk a few times. It took me a while to realize the only thing getting drunk does is give you a headache in the morning. It doesn't make you forget a thing."

His seriousness surprised her, and she looked at him more closely. Unlike Cabot, he'd talked very little about the war. "There must be many things you want to forget," she observed quietly.

When he faced her again, his eyes were sad, and her heart went out to him. He set his cup on the small black walnut table, then put his arm on the back of the sofa behind Michaela. His smile was gentle, with no hint of the teasing that usually lurked around the edges of his mouth. She felt him relax.

"Yes, Michaela, I have seen and done a lot of things I'd like to put out of my mind forever."

Watching his lips as he spoke stirred the new sensations she had experienced when he'd kissed her. She wondered if he would kiss her again. Should she let him if he tried? No! She had already acted shamelessly. Kate would be furious if she knew Samuel had kissed her even once.

"You must have liked it. Your cup is empty. How do you feel?"

Michaela looked down and saw a scant trace of golden

brown liquid in her cup. When had she finished the coffee? The delicate flower-printed cup rattled in the saucer when he took it from her hands and set it down. Michaela looked into Samuel's brownish-gray eyes, now dark with memories.

She pondered his question. How did she feel? As if she hadn't a care in the world. As if she'd never again be frightened to stay alone in the bank. As if she had been insane to think she could marry Cabot when Samuel's kisses made her tingle all over. But she didn't want to say all those things to Samuel.

"Warm." Which was also true. "I feel relaxed to the point of not wanting to move a muscle."

"Brandy can do that to you. I'm beginning to feel the same way."

The fire danced wickedly in his eyes, making Michaela suddenly feel vulnerable. "Why did you give me the brandy?" she asked. Her manner wasn't accusing, only questioning.

"Why did you take it? You could have refused." His words were unexpectedly husky.

Once again he had turned the tables on her. "I wanted to know what it tasted like. What was your reason?" She wasn't going to let him avoid her question. She expected him to be truthful, too.

He moved close to her. That charming, seductive smile spread across his face again. "So I could have my way with you."

She blinked; his words surprised her. "I don't believe you."

"Why not? You're beautiful. So lovely, I can hardly keep my hands off you." His gaze went no farther than her eyes. "During dinner, while you listened to Cabot's speeches, I was watching you." He leaned closer still. "I watched your lips move, and I thought, I've got to feel those lips beneath mine. Once I felt them, I wanted to feel your breasts pressed against—"

"Stop!" Michaela jumped from the sofa so fast, her head spun for a moment. Samuel caught her arm. "Don't talk to me that way." The words were forced past short breaths that came too rapidly. Everything was happening too fast. Her feelings were too new. He was doing things to her that he shouldn't.

"Why? Why don't you want me to tell you how you make me feel?" He still held her gently, with no pressure.

From the front of the house, Michaela heard sounds of Cabot and her father coming back inside. She jerked away from Samuel and poured coffee into a fresh cup. Her throat was suddenly dry, and her hands shook. The liquid steamed, but still she drank it, letting it burn her throat.

"Settle down, Michaela," came Samuel's reassuring voice. "You sit there on the sofa. I'll stand here in front of the fire. If you take that scared look off your face, no one will know what we said, or that I kissed you."

She didn't need him to tell her that. Turning angry eyes upon him, she ordered, "Don't scold me like a child after you have treated me like a woman!" She sat on the sofa so quickly her hoop bowed and her skirt flew into the air, showing her petticoats. Refusing to look at Samuel again, she held her cup and saucer steady in one hand while covering her petticoats with the other.

Why couldn't the man behave like a proper gentleman? Cabot had always treated her with respect. Samuel simply had no manners. Imagine his kissing her and encouraging her to drink strong spirits. What nerve! *But you liked it,* a little voice reminded her.

"It's not fit for man nor beast to be out tonight," Padraic stated as he stomped into the warm room and stood in front of the fire next to Samuel.

Cabot almost floated into the room, so light was his step. "There, that didn't take long, did it, my dear?" he questioned as he seated himself on the sofa beside Michaela.

The heavy smell of tobacco smoke clung to his breath and clothes. Michaela had never found the scent offensive before, but tonight she did. She had discovered she preferred the smell of shaving soap and the taste of brandy.

"No, not long at all," she answered quietly, and drank from the cup again.

"You've been standing too close to the fire," Cabot said. "Your cheeks are red from the heat. You must be careful to guard your delicate skin."

I'll wring his neck if he touches her, Samuel thought as Cabot talked about Michaela's brandy-warmed skin. Maybe he wouldn't have wanted her so much if she hadn't caressed his lips so innocently with her tongue. That had sent heat through him like no other woman's touch ever had. Holding her in his arms tonight had made him sure of one thing. There was no way he would let Michaela marry Cabot Peabody.

"Does it look as though the storm will clear?" Samuel asked in an easy tone of voice. He was speaking to Padraic but kept his eyes on Michaela.

"Not before morning. The downpour is fierce and the

wind is up. I was just telling Cabot that I'll have to offer you both beds for the night."

"Oh, I see you've finished your cigar." Kate glided into the room as quietly as a mouse. Cabot jumped to his feet. "Shall I get fresh coffee?" she asked Padraic.

"Right now I think we should find Bessie and have her prepare rooms for our guests. No one can go out in that rain."

Samuel watched Kate smile at Padraic. He saw that she wanted the banker's approval. The smile Kate gave him would have melted any other man's heart, but Padraic didn't seem to notice it. What a pair they made. Kate was all softness and sweetness and Padraic so rough and uncouth. Samuel hadn't made up his mind clearly whether or not the man was honest.

"That's already been taken care of," Kate replied. "I knew you wouldn't send our guests out on a night like this. And I do hope you don't mind, Mr. Brennen, but I took the liberty of having Bessie lay out two of your nightshirts for them."

Samuel couldn't help but chuckle inside when he imagined Cabot putting on Padraic's nightshirt. Cabot was at least five inches shorter than the older man and close to one hundred pounds lighter.

"You are a capable woman, Kate dear. Have you left nothing for me to attend to?" Padraic asked.

"Yes, I'll say good night to our guests and leave you to show them to their rooms." Kate turned to Michaela. "Why don't we put Cabot in the room on the left at the top of the stairs and Samuel down the hall beside your father."

Michaela set her cup on the silver tray and rose from

the sofa. "I'm sure that will be fine. Thank you for taking care of everything."

"It was my pleasure, dear." Kate turned to Cabot, who was still standing beside the sofa. She extended her hand. "It's always a delight to see you. Do keep us posted on your political career."

Cabot bowed and kissed her hand. "Indeed I will."

Kate turned to Samuel. Her eyes glistened softly. "What an honor it was to meet you, Samuel Lawrence. Your dedication to the Confederacy will be remembered for a long time. I do hope we have the pleasure of seeing each other again."

Samuel took her hand and squeezed it gently before bringing it to his lips. "The war changed many things in the South, Kate. I'm glad to see it didn't change our gracious and beautiful women."

After a final smile of appreciation to Samuel, Kate said good night and left the room.

Padraic turned his back on Cabot and Michaela and faced the dying fire. In a low voice he said to Samuel, "Well, what do you think?"

A knot of uncertainty twisted in Samuel's stomach. He didn't like being vulnerable. His eyes roamed over the room, ever so often alighting on Michaela's face. Cabot had trapped her with one of his long speeches, and, being an angel, she was listening.

"About what?" he asked at last, turning around to face the blue-and-yellow flame.

"Come, come, Mr. Lawrence. You sound as if we had never talked yesterday."

Samuel rubbed his palm across his lips. On his hand, he caught a lingering trace of Michaela's perfume. It was as sweet and tempting as she was. He took a deep breath. The scent haunted him as he closed his hand and stuffed it in his pocket. He wanted to pull her close and breathe in the smell of her once more. He couldn't remember ever having such a driving desire for a woman before.

"I just wanted to know if I should deposit some money into an account for you."

The fire grew hotter on Samuel's face. Yes, he needed that money for Twin Willows. He'd take it, but he'd pay back every dollar. With interest. He didn't want to barter for Michaela's hand in marriage. She was too special for that.

He looked into Padraic's eyes. "Do it."

"Give me a couple of days, then stop by." Padraic cleared his throat and turned around. A loud burst of thunder forestalled his speech for a moment. "Michaela, would you be so kind as to show our guests to their rooms. I have a couple of things to check on before I go up."

It was unusual for Michaela to be given so much time alone in the company of men. Maybe her father was beginning to realize that she could take care of herself.

"Of course, Papa." Michaela reached up and kissed her father's round cheek. "Will you be long?"

"No, I'll be up presently. You run along to bed, dear."

Good-nights were issued, and Michaela, Cabot, and Samuel headed for the stairs. They had walked as far as the entrance when Michaela suddenly turned back to her father. He was still standing before the fireplace. "Don't forget to put out the lamps before you come up, Papa."

Padraic laughed loudly. "Do you think I'd forget after the tongue-lashing you gave me the last time? Silly girl."

Michaela smiled fondly at her father, and, lifting the skirt of her silk dress, she stepped on the first stair with Cabot beside her and Samuel behind her. They walked up the wide stairway in silence. A large painting of someone Michaela didn't know hung halfway up the wall. Her father had foreclosed on the house, and most of its furnishings were left by the indebted owner. Michaela thought she would redecorate eventually, but for now she was content to leave the house intact.

Bessie had lit the lamps at the top of the stairs. They dimly lighted the long hallway. There were six bedrooms in the two-story Colonial, three on each side of the passageway. Michaela stopped at the first door on the left, the one Kate had said was made up for Cabot.

"Michaela, my dear, let's show Mr. Lawrence his room so that we may have a moment alone before we retire."

A quick glance at Samuel told Michaela that he was not happy about Cabot's suggestion. This gave her the perfect chance to get back at him for the way he had treated her earlier in the evening.

"That's a splendid idea. Wait here, I'll be right with you." She smiled sweetly at Cabot. "Follow me, Mr. Lawrence," she added in a clipped tone as she started down the hallway at a brisk pace.

Finally she stopped in front of the last door on the right. It was dark and smoky in this part of the hallway, but Michaela knew Samuel's eyes crinkled with humor. She had been his source of amusement all evening.

"This is your room, Mr. Lawrence. I hope your sleep is fitful and the storm keeps you awake all night."

"Oh, I'll be awake all night, but it won't have anything to do with the storm."

She started to move on, but he placed a gentle hand on her arm and held her back. "Don't touch me!" Her voice was low and angry. She wasn't in the mood for any more of his forwardness.

He let her go. "All right, but not so fast. First, I'm sorry I treated you like a child. Believe me, there isn't anything about you that reminds me of a child."

Michaela moistened her lips. Should she forgive him? In the dim light she looked into his eyes. Yes. "Apology accepted," she answered in a softer tone.

"Which room is yours?" he asked.

She could feel his eyes scanning her face as if he were trying to memorize it. She swallowed. "The first one on the left," she said, then added quickly, "I always bolt my door at night." Her answer sounded more like a challenge than information.

He smiled with that easy manner she'd come to expect from him. "That's a good idea."

"It comes from—never mind." She shook her head and clamped her mouth shut, not wanting to tell him about the many different places she had slept in, lying awake in the darkness wondering if anyone would try to harm her or her father.

Samuel reached up and briefly caressed her cheek with the back of his fingers. "Sweet dreams, Michaela." He turned away and went inside the room.

When the door was shut, Michaela walked slowly back toward Cabot. She passed her own bedroom door and wished she could go inside without having to speak to Cabot again tonight. She wanted time alone to think about the things that had happened throughout the evening, but most of all she wanted to ponder Samuel's disturbing kisses.

"I'm not happy about his staying the night in this house," Cabot said in a quarrelsome manner when she approached him.

Michaela didn't want to discuss Samuel with Cabot. They were just too different. "Nonsense." She sighed heavily. "No one can travel tonight."

"It's not that I think Mr. Lawrence is a bad sort, but surely his crass behavior proves he's not of the cavalier ancestry he'd like you to believe. Instead, I suggest his origins are from the plebeian class. To understand the amazing endurances of what was from the start a dubious tradition of aristocracy, one must go back to the origin of the plantation system."

"Cabot, do you mind if we discuss this tomorrow? I'm really tired," Michaela pleaded when he took a breath. She knew there was no way Samuel could hear him through the thick wood door, but for some reason she felt as if he were still watching them.

"Yes, of course you are. I should have been more considerate." He placed his hands on her shoulders and looked into her eyes. "I had intended to speak to your father about us tonight, but . . ." He bent his head to kiss her. She thought she would let him until just before his lips met hers. Suddenly, once again, she had the odd feeling someone watched her. She turned her head to let his lips graze her cheek.

"Good night, Cabot," she said quickly, and stepped away.

"Good night, my sweet."

Michaela watched him close his door and heard him throw the bolt before she walked away. Tonight had been the most interesting she'd had in a long time.

When she stood in front of her door, she looked across at Samuel's. He couldn't have been watching—still, she had the eeriest feeling. It was better to put it to rest. Slowly she walked toward his room. Her feet were silent on the carpet, but her dress rustled around her legs.

As she approached his door, she drew a quick breath of relief. The door was shut tight. He couldn't have seen her with Cabot. She smiled and turned to go back to her own room when the door swept open and Samuel whisked her inside.

Four

A *SURPRISED* breath choked in Michaela's throat when Samuel shut the door behind her, gently pushing her against it. His hard, lean body flattened her hooped skirts and pressed closer to her than any man ever had. Their eyes met in the dim light. In an instant anger replaced shock.

"What are you doing?" Her temper flared with excitement when she saw Samuel smiling down at her boldly. All evening she had let him be free with her, and now he intended to continue his unseemly behavior. Well, she had had enough!

Pushing with all her strength, she broke his hold. "How dare you accost me in such a manner," she snapped. Her hands settled around her small waist. Through her anger, Michaela noticed that Samuel's eyes were no longer on her face, so she followed his gaze. To her dismay, the bodice of her dress had been disarrayed in their brief struggle, and most of one breast was showing.

"Oh!" she gasped as she straightened her clothing, covering herself. Sparks of outrage glittered in her eyes. "You're an impossible man. Papa will disown me if he finds us here in your bedroom."

Samuel leaned lazily against the door, resting his arm on the brass knob. He met her flashing emerald eyes unwaveringly. "I think not. You're too lovely to disown," he said in a low, clear voice.

Light from the low-burning lamp threw larger-than-life shadows that shivered on the wall. Was the room warm, or did the rush of heat that enveloped her come from the look in his eyes? Michaela touched the back of her palm to her flushed cheeks.

"You have compromised me for the last time this evening," she said. "Now step aside and let me out of here."

"Not until you answer one question."

"I will not. You've had your last answer from me." Her voice was strong. She didn't intend to back down.

"Did Cabot kiss you good night?" he asked.

"That's no concern of yours," she replied indignantly.

He moved closer to her. "It is if you want to leave this room."

Michaela took a step backward. "I'm not afraid of you, Samuel Lawrence." But she was. She didn't fear being hurt. She feared the wonderful way he made her feel. When she was in his arms nothing else mattered.

"Good. I don't want you to be afraid of me. The last thing I want to do is hurt you." A wicked light danced briefly in his eyes.

Samuel continued to inch toward her, and Michaela kept easing away from him until the backs of her legs hit the side of the bed. She could go no farther. He had trapped her once again.

Not waiting for her compliance, Samuel slid his arms around her waist and pulled her closer. "See, I'm not going to hurt you. Now answer my question. Did Peabody kiss you tonight?"

Michaela parted her lips to speak, then caught herself. No, he wouldn't persuade her to tell him. What she did was none of his business, and she wouldn't give in to him. She clamped her lips shut.

"You leave me no choice." With the ease of a man accustomed to getting what he wanted, Samuel claimed her lips with soft persuasive pressure.

It wasn't easy to remain still in his arms while the seeds of passion burned inside her, but she did. His lips were gentle, teasing, loving. She closed her eyes and inhaled slowly. For the time being, she was content to let him have his way. She liked the strength she felt in his arms. She liked the smell of him, the taste of him.

His lips left hers but continued to place hot little kisses on her cheeks, over her chin, and down her neck, lighting little fires wherever they touched her. It was an assault on her senses, and she found herself anticipating the next kiss as the last singed her flesh.

At last he lifted his head, his eyes dark with passion. Huskiness shaded his voice as he said, "I couldn't let you go to sleep with Peabody's kiss on your lips, or with his touch upon you."

She looked at him in the half-light and realized he no longer held her. She was free to move away from him, but she didn't. With some reluctance, she admitted to herself that she enjoyed Samuel's caresses. She was wretchedly torn between what was supposed to be the right way to behave and the way Samuel made her body respond to him. She closed her eyes. Maybe if she remained still, he would grant her silent wish and kiss her again.

A soft chuckle rumbled in Samuel's chest. "Does the beautiful lady want another kiss?"

Michaela's eyes flew open. Her haughtiness returned. She took a deep breath, but all she could murmur was, "You know this isn't proper."

"I believe," he assured her, "that society allows me the right to steal a few kisses from my fiancée." Without waiting for her reaction, he walked over to the marble-topped mahogany dressing table, taking off his tie as he went.

Michaela's skin tingled, and her gasp wouldn't emerge from her tight throat. "What—what are you talking about? I'm not your fiancée." She followed him to the dresser and watched him in the mirror while he slipped the tie from around his neck. The lamp burned brightly, highlighting the blond streaks in his hair.

"I intend to marry you, Michaela," he said, pulling off his jacket and throwing it over the back of a gold brocade slipper chair.

"That's absurd. You don't know me. I don't know you!"

They watched each other in the mirror. "Not a valid excuse. Most couples marry without knowing each other properly." He unbuttoned his shirt.

"Well, I don't! Be-besides, I'm a difficult person to live with."

"Everyone is difficult to live with because we all basically want our own way."

Michaela tore her eyes away from Samuel and glanced at her reflection in the mirror. Her eyes gleamed and sparkled. Her cheeks were bright pink. What was he trying to do to her?

"I don't approve of arranged marriages, and I don't approve of you... What are you doing? Why are you taking off your shirt?"

"I'm going to bed, Michaela."

His words startled her. "You can't do that."

Samuel turned away from the mirror and faced her. His shirt was open to the waist, and he started on his cuffs; a serious look dominated his features. Light brown furlike hair covered his chest. She was tempted to reach out and touch it to see if it felt as soft as mink.

Samuel looked directly at her. "I'm going to marry you, Michaela." He pulled the tail of his shirt from his trousers. "And, if you stay in this room much longer, it will be sooner than I planned."

Michaela clenched her hands into fists. Frustration and anger fused together inside her. First he forced her into his room and now he was throwing her out.

"You arrogant man. It's impossible to talk to you! Cabot was right. You have no manners." She spun around, skirts flying, and headed for the door. As she reached for the handle, she turned back and announced sharply, "Cabot also wants to marry me, and his manners are impeccable. You, Samuel Lawrence, are the last man in the world I would marry."

Jerking open the door, she rushed outside, slamming it shut behind her. The sound reverberated throughout the long hallway. Realizing what she had done, Michaela lifted her skirts and ran to her room, wanting to get away before someone got up to investigate the noise.

Once inside, she hurried to the dresser and pulled the cord to summon a maid to help her undress. Seating herself in front of the mirror, she took the pins and ribbon out of her hair and brushed it vigorously.

When her arm tired and her scalp tingled, Michaela laid down the brush. She sat quietly for a moment, pondering her reflection in the mirror. The corners of her pink mouth, reddened after Samuel's demanding kisses, began to quiver. A dozen thoughts swirled in her mind, but she continued to sit there thinking first of Samuel, and then of Cabot, and then of Samuel again.

Samuel Lawrence was a man to be reckoned with. He was a man she couldn't ignore. A big man, a perplexing man. But did she want to tackle that big a challenge? Michaela watched her mouth widen into a smile.

The next morning Kate was up while it was still cold and last night's rain lay sparkling on the grass. She stood in the breakfast room doorway waiting for Padraic to arrive. She had no doubt that he would be the first because she had stopped and listened at each door before coming down. Only at Padraic's room did she hear the noise of bustling. It wasn't surprising. Since she'd known him, he had always been an early riser. She liked that trait, along with many of his other qualities she'd become accustomed to in the three months she'd lived in the Brennen household.

Watching the hallway, she willed him to hurry down the stairs. She simply had to speak to him before the guests arrived.

The new cook was busy in the breakfast room setting up the buffet Kate had ordered. There was no better way to serve guests properly in the morning than by keeping the food warm over lighted candles.

At last she heard Padraic's heavy step on the stairs, interspersed with an occasional grunt. It would never occur to him to be quiet in case their guests were still sleeping.

Kate was worried. Padraic was—She stopped herself. When had she come to think of him as Padraic? She had to be careful that she didn't slip and call him by his Christian name in front of anyone. That would never be acceptable as long as he was her employer.

"Ah, Kate, this is a surprise. You don't often rise before I do." He combed at his thinning hair with his hand.

"Yes, I know, Mr. Brennen, but I must speak to you this morning before the others come down." Quickly she glanced over her shoulder into the breakfast room. "Let's step over here where we can have privacy. The cook is still setting the table."

Padraic followed Kate to the round window at the end of the hallway. Gray clouds still lingering after last night's storm blocked the sunshine, and a draft of cold air slipped through a crack somewhere in the window.

"What is it you want to say?"

Primly, Kate clasped her small hands together in front of her blue wool dress, then looked up at Padraic with determined hazel eyes. "The order you gave me yesterday about giving Michaela and Samuel time alone is highly improper. I want you to know that I won't do it again.'' Her eyes remained firm, and her chin had a decided lift.

"What harm did it do to give them a few minutes alone to get to know each other?" he asked in a perturbed tone.

Taking a cautious breath, Kate replied, "That kind of behavior will only damage Michaela's reputation. Last night I was able to get away with it because of the storm and having the extra rooms prepared. But if it happens again, Samuel will think we are trying to force him into a situation of compromising Michaela so that we have reason to demand he marry her."

"Nonsense." Padraic dismissed the idea with little consideration. "Samuel wouldn't think that at all."

Kate took a step closer to him. "It's not nonsense. If we allow her freedoms no other properly chaperoned young woman has, Samuel could think she has already been compromised, and that we are trying to trick him."

"Enough!" He raised his hand into the air. "Anyone can look at Michaela and know she hasn't been touched."

"No, only you can." Kate was adamant. "You are her father and you love her." Her voice softened as she continued. "You can't know how others will perceive her. We must guard her against any possible acts that may damage her hopes for a good marriage." She took another deep breath, and her gaze held his eyes firmly. "Protecting her reputation is my job. Now, I'm asking that you remove the restrictions you placed on me yesterday and allow me to do my job properly so that Michaela will not suffer."

"Yes, yes. You're quite right. I don't know what I was thinking to even suggest such a thing." He rubbed the back of his neck with his large hand and continued down his shoulder. "Come. Let's see if the cook has breakfast ready yet. I feel in need of some nourishment."

Samuel quietly eased the bedroom door shut. Stretching his arms up over his head, he bent from side to side to loosen his tight muscles. He felt good. Sleep had come to him immediately after lying down, and, contrary to what Michaela had hoped, it was restful. He was light on his feet as he hurried down the stairs, heading for the kitchen to see if anyone else was up and about.

At the sound of voices coming from a doorway just before the kitchen, he stopped and looked inside. Padraic pushed away an empty plate with one hand and patted his round full stomach with the other. Kate sat to his right with only a cup of coffee in front of her. Watching the two, Samuel wondered whether or not there was anything between them. The gentle looks Kate gave Padraic were no true indication of how she felt because she looked that way at everyone.

"Good morning," he said, stepping inside the small room that had windows on three sides.

Padraic grunted his greeting while Kate made hers very formal with a pleasant smile. "Good morning to you, Samuel. I trust you slept well."

"Yes, I did."

"I'm going to ask that Kate remain to keep you company through breakfast, Samuel. I have some paperwork to attend to in my study." Padraic pushed back his chair and rose with the strength of an agile man.

"Before you leave, Padraic . . ." Samuel tried out the man's first name. It rolled easily from his tongue, giving him confidence. "I'd like to invite you and Michaela out to Twin Willows for a visit." He turned to Kate. "And I'd like you to come, too. I know you'll get along very well with my mother."

Kate's pleased smile thanked him for the personal request.

Padraic rubbed beneath his chin with the backs of his fingers. "A trip to Twin Willows? I think that can be arranged. Let me give it some thought and get back to you later in the week."

"Certainly," Samuel said, and watched Padraic leave the room.

Kate rose from the table and picked up her empty cup. "Please help yourself to breakfast, Samuel. We don't stand on ceremony in the morning. Things are too rushed." She added more coffee to her cup and went to stand in front of the window, looking thoughtfully at the gray day outside.

Although his eyes followed Kate, Samuel was thinking of Michaela. If he could get her to Twin Willows, and spend some time alone with her, he knew it would be easy to make her fall in love with him and want to marry him.

Michaela was up early. Her night's sleep had been fitful. After slipping into a morning dress of yellow crushed velvet, she twisted her long auburn-streaked hair into a hasty but neat chignon at the nape of her neck. She wanted to make sure the breakfast room had been prepared for a buffet. Last night she had paid too much attention to Samuel and not enough to her duties. She should have made sure the new cook knew what to do.

The house was chilled from the evening's storm, and the morning fires had not yet warmed the air. Michaela pulled her beige knitted shawl tighter. With eager steps, she crept down the stairs, across the marble foyer, and into the breakfast room. She froze at the doorway. Much to her dismay, she wasn't the first one up.

Kate looked up and smiled. "Good morning, Michaela. I was just telling Samuel that I was sure you would be the next person down."

Michaela glanced briefly at the two. A tiny chill shook her body. Seeing them together made her feel odd. Surely it wasn't jealousy? She berated herself at the thought.

Grinning like a well-fed cat, Samuel helped himself to a serving of scrambled eggs from a silver platter. Kate stood in front of the window holding a cup of steaming coffee— and she was smiling. Nothing could warm a room like a smile from Kate. Michaela had never seen her in a bad temper or worried about anything. She was always calm, always in command.

"Good morning to both of you," Michaela answered pleasantly, keeping her eyes on Kate for a few moments before letting them drift to Samuel. "I trust you slept well, Mr. Lawrence, and that the storm didn't keep you awake." She couldn't keep an undercurrent of curiosity out of her voice. He was still by far the most annoying man she had ever met.

"Not at all, Michaela." He set his plate on the table. "And I thought you had agreed to call me Samuel?"

Michaela glanced at Kate before answering. The older woman was watching her closely. When Samuel was around, it was easy to forget that anyone else was in the room. "Yes, of course. How could I have forgotten?"

Michaela pasted a smile on her face and walked over to the buffet table. She wasn't hungry, but filling a plate gave her something to do. Out of the corner of her eye, she watched Samuel standing near the table and holding out a chair for Kate. When she was seated, he walked back to the buffet and poured a cup of coffee. As he replaced the silver pot, his arm touched hers, sending a sweet rush of heat through her. Why did his touch always start a fire of longing inside her? Her reaction to him couldn't be natural.

"And how did you sleep, Michaela?" Samuel asked.

Turning defiant eyes upon him, Michaela remarked, "Like a baby."

"Interesting," he drawled, plainly teasing her. "The few babies I've known awaken several times during the night to be fed." Without giving her time to retort, he added, "But my knowledge is limited."

No, he couldn't have known that she lay in her bed wishing she were back in his arms. The tautness of her body increased. "It most certainly is," she agreed. How could he possibly have known that she had a miserable night?

Quickly Michaela turned away from him and put her plate on the table. Samuel held out her chair politely, and she gave him a stilted thank-you.

"Most babies sleep very soundly," she continued when Samuel had taken the seat in front of her. "Isn't that true, Kate?"

"Oh, you're both right. When a baby is put to bed one

never knows whether he'll awaken several times for a feeding or sleep through the night.''

It was just like Kate to be diplomatic. But her answer didn't soothe Michaela's heated temper. She was of no mind to be generous to Samuel. His treatment of her last night and his bold statement that he intended to marry her still hung heavily around her. Threatening.

Michaela watched Samuel eat heartily. It appeared that he had slept well last night, and that angered her all the more. She watched him butter another large biscuit, then add a spoon of rich blackberry preserves to the center before taking it to his mouth for a bite. His eyes caught her watching. The knowing look he gave her made her immediately give her attention to her breakfast.

Refusing to glance at him again, Michaela turned to Kate and deliberately changed the subject. ''Has Papa been down?''

''Oh, yes. You just missed him. He's in the study, though, if you need to speak to him before he goes to the bank.''

''I've invited you and your father out for a visit,'' Samuel told her.

Michaela's eyes shot up, and her hand flew to her chest. ''To Twin Willows?'' Did this mean he had spoken to her father about marriage?

''Yes. The plantation isn't what it was before the war, but I can promise you that my mother and sister, Davia, will make you feel welcome.''

She was leery. Why did he want them to visit Twin Willows? A swarm of conflicting emotions whirled inside her. Did she want to go? No, he was too arrogant and too opinionated, too sure of himself and of her. Yes, he was a challenge.

"What did Papa say?" Her voice was soft. Samuel watched her with his brown eyes, making her skin prickle pleasantly.

"I believe he's going to arrange it for some time next week."

Her heartbeat increased rapidly. She was excited, yet worried. "What do you think, Kate?"

"It will do Mr. Brennen good to get away for a few days."

Samuel laid his linen napkin on the table. "If you'll excuse me, ladies, I have to be on my way. Michaela, please pass along my thanks once again to your father for his hospitality. And tell him I'll be looking forward to your visit."

A gentle feeling tugged at her heart. Michaela couldn't tell what Samuel was feeling, but her own pulse raced at the thought of going to his home. Suddenly she didn't want him to leave. "I will," she said quietly.

Samuel reached for Kate's hand, and when she held it out, he kissed it. "You're an enchanting woman, Kate." He smiled.

"And you are a true gentleman."

The short hairs of Michaela's nape bristled. She didn't like the way Samuel and Kate looked at each other. At the doorway, Samuel turned his eyes upon Michaela and with a devilish grin said, "Until we meet again."

Before Michaela had time to recover from Samuel's exit, Cabot made a hasty entrance. He held a handkerchief over his nose and sneezed loudly. "My apologies, ladies. It seems I caught a nasty cold last night while standing outside." He sneezed again, a loud, shrill noise. His head jerked, sending dark hair flying across his forehead.

"You sound simply dreadful. I'll ask the cook to make you some hot tea right away."

"Thank you, Kate. I will have a cup before I go, but I won't take time to eat. I must get to the doctor before this wretched stuff turns into pneumonia." He coughed into the white handkerchief while he pulled out a chair and sat beside Michaela.

"I'm so sorry this happened, Cabot. Do you always catch colds so easily?" Concern filled her voice.

Removing the handkerchief, he revealed a rosy red, glowing nose. "No, my dear, have no fear that you have a man with a weak constitution on your hands. It was simply the damp air that brought this on." His voice sounded faint and nasal.

Michaela was worried. Cabot didn't look good. "I do hope this doesn't send you to a sickbed."

He smiled and patted the hand that rested on the table. "I'll make certain it doesn't, my sweet. I wouldn't have you worry a moment ov-ov-" He sneezed again.

"Perhaps I shouldn't wait for the tea after all." Cabot rose from the table, and Michaela joined him.

Cabot wasn't faking. His pale lips and red nose really made him look ill. "Should I ask Papa's driver to take you to the doctor?"

"Yes, that would be splendid. I don't relish a long walk on a dreary day, especially when there's the possibility of this head cold moving into my chest."

"Sit back down and wait for your tea. I'll go speak to Papa."

"Michaela." He touched her arm. He so seldom touched her that she jumped slightly. "While we have a moment away from Kate, I wanted to ask you if—if—" A sneeze, followed by a fit of coughing, stopped his words.

"Don't worry about anything right now, Cabot," she said in a firm voice. "We'll talk later. You must get to a doctor for medicine, then go straight to bed."

Michaela turned away quickly and went in search of her father.

Five

*I*T was well past noon when Samuel arrived at Twin Willows, cold and damp from a light misting rain that had plagued him the last half hour of his journey. Spring was just around the corner, although the Georgia sun didn't know it. It had remained covered by gray storm-threatening clouds the entire day.

Samuel hoped that so much rain this early in the season meant that March would stay dry so seed could be planted. Sometimes getting the seed in the ground was the easy part. Keeping it there through heavy rainstorms was hard. The seed or young plants could easily be washed away in less than an hour.

When the big white house with black shutters came into view, Samuel could see smoke coming from the three chimneys. It would be warm inside with hot coffee simmering on the stove. Laughter would shine in his mother's eyes when he told her about the loan.

Samuel dug his knees into the sorrel-colored horse and rode past the house and out to the barn. The large doors were open and a faint trail of smoke drifted out, clinging heavily to the moist air. Samuel didn't dismount until he was inside the spacious barn.

"Good day to ya, sir," Henry called as he plucked a handful of feathers from a headless chicken, then dunked it in a kettle of steaming water. "I'll take care of dat horse far ya, jest as soon as I'z gets through with dis chicken."

Nodding, Samuel pulled off his black leather gloves and left the horse in his stall. He shed his damp jacket only to find that the rain had soaked through, wetting his shirt. The stench of scalded feathers hid the barn's usual smell of horse and hay. Wrinkling his nose at the foul odor, Samuel walked closer to the tall lanky man and the fire.

"I have some good news, Henry. I was able to procure a loan. We'll have enough money to put in three hundred acres of corn and get the mill started."

"Yessir, that's shor nuff good news." His head bobbed with acknowledgment.

Henry never smiled, but Samuel knew by the light in the old man's eyes that he was glad. This had been a long time coming, and it was going to mean a better life for all of them.

"I'll be going back into town in a couple of days to get the supplies and hire some workers for the mill. Have you heard if any of the Jackson boys are still in the area?" Holding his hands out toward the warmth, Samuel moved still closer to the fire burning beneath the black iron kettle.

Henry pulled the chicken out of the water, and Samuel stepped back. "No, sir. I don't get around like I used ta, but I'll see what I can find out far ya." He started plucking feathers once again, carelessly letting them drop and settle around his feet.

"Thanks. I'd appreciate it, Henry. The Jacksons are good field hands—hard workers. I know we can get that corn in the ground by the first of April if I have any two of those brothers."

"Jest leave it ta me. If I can use the mare t'night, I'll do myself a little ramblin' and see whats I come up with."

"Just don't leave before supper's ready. I don't want Mama trying to roast that chicken."

His head bobbed slowly once again, and he closed his eyes briefly. "Yessir. I knows what ya mean."

Davia met Samuel in the foyer, and he gave her a gentle hug. "How's it going, Muffin?"

"Mama won't let me go out because of the rain," she complained.

"Your mama's right. You could catch a cold in that kind of weather." Samuel ran his hand over more than a day's growth of beard, and his thoughts slipped to Michaela. She'd looked especially tempting this morning, with her eyes clear and her cheeks naturally blushed. She was still angry with him about last night, but that didn't worry him. If she hadn't cared that he'd been so free with her, that would've worried him. No, she was innocent when it came to men, and that pleased him. His only worry was the possibility that Cabot might be getting the same passionate response when he kissed her. Damn, he didn't like that thought. Why was she so evasive when it came to that prig?

"Guess the storm kept you away last night," Davia said as she looked up at him with her big brown eyes.

"What? Oh, yes, it did. You weren't afraid, were you?"

Her hands jerked to her waist, and she lifted her chin

proudly. "Have you ever known me to be afraid of anything?"

Samuel pretended to think about it while he hung his damp jacket on a brass horn. "Seems to me there was a certain snake that had you screaming for your life one time."

"That doesn't prove anything. Anyone with good sense in their head would run from a snake," she said defiantly, then added, "And I wouldn't have run if I'd had a gun in my hand. I'd have shot him."

Samuel chuckled under his breath but pointed a firm finger at her. "You let Mama hear you say a thing like that and she'll tan your hide, then not let you come down to dinner for a week."

Davia grinned. "So where did you spend the night?"

His feet were cold, his boots and pants were wet, and his little sister was standing in front of him, playing the part of his keeper. "Now, do you really think that's any of your business?" he asked, allowing a scant trace of reprimand to enter his tone.

Clasping her hands together behind her back, Davia swung lightly back and forth. "Was she pretty?"

Samuel snapped around to face a knowing grin. She was baiting him. "You little imp. Where do you get such notions?"

"Maybella Owens said the reason you wouldn't court her is because you have a woman in town." She lowered her voice to a secretive whisper. "And that sometimes you stay the night with her."

"That's nonsense. I don't court Maybella because she's only fifteen years old. When I take a wife, I'd like her to be a little older than that. Maybella is just jealous." He started to walk away but stopped after only a couple of steps and turned back to his sister's gaze. "And furthermore, I don't think she's the kind of girl you should be spending time with."

"Samuel, I thought I heard your voice," Evelyn Lawrence called as she entered the foyer from the library with a dusting cloth in her hand. Although her red dress was faded and worn, she was carefully groomed, her light brown hair drawn into a perfect bun on top of her head.

Samuel kissed her soft cheek and said, "Mama, I have good news. Let's go into the kitchen where I can have a cup of coffee, and I'll tell you all about it. I'm chilled to the bone."

"What good news, Sam?" Davia asked eagerly, pushing herself between Samuel and her mother.

"Never mind that right now. Samuel needs to get into some dry clothes."

"The clothes can wait. My news can't. I've been bursting at the seams all the way home."

Evelyn smiled. "All right, but come sit by the stove and warm yourself."

Davia started to follow Evelyn into the kitchen, but Samuel stopped her by placing a firm hand on her shoulder. He spoke quietly so his mother wouldn't hear. "We'll finish our conversation later. You're getting a little too big for your britches."

She stuck out her tongue. "I don't wear britches."

"Did either of you see Henry?" Evelyn asked as they made their way down the hallway.

"He's in the barn dressing a chicken for dinner," Samuel said.

"He wouldn't let me watch," Davia complained.

"I don't think you'd find it a pleasant sight, Muffin," her brother remarked.

"I already saw him one time. He took the chicken by the neck and started twirling it around in his hand." Davia demonstrated the act by the movements of her hand. "The chicken's wings started flapping, and—"

Evelyn spun around quickly, turning angry brown eyes upon her daughter. "That's enough about watching a chicken being killed, young lady. If I hear one more word about it, you'll go to bed without one bite of dinner."

Davia clamped her lips together and placed her hands behind her back, but her eyes twinkled with mischief. She knew such gruesome details bothered her gentle mother. Although she loved to tease, she also knew when to stop.

The large kitchen was warm, and Samuel welcomed it. His shirt still clung damply to his chest, and his pants felt like a second skin. While Evelyn poured the coffee, he and Davia placed three chairs in front of the stove. When he was settled in the bow-back armchair, he pulled off his wet boots and propped his feet on a low stool Davia had set before him. The heat made his chilled toes tingle.

Evelyn handed him a steaming cup of black coffee, then sat down beside him. "Now, tell me what news you have."

"I got the loan we needed—on my terms."

With joyful oohs and ahhs, Davia and Evelyn hugged and kissed Samuel, almost spilling his coffee. "Take it easy," he warned, basking in their delight.

"Samuel, I can't tell you what wonderful news this is," Evelyn said softly. The sparkle in her eyes gave light to the gray day. "Thank God. I knew He wouldn't let us down."

"Both of you sit back down and I'll tell you everything I have planned."

Evelyn and Davia returned to their chairs, allowing Samuel time to sip his much needed coffee. It was strong and bitter. His guess was that it had been brewing half a day.

"I've got to go back into Atlanta in a couple of days to get the money. While I'm there I want to buy enough seed corn to plant three or four hundred acres, and I need to hire workers, too."

"Oh, dear," Evelyn said in a concerned voice, her eyes watching Samuel closely.

"What is it?" he asked.

"You know I don't question you on most things, Samuel, but wouldn't it be best to plant cotton?"

"Not when everyone is planting cotton. No one's planting large crops of corn because they think they'll make more money with cotton. By the end of June when the corn is harvested, it will be in big demand, and we'll get a good price for it."

"Are you certain, Samuel?" Worry clouded her gentle expression.

"Listen, Mama." Samuel set his cup on the floor beside his chair and took her hand in his. "If everyone plants cotton, there will be a surplus, and prices will go down; and if only a few people plant corn, there won't be enough on the market. Since everyone needs to eat, they'll pay well for our crop."

Evelyn smiled gently and patted Samuel's hand. "I see what you mean, and I do trust you, Samuel."

"Good. I hope to hire several mill workers while I'm in Atlanta. There are enough men out of work, so I shouldn't have any trouble. And I'm going to hire a woman to help you in the house."

"You don't have to do that, Samuel. We're getting along just fine. You use that money for something more important. I've learned how to cook and wash and iron."

Instinctively Samuel rubbed his neck. He knew how well his mother could starch and iron a shirt. "Yes, but you shouldn't have to do those things. Besides, you'll need help because we'll have guests staying with us for a few days."

"Visitors? Here at Twin Willows? Oh, Samuel, we can't possibly entertain anyone now. The house hasn't had a good cleaning in years. We don't have the proper foods or maids to care for guests. Look at our clothes." Evelyn rose quickly, and spread out her skirt for him to see. "Your sister and I haven't had a new dress in years. I'm not complaining. It's just that we can't possibly receive visitors dressed like this."

Samuel stood up and laid loving hands on his mother's shoulders. "Mama, don't you worry about pretty dresses. I'm going to see that you and Davia get new clothes."

Her eyes brightened. "Will there be enough money?"

Smiling, he nodded. "Plenty, I promise. It will take a while before we get the house the way it was before the war. Some things won't ever be the same, but this loan is going to give us a start, a chance to rebuild."

"Who's coming, Samuel?" Davia asked from behind them.

"The Brennens," he said, turning to face his sister. "Padraic, his daughter, Michaela, and her chaperone, Kate Spencer. Padraic Brennen is the banker who's lending me the money."

"What about his daughter, Mickala?"

"No, it's Michaela. Mi-kay-la."

"Why's she coming?"

Davia's tone was sharp, and Samuel knew he had to be careful. She wasn't used to sharing him. "Because I want her to come. She's a very beautiful young woman. I think you'll like her."

"Is she the woman you spent the night with?" Davia asked accusingly.

"Davia, hush your mouth!" Evelyn ordered. "That was a rude thing to ask. Apologize to your brother this minute."

"No, Mama. It's all right," Samuel cut in to take care of the problem. "I did stay in the Brennen home last night. Not that it's any of your business, Davia. But it would hardly be fair to say I spent the night with Michaela, considering the fact we slept in separate rooms."

Davia dropped her chin, contrite. "I'm sorry," she apologized.

Samuel raised her chin with one gentle finger. "As well you should be. Michaela Brennen is a very nice young lady."

The back door opened and Henry stepped inside. A headless, plucked chicken dangled from his dark hand. "You ready fo' me to start da dinner, Miz Lawrence?"

Three days later Samuel walked into Padraic's bank. He stood in the doorway for a moment, checking the room with a sweeping gaze. His reflexes hadn't left him, and wartime habits died hard. He didn't recognize the teller behind the counter, and since Padraic wasn't in view, he headed for his private office.

"Just a minute, sir. May I help you?" The teller left his position and scooted mouselike from behind the counter to stand between Samuel and Padraic's door.

Unimpressed, Samuel said to the shorter man, "I'm here to see Mr. Brennen."

The small, balding man sniffed and pulled at the hem of his dark blue waistcoat. "I see. Is Mr. Brennen expecting you?"

"Yes," Samuel said firmly.

"Well," the teller insisted, "you'll have to wait here and let me announce you. Mr. Brennen may be busy."

Samuel tapped his booted foot on the floor while the man opened Padraic's door and closed it solidly behind him.

"Send him in, you ninny," Samuel heard Padraic bellow through the door.

The flustered teller came out quietly, clearing his throat. Summoning up his lost dignity, he said, "Mr. Brennen will see you now," then hurried back to his post behind the counter.

"Samuel, come in, come in. I've been expecting you. Close the door and sit down. I can't tell you how delighted Michaela is about the invitation to Twin Willows. She's simply ecstatic."

Samuel would have liked to think that Padraic was telling the truth, but Michaela hadn't seemed too happy with him when he'd left her house a couple of mornings ago.

"Take a look at this." Padraic handed him a single sheet of paper. "I've deposited the amount you asked for into an account in your name. You're free to draw the money out at will and spend it on whatever pleases you."

The thin sheet of coarse paper was heavy in Samuel's hand. He'd been trying to get a loan like this since the winter of '65. Now, a year and a half later, he had it.

"Go ahead, and read it. It states simply that the money is yours and that you will be forgiven the debt if it's not paid back in three years."

"I'll pay you back," Samuel said.

"Splendid. If you decide to, I will gladly accept payment."

Samuel looked at the paper. Everything was in order. "I'll make the first payment when the corn is in at the end of June."

"That's satisfactory, but remember, there's no hurry," Padraic insisted. "Now, how long will you be staying in town?"

"At least until tomorrow. I've got to buy supplies and hire some workers."

"Good. It's a wonderful opportunity for you to have dinner with us. And you're invited to stay the night. No need to go to a hotel. I'll go home at lunch and ask Michaela to have a room made up for you."

Samuel remembered how tempting Michaela looked with her long hair streaming down her back in curls. He remembered the sweet taste of her lips and the haunting smell of her soft skin. Yes, he wanted to see her again. "What about Peabody? Is he coming?"

"No, the dear man is out of it," Padraic said, suppressing a grin. "Seems he caught a chill the last time he dined with us and has taken to his bed. Poor soul must be on the puny side."

Samuel folded the paper and put it in the pocket of his wool jacket. "In that case, I'll come."

"Splendid. We usually dine at seven."

"I'll be there."

With all his errands behind him, Samuel stood beneath a newly installed gas-lit street lamp in front of the two-story Colonial on Peachtree Street. He combed through his hair with his fingers. He wanted to look presentable for Michaela Brennen. Since their first kiss she hadn't left his thoughts. One moment she'd kissed him with the passion of a grown woman, then only a few minutes later she had been an eager young girl wanting her first taste of brandy. In anger she had been a strong, worthy opponent. In his arms she had been ready for love. What more could a man ask in a woman?

The thought of her green eyes flashing at him sent him running up the steps two at a time. He was ready to see her again. She was the woman he wanted. Three solid hits on the door knocker announced his arrival.

A maid showed him into the parlor, where Padraic, Kate, and Michaela were waiting. She was as lovely as he'd remembered. The dress she wore resembled the color of an apple just before it ripened, her lips a rich, rosy shade of pink. Their eyes met, and Samuel knew she was no longer angry with him for forcing her into his room. He couldn't take his eyes away from her while he responded in kind to Padraic's polite greetings; and when she held out her hand, he dropped a kiss upon it gently.

"Michaela, it's good to see you. You look lovely tonight." He let his eyes tell her he meant every word.

Michaela smiled. "Thank you, Samuel. Please sit down."

Samuel sat on the sofa as close to Michaela as he

could get without fear of Kate's wrath. The smell of cloves and cinnamon teased him. He leaned closer to Michaela and inhaled deeply. The scent came from her hair. He had to suppress the temptation to reach over and strip the pins from her hair and let it fall to her white shoulders so he could bury his face in it. After they were married, he would tell her always to wear her hair down for him.

"About this invitation to Twin Willows—how long a visit did you have in mind?" Padraic asked as he stood warming himself in front of the blazing fire.

Reluctantly, Samuel turned his attention to Padraic. "A few days, perhaps, I don't know how long you can stay away from your work."

"Mmm . . . I may be able to take three days off toward the end of next week. Will that be a good time for you?"

"Excellent, in fact. By the middle of March, I should be busy getting the fields ready for planting."

"We'll plan on it. Now, why don't we go in to dinner?"

Samuel rose and reached for Michaela's hand. "Allow me," he said, and helped her from the small sofa.

Michaela smiled and slipped her arm through his.

Tonight, Samuel thought, Michaela would see a different man. She had accused him of having no manners, unlike the pompous Cabot Peabody, who knew just how to treat a lady. Well, he would be the perfect gentleman—until he could get her alone.

Through dinner, Michaela was content to listen to Samuel and her father exchange views on subjects from politics to horses. This time she saw Samuel with different eyes. He was turning out to be a very interesting, desirable man.

She didn't really know anything about him, yet she felt she knew everything. She remembered the way his lips had felt pressed against hers and how firm and strong his muscular body had been when he'd held her. His teasing smile was especially pleasing. She liked the clean smell of his shaving soap and the color of his hair. Right now she wanted nothing more than to be close enough to run her fingers through it.

He had such good manners when he ate, although his appetite was hearty. He didn't pick at his food curiously as Cabot did. And his laugh was a fresh, wholesome sound filled with genuine delight. She had seldom heard Cabot laugh.

When dinner was over they retreated to the parlor for coffee. Padraic excused himself for his usual smoke on the porch. Michaela had hoped Kate would remain in the kitchen and bring out coffee as she had the last time Samuel visited. But there was no such luck this time. Kate was right there doing her duty. She wasn't going to give Samuel and Michaela one moment alone.

After Bessie brought in the coffee, Michaela poured a small amount of brandy into Samuel's cup before giving it to him. She was tempted to put a few drops in her own cup; but with Kate's watchful eye on her, she decided it wouldn't be wise to be so bold.

"I hear Peabody is under the weather," Samuel said, taking the cup from her.

Michaela wasn't sure whether or not Samuel's comment had a sincere note of concern in it. "Yes, he caught a chill. The doctor says he may have a touch of pneumonia."

"That's too bad," he replied, then took a big sip of the coffee. He smiled at her. "Just the right amount."

His pleasing smile warmed her as surely as if she'd sipped the liqueur and let it coat her throat. "I had a note from Cabot yesterday. He's feeling better. He said he's going to stay in bed a few more days to make sure there's no chance of a relapse."

"That's a good idea. I've never had pneumonia, but I saw a lot of it in the winters of sixty-three and -four. He's best not to take it lightly."

Samuel's mention of the winter of '63 brought back memories Michaela didn't want to think about. She and her father had spent most of that winter begging for work, food, and a place to stay the night. With firm resolve to forget those days, she pushed the memories from her mind.

She listened as Samuel spoke briefly with Kate about the war. He was articulate, persuasive, and compassionate. He didn't assume to be an authority on the subject the way Cabot did, and she liked that.

Padraic joined them a few minutes later and announced it was time to retire.

Michaela had hoped the four of them would walk upstairs together, but much to her consternation Samuel touched Kate's arm and pulled her to one side. Michaela had no choice but to continue up the stairs with her father.

"Kate, I was hoping you could suggest someone I could hire to help out at Twin Willows. I'd like a woman who can do some of the household chores as well as cook," Samuel said. "I'll give her room and board, but

I'm sorry to say that I can't pay her very much at this time.''

Kate placed a slim finger over her closed lips and pondered his question. Suddenly her eyes brightened. ''I may have just the person for you. I'll speak to her tomorrow and have her come out to Twin Willows the day after.''

''Thanks. I'd really appreciate it.'' He reached down and kissed her cheek. ''You're wonderful, Kate.''

''Stop that. You'll make an old woman blush if you're not careful.''

''You're not old. You're beautiful,'' he insisted.

''Enough of your flattery. The woman I'm thinking about may not even consider your proposal. Don't go thanking me until I've done something. If Velvet isn't interested, I'll make other inquiries for you.''

''That's all I ask. And I do thank you.'' Samuel reached for Kate's hand and kissed it gently.

Upstairs, Michaela sent her maid away as soon as her corset was untied. She quickly shed everything else she was wearing and slipped a white cotton gown over her head. She left untied the ribbons that would have held together the opening of the gown's bodice and sat down at her dressing table. One by one she took out the hair pins, letting her hair fall.

Why had Samuel asked to speak to Kate alone? What could he possibly have to say to a woman old enough to be his mother? Did he have designs on Kate? Kate was a very beautiful woman—soft-spoken and kind. But she was her father's age! The possibility of Samuel being interested in Kate set her teeth on edge. And Michaela had secretly hoped Kate and her father might one day . . .

That was a hopeless thought. Padraic was too rough, too loud, too overbearing for a gentle woman like Kate.

With a sigh, Michaela dropped her hairbrush to the dresser. Maybe she wasn't being fair. Her father had a wonderful sense of humor, something a lot of men lacked. He was generous and loyal to his loved ones. Yes, now that she thought about it, her father had several admirable qualities. She smiled. And she did love him very much.

Michaela stared at her reflection in the mirror, intent on deciding what kind of woman Samuel saw when he looked at her. Bemused, she let herself gaze at the eyes reflected there, faintly mesmerized with watching herself so closely.

A light knock on her door penetrated her concentration. Was Kate stopping by to tell her what Samuel had wanted? Michaela jumped from her stool, almost knocking it over, and rushed to the door. "Who's there?" she whispered, her lips pressed against the cold wood.

"Samuel."

Michaela jerked backward. Samuel? She bent to the door once again and whispered loudly, "What are you doing? What do you want?"

"I have to talk to you. Open up and let me in."

"Are you insane? If anyone catches you in my room, you'll be shot and I'll be ruined for life."

"Everyone's light is out but yours. If you'll open up and let me in, no one will hear us."

"No. Go away. I don't have anything to say to you that can't wait until tomorrow." Her voice stayed low, but her tone had lost its firmness.

"Michaela, if you don't open this door, I'm going to

yell so loud your father will come out to see what's going on.''

This was madness. First he tried to compromise her by dragging her into his room, and now he was trying to gain entrance to her room. He knocked louder. Michaela took a deep breath. He wasn't playing by the rules. He never had.

"Wait a moment," she whispered, and ran to her bed for a robe to cover her gown. Hastily she tied the sash of the green velvet robe as she rushed back to the door. With cold, trembling fingers, she threw the lock on the door and opened it just wide enough for Samuel to slip inside.

Samuel shut the door quietly and leaned against it while Michaela scampered to the far side of the bed, putting its width between them.

"What do you want?" she asked in a firm but breathless tone.

"I want to hold you in my arms and kiss you." Neither his words nor his eyes held back his passion.

Michaela gasped at his forwardness . . . yet it excited her. "You—you said you wanted to talk to me."

"I do." He started toward her.

"Don't come near me, Samuel." She put out her hand to warn him away. "You said you wanted to talk, and I'm going to hold you to your word."

He rounded the foot of the bed and didn't stop until he was mere inches away from her. "All right, we'll talk. I couldn't go to sleep tonight until I held you in my arms and kissed you." He smiled down at her. "That's what I wanted to tell you."

Michaela looked into his eyes. He seemed sincere. She

didn't want to tell him no. "But it's not right," she whispered hoarsely. "You shouldn't even be here in my room."

"I can't very well do this in front of your father." He slid his arms around her, pulling her to his chest, letting his lips claim hers in a soft, tempting kiss. Michaela yielded as soon as he touched her. He tilted her head back, and her hair fell from her shoulders to shimmer down her back.

She wasn't supposed to allow this. Michaela knew she should run or call for help, but all she could do was enjoy his embrace, his kiss. Without her corset and big skirts to interfere, she was sure she felt every muscle in his body. She felt strength in his arms, passion in his lips, tenderness in his kiss. A sweet thrill trembled through her. Being close to him like this was so different from being held while wearing so many clothes. It was more desirable, more enticing. It was what she wanted. And it was wrong.

With that realization, she twisted her face away from his lips, although she remained locked in his arms, fitted firmly against his hard maleness. "You shouldn't be in here. I'm not properly dressed." Her voice was husky, undemanding.

"I know."

Samuel was pursuing her ardently, and she loved it. Her breath came unevenly as he brushed a stray length of her hair away from her shoulders. Her heart pounded in her own ears. Her knees trembled with the weakness of desire.

"You're so beautiful I can't keep my hands off you. I want to touch you." His lips claimed hers once again while his arms pulled her still closer, held her tighter. They clung together for a moment in a long, deep kiss. The spark that kindled between them fanned to a bright roaring flame.

Michaela tried to find words to make him stop since she had neither the strength nor the desire to push him away. "You shouldn't be kissing me like this," she whispered against lips that swallowed the sound of her protests.

"Don't you like it?" His voice was intense, his brownish gray eyes glowing in the faint light of the room.

"Yes." Her answer was more of a moan as his lips slipped down her neck, leaving a tiny trail of moisture that caused her skin to chill when the cool evening air touched it.

"How do my kisses make you feel?"

"I don't know," she admitted breathlessly. "It's like—" She sighed. "It's—like I want something more."

"Something more than kisses—like this." His voice was husky as he reached up and gently cupped her breast in his hand, applying the merest hint of pressure.

Michaela drew in her breath sharply. Yes, like that. No one had ever touched her there. She hadn't expected his caress to give such pleasure. She tried to fight the constantly mounting sensations. Her eyes locked with his, asking him to explain this new feeling that had caught her in its web.

Samuel answered with his touch, caressing her gently. Michaela closed her eyes. Her abdomen tightened. With his free hand, he untied the ribboned sash of her robe and pushed it and her gown aside. He kissed her exposed shoulder, letting his lips grace her skin as softly as butterfly wings.

Even though Michaela kept her eyes shut, she was keenly aware of everything Samuel was doing. She was too intrigued with the new, unknown sensations to object. Gently Samuel pushed the robe and gown farther down her arms, exposing her breasts.

"You're as beautiful as I knew you'd be," he whispered, shaded passion outlining his voice. He reached down and kissed the warm skin between her breasts. She trembled with increasing desire for him, wanting him to do more. She moaned provocatively, slipping her arms around his neck and cradling his head against her bosom.

Samuel closed his lips around her nipple, pulling it gently inside his mouth as his hand swept across her buttocks to press her against his hardness.

His loving action was so new that Michaela gasped, stiffened, then pushed him away. "Wh-what am I doing? I must be mad!" Cheeks flaming, she pulled her robe and gown together and turned her back on Samuel. She was too eager to discover the pleasures a man and woman share. It was Samuel's fault. He'd turned her into a wanton! A woman of the night!

"Michaela." He laid his hands on her shoulders, and she jerked away.

She pivoted around on one foot and glared at him. "Stay away from me. You make me do things that aren't proper. Don't come near me again." She ran a shaky hand through her long hair.

Samuel's eyes turned hard. "There's nothing wrong with what happened. I'm going to marry you."

"Ha! I'm not marrying you. I'm going to marry Cabot."

Suddenly he pulled her into his arms and pressed her close. "Has Cabot ever made you feel the way I do?"

"That's none of your—"

"Business!" he finished for her in an angry voice. "It is my business. Dammit, Michaela, I want you."

Michaela wrenched free of him and spun away. Why had she told him she was going to marry Cabot? She wanted to laugh at the absurdity of that idea, but she didn't have time. In a commanding voice she said, "What I feel for Cabot is none of your concern. Now get out of my room or I will call for my father."

Samuel took a deep breath and moved backward a couple of steps. "I'm going to make you forget about Cabot Peabody." He turned and strode confidently out of the room.

When the door was shut, Michaela realized her chest hurt from holding herself so erect. That man could bring out the worst of her temper. But he could also make her feel so very much alive.

She turned and looked at herself in the mirror, then timidly placed a hand over her breast, cupping it gently the way Samuel had. Samuel might not know it, but he'd already made her forget about Cabot.

Six

*T*HE smell of frying bacon and strong coffee quickened Samuel's step as he walked into the warm kitchen. Velvet Dickerson stood at the wood-burning stove, her back to Samuel, humming a happy tune while the bacon hissed and crackled in the pan. Her bun of dark brown hair was arranged neatly, even though a few hairpins showed around its edges. The sash of her calico-printed apron had been tied into a tiny bow at the center of her waist. One of the things Samuel liked about Velvet was that she was always humming, singing, or smiling.

If she had heard him come in, she didn't bother to turn around and acknowledge him. A tall woman with a large frame, Velvet was a welcome addition to Twin Willows. Without her they would never have been ready for the Brennens' visit.

"You want your eggs fried or scrambled, Mr. Lawrence?"

Samuel grinned to himself. She'd heard him come in after all. Velvet had only been with them for a week, but he had already decided she was the kind of woman who wouldn't let much get by her.

"I think I'll have them the way you cooked them yesterday," he answered.

"I thought as much," she said with a pleasant smile. "They'll be ready by the time you pour coffee."

"Am I the first one up?" he asked. He picked up the heavy black pot and poured the hot liquid into the waiting cup. He inhaled deeply. There was something especially pleasing about the smell of coffee on a chilly morning.

"Missy has already had her breakfast. I sent her back upstairs to change. She came down in one of her new dresses. I told her I needed her to help bake pies, and I didn't want flour all over that pretty dress. Your mama and I were up until after midnight getting the last one hemmed. But we made it." Velvet turned and faced Samuel with clear blue eyes. "Mrs. Lawrence works hard, but she's not fast."

Samuel chuckled. "You're right about that. No one works harder than Mama," he agreed, and sat down at the table.

Velvet placed a plate with two eggs, three strips of bacon, and two large golden-topped biscuits in front of him. He thanked her and silently thanked Kate as well for sending Velvet to work for the Lawrences. Not only could she clean and sew, she was also an excellent cook. Henry was very happy to give up his cooking duties in the kitchen and go back to tending the grounds and preparing the land for a spring vegetable garden.

"Hi, Sam." Davia scampered into the room, wearing a faded blue dress. Her happy face told him she wasn't rejecting Velvet's authority. That was another indication that Twin Willows was indeed lucky to have a new housekeeper, seamstress, and cook.

"I hear you're going to help make pies this morning?" Samuel bit into the hot biscuit he'd filled with fresh-churned butter and blackberry preserves.

"I guess so. I'd rather go out riding. Can we?" She stood before him, her big brown eyes shining. She cocked her head sideways and gave him a wistful look.

"Not today. We've got too much to do before the Brennens get here."

"That's all I've heard for the past week." Her tone indicated that her patience was running out. "What time can we expect them?" she asked.

"Oh, I'm sure they'll be here by dinner. Plenty of time for you to help with the cooking before you have to change. It's a long journey from Atlanta by carriage."

"Does Michaela ride?" Davia asked.

Samuel sipped the hot coffee and cut into his eggs. "I'm not sure. You'll have to ask her when she gets here."

"I bet she can't," Davia declared. "Maybella said she knows Michaela. She's seen her in town."

Samuel didn't look up from his plate. "Has Maybella met Michaela?"

"No, but she's seen her three times. They passed in the street just last Saturday."

Because of the way Davia pronounced each word with

unaccustomed slowness, Samuel looked at his sister. What was she going to say next? Obviously Maybella had told Davia something she was itching to tell him. He might as well ask. "What else did Maybella say about Michaela?"

Davia glanced at Velvet before leaning closer to Samuel. "She was walking with a man, and she was smiling," she whispered, then cut her eyes around to see if Velvet was listening. "And she had her arm hooked through his. Maybella said the man wasn't old enough or big enough to be her father."

Her words hit Samuel in the pit of his stomach, and he tried to hide his irritation by taking another bite of his biscuit. So, Michaela was still seeing Cabot Peabody. Damn!

Trying not to listen for carriage wheels, Samuel sat at his desk in the library later that day working on his account books. Velvet, his mother, Henry, all of them, had worked diligently for a week to get the house cleaned, the furniture waxed, and new clothes made. They were all tired. Even Henry had complained that morning about having to chop extra firewood and carry it up to the guest rooms, dress two chickens, and peel a tub full of sweet potatoes.

Samuel couldn't tell them that he worked everyone so hard because he wanted Michaela to like Twin Willows. She had to. His home had to become as important to her as it was to him.

He hadn't been idle while the others toiled at the house. He'd spent his days going over the farm land, testing the soil to see which acreage would be best to plant the seed corn. Henry had managed to locate two of the Jackson boys, and they'd agreed to work for a wage and place to live. Repairing one of the houses in the old slave quarters was still a chore that had to be done before the workers arrived next week. He and Henry would have to get busy with that job as soon as the Brennens were gone.

How was he going to repair a run-down house, get the corn seed in the ground, and plan a wedding all in the next couple of weeks?

Michaela wasn't aware the carriage had reached Twin Willows until it came to a halt. A stab of apprehension grabbed hold of her. What would Samuel's mother and sister think of her? Would they like her? Would she like them? She shook her head. It didn't matter. She wasn't going to marry Samuel. And she definitely wasn't going to allow him in her room again. She didn't care if he shouted the house down.

Padraic pushed open the carriage door and stepped out. She couldn't see Samuel from her position inside, but she heard him. There was a smooth, warm quality to his voice that made her heartbeat quicken. She also heard female voices as her father was introduced. Padraic turned back to help Kate. Her full burgundy-colored skirt caught on an exposed nail, and it took a moment for Michaela to free it.

At last Padraic reached into the carriage for her hand. She lifted the hem of her skirt just enough to show all of her ankle-high boots so she could watch her step. When her feet touched the ground, she let go of her dark blue dress and looked up into Samuel's waiting brown eyes.

What she saw in his face made the long, bumpy carriage ride worthwhile. His look warmed her like a fire on a cold night. Maybe she should marry him. If she didn't, she had a feeling she would end up in his bed anyway. The truth was difficult to bear, but she had to admit it. She wanted to be in Samuel's bed. That admission suddenly made her feel vulnerable.

A large ball of bright sun shone low in a cloudless western sky. The breeze was cool but not cold. The big white house with its black shutters shimmered in the late afternoon sunshine. So this was Samuel's home.

"Hello, Michaela. Welcome to Twin Willows."

Just the sound of his voice, that knowing grin on his lips, set her to remembering what it was like to be held in his arms, pressed close to him. She took a light, steady breath, hoping he felt as flustered as she did.

"Good afternoon, Samuel, and thank you again for the invitation." She extended her gloved hand, and he kissed it without taking his eyes off her face.

Still holding her hand, he turned and said, "Let me introduce you to my mother, Evelyn Lawrence, and my sister, Davia."

"It's a pleasure to meet you," Michaela said to his mother, then turned her attention to Samuel's young sister. Davia, whose eyes were the same unusual shade of brown as her brother's, was watching her closely. In contrast to her mother's pallor, Davia's cheeks were radiant with color and life. Her eyes held a hint of deviltry that challenged Michaela. She doubted there would ever be a dull moment around Davia, and she took an instant liking to her.

"Do you ride?" Davia asked as soon as Michaela's eyes met hers again.

"I don't sit a horse well. I've seldom had the opportunity, but yes, I do like to ride."

Instead of the news delighting Davia, as Michaela had hoped, it seemed to upset her: the young girl's bottom lip puckered, and her forehead creased with a frown. Michaela realized Davia didn't want any competition. If they were going to be friends, Michaela would have to watch what she said until Davia knew she could trust her.

At Samuel's urging they all moved inside, leaving Henry and Padraic's driver to carry in the luggage and see to the horses.

When they were seated in the parlor, Velvet came in carrying a large tray laden with steaming coffee and an assortment of tea cakes, and she and Kate talked for a moment. Michaela noticed that Davia stayed close to Samuel yet kept her eyes on her. It was apparent that Davia knew a relationship had developed between the two of them.

Michaela looked at the handsome planter and wondered what he had told his sister about her. As she watched him, she wondered also if he would try to slip into her room that night or drag her into his. Just thinking about the possibility made her breathless. No, she told herself sternly. If he came to her door, she would not let him in under any circumstances. He'd made a wanton of her once. She wouldn't let him do it again. She didn't want him to hold her in his arms and kiss her the way he had the last time they were together.

Then Samuel lifted his eyes to hers, and despite

herself, she knew she wanted him to hold her in his arms and kiss her exactly as he had kissed her the last time.

"You didn't answer Mrs. Lawrence, Michaela," Kate said in a quiet tone that betrayed a note of dissatisfaction.

Michaela cleared her throat and turned her attention to Samuel's mother. "I'm sorry, I was just admiring this room. It has such a warm feeling about it. It's so lovely. What was the question?"

"I'm glad you like it, dear," Evelyn replied. "Would you care to have cream and sugar in your coffee?"

"Oh, yes, both please."

She watched the older woman put a scant spoon of sugar in the light brown liquid, then add a small portion of cream. Michaela took the cup and looked around the room, determined she wouldn't be caught staring at Samuel again.

The dark mahogany of the settee Evelyn occupied was in excellent shape, but the material on the scrolled arm had worn thin. Against the far wall stood an early Chippendale sideboard. The beautifully carved mantel and exquisite cornice boards seemed untouched by time. A quick glance around the rest of the room confirmed what she'd been thinking: the war had robbed Samuel's home of its treasures. Many Southerners had sold or given most of their fine pieces of furniture, paintings, silver, and jewelry to help the cause or to buy food for the troops. Samuel's family was obviously no exception.

"I hope you didn't get too cold on the drive out?" Samuel asked Michaela when, despite her determination, her eyes lighted on his handsome face once again.

"Oh, no. We stopped once for refreshments, so it was

quite a pleasant day." Actually her feet had been cold the entire trip and were only now starting to feel warm again.

"She's quite right, Samuel," Padraic added. "It was an excellent day to travel. The sun has dried the roads and left very few potholes."

For politeness' sake Samuel asked, "And how is Peabody? I believe he was under the weather when I spoke to you last week."

Michaela saw sparks of jealousy in his eyes when he mentioned Cabot's name, although he managed to keep it out of his voice. Samuel's question made it clear that he still considered Cabot a rival for her attentions, and that pleased her greatly.

"How kind of you to ask." She smiled at him, hoping to irritate him. "Yes, he was ill for a time. I'm pleased to say that he's doing very well. I saw him just last evening." Her smile widened.

Michaela knew Samuel wouldn't like hearing that, but she couldn't help teasing Samuel. She wanted him to wonder if Cabot had kissed her. If he did, he might be tempted once again to steal into her room and wipe the memory of Cabot's lips from her mind, to fill her only with his scent, his taste, his touch, his words, and his face.

"Michaela?"

"Oh, I'm sorry, Kate. What did you say?" Michaela felt a blush creeping up her cheeks. Once again she'd been caught not paying attention.

Kate gave her a disapproving look, and Michaela lowered her eyes. "I think Mrs. Lawrence is right. You must be tired. You can't keep your mind on the conversation." Michaela reddened further, and Kate turned to

Evelyn. "Yes, thank you, we would like to go up and rest. What time should we be down for dinner?"

"Seven," Evelyn said softly.

Padraic rose with a grunt. "And I should go speak to the driver before he leaves. I want to make sure he's here bright and early Friday morning."

Samuel stood up and stopped Padraic. "But if you leave Friday, that won't give you two full days here. I was expecting you to stay through the weekend."

At the sound of Samuel's tense voice, Michaela was forced to look at him again. He wasn't happy about the shortness of the visit. A wrinkle creased his forehead.

"I know. Such a shame it is, but I can't possibly be away from the bank on Saturday. You know how it is. The busiest day of the week, and there's simply no one I can trust."

"I think Henry has all the luggage in the rooms now," Evelyn said. "Davia, why don't you show Michaela and Kate to their rooms. Samuel, I'll let you take care of Mr. Brennen. Do let us know if you're in need of anything."

Samuel nodded, and Kate said, "Thank you for the coffee, Mrs. Lawrence. It was so nice."

Smiling broadly, Evelyn responded, "Dinner will be ready by seven. Don't feel you have to rush down before then."

Michaela watched Samuel walk out with her father before joining Kate and Davia. The last thing she wanted to do was rest. She wasn't tired, but she followed Davia's bouncing steps up the stairs and listened to her question Kate.

"You're Michaela's chaperone?"

"That's right," Kate answered patiently, keeping step with the younger girl.

"I don't have a chaperone," she stated proudly, glancing back to make sure Michaela had heard her.

"You have your mother," Kate informed her as they reached the curve in the grand staircase.

"You live with Michaela and her papa?"

"Yes, for almost four months now."

"What happened to her mother?"

Michaela had reached the top stair when Davia's question hit her. She grabbed the banister and held on tight as a vision of her mother lying dead raced across her mind. Looking up, Michaela saw Kate and Davia staring wide-eyed at her. She shook her head gently to clear the images that so readily came to mind. They hadn't been that vivid in years.

Kate regained her composure quickly and answered Davia. "I believe she died when Michaela was a young child."

"No, she didn't." Michaela's voice was raspy as she corrected Kate. Looking into Davia's inquisitive eyes, she responded, "She was killed by an Englishman's bullet when I was your age. I don't consider you a child. At thirteen, you're a young woman."

Samuel's little sister gazed at Michaela with the same bleakness in her eyes that filled Michaela's. "My papa was killed by a Yankee's bullet," she said softly.

"Well, I don't believe this is the place or the time to talk about this subject," Kate interjected. "Now, Davia, which room is Michaela's? I do believe she needs to rest."

Michaela watched the two of them walk down the

hallway. She realized she was breathing deeply, and her hands had made fists. Thinking of her mother's death would always cause her pain. Kate didn't want to hear about her mother or Davia's papa. Kate never wanted to hear anything sad or depressing. Rubbing her eyes with the back of her hand, Michaela followed them. She and Davia had more things in common than just Samuel. A lot more.

Three rooms down on the left, Davia stopped and pushed open a door. "This is where you'll be sleeping," she said to Kate.

The three of them walked into the large room. A low-burning fire and late afternoon sunshine added their warmth to a room decorated in pale pinks and lavender. The field bed had a canopy and attractive flower-printed coverlet. The dresser was rosewood with a matching mirror attached to it.

"This door connects to your room, Michaela." Davia smiled as she swung open a door that led to a much smaller room with one window. The room was decorated in deep shades of reds and greens. The bed was narrow, and the only other furniture was a squat bureau against the far wall with a plain wood-framed mirror hanging over it.

Kate looked at Michaela and gave her a quick wink. "Oh, well, since my things have already been placed in this room, I think I'll use it and let Michaela have the larger. Anyway, I'm not fond of pink. You don't mind, do you, Davia?"

If Kate's words had been any softer or kinder, Michaela would have burst forth with the smile she was suppressing. She was certain now that Davia was jealous and had every intention of trying to make her visit a miserable one. That didn't bother Michaela. She admired Davia's spirit and knew she was going to enjoy getting to know Samuel's little sister.

Davia crinkled her nose. The look she gave Kate said that she knew she'd been outsmarted this time. "I guess not," she answered, and glanced up to see Michaela's reaction.

Michaela kept her smile to herself and said, "Please tell Mrs. Lawrence the rooms are lovely and how delighted we are to share your home for a few days."

Davia didn't acknowledge her compliment but walked back into Michaela's room. "There's fresh water in the pitcher. If you need anything else, just let one of us know."

After the door was shut, Michaela and Kate burst into laughter.

That evening, Samuel waited in the parlor for Michaela to come downstairs. Padraic sipped a glass of sherry, and Evelyn sat on the sofa, showing Davia how to do an embroidery stitch. As usual, Davia was complaining. Samuel didn't know much about young girls, but he was certain Davia's lack of interest in sewing and cooking wasn't typical. Not many men cared whether or not their wives could ride a horse or shoot a rifle; however, they'd want wives who knew how to manage a household.

He smiled to himself when he realized the direction his thoughts had taken. What was he thinking? He couldn't care less whether or not Michaela could cook and sew. Housekeepers like Velvet could be hired to do that kind of work. The only thing that was important to him was the way he felt when Michaela looked at him, when she was in his arms with her lips against his.

Closing his eyes, he took a deep breath. He wanted to be alone with her. He couldn't have argued with his mother about which room should be Michaela's. Naturally his mother would choose the proper one, but it wouldn't be easy to sneak in or out of her room with Kate nearby. He'd find a way to see her tonight. He just hoped she knew that he was going to and would make sure the door between her room and Kate's was locked.

As if on cue, Kate and Michaela walked into the parlor. Samuel didn't even look at Kate, although he knew she was there. Michaela wore a brandy-colored dress with a heart-shaped neckline. The deep color against her creamy white skin made his throat go dry. A gold brooch, tied snugly with a brandy-colored ribbon, rested in the hollow of her throat, right where he wanted to put his lips and feel her heartbeat.

When their eyes met, Samuel knew he'd have to kiss her before the night was over. And he'd speak to Padraic before they went back to Atlanta. He didn't want to give Peabody a chance to touch her again. Michaela was going to be his bride before spring was in full bloom.

Later that night Samuel lay on his bed waiting for all the sounds of the night to subside. When he felt certain everyone was asleep, he crept to Michaela's door and knocked very lightly several times. He only had two days to convince her to marry him.

Another knock and he was rewarded with hearing the soft click of the lock. The door opened mere inches and Michaela's beautiful face came into view. Samuel bent closer to the opening and whispered, "Come out here so we can talk."

She shook her head furiously, then whispered back to him, "No. It's too risky. Kate's a light sleeper."

Samuel felt a moment of apprehension. His questioning eyes sought and held hers. "She won't hear us if you come outside."

Michaela moved closer to the door. "I can't. You shouldn't ask."

Hoping not to startle her, Samuel reached inside the door and caressed her face. "I want to hold you. Please, Michaela, come out here."

When she lowered her lashes over her eyes, he knew she was weakening, and his hopes soared. He wanted to kiss her so badly that he was trembling. Even with the door between them he could feel her warmth and smell her sweet scent.

She lifted her lashes. Her eyes were filled with disappointment. She touched the hand that rested on her cheek. "I can't do this. Go away and don't ask again. Please."

Samuel tried to hide his frustration. They were less than a foot apart and he still couldn't hold her. He sighed. "All right, not now. But I want you to promise to meet me at the barn eleven o'clock tomorrow morning."

Her eyes widened. "Why?"

He smiled. "We're going on a picnic. Just the two of us."

"But I couldn't possibly get away from Kate."

The excitement in her eyes pleased him. "I'll take care of Kate. Just promise you'll be there."

Michaela bit down on her bottom lip for a moment, then looked up and smiled at Samuel. "I'll be there."

Seven

"I REALLY shouldn't be doing this," Michaela said as the rickety buggy left the barn. "Kate will be furious."

Samuel smiled at her with complete confidence. "Well, if she insists I've ruined your reputation, I'll simply have to marry you."

"That, Mr. Lawrence, is one of those things that is easier said than done." She hadn't forgotten his promise that she was going to marry him. However, she wanted it to be her choice, and Cabot had to be considered. He wanted to marry her, too. But Samuel's kisses made her yearn for more, while Cabot's left her feeling there was no more to kissing than the pressure of his lips against hers.

"What was I supposed to do?" Samuel continued. "Kate didn't leave your side for one minute yesterday. You wouldn't come out of your room last night and talk to me, and you leave tomorrow. I had no choice except to kidnap you if I wanted time alone with you. Besides, what could be more harmless than a picnic?''

"I'm afraid Kate won't see this picnic as harmless, and she could very well decide that you should marry me.''

Samuel cut his eyes around to her and grinned. "That would be my pleasure.''

Michaela took a deep breath and clasped her hands together in the lap of her velvet skirt. "A forced marriage is not to my liking. I want it to be my decision whom I take for a husband.''

Chuckling lightly, Samuel asked, "If you really thought we might have marriage forced upon us, why did you agree to come away with me?''

Their eyes met, and Michaela realized his question was very important. Why had she come away with him knowing it could irreparably damage her reputation or force her into marriage? Looking into his gleaming brown eyes, she knew there was only one answer. "I decided it was worth the chance.''

With a satisfied nod, Samuel turned his attention back to the horse. Michaela was silent while she reconsidered her words. It was true she was willing to risk her reputation for a few minutes alone with Samuel. But did that mean she was in love with him? At one time, she thought she might be in love with Cabot. Now she was certain she didn't love Cabot, but she wasn't convinced she was in love with Samuel. Their physical attraction for each other went way beyond her wildest dreams, but did that prove love?

The brisk morning air nipped her cheeks and lightly stung her eyes, but the brassy sun high in the light blue sky warmed her. The carriage squeaked and creaked over the rough terrain, and the horse gave an occasional snort.

Last night's misting rain had left the earth smelling sweet. Budding trees and sprouting grass, the first telling signs of spring, surrounded them.

"Where are we going?" she asked after a long silence.

"Oh, about a mile over that hill is a small lake. I thought we'd have our picnic there."

"Is it part of Twin Willows?"

"Yes. The lake's not big, but the water is clear. It's a perfect place to swim in the summer. I like it because it's quiet and peaceful. I think you'll like it, too." He smiled, then asked, "Can you swim?"

She laughed lightly. "No, but I have a feeling you'd love to teach me."

He whistled through his teeth, and his eyes scanned her face longingly. "If only it were warm enough today."

Michaela glanced away. Every time she looked at him she wanted to touch him. Being this close and not touching him was agony.

"I like your home very much." Determinedly she changed the subject. "You have so many flowers blooming in the garden."

"The gardens are Henry's domain. Until Velvet came, Henry had to help with a number of chores inside the house. Now he devotes his time to the vegetable and flower gardens.

"This is the way to the lake," Samuel continued as they left the ruts in the dirt road and headed between the trunks of two large trees, budding with life. Moments later shining blue water came into view. The sun's rays glanced off the still water of the lake with blinding brilliance. As soon as they hit the shade trees the air grew cooler. The horse picked its way slowly through the small trees and bushes for a few minutes until they came to another clearing with the beautiful blue lake sparkling like polished silver in the background.

Samuel tied the horse to a tree, then helped Michaela down, putting his hands on her waist and holding her for a brief moment. "You spread the blanket while I water the horse," he told her.

The sun was quite warm, so she took off her cloak and laid it beside her on the blanket. Samuel lifted the basket of food out of the carriage and joined her.

"What will we do if Papa and Kate come after us?" she inquired as Samuel sat down on the blanket.

"What can we do other than ask them to join us? I'm sure Velvet packed plenty of food."

Michaela laughed. "Do you always make light of serious matters?"

"No, not always." He moved closer to her. "I don't want to spend one minute of the time we have together worrying whether or not your papa will come charging through that brush with a shotgun. If it happens, then I'll worry about it."

How could she do anything but smile at such self-confidence? Michaela's breath quickened when he reached over and softly touched his lips to hers. His arms closed around her gently, enveloping her in warmth and strength. With slow movements he untied the bow of satin ribbon at her throat and let her bonnet fall to the blanket behind her. Lost in the gentle pressure of his kiss, Michaela sighed contentedly.

When he drew away from the kiss, the crisp wind dried her moistened lips. Their eyes met. Michaela knew the bond between them was great, the attraction so intense that she had to be in love with him.

"I've been waiting for a long time to do that," he said in a husky voice.

"It was very nice," she answered demurely, and lowered her lashes over her eyes. She didn't want him to think she was a wanton or lady of the night, but she wanted his kisses and caresses.

Samuel touched her chin with the tips of his fingers, and she looked up at him. "Your kisses are more than nice." He cleared his throat and ran a hand through his hair. "I think we'd better get the food out just in case your father does decide to come after us."

Michaela dug into the picnic basket and pulled out a loaf of bread wrapped in a linen napkin. He was right; she didn't want her father to catch her kissing Samuel.

"Your mother's very nice, and Davia, too. She's not willing to admit it yet, but we have a lot in common."

"Oh, I can see it. You're both strong-minded, outspoken. And you're both beautiful."

She smiled. "Yes, but there are other things, too. More personal things. Your father was killed by a Union soldier?"

"Yes, shortly after the war started. In a way he was lucky not to have suffered. I know plenty of men who did. I'm surprised Davia mentioned it to you. She doesn't usually talk with anyone about her father."

"I can't say we were actually talking about it. She mentioned it in passing when she asked about my mother."

"Your mother? I'm afraid I don't even know about her." His voice was gentle.

Michaela felt a flutter in her stomach. Why had she brought up this subject? She pulled a wedge of cheese out of the basket. "My mother was killed by an Englishman. We'd gone for a walk in the park. We didn't know that some men had planned an uprising. When the shooting started we tried to get away to safety, but my mother was shot in the chest before we could make it to the trees."

Samuel took the hunk of cheese from her hand. "I'm sorry. It must have been terrible for you."

The caring in his expression warmed Michaela. "At times, it seems as though it happened only yesterday."

"Do you want to talk about it?"

She shook her head and continued to unload the basket. "Papa thinks it best if we don't discuss it. He thinks that will make the memories fade."

"Have they?"

Michaela looked into his eyes and appreciated the tenderness she saw there. "No. I still remember the shouts and cries of men and women running through the park. The screams. I hear the sound of bullets as they whiz past my head . . . and my mother lying so still with blood staining her white blouse." She shuddered.

Samuel slid his arms around her waist and pulled her against his chest. She felt the heat of his body, the scratchy wool of his jacket, the crisp linen of his shirt.

"Shh, don't say any more," he muttered, his breath warming her cheek. "Your mother's safe in heaven now, and you are safe with me." He kissed the top of her head, then said, "For the rest of this picnic we're only going to talk about happy things. Why don't you pour the coffee while I cut the bread and cheese."

As the cool breeze whipped at loose strands of her hair and the sunshine kept them warm, Michaela and Samuel ate their lunch. When they'd finished off the cheese and bread, they ate a piece of sweet cake that Velvet had packed for them.

Samuel feasted on Michaela's beauty while they ate. He loved it when she laughed at his tales of childhood pranks. She threw bread at him when he told her she didn't pronounce her *c*'s correctly, and he promised her a dunk in the lake when the water was warmer.

"You're so lovely, Michaela," he said when the meal was finished.

She turned from putting the napkins in the basket and looked at him with her vibrant green eyes. He hadn't meant to tell her that. He was trying hard to keep the conversation light and his hands to himself. It appeared his willpower was weakening. If Padraic was coming after them, he'd have been there by now. Still, he knew he couldn't keep her out much longer.

"Thank you, Mr. Lawrence." She smiled.

"Why do you sometimes call me Mr. Lawrence?"

She laughed. "Let's see. I believe I call you Mr. Lawrence when you've said something that makes me very angry with you or very pleased."

Samuel pushed the picnic basket aside and moved closer to her. "And what do you call me when I do this?" His lips took possession of hers in a fierce and demanding kiss.

Beneath his lips, hers shaped his name with a whispering soft voice. His hand slid to the back of her neck and held her firmly. As desire for this woman ripped through him, she lifted her mouth with an eagerness every bit as intense as his own. Her lips parted willingly to admit the thrusting strokes of his tongue. Samuel was lost in the feel of her, her smell, her taste. Every hasty breath she took made him want her.

Her name slipped like a blessing from his lips as he pressed closer, trying to feel more of her. Gently he pushed her to the ground, leaving one arm under her head for a pillow, and pressed the length of his body to hers.

Samuel was no stranger to a woman's body, but no woman had ever aroused him so fully, so quickly. No other woman had ever felt so good in his arms, fit so naturally against him, made him feel so protective, made him want to hold her forever. Only Michaela.

The high collar of her dress hid her creamy skin. He wanted to kiss her neck and her shoulders; but knowing the perils of unfastening her dress, he merely skimmed his hand across the bodice. Trembling with desire, he caressed the full swell of her breast. Michaela moaned as his lips pursued hers with reckless abandon.

With all the control he could summon, Samuel pushed away from her and sat up. His breathing was shallow, ragged. As Michaela straightened her clothes, he wiped his mouth and tried to calm his breathing. Padraic trusted him not to dishonor her, and he wouldn't. But, damn, he had to marry her soon!

He turned and reached for both her hands. "Come on. I'll help you up. I think it's time we were going."

"Mr. Brennen, I must speak to you at once." Kate found Padraic on the back porch napping on one of the chairs.

"Ah—what's the matter?" Stretching, he rose from the chair and squinted as the sun caught him full in the face.

"It's Michaela. I think she's run off with Samuel." Her tone and voice showed how worried she was.

"My dear woman, what in heaven's name are you going on about—run off?" Padraic cleared his throat and straightened the jacket of his tweed suit.

Kate was breathless and shaky. "While I was looking at some of Velvet's handiwork, Davia came rushing in to tell me she saw them leave in a carriage not more than ten minutes ago. It took me all this time to find you."

"Nonsense."

"What do you mean? I can assure you Davia knew what she was talking about. I can't find either of them, and Velvet confirmed that Samuel asked her to pack him a picnic lunch."

"No, no. I mean it's nonsense that they've run off. They've simply gone on a picnic. It's all perfectly fine."

"Fine!" she cried. "How can you say it's fine? We must go after them immediately."

"Go after them?" he questioned. "Surely not. They would probably be on their way home by the time we found them."

"Your daughter's reputation is at stake here. You let Michaela go off alone with Samuel?" Kate clutched desperately at the folds of her wool skirt. "How could you? This is highly improper. Why did you hire me as a chaperone if you were going to let her have all the freedom she wanted?"

"Now, now, calm down, Kate. Please." Padraic tried to soothe the woman who paced back and forth in front of him. "I didn't say I let her go out alone with Samuel, only that she'll be perfectly safe with him."

"You hardly know Samuel. Besides, that's not the point. It's what people think that matters." Kate rubbed her forehead in a distressed manner. Padraic had his good points, and she was sure he loved his daughter. He simply didn't realize what harm this would do. "What will everyone say? This will ruin her chances of a good marriage, and it will be all my fault for not taking proper care of her."

"Who's going to tell?" He snorted. "You?"

His words brought Kate up short. Her eyes widened in shock. "Me?" she asked, surprised he'd imply such a thing, let alone come right out and say it. "Mr. Brennen, I would never spread gossip on my own charge."

"Neither will I. I'm also certain we can count on these good people not to discuss it." Padraic grabbed his lapels and pursed his lips. "Well, maybe except for that little lass who told you. Perhaps you should ask her mother to speak to her."

Kate took a deep breath and lifted her chin with a haughty air. "If you don't intend to go after Michaela and save her, I'll have to."

"You're making too much of this. What harm can there be in a picnic? Good heavens, I don't want Michaela to feel as if she lives in prison."

Kate eyed him with defiance. "Then I must take care of things." She turned and stalked away.

Fuming with frustration, Kate walked toward the barn. She knew Padraic loved his daughter. He simply didn't know what was best for her.

Kate had to think of herself, too. When Michaela married she would have to leave the Brennen household. That thought caused a quickening of her breath. She didn't want to leave. She'd been very happy the last few months, but she had to be realistic. She'd never get another post if it became known that she'd let her charge stay out alone with a man.

The barn door was heavy, but she managed to open it. It was too dark to see clearly, so she opened both doors and called out, "Hello," as she walked inside. A close scrutiny of the smelly barn revealed one horse and two saddles. She supposed it was possible that the Lawrences had only one carriage. And Samuel and Michaela were using it. With an exasperated sigh, Kate whirled around, her skirts flying, and headed out of the barn.

She had to find that man who worked for the Lawrences. What was his name? Harry or Henry? She'd have him saddle the horse, and she'd go after Samuel and Michaela by herself. She'd find them, and when she did she wouldn't let Michaela out of her sight again.

Two hours later Kate was still at Twin Willows, only now she was sitting on a rocker on the front porch waiting for Samuel and Michaela to return.

Henry had informed her that the horse had a loose shoe, and if she rode him, irreparable damage would occur. Knowing very little about horses, Kate was forced to take the man at his word.

When the carriage approached the front porch and Samuel helped Michaela step down, Kate rose from her chair and went to meet them. A quick glance at Michaela told Kate how happy she was. Kate didn't want to deny her the opportunity to be with the young gentleman. However, she simply had to obey the rules.

"Michaela, would you please wait for me in your room. I'd like to speak to Samuel alone before you and I talk."

"Certainly, Kate." Michaela turned her attention back to Samuel. "Thank you for a wonderful picnic. I'll see you at dinner."

When Michaela was safely inside, Kate turned on

Samuel with the fire of anger in her eyes. "You have compromised my charge, and I'm most unhappy about it. I want a full explanation of what went on and why you have been so careless of her reputation."

Samuel didn't blink an eye at her assault. "Kate, I appreciate what you did for me. Sending Velvet our way was a godsend, but this is my business."

Refusing to back down, Kate answered, "I won't have you ruin her reputation so she can't make a proper marriage. If this ill-conceived rendezvous gets out, she'll not live it down, and it will be my fault."

"Don't worry, Kate," he said with confidence as he brushed a lock of wind-tossed hair out of his eyes. "She'll have a proper marriage. I intend to marry her."

Samuel walked off, leaving Kate standing on the porch with her mouth open. He didn't need Kate to remind him how close he had come to making love to Michaela. Dammit, he couldn't help it. Everything about her excited him, and she was so responsive to his loving. He knew Michaela would be totally free and giving with her love when they were married.

He stopped at the fence that was connected to the barn and leaned heavily against the boards. It pleased him to know that he could make Michaela feel so good, she purred with pleasure. But he didn't want to be so besotted by her that he couldn't think of anything else. Still . . .

"How long you going to hold up that fence?"

Samuel jerked around, and his head snapped up. His eyes caught the glaring sun. A man sat on a horse in front of him. Samuel tensed. He'd been so wrapped up in thoughts of Michaela that he hadn't heard the horse approach. He was getting soft, losing all his military training. That thought didn't make him happy; neither did a man who was able to sneak up on him.

"Can I help you?" Samuel asked in a lazy voice, leaning back against the boards once again, hoping to appear calm.

"Don't you remember me?"

The man's words didn't remove the threat because Samuel didn't recognize the voice. He took a step to the left so the rider would be between him and the sun. Suddenly his eyes lighted with recognition. "Riverson? George Riverson, you ol' river rat! What are you doing in this part of the country?"

"Looking for you." Riverson jumped off the horse and the two men laughed, shook hands, and slapped each other on the back.

"You're a little thicker around the middle, aren't you?" Samuel playfully hit Riverson in the stomach.

"Yeah, yeah, noticed, did you?" Riverson threw a punch at Samuel, and he ducked.

"Who was that woman I saw you riding with? Don't tell me you've gone and got yourself hitched. You know better than to tie yourself down to one woman. What'd I teach you when we were in Charleston?"

Samuel grinned as the memories flooded back. They'd spent a week there waiting for the rest of the rough riders to join them. Riverson had taught him a few things about drinking, cards, and women. "We had a good time all right."

"Good time! Hell! We had every woman in town panting after what was in our britches."

Samuel laughed. "Not quite." Modesty about his women was never Riverson's strong suit.

"What did you want to go and get married for? Did you get her in trouble?"

The grin faded slowly. Riverson was an old friend, and he'd be glad to talk over old times, but Michaela had to be left out of it. "We're not married yet, and she's not in trouble. Come on, let's go up to the house and I'll introduce you. You'll stay for dinner?"

"Naw, Sam. I didn't come here to barge in on you. I just had something I wanted to talk over with you." Riverson's attitude changed quickly. He twisted his hat between his hands and refused to look Samuel in the eyes. That was Samuel's first clue that all was not well with his old Confederate comrade.

"I won't hear of it. You're staying for dinner, then we'll talk. It's probably been a while since you've eaten a decent meal."

Riverson looked up at Samuel and smiled nervously. "It's been a while since I've had a home-cooked one, that's for sure."

"I knew it. Come on. You can wash while I get you something for that dry throat."

"A shot or two of strong Southern whiskey would go down mighty easy right now." Riverson laughed and clapped Samuel on the shoulder as they walked toward the house.

Later that night, Michaela watched Samuel's friend with mild curiosity while Davia kept him busy talking. It was clear that Davia was fascinated by his war stories and the fact that he'd been to Texas. But there was something about the man that gave Michaela an uneasy feeling.

She glanced at Kate, who wasn't even pretending interest in George Riverson's tales. After a thirty-minute lecture on why she shouldn't be left alone with a man, Kate had been very quiet but always present. Michaela had wondered all afternoon what she and Samuel had said to each other, but she hadn't garnered enough courage to ask.

Even though Davia seemed to be the only one interested in his war stories, George Riverson continued to look around the room as if he were expecting something to happen. That made Michaela jittery.

He was bearded, as were most of the men who'd fought in the war. He wore clean clothes, and he was extremely polite. She couldn't fault him on his dress or manners. Still, there was something. He appeared nervous, and that made Michaela edgy. She decided to concentrate on what he was saying rather than the way he was acting to see if she could pick up on why he was troubled.

"Shortly after I met up with Sam we were sent on this special mission, along with a few other men, for President Davis. I can't tell you where we went because that's still secret. Anyhow, we rode hard the first day, each of us had our own thoughts about what we had to do so we didn't talk much. By nightfall we were all hungrier than a pack of starving wolves. But there was a problem. There we were with our saddlebags bulging with bacon and beans, and not a one of us knew how to cook."

Davia giggled and cupped her hands over her mouth. Evelyn smiled indulgently, and Michaela's curiosity grew.

As Michaela knew she would, Davia asked the obvious question. "Who did the cooking?"

"I was hoping you'd ask. I've been wanting to tell this story on Sam for a long time."

Davia squealed with delight. "Sam did the cooking?"

George Riverson laughed, too. "Well—he was the youngest in our group, so we sort of ganged up on him, if you know what I mean. But did we ever make a mistake. It was the sorriest fixin's any of us had ever tried to eat."

"As I recall, you cleaned your plate." Samuel spoke from the doorway, and, laughing, everyone looked his way.

"We had to. Our stomachs were emptier than a water bucket shot full of holes," Riverson declared with a generous smile made warmer by the friendship that showed in his eyes.

Michaela watched Samuel carefully. She loved the way he walked into a room, the way his arms swung ever so slightly, the way his legs moved from the hips, barely bending at the knees. She'd been impressed with his air of confidence the first time she saw him in the bank, and he hadn't disappointed her once. When his eyes met hers, they shared a smile.

"Don't believe a word this man says," he told Riverson's audience. "He'll say anything to hold the attention of four beautiful ladies."

After dinner, Samuel and Riverson retired to Samuel's office on the other side of the house for a glass of brandy and the talk Riverson wanted. Padraic excused himself for his usual smoke on the porch.

All through dinner Samuel had tried to fool himself by coming up with a hundred different things Riverson could want to discuss. But now that they were alone, he was sure there could be only one reason for Riverson to come to see him. It must be something to do with the bank robberies. Out of the seven men who'd participated in those ill-fated robberies, Riverson was the one Samuel liked best. Riverson was a drifter who'd been a few places, seen a few things Samuel hadn't, and had taught him how to survive.

The two men sat on chairs flanking the fireplace. Samuel didn't bother with a fire, knowing the brandy would warm them within minutes. Riverson was still as nervous as a cat who'd had his tail caught under a rocking chair.

"I'm glad you didn't mention anything specific about how we ended up together." Samuel decided he would be the one to open the conversation. "My family doesn't know anything about that part of my war activities, and I'd rather they never knew. It's not something I'm proud of."

"I didn't expect you had told them. It wasn't the sort of thing you came home bragging about when the war was over." Riverson took a drink of the liquor and winced. "Whew! This is good stuff."

Samuel smiled, remembering when he'd given Michaela an ounce of brandy in her coffee. He hadn't had the chance to talk with her since the picnic; and by the look on Kate's face, he wasn't going to get a chance if she could help it.

Riverson took another drink and sighed his appreciation. "We've got trouble, Sam."

Samuel tried not to react, but he felt a muscle working in his jaw. He had a feeling this had something to do with the presidential pardons. The war had been over for two years. He hadn't asked the president for a pardon and knew he wouldn't as long as the provisional governor allowed him to keep Twin Willows intact. He was aware of the dangers of not seeking the amnesty that was offered, but he wasn't going to take that oath until he was forced.

"What kind?" he finally asked.

"This." Riverson took a piece of dusty-colored parchment out of the pocket of his brown leather vest and unfolded it. His hand shook as he handed it to Sam.

Samuel recognized the paper immediately, and his insides lurched. It was half of the map he'd drawn up four years ago that told where the Union money was buried. His chest tightened. He was wrong. This didn't have anything to do with a pardon.

"You have half of the map? Who'd you get it from?" His voice was low and husky as a part of his past flashed before him, causing him to flinch.

"Shareton slipped it to me before we split up. Said he didn't want no part of it."

Samuel brought his feet down from the stool with a thump. "Neither do I."

"You may not have a choice." Riverson shifted uncomfortably on his chair, almost sloshing the brandy out of his glass. "There were five of us left after the first few robberies. Now there are only three."

Samuel sipped his brandy, holding the amber liquid in his mouth, letting it sting and burn his tongue for a moment before he swallowed it. "I didn't know. I haven't kept up with anyone. And I don't have the other half of the map. I can't help you find the gold."

Riverson chuckled and wiped sweat from his forehead

even though the fire hadn't been lit. "I don't want the money. Hell, it's damn Yankee money anyway." His eyes narrowed decidedly, and he held Samuel with an impassive gaze. "Shareton and Thomas died of gunshot wounds to the belly. Both of them were killed in the last two months."

The brandy burned in Samuel's stomach. "I'm too tired to play guessing games. Just tell me what the hell you're talking about."

"I don't know what happened to the two men we sent back to Alabama with all that money we'd stolen in the first three robberies. Far as I can tell no one ever heard from them. But I kept in touch with Shareton, both of us being from Virginia." Riverson finished his brandy and got up and poured another, more than Samuel had given him the first time.

"About a month ago I got a letter from his widow. I was feeling real bad about it, so I went to pay my respects." He took a big gulp, then coughed twice. "Wow!" He wiped spittle from his mouth with the back of his hand and sat back down. "It was scary, let me tell you, Sam. She told me how Shareton had heard just a couple of weeks before that one of his old army buddies had been killed the same way. I got suspicious; there was something creepy about the whole thing, so I did some checking. She was right. Thomas took lead in the gut, too." He looked Samuel square in the eyes. "I think Rufus Tully killed them trying to get his hands on that." He pointed to the paper Samuel still held.

Samuel swallowed hard. "I think you're getting soft, Riverson," he told his old friend, but he didn't for a moment believe his own words.

"Tully spent two years in an Alabama prison camp for killing a man over a twenty-dollar card game. He got out two weeks before Thomas was killed."

Rising from his chair, Samuel added more brandy to his glass. He'd never liked Tully. The man had a mean streak that he had come up against more than once in the three months they rode together. In fact, he'd almost killed the bastard a couple of times. For the first time he was getting scared—for Michaela, his mother, and Davia.

"That still doesn't mean anything." Samuel tried to reinforce doubt in both their minds.

"Maybe not, but I always liked you, so I thought I'd tell you what I'd found out. I think Tully killed Thomas and stole his half of the map, and now he's after this half. Everyone thought Shareton had it when we left, so that's the reason Tully went after him. I would have just waited around and given him the map if I thought that's all he wanted, but I have a feeling he's going to get rid of anyone who knows about it after he gets his hands on it. You and me are the only ones left."

Samuel stood still, looking into the empty fireplace, trying to decide whether or not Riverson was a madman or a true friend.

Riverson rose from his chair and drained his glass. This time he didn't cough. "You keep that map. If he comes looking for it, give it to him. Maybe if he sees you're not interested in him or the gold, he won't think it's worth another killing. I'd hate to think you'd never get to marry that pretty woman you got waiting for you."

Samuel looked at the piece of paper still held between his fingers. He didn't doubt Tully's capacity for killing over a few thousand dollars. "Let's burn it," he said.

"Then no one will get the map or the gold. It won't do him any good to kill me. He won't get the gold either way."

"Whatever you say. Sounds reasonable, but Tully's not a reasonable man."

Samuel struck a match, lit the paper, and threw it into the fireplace. In silence they watched it go up in smoke and fade into a heap of gray ashes.

Riverson placed his glass on Samuel's desk. "I don't go looking for trouble. This time, I'm afraid it's looking for us."

"I hope you're wrong." Samuel sipped his brandy again, knowing he was drinking too much. His head was buzzing.

"So do I, Sam."

"What are you going to do?" Samuel looked at his friend. A sudden concern for Riverson's welfare gripped him.

"Same as always. Run like hell."

They laughed.

"Is it okay if I bunk in the barn?"

"Hell, no! Mama's prepared a room for you here in the house. I can't let you sleep in the barn."

"Thanks, Sam, but no. I want to be out of here by first light, and if I get in a soft bed, I may find myself hanging around too long."

Samuel nodded. "Where you headed?"

"Texas. They got some mighty fine looking women out there. Too bad you can't go with me. It could be like old times."

Samuel didn't want the old times back. He had exactly

what he wanted. "Why don't you find yourself a good woman and settle down?"

"I just might give it a try when I get to Texas." Riverson smiled broadly. "Now that I've seen how happy you look with your little woman. I just might give it a go someday." He reached for Samuel's hand, and the two men clasped hands with equal respect. "You be careful."

If what Riverson suspected was true, Samuel had cause to worry. "I will. Thanks for making the trip by here to warn me."

"Ah, hell. It was on my way to Texas anyway."

Samuel followed Riverson outside and saw the red tip of Padraic's cigar glowing in the dark before the stale odor struck him. After his final good-bye to Riverson, he retraced his steps back to where Padraic was sitting in the darkness on the far end of the porch. Now was as good a time as any to say what was on his mind.

"I want to marry Michaela." It wasn't his intention to be so blunt, but he had too much on his mind to play word games.

"Is that so?" Padraic asked in a tone that sounded as if the subject had never been discussed between the two of them.

Samuel leaned back against the large column and watched Padraic blow smoke out of his mouth. The man's answer wasn't to his liking. "Isn't it what you wanted?"

"Oh, yes, indeed I do. The name Michaela takes in marriage has always been of utmost importance to me. This is precisely the reason I left my work and came to Twin Willows for a visit. I was hoping such would be the case. And I wanted to look over your home to see if I thought Michaela would be happy living here."

"And . . . ?"

"With time and more money I believe you could make something of this place."

Fine hairs stood up on the back of Samuel's neck. "Twin Willows came out of the war as scarred as the men who fought for it. Bringing it back to its prewar condition is my responsibility, and I intend to see that's accomplished. I can assure you, Michaela won't suffer because of it."

"Oh, I have complete faith in you, Samuel. I've no doubt you'll have this place thriving in a few years."

Padraic gently rocked the swing where he was sitting. "Tell me, have you asked Michaela to marry you?"

Samuel wiped his eyes, wishing he hadn't drunk so much brandy. He was tired, and the liquor was making him drowsy. "No, not in so many words," he responded. "I intend to tonight. With your permission, we'll go for a walk and I'll ask her. I think she'll agree."

"I don't know." Padraic chewed on the cigar. "We shall see. She's still quite fond of Cabot Peabody."

"That prig!" Samuel's mouth tightened. He shuddered at the thought of Peabody touching Michaela. And the merest hint of her marrying him had his stomach quaking with rage.

"That prig is a highly intelligent man," Padraic countered with smoke issuing from his mouth. "And he's gaining support for the nomination. You can't afford to overlook his credentials."

Samuel thought about the first time he'd seen Michaela and Cabot in the bank. They'd been holding hands, and he'd known she'd let him kiss her. Still, he didn't want to believe she'd responded to Peabody the way she had to him.

Padraic and Samuel studied one another for a short time. Finally Padraic said, "It's no matter about Twin Willows. Michaela's dowry should be a great help to you."

"What?" Samuel leaned forward.

"Well, as her husband you'll be entitled to a generous dowry. What do you say to fifty thousand and a small house in Atlanta."

"I don't want your money or your house. Whatever you'd give, put in Michaela's name should she ever need it. I don't want anything from you except Michaela."

"You're not being realistic. You deserve the money as her husband, and it'll make her life easier."

"She'll have to learn to live with what I can give her. I won't be taking money from you."

Even though their conversation was serious, Padraic didn't move from his relaxed position on the swing. He didn't appear in the least perturbed by their conversation, only content to sit back and enjoy his cigar.

"Why should she have to do without when I have more than I need? We once agreed that neither of us is a fool. Don't give me reason to change my mind about you, Samuel."

"I'm not a foolish man, Padraic. I'm a proud and honorable one. Michaela won't go lacking when she's my wife."

"Very well, have it your way."

Samuel leaned back once again and watched the glowing tip of Padraic's cigar. His muscles tensed. He was in love with Michaela, and that made him vulnerable. He wanted to marry Michaela, but he still wasn't sure how she really felt. It was time for him to find out.

"I'd like to talk to Michaela before it gets any later. Perhaps you should go talk to Kate."

"Kate? Whatever for?" Padraic gave Samuel a perplexed look.

Samuel smiled. "If you don't speak to Kate, she won't let us out of the house."

"Of course she will." Padraic laughed, his round middle shaking with each gusty breath. "Every young woman is entitled to a few moments alone for a proposal."

"If you don't mind, I'd rather you go speak to her. I don't think she's forgiven me for this morning."

"Certainly. Indeed I will. This is cause for a celebration. We'll plan the engagement party while we're still here. You should be engaged at least six months. What do you say to a late fall wedding?"

"I say that's too far off. I want to marry her as soon as possible."

"Now see here," Padraic said, coming to his feet. "I'm sure Michaela will want a proper engagement and wedding." A defensive crispness had entered his voice.

"I promise the wedding will be proper." Samuel headed for the door. "But I don't intend to wait half a year to marry her."

Eight

"IS it too cold out here for you?" Samuel asked as he settled onto the swing beside Michaela, close enough for her to feel the warmth of his body.

"No." She turned to him, smiling. "I'm quite warm."

Michaela noticed that the moon was partially covered by dark purple clouds. The chill wind whipped around them, forcing her to pull her lightweight cloak tighter. The kerosene lamps that hung on each side of the entrance to the porch cast a warm glow on Samuel's hair.

While she still looked into his eyes, Samuel said, "Michaela, earlier tonight I told your father that I want to marry you."

Even though she expected this was the reason they were allowed to be alone, his admission made her heart flutter and tighten the words in her throat. "I—I thought as much," she said, and cleared her throat with a light cough.

Samuel took her hand and held it in the warmth of his. "Will you marry me?"

"I don't know," she whispered.

He jerked back as if she'd struck him. "What? You don't know?"

It didn't take much to figure out that he wasn't happy with her answer. Leaving the security of her papa's home and starting a new life was not an easy decision to make. "I have to think about it," she answered, knowing that was the proper thing to say.

"You have to think about it?" he questioned with a look of incredulity on his face. He squeezed her hand. "Michaela, do you know just how close we came to making love this afternoon?"

Michaela cleared her throat once again. He was making her nervous, and she didn't like it. He had no reason to question her so blatantly, to remind her of their forbidden kisses and caresses.

"Yes, of course I do," she said with defiance, knowing that she wasn't telling the truth. Her knowledge of making love with a man was limited to exactly what had happened between the two of them earlier in the day. She pulled her hand from Samuel's and turned away from him. He wasn't being a gentleman about this. Wasn't he supposed to take "I don't know" as an answer and give her a couple of months to make a decision?

"Has Peabody ever gotten that close to loving you?"

Michaela's head whipped around, facing him once again, this time with anger in her eyes. "No! Unlike you, he's a gentleman."

"Right," he responded quickly in a rough voice. "I forgot he does everything the proper way." They glared at one another until Samuel's eyes softened; and when they did, so did his voice. "Michaela, does his proper way of kissing you make your heart hammer in your chest the way it did this afternoon when I kissed you?"

She didn't want to answer him. He had no right to ask, but she found herself slowly shaking her head and saying, "No."

His face moved closer to hers. "Does his touch make you tremble with pleasure? Does the thought of him quicken your breath or fill you with anticipation?"

His voice was low, seductive. Lamplight was shining in his eyes, bouncing off his hair, making him very appealing. She wanted to reach up and touch her lips to his, experience the glorious feelings that engulfed her every time he kissed her.

With tenderness, he answered her silent plea and covered her cool lips with a warm kiss. One arm circled her waist while the other wrapped around her shoulder, pulling her tight against his chest. She closed her eyes, wanting only to be more aware of his touch and taste.

"Marry me, Michaela," he whispered as his lips left hers and traveled over her cheek.

He was intoxicating, making her tremble with desire. But why didn't he declare his love for her? He wanted to marry her. She was sure of that. Could it be he didn't love her, or was he just afraid to admit it? Her heart wanted to say yes, but her mind jumped ahead and she murmured, "No."

Samuel went still.

Michaela pushed away from him and folded her arms

in the warmth of her cloak. "What I really mean is that I must talk to Cabot first."

"Why? Why must you talk to him? You only need your father's permission to marry me." His voice didn't hide his agitation.

"Cabot wants to marry me, too, and I need to speak to him before I give you an answer."

"No, you don't. It's none of his damn business what's between you and me." Possessiveness edged his voice. "The only thing you need to do is tell me now that you'll marry me."

"I'm sorry, Samuel. I have to talk to Cabot." She squared her shoulders. Cabot had been her friend too long for her to treat him in such a careless manner. "If you want an answer from me, you'll have to wait at least two weeks."

Samuel ran a hand through his hair and sighed. "I'm not opposed to compromise. If you must speak to Peabody, one week is all I'll give you to tell him you're going to marry me." He pulled her into his arms and kissed her quickly, passionately.

Michaela was flushed with happiness as they walked back into the house. Yes, she loved Samuel, and she wanted to marry him. But she didn't have to tell him that right now. He could wait at least a week.

The first night they were home, Michaela waited for Kate to retire before she approached her father. They hadn't really talked since Samuel had asked her to marry him. She wanted to know what he thought and how she felt about her marrying Samuel instead of Cabot.

The fire burned low in the grate, and the room had a

warm, cozy feel to it. Sitting in a big silk-covered chair with scrolled arms and flaring wings, Padraic studied some papers in his hand, his newly acquired eyeglasses perched on the bridge of his nose. Michaela gazed at her father intently. They'd gone through many hardships together when they'd first arrived in the States. Fate had dealt them a hard blow when her mother was killed and they were forced to flee Ireland in search of a safer life, only to be caught in the war between the North and South. They were homeless, frightened, and penniless, but they'd had each other. Now things were changing. She was planning to move away from the security of her father and place her trust in the hands of another man. She was going to become the mistress of her husband's home, Twin Willows.

Easing out of her chair and walking toward him, Michaela said, "Papa, may I talk to you?"

Padraic laid his papers on the table beside his chair and took off his reading glasses. "What is it, Kayla?"

Michaela smiled. He hadn't called her Kayla in a long time. It was his pet name for her. She knelt by his chair in front of the fire, the folds of her skirt fanning out around her, and looked up at him. "I'm no longer a child, Papa. I've two men who want to marry me."

He smiled proudly and hurrumphed at the same time. "That's because you're a beautiful and intelligent woman. You'd have a dozen asking if you'd ever give them a notice. So let's talk. What do you think about these two men who want to marry you?"

"I think I love both of them."

"This sounds serious. You can only marry one of them. You will have to make a choice." Padraic brushed at her auburn-streaked hair, although not a strand was out of place.

"I enjoy being with Cabot. We talk about books and politics. He's taught me a lot about the war, its causes and effects. He has good ideas for reform, and I know he'll serve in Washington one day. I guess the best way to put it is to say I'm quite comfortable with him." She laid an arm on Padraic's knee and rested her chin in her palm. "I don't have that kind of relationship with Samuel."

"What do you mean?" Padraic asked in a troubled voice. "Has he ever done anything to make you feel uncomfortable?"

Michaela brushed an imaginary piece of lint from her father's pants leg. "No, no. It's just that when I'm with Samuel, my stomach knots, my heart flutters, and I lose my breath. I worry that I won't say or do the right thing. When I dream, I dream of Samuel. When he's not around I want to be with him, see him. Does all this mean that I love him?"

"What do you think it means?" Her father threw the question back to her with his green eyes twinkling.

She smiled. "I think it means I love him."

"Then what do you feel for Cabot?"

"Oh, I think that's love, too, only a different kind. More like what I feel for you and Kate."

Padraic chuckled, his round stomach shaking lightly. "I think you are a very bright young lady." He reached over and kissed her cheek as Michaela rose from her kneeling position.

"Do you think I'll be happy if I marry Samuel?"

"Ah, Kayla. You must remember that happiness comes from inside you." Padraic stood and pointed to her heart.

"Don't let your happiness depend on anyone else. If you do, you'll be disappointed. Besides, it's too heavy a burden for anyone to have to carry around. Remember some people have made their own lives miserable trying to make others happy."

Making her way to her bedroom later that night, Michaela thought about her father's parting words. She shouldn't look to anyone to give her happiness. It should be found inside oneself. If that were true, why did she feel such a need to see to it that Samuel was happy?

Three days later Michaela waited in the late afternoon waning sunshine for Cabot's arrival. The air had a slight chill, but the velvet dress she wore kept her warm. Spring had come to Atlanta, giving a new coat of green to the trees and shrubs.

Peering once again down the street, Michaela looked for Cabot. She'd sent a message to him that she'd like him to stop by on his way home. The fact that he would be unhappy with her news left her with a feeling of apprehension. It wasn't going to be easy telling him that she was in love with Samuel and intended to marry him.

Would it be more difficult for him if she told him that she thought of him more as a brother than a husband, or should she simply tell him that she wanted to remain his friend? As Michaela watched a carriage pass by, she realized what a foolish thought that was. It would be almost impossible to stay friends with Cabot when he and Samuel wouldn't even exchange polite words. But she would try.

The sun was fading fast, and dusk lay quietly on the horizon waiting for twilight and darkness. Spring was bringing warmer temperatures, beautiful flowers, and gentle rains.

Michaela turned from her search of the sidewalk and saw Kate sitting in the parlor where she could glance out the window to the swing. Smiling to herself at Kate's dutiful presence, Michaela looked up the quiet street and saw Cabot walking toward her. He had a bounce to his step; he was clearly happy about something.

"Michaela." He took her hand and kissed it, then joined her on the swing. "It gave me such pleasure to see you waiting on the porch, looking for me. Where's Kate?"

"Oh, just inside." She pointed toward the window. "She's not far away." In fact, Kate had seldom left her side since they had returned from their visit to Twin Willows.

"I can't tell you how delighted I was to receive your invitation. I've hardly had a moment to myself these last few days. President Johnson and Congress are almost at war over the reconstruction policy, pardons, and reconciliation of the Southern states. If that were not enough for me to deal with, representatives of the Radical Republicans consider themselves experts on reconstruction legislation, yet they lack harmony among their number. We have the same weakness in our own party as exists between the Union and the Southern states."

Michaela was momentarily lost for words. Politics was of great importance to Cabot; however, she had readied herself to talk about another subject. "It sounds as though you've been very busy, Cabot," she managed to say while she tried to remember what she'd heard about Johnson's reconstruction plan. She prided herself on being able to talk intelligently with Cabot about political matters. Unfortunately politics hadn't been on her mind recently.

"The worst of it is that this split within the Republicans is hampering efforts for restoration, and that will weaken my support in the elections."

"I'm sorry to hear that. Surely by election time things will be more orderly."

He sighed. "I doubt it. History teaches us that pursuing harmony during a postwar period is struggling toward an elusive objective that's seldom reached without first creating more disorder."

Michaela bit down on her bottom lip. She wasn't quite sure how to get Cabot off the subject of politics and tell him she was going to marry Samuel.

"I'm leaving for Washington on Thursday to meet with some representatives of both sides. I find myself caught between the two."

"That's a wonderful idea, Cabot. I hope you'll accomplish many things." Michaela groaned inwardly as she gave the trite answer. She couldn't talk politics with Cabot when marriage to Samuel was on her mind. "Actually, Cabot, I asked you over because I have something important to tell you." She took a deep breath. "Samuel Lawrence has asked me to marry him."

"What! My God, the gall of the man." Cabot was flustered with indignation. "That penniless Confederate rebel asked you to marry him?" He laughed with confidence. "My dear sweet Michaela, I'm sorry you had to endure his attentions. I was afraid something was afoot when he asked you and your father to visit his home. I do hope it wasn't too dreadful for you."

Michaela's heart pounded in her chest. She hadn't expected this meeting to go well, and it wasn't. "I'm going to accept."

Cabot's blue eyes lost their humor, and his face turned a faded shade of pale. "No."

Determined to remain calm, Michaela responded, "Yes."

Suddenly Cabot grabbed both her hands in his and jumped off the swing, kneeling in front of her. "No, Michaela, you must not marry him. I want to marry you. You know that I need you as my wife." His eyes stared into hers with growing concern, his hands clutched desperately at hers.

Michaela was struck by the thought that Cabot hadn't confessed an undying love for her, either. Was it so difficult for men to say "I love you"? "I'm sorry, Cabot. I love Samuel, and I'm going to marry him."

"You don't know what you're saying. He has nothing to offer you but a vast amount of land that will have to be auctioned off one day; then he'll have nothing. I can give you a beautiful home, social position, and children. Anything you want I'll provide for you."

"Get up, Cabot, please." He returned to the swing but didn't let go of her hands. "You don't understand. I love Samuel, and I think he loves me."

Cabot's lashes were blinking like lights on a ship. "You think he loves you? You don't know for sure? Then let me tell you. He doesn't love you, Michaela; I do. I want you to be my wife."

Michaela didn't waver from her opinion. "But I don't love you the same way, Cabot. I love the books you bring me to read. I love talking with you about politics, and other things."

He squeezed her hands, a beaming smile on his face. "I knew you loved me, Michaela, I just knew it."

"I do, as a friend, and that's very different from the way I love Samuel." Her voice grew softer, her eyes took on a dreamy quality. "I dream about him. I think about his kisses. I get excited at the thought of seeing him, and I feel empty when he's away."

"You don't know what you're saying." His voice roughened. Grabbing her shoulders with a jerk, he pressed his lips to hers, grinding the two together.

At first Michaela let Cabot kiss her, hoping to help appease his wounded pride. When it appeared he didn't intend to stop, she pushed at his chest. He held her tighter, bruising her lips beneath his. With all her strength, she pushed at him again and broke free. She bounced off the swing and away from him.

"How dare you kiss me that way without my consent!" she said in an angry voice. She made a pass at her hair with her hand, then brushed at her skirt while she regained her aplomb.

Cabot was quick to his feet and his apology. "I'm sorry, Michaela. Of course you're right. My behavior was inexcusable. I shall never forgive myself for being so boorish."

Cabot looked so defeated, Michaela immediately regretted her tone. She really couldn't blame him for his rude behavior. She was in fact putting him aside for another. A sigh parted her lips. "Let's forget it ever happened. I'd like us to remain friends. I'm going to marry Samuel, and you can't change that."

Contrite, Cabot agreed immediately. "Very well, if

you insist upon marrying Mr. Lawrence, I offer my congratulations and best wishes.''

"Thank you.'' Michaela lowered her lashes for a moment, then looked back into Cabot's blue eyes. "I'd like you to be Samuel's friend, too.''

Cabot sighed heavily and pulled on the tail of his jacket and straightened his cravat. Clearing his throat, he said, "Of course you and I will remain friends—always, Michaela. However, Samuel is a different matter. I doubt I shall ever consider him a friend.''

She believed him, yet she wanted to try. "Will you come to the wedding?'' she asked almost shyly.

"I don't think so.'' He walked toward the steps, then turned back. "It's asking a lot of me to watch you marry another man, especially one I feel is so wrong for you.''

Michaela understood but said, "I hope you'll change your mind. I'd like you to be there.''

"And what about Samuel?'' His words were cutting.

"I can't speak for him. I'm asking for myself.''

Cabot rubbed his chin thoughtfully for a moment while he watched Michaela. "Maybe I will come. That should make his wedding day one he shall always remember.''

Taking a step forward, Michaela reached out to him. "Oh, Cabot, you wouldn't start any trouble, would you?'' she asked, fearing she may have done the wrong thing in asking him to come.

Cabot touched her cheek and gave her a comforting smile. "No. I won't start anything. However, rest assured, if Samuel does, I'll oblige him.'' He turned and hurried down the steps.

His parting words worried Michaela. She was certain Samuel wouldn't be happy to see Cabot at their wedding.

Maybe she had acted unwisely in inviting him. No, she and Cabot were friends and had been for a long time. Cabot and Samuel simply had to learn how to be civil to each other. The war had been over for two years. It was time both of them realized it.

Dinner was progressing with agonizing slowness at the Brennens' house. Samuel had made it through the green-pea soup, the rare roast beef, and the boiled potatoes, and the peaches, which were smothered in a brandy sauce, had finally been served. Any other time he would have savored every morsel, including the sweet cake in its thick, sticky sauce. But tonight his stomach twisted in knots and his food wasn't going down easily. In a very short time Michaela would tell him whether or not she planned to marry him.

As he pushed the peaches around in the dish, his eyes kept lighting on Michaela's face. Occasionally he would catch her watching him, and he would smile at her. He'd been fairly confident that she would marry him until he'd arrived at her house an hour ago. She'd treated him with cool indifference, and that put him on edge. Even if she said no, he'd find a way to make her change her mind. No woman had ever haunted his dreams and thoughts as Michaela had.

"It was such a pleasure to visit your home, Samuel, and I particularly enjoyed seeing Velvet again."

"As I've told you before, Kate, Velvet is indeed a welcome addition to Twin Willows. We're all wondering how we survived so long without her."

Kate laughed politely, and Samuel looked at Michaela. It was time to make his move. He had to make the ride back to Twin Willows tonight and then be up at daybreak to plant the corn. Henry and the Jackson boys were good workers, but he needed to be there to get them started.

"Padraic, if you don't mind, I'd like to have a few moments alone with Michaela out on the porch?"

Laying his spoon aside, Padraic looked up at Samuel. "Certainly, Samuel, go ahead, but only a few minutes. Kate will keep an eye on you." He rose from his seat. "I'll be in the study should you want to talk to me later."

As if they had rehearsed it, they all rose at the same time and left the dining room.

"I'll be in the parlor, Michaela. Don't forget your shawl. It's still quite chilly." Kate gave instructions as they walked into the foyer.

Samuel knew what Kate meant. She had every intention of sitting in the parlor where she could look out the window and see exactly what went on in the swing.

After helping Michaela with her wrap, Samuel put his hand to the small of her back and they walked outside. As soon as the night air touched his face he shut the front door and swept Michaela into his arms, bringing his lips down on hers with the passion absence had built inside him. Michaela struggled for only a moment before she accepted and returned his intense embrace.

Samuel let his lips glide along her cheek and down the warm column of her neck, breathing in her sweet scent, tasting her creamy skin, hearing her soft moans of pleasure.

"I've been waiting six long days to hold you like this." He kissed her again, letting his tongue slip into the moistness of her mouth.

"I've been waiting, too," Michaela answered when

Samuel gave her a brief reprieve. "Your kisses do strange things to me."

Samuel chuckled and hugged her tighter. "Your kisses do wonderful things to me. That's the way it's supposed to be between two people who are going to be married."

"Shouldn't those feelings come after you're married instead of before?" she asked.

This time Samuel laughed. "If you don't feel them before you marry, I can assure you marriage won't automatically make your breath grow short, your stomach quake, or give you an insatiable appetite for kisses."

He pulled her close once more and looked into her eyes. "When are you going to marry me, Michaela?"

Michaela pushed out of his arms and said, "You'd better let me go. Kate will be looking out the window any moment now. Come, let's sit on the swing."

He didn't care whether or not Kate saw them. He'd missed her, and he didn't want to let her go. A week was too long to be without her sweet lips on his. Reluctantly he let her go and followed her to the swing. Through the parted drapes he saw Kate arranging her embroidery on her lap. Samuel pulled at his shirt collar. A couple of kisses from Michaela and he was hot. He opened the two top buttons of his high-necked shirt. He'd never wanted a woman so badly.

"Well?" he asked as he picked up Michaela's hand and squeezed it. "When are you going to marry me?"

Michaela smiled up at him. "Shouldn't you ask *if*, not *when*?"

"I decided I was going to marry you a long time ago. It's always been a matter of when."

"You're too self-confident, Samuel Lawrence. I shouldn't agree to marry you—but I will," she finished softly.

He reached over and kissed her tenderly on the lips. "Next week?" he asked, squeezing her hand again.

"No," Michaela said, and shook her head. "I couldn't possibly be ready by then."

Samuel wanted her right now. He didn't want to wait a week. His lips moved convincingly over hers while his hand ran up and down her arm, sending bolts of desire speeding through him. A knock on the window pane made them jerk apart, and Samuel cleared his throat as he moved to the other end of the swing. They looked at each other and laughed.

"Kate really takes this chaperoning seriously, doesn't she?"

"Oh, yes. She's very good at what she does."

He loved the way her eyes sparkled when she laughed. "Michaela, I don't want to have to wait a week to marry you, certainly not any longer." He ran a hand through his long hair and down the back of his neck.

"Samuel, you don't understand." She touched his arm, and he liked the feel of her warmth. "I must have a dress made, a trousseau, invite the guests, arrange for the food, the church, and there's too many other things to mention that have to be done."

"I can handle some of those things. I want the ceremony at Twin Willows—that takes care of the church— and I'll arrange for the minister."

Stunned, she said, "Priest. And I think Papa will want me to marry in the church."

"All right, a priest is fine with me, but, Michaela, Twin Willows will be our home. That's where we need to start out life together. Besides, it will make my mother very happy because she and my father were married there. If you like, I'll speak to Padraic."

"No, no. I'll speak to Papa. If I agree to the wedding at Twin Willows, you'll have to agree to give me extra time to get ready. We'll marry the first Sunday in May."

Samuel thought for a moment. May was more than a month away, but that would give him time to get all the seed planted and the mill running. "All right. The first Sunday in May it is. Now give me another kiss before Kate comes back to the window and calls us inside."

Once again their warm lips met with tender passion. This time Samuel kept his emotions under control and made the kiss brief.

"There's one other thing I want to discuss with you before you go." Uncertainty laced her voice. "I want to invite Cabot to the wedding."

"Never—I'll see him in hell first!" Samuel swore again under his breath as he rose from the swing. "I'm sorry, Michaela, that's impossible."

"Why? He's my friend," she protested, following him to the edge of the porch.

Samuel turned on her with anger. "You know how we feel about each other, so why would you even suggest it? I can assure you Cabot will feel the same way I do."

"No, you're wrong." She grabbed his sleeve and held him. "He's already promised me he'd come."

"Dammit, Michaela, you asked him without consulting me first?" His voice rose in anger, and he jerked away from her.

She took a step backward, but her voice remained firm. "He's *my* friend. I didn't need to consult you."

"I won't have that carpetbagger Republican at my wedding. You'll have to uninvite him." A slight sneer lifted one corner of his lips.

Michaela held her chin high. Her eyes glowed in the soft gaslight from the street corner. "I can't do that," she said softly.

Samuel rubbed his hand across his mouth and stared at the beautiful woman he wanted so desperately to take to his bed and love. "I'd do anything for you—except this."

"Then there won't be a wedding."

Her voice was as soft as the breeze that fanned his face, but it struck his chest with the force of a cannon.

"Fine. There won't be a wedding."

Their eyes locked in anger. A night bird whistled, the wind blew in a chill, and the stars twinkled against a black sky. Their anger quickly melted into acceptance, which flowed into desperation. The longer they stared at one another, the closer they came together. Their kiss was sweet, gentle, giving, receiving, believing, forgiving.

Samuel's heart felt as if it would pound out of his chest. He knew without a doubt that he loved this woman. Her happiness was more important than his own. He hugged her as tightly as he dared for fear of cracking a rib and whispered into her ear, "I want to marry you, Michaela. Cabot can come and anyone else you wish."

Their lips met in a long, passionate kiss that ended with a tap on the window pane.

Nine

S A M U E L ' S eyes popped open as the first threads of twilight seeped through the parted drapes. The distant crowing of a rooster was the only sound he heard. He lay in his bed for a moment, waiting for the last vestige of sleep to slip away from him. Sitting up, he noticed a slight chill to the room, not unusual for early May. He also felt the ache of strained muscles. He'd been working fourteen hours a day in order to get all the seed in the ground and the mill operating before today.

Without the help of Henry and the Jackson boys he'd never have made it. Now it was time to sit back and let nature take care of the tender kernels with sunshine and spring rains, and to let his new foreman take care of the gristmill.

What was he doing thinking of the plantation on his wedding day? Because if he didn't have a plentiful crop of corn, there wouldn't be enough money to pay Padraic.

Samuel smoothed his ruffled hair away from his forehead with both hands and realized how long it had grown. He'd meant to get it cut before today.

The news George Riverson had brought crossed his mind, and he rubbed his whiskered chin thoughtfully. It had been close to six weeks since his visit. He had a feeling that if Tully was nearby, he would have made his presence known by now. Still, the possibility remained. And Tully was the kind of man who would kill for what he wanted.

Samuel shook his head and wiped the sleep from his eyes. He wasn't going to let George Riverson or Rufus Tully spoil this day for him. Michaela should be the only one on his mind.

He lay back against his pillow and remembered how good she'd felt in his arms the last time he'd held her, so soft, so fresh smelling. God, he wanted her, loved her, and it was time he told her he loved her. Tonight she would be his forever.

Samuel threw back the covers and jumped out of bed, whistling as his bed-warmed feet hit the cold floor. He reached for his work clothes and pulled them on with haste. There were still many things to be done before the Brennens arrived. Michaela had promised him they would leave Atlanta in time to arrive at Twin Willows by noon. That would give her plenty of time to rest before she had to dress for the wedding at four. He'd agreed to stay away from the house during that time. She was adamant that he not see her the day of the wedding before the ceremony. He didn't mind humoring her as long as she was his when the day was over.

Samuel walked to the window and pushed back the faded curtain panel. The eastern sky was alive with the beauty of dawn. He rubbed his arms to dispel the chill of the room and smiled. It was going to be a beautiful day for a wedding.

A few minutes later he walked into the kitchen. The smell of baking bread permeated the warm room, the enticing aroma causing his stomach to growl with anticipation.

"Good morning, Velvet," he said, walking directly to the coffee pot and pouring himself a cup.

"Yes, a fine morning it is, Mr. Lawrence. A perfect day for your wedding. I haven't been this excited since before the war. I didn't sleep a wink last night."

Samuel chuckled. He knew his mother felt the same way. Davia was the only one who hadn't taken the news well. She'd sulked in her room for a full day. When she'd finally agreed they could talk, he'd tried to make her see that having Michaela around would be like having a sister. Davia had balked at that idea, continuing in her belief that Michaela would usurp her position at Twin Willows. Samuel had decided the best thing was to let Michaela win Davia over. He had no doubt she could do it.

"Is that bread ready to come out of the oven? I'm hungry as a bear." He came up behind Velvet and peered over her shoulder to see what she was cooking.

"No, and you couldn't have any if it was. This is for your wedding feast. I've got biscuits and eggs for you this morning. No time to fry bacon today, too many things to do. Did you see that list your mama gave me for food? Fillet of braised beef, chicken croquettes, oysters vol-au-vent . . . It's a good thing Mr. Brennen's having the cake baked in Atlanta. I'd never get everything done if I had to do a cake, too."

Samuel laughed again as he filled four biscuits with

butter and green-apple preserves. "Don't worry, I've already spoken to Henry about helping you."

"Humph! All he can do is complain that I work him too hard. I've never seen anybody peel potatoes slower than he does. Besides, he's already been to the door this morning and told me he asked Bo Jackson's missus to help me so he could make sure the gardens were ready for the ceremony and then cut the flowers to decorate the house. She's on her way over here now."

"I didn't know Bo had a wife," Samuel commented as he served his plate.

Velvet shot Samuel an impish grin. "I didn't, either, but I didn't ask any questions. I don't tend to anyone else's business. I'm just glad to have someone help me other than that grumbling yard man."

Chuckling to himself, Samuel continued to eat while Velvet carried on with her own form of complaining.

A few minutes before four o'clock Michaela slipped her wedding gown over her silk-and-lace undergarments and the whalebone-ribbed corset. She stood quietly while Kate closed all thirty-one satin-covered buttons that outlined her spine. The dress was the most beautiful Michaela had ever seen. The material was pearl white silk, accented in places with fine satin. The lower skirt was trimmed with five rows of narrow ruffles with satin piping, and three satin bands circled the waist. The overskirt was made of gossamer silk tulle and richly embroidered with satin floss in a pattern of white lilies. The high-necked bodice and long sleeves were made of silk covered with delicately woven lace.

As Kate put the finishing touches to Michaela's hair, Evelyn came in wearing a dress of deep blue silk with black velvet cuffs and carrying a handful of pale pink and white flowers. She smiled with delight as she looked at Michaela. "You are so beautiful. I will be proud to call you my daughter-in-law."

"Thank you, Mrs. Lawrence. I'm very happy to be a part of your family."

Evelyn smiled her appreciation and said, "Oh, before I forget. Samuel sent these up. He asks that you wear them in your hair." She held out the delicate blossoms.

"Oh, but Michaela has this lovely headpiece, and it will crush the flowers if we put them in her hair," Kate said. "Although it was so nice of Samuel to think of it."

Michaela looked at the magnificent wide-brimmed hat made of silk and net. It was truly an exceptional creation with tiny white satin roses outlining the crown. Her heart constricted. Samuel wanted to see the fresh flowers in her hair.

"No, Kate," she said softly. "I will accept my bridegroom's gift of flowers and wear them as my headdress."

Kate stiffened perceptibly. "But, Michaela, your face must be covered," she argued.

Michaela grabbed the hand-made veil from the bed and looked at it closely. "Mrs. Lawrence, do you have a pair of scissors? We'll cut out the net and pin it in my hair here." She showed them with her hands what she was talking about. "Then we can outline it with the flowers like this. Do you think it will work?"

Evelyn laughed with genuine pride. "Of course it will work. That's a wonderful idea, Michaela. I'll be right back with the scissors."

While Evelyn hurried from the room, Kate and Michaela stared at one another. "That is a very expensive headpiece," Kate reminded her, but with no reprimand in her voice.

Michaela smiled. "I know, but it won't please Samuel as much as my wearing his gift. And that lowers its value considerably."

The sun was hanging low in the western sky as Rufus Tully reined in his horse a short distance from Twin Willows. A crowd of about twenty-five stood on the front lawn of the mansion. It appeared that the man he'd spoken to in Atlanta was right when he'd said Sam was getting married today. He laughed lasciviously. So his old army pal was tying the knot. Hell, he'd figured Sam would've married right after the war like most men.

Tully wiped his forehead and neck with his damp handkerchief while vagrant sounds of laughter and voices filtered his way. Damn, it was a long ride back to Atlanta, but now that he was here, he had second thoughts about riding in and disrupting the wedding proceedings. Seeing him was sure to ruin Sam's day, and he kind of liked that idea, but on the other hand, the fewer people who knew he was here, the better.

Tully reached into the inner pocket of his leather vest, pulled out a rumpled sheet of parchment, and opened it. The markings had faded, but a trained eye could follow the directions written there. All he needed was the other half. Refolding the paper, he put it back in his pocket.

He scratched his bearded chin and neck with the backs of his fingers, contemplating the merits of attending a wedding feast with free-flowing whiskey against a long, dry ride back to the nearest saloon on a tired, cranky old horse.

He'd have felt better about all this if he could have found Riverson. Shareton said he'd given his half of the map to Riverson, and don't many men lie when a gun is pointing at their gut. Well, hell, if he couldn't find Riverson, he'd go for the last one on his list. Sam.

Tully laughed and pulled on the reins, turning his horse around. No, he wouldn't mess up Sam's wedding night. It was best to give him a little taste of his woman so he'd know what he would be missing. In fact, maybe he'd be nice this one time and give the bride and groom a couple of days before he ruined their life.

As soon as Michaela was pronounced Mrs. Samuel Lawrence and kissed appropriately, the wedding feast started. Samuel pulled her away from well-wishers and ushered her into the living room, where the furniture had been cleared to make a ballroom.

At the sound of the waltz, Michaela went willingly into Samuel's arms, the place she'd wanted to be for more than two weeks. Samuel was very handsome in his new black suit of lightweight wool and his gray-and-black-striped cravat. Her heart swelled with love and pride as she looked into her husband's eyes and remembered the beautiful ceremony among the flowers and under the dogwood trees.

"I couldn't wait any longer to hold you," Samuel said, dancing closer to her than was acceptable. "I know you must be hungry, but the only way I could think to get you in my arms was to whisk you to the dance floor."

"I don't mind. I want to be near you," she said.

"Thank you for wearing the flowers in your hair." He smiled. "You are without a doubt the most beautiful woman I've ever seen, Mrs. Lawrence, and I'm wondering how I'm going to get through the next three or four hours until we can go upstairs and be alone."

"I should go up a few minutes before you and prepare

myself," she said, looking into his dark brown eyes, experiencing no fear of the moment when she would really become his wife.

"Don't," he said in a raspy voice.

"Don't what?" she asked, frowning.

"We'll go up together. I don't want you to change until I'm there to help you. I'm going to take great pleasure in undoing each and every one of these tiny buttons running up and down your back." His hand caressed the length of her spine as he spoke, sending chills of pleasure through her.

Michaela's breathing was shallow. "Th—that's not the way it's usually done," she argued while her mind played the picture of him undressing her.

"I know." His dark eyes sparkled. "But I'm not going to let anyone take this dress off you but me. And I'm going to enjoy every moment of it." He chuckled lightly and squeezed her hand. "Why are you blushing? You're a beautiful woman, and I intend to look at you every morning and every night."

Her color deepened, and heat rose up from the pit of her stomach and drenched her with warmth. She took a deep breath to calm her erratic heartbeat and said, "Then I intend to look at you every morning and every night."

Samuel laughed heartily. He twirled her around as the music came to a stop. "Nothing would make me happier." He planted a chaste kiss on her lips before turning her over to her father, who'd stepped up behind them.

A few minutes later, while dancing with Davia, Samuel saw Michaela dancing with Cabot. A knot of jealousy formed in his chest. Cabot was holding her too close. Probably caressing the palm of her hand, too. He stiffened when he realized how desperately he wanted to rush over and snatch him away from her. But he knew better than to create a scene at his own wedding. In fact, Cabot was probably hoping he'd cause a disturbance.

"What's wrong, Sam? You're holding my hand so tight, you're hurting me," Davia complained.

Samuel looked down at his little sister, dressed in the finest frock she'd had in many years. "Oh, sorry, Muffin. Guess I'm rusty on the dancing."

"No, you're not." Her eyes snapped with irritation. "If you'd stop looking at *her*, you wouldn't keep stepping on my toes."

"She's my wife, and you're going to have to get used to that. This will be her home as much as it's yours."

"Good. She can help Velvet with the cleaning and the cooking." She pouted for a moment.

"I'm sure she'll gladly help."

Davia swung her head around and looked at Michaela. "Who's the handsome man she's dancing with?"

Samuel felt a chill go up his back. It never dawned on him that Davia would think of Peabody as handsome. "You don't want to know," he answered ruefully.

"Yes, I do." She turned back to Samuel. "I'd really like to meet him. Will you make the introductions?"

Stunned, Samuel growled at Davia without shifting his focus from Michaela and Cabot. "He's a Republican bast—" He bit his lip and took a deep breath before looking down at his sister. "Besides, you're only thirteen. Just take my word for it. You don't want to meet him. Come on, let's get something to eat." He fumed all the way to the buffet table. Dammit! The last thing he wanted was his little sister making eyes at Cabot Peabody.

As the evening wore on, Samuel became less tolerant of all the eating, drinking, and dancing. Every man in the house had danced with Michaela at least twice, and he was ready to stop sharing and have her all to himself. There was only one thing to do. It was time to take matters into his own hands.

He found Henry in the kitchen stuffing a bite of meat pie in his mouth.

"I'm awful sorry, Mr. Lawrence, but I'z starving ta death. I hain't had time ta eat all day."

"Don't get up, Henry," Samuel told him. "Just tell me where you're keeping the champagne. I want a bottle and two glasses."

Henry smiled and wiped his thick brown lips with the back of his hand. "You jest wait here. I knows what ya want." Henry went out the back door and came back a moment later. "Here's da bottle. I'll open it while you get da glasses offa that shelf."

Samuel smiled. "Thanks, Henry. When you finish your dinner, would you make up a tray and bring it to my room? I've noticed that Michaela hasn't eaten all evening."

"You jest leave it up ta me. I'll fix her a real nice dinner."

Less than two minutes later Samuel walked back into the ballroom and searched the crowd for Michaela. He spotted her talking to Kate on the far side of the room. Weaving his way through the crowd, with the bottle and glasses in hand, he headed toward his bride.

Samuel closed the door to his bedroom, shutting out the noise of the party that was still going on below and would for several more hours. Michaela stood just inside the room and looked around. One low-burning lamp and blazing coals in the fireplace lent a seductive glow to the room. The bed covers had been turned down, and the white cotton sheets shone in the dim light with a silky iridescence. A small vase of spring's first violets sat on the dresser. Samuel's room was so warm and subtle that Michaela relaxed immediately.

"Come over here and sit down." Samuel ushered her farther inside the room and seated her on the slipper chair by the fireplace. Michaela kept her back straight and chin high. The stays in her corset wouldn't allow her any other posture. Quietly she watched as Samuel poured a little champagne into each glass before setting the bottle aside.

When he handed her the glass, he said, "To us."

Michaela nodded her head in agreement and took a sip of the bubbly liquid. Her throat was dry, and she liked the cool, crisp taste, so she took another sip.

"Don't drink it too fast," Samuel said, a lazy grin playing at the corners of his mouth.

"It's very good," she answered, looking up at him. "And I'm more than a little thirsty."

Samuel took the glass from her and placed it on the lamp stand beside the champagne. "I know you didn't eat anything tonight. I asked Henry to bring up a tray for you. Until you eat, I think it's best you not drink any more."

"Thank you. You're right. I've been too excited to think about food."

She watched Samuel's eyes travel over her face and down her body. At his request she was still in her wedding gown, the flowers he gave her still adorned her hair. He was simply looking at her, yet the light in his eyes filled her with warmth and anticipation.

"You are so lovely," he said huskily, looking into her emerald eyes. "I feel so lucky."

Michaela's heartbeat quickened. "So do I," she answered.

With his fingers he caressed her cheek, letting his hand slip down the contours of her neck, over her collarbone and across her breast, and down to rest on her waist. Michaela's breathing was as slow and laborious as Samuel's movements.

"You are so beautiful. . . ." Love and desire shone like a fire in his eyes.

"And you are—" A light knock on the door cut her sentence short.

"Stay seated. That will be Henry."

Samuel and Henry rearranged the furniture so that they had the food-laden tray sitting on a small table in front of the fireplace with two chairs on either side of it.

When Henry left, Samuel joined Michaela at the make-shift dining table. "Now, this is the way a wedding feast should be served. The bride and groom alone with no one else around."

"I think I like it best this way, too. There are too many people downstairs who want attention." Michaela was just beginning to realize how truly lucky she was to have married Samuel.

He laughed and picked up a fork. Piercing a small smoked oyster, he offered it to Michaela. "It appeared to me that you were the one getting all the attention. I counted at least five different men who danced with you."

Michaela opened her mouth and took the delicacy. "Mmm . . . this is very good." She moistened her lips and tasted the lightly sweet champagne.

"Try this," he said, and offered her a tiny bite of beef that had been smothered in a Burgundy sauce. Michaela smiled engagingly at him. "Are you going to feed me?" she asked.

"Oh, yes," he said huskily. "I'm going to feed you all night."

When the tray was empty, Samuel gave Michaela her unfinished champagne and they moved away from the table to stand before the fire. "Feel better?" he asked.

"Much better. I didn't know I was so hungry. And I've had enough of this," she said, returning the glass to Samuel.

"So have I."

Samuel put the glasses on the mantel and turned back to Michaela. He reached down and kissed her lips lightly, for a moment, not touching her anywhere else. While his lips made exotic little movements over hers, he reached up and started pulling the pins and flowers from her hair, letting them both fall to the floor. His actions were so tantalizingly slow, Michaela closed her eyes, surrendering to the marvelous feel and taste of his lips on hers and the motions of his hands in her hair. When all her hair was down he arranged it over her shoulders, then took a step back and looked at her.

"You should always wear your hair down," he whispered, gazing into her eyes.

"I—it's not proper to wear it down in public." Samuel was making her feel very beautiful, very desirable.

"Here, in our bedroom, anything is proper. Wear it down for me whenever we're alone."

"Yes," she answered, wanting to fall into his arms and be crushed against him. She appreciated his consideration in taking things slowly, but intuition told her something wonderful was going to happen, and with each breath she took, each second that Samuel delayed, her anticipation mounted.

"Are you frightened?" he asked.

"No," she whispered.

He pulled her close, bringing their faces mere inches apart. "Michaela, before I take you to bed I want you to know that I love you." She smiled, and he went on. "I think I loved you the moment I saw you in your father's bank."

"I love you, too, Samuel. I'm so happy we're married."

He cupped her face with his large hands. "What about Cabot?"

"Cabot?" She stiffened. What did Cabot have to do with this moment?

"Do you love Cabot?" His expression was intense.

She swallowed hard. It was time to let Samuel know he had no reason to be jealous. "Cabot is a friend. That's all he has ever been and all he will ever be. Only a friend, Samuel."

Samuel hugged her to him and brought his lips down on hers hungrily. She returned his kisses with the same fervor. His hands ranged up and down her back, the feel of silk singing against his roughened palms.

"Let me look at you for a moment." His voice was raspy as his loving eyes appraised her. "You are so lovely. The most beautiful woman I've ever known."

Michaela smiled, wanting to be worthy of his words. She stood, slender and erect. She wanted to please him. The flowers were gone from her hair, her dress had a few wrinkles, but she had the feeling he was looking inside her, and she wouldn't be caught lacking the courage to be his wife.

With care, Samuel placed his hands on her shoulders and turned her around. Heat from the burning embers warmed her face as he moved all her hair to one shoulder and started undoing the little satin-covered buttons. When he was halfway down he pulled the material aside and kissed her back between her shoulder blades. Michaela shivered. She'd never felt anything so enticing before in her life.

He unbuttoned a few more and kissed her back again, this time letting his moist tongue taste her hot skin. Michaela gasped, a sweet, sighing sound. Her heart was beating so fast, she was fearful she wouldn't be able to catch her breath. As Samuel's lips made love to her back, his hands slid under her arms and outlined her breasts. He squeezed them gently, stroking, caressing, exploring. Michaela went weak with desire. Tilting her head back, consumed by the exquisite sensations rippling through her, Michaela closed her eyes and enjoyed her husband's touch.

Samuel's legs trembled with wanting, his manhood throbbed with expectancy. While he rained kisses up and down her backbone, he finished unbuttoning the dress, then helped her step out of it. He threw it across the slipper chair behind him. With her back still toward him, he untied the ribbon that held her hoop and petticoats around her waist and threw them aside before turning her around to face him once again.

He whistled under his breath. She had on a corset that emphasized every curve. The strapless silk pushed most of her breasts up and out of the cup, which was outlined with a delicate lace. Samuel's throat went dry. Did she know how tempting she was wearing only her undergarments?

Her skin glowed in the pale light. For a moment he simply stood still and loved her. Slowly his gaze moved back up to her face, and he whispered her name as his hand moved leisurely, caressingly, down her breast and across her stomach. Their lips met, then their tongues, as passion mounted within Samuel's loins.

Reluctantly he stepped away from her softness and untied his cravat, tossing it on top of Michaela's discarded wedding dress. Next came his coat and shirt. Shaking with desire, he yanked off his shoes and socks, then quickly helped Michaela with her pantaloons, slippers, and stockings. He'd take the corset off later.

Michaela went into his arms eagerly, hungrily, passionately. The touch of her soft hands on his bare skin, running over his shoulders, down his back to the waist of his pants, sent flaring heat coursing through him. The lace of her corset lightly scratched his chest, just enough to incite his desire. His hands moved to circle her small waist, and his lips slipped to the swell of her breast. He licked, nipped, and kissed their fullness. She was so soft, she tasted so good, he felt his control snapping. Her moans and sighs spiraled him further, made him grow harder. With unsteady hands he lifted her breast out of the lacy cup of silk and found the tip, sucking it slowly into his mouth. He groaned an impassioned breath. God, she was wonderful. He had to finish undressing them before he exploded.

As he continued to make love to her breast, he untied the ribbons of her corset. When the hard-ribbed undergarment fell away, all she was wearing was a beautiful pearl-colored silk chemise. Samuel swallowed with difficulty and picked up his bride and laid her on the bed. His want of her was so fervid, he was suddenly afraid of hurting her.

The cool sheets touched Michaela's back, and she shivered even though her skin was burning. She kept her eyes on Samuel as he crawled into the bed beside her and slipped his arm underneath her head. "Shouldn't we turn down the light?" she asked.

"No," he said huskily. "I've waited too long to look at you. You're so lovely I don't want you to be hidden by darkness, ever." He kissed her lips, her cheeks, her eyes, her breasts, slipping the chemise over her head and tossing it to the floor.

Michaela responded with a knowledge she didn't know she possessed as she reached for the buttons on Samuel's pants. He patiently let her undo the buttons, then helped her slide them off his hips and down his legs to be kicked away. Then he reached down and pulled the crisp sheet halfway up their entwined legs.

Samuel took his time and became familiar with Michaela's body, getting to know her, loving her, committing her to memory. Michaela gloried in her husband's loving touch, letting him teach her that intercourse wasn't necessary for making love. She marveled at his gentleness, at the things he knew to do to make her body respond so deliciously to such exquisite torture. When she asked, he showed her how to please him with the same intensity. The sharing, the taking and the giving between the two of them, could only reinforce their love.

Now Samuel could no longer hold off his need for release, and when Michaela stiffened slightly at his entry, he soothed her with loving words, with kisses and caresses, slowly moving inside her until she regained her earlier passion and they became one, husband and wife, lovers.

"Sweet, beautiful Michaela, I love you," he whispered passionately into her warm, soft neck, cuddling his bride in his arms, content to bask in the glowing aftermath of lovemaking that surrounded him like a gossamer haze.

"Do you mean that?"

Samuel raised himself on one arm. With a lazy smile he looked into her eyes. "Of course I mean it. I love you. You're mine, and no one can take you away from me."

Michaela reached up and touched his cheek. "I love you. Very much. Can we do that again?"

"What?" he asked, that easy smile coming to his lips again, a throaty chuckle rumbling deep in his chest.

"You know," she insisted, feeling suddenly shy.

His expression gentled at her sensitivity. "Yes, I know." He brushed her hair aside, exposing her delicate ear. "Say the words, Michaela. If you want to make love, I want you to feel comfortable saying, 'Samuel, I want to make love.' Can you do that for me?"

Smiling, Michaela whispered, "Samuel, I want to make love to you."

His answer was to cover her lips with his, to join her body with his, to make love to her twice more before they slept on their wedding night.

Ten

TH E next morning they made love again.

Michaela was a little anxious about making love to her husband in the bright light of day, but Samuel calmed her fears and caressed her eager body until all her objections vanished in the intensity of passion.

When they came down for breakfast, some of their guests were preparing to leave. Samuel and Michaela thanked everyone for the gifts and for helping to make their wedding day perfect. Michaela was happy to hear that her father and Kate had decided to stay over for another night.

After breakfast Samuel left Michaela talking to his mother and went in search of Padraic. He found him taking a midmorning nap on the back porch.

"Padraic."

One eye opened, then the other. "Ah—oh, yes, Samuel," Padraic stammered, and cleared his throat as he roused himself. "Good morning to you."

"It's a very good morning, sir." Samuel walked over to the edge of the porch and leaned against the white rail. He saw smoke curling above the barn and knew Henry had the pig roasting for the barbecue later in the afternoon. After that, most of the guests would leave. That idea appealed to him. He wanted Michaela all to himself. Even now he wanted to find her and take her upstairs and love her again.

He turned back to face Padraic. "I want you to know that I love Michaela. I'm going to do everything in my power to make her happy."

"I never expected less from you, Samuel." Padraic rose from the chair, the wood creaking beneath his weight, and went to stand beside Samuel.

"I don't want her to ever find out that you offered me money to marry her." Samuel's voice had a ring of desperation.

Padraic hooked his thumbs in the small pockets of his waistcoat. The two men stood head to head. "I couldn't agree more. She'd never forgive either of us. However, I must say again, I don't want her doing without what she wants or needs. I couldn't bear for her to be left wanting when I have so much to give. If you need money, you must come to me."

"For a loan, yes; for a gift, no."

"Any way you want to handle it will be fine with me. Just let me know if you need more money."

"Thanks, but if we have a wet spring, there won't be a problem. I've planted four hundred acres in corn. By the end of summer, I should make my first payment to you." Samuel smiled and extended his hand to his father-in-law.

"I knew I wasn't making a mistake when I offered you

that money to marry Michaela.'' Padraic patted Samuel's shoulder and shook his offered hand heartily.

''In a way I'm glad you did. It gave me the opportunity to meet her. I'm going to make her happy.''

''Oh, I've no doubt of that. She was simply glowing this morning. Yes, I'm pleased. Quite pleased indeed.''

Furious, Cabot tiptoed away from the house. So Padraic had paid Samuel to marry his beautiful daughter! Why couldn't he have heard this before the wedding? That little bit of information would have stopped the marriage before it began.

He hadn't heard everything that was said, but he'd heard enough to know that Padraic had paid Samuel to marry Michaela and that he was going to continue to give Samuel money whenever he needed it. Cabot's hands balled into fists, and his heart pumped angrily in his chest. He would have married Michaela for love! He had wanted to marry her even though Padraic Brennen had never given one cent to support his political aspirations. Bemused, Cabot took a deep sighing breath, trying to understand why Mr. Brennen would want to sell his daughter to a penniless Confederate land baron.

When he reached the front of the house he saw Michaela saying good-bye to some of her guests. Good, she was busy. This would give him time to decide exactly what he was going to say to her.

Michaela must be told. Yes, he was sure of that. Then it would be up to her what she did. A satisfied smile twisted Cabot's lips. He couldn't have Michaela; she was legally married to Samuel, and he was certain that the marriage couldn't be annulled. But once Michaela discovered Samuel had been paid to marry her, Samuel wouldn't have Michaela, either. She would be sure to ban her husband from her bed.

Cabot chuckled. Should he stay around to see the look on Samuel's face when Michaela confronted him? He sniffed. He'd think about it.

"Democrats, they can't be trusted," he said aloud as he waited to catch Michaela alone.

"I beg your pardon?"

Cabot spun around at the sound of the feminine voice. "Oh, good day to you, Miss Lawrence." Flustered at being caught talking to himself, he reached up to tip his hat to the young lady and then realized with embarrassment that he wasn't wearing one.

Davia Lawrence smiled at him coquettishly. "Please call me Davia, and may I call you Cabot?" she asked.

Suddenly amused by this girl with the beautiful, expressive brown eyes, Cabot answered, "Indeed you may, and it will be my pleasure to address you as Davia."

"Are you a friend of Michaela's?" she asked.

Cabot's eyes strayed back to the front porch where Michaela stood talking with a couple of ladies. "Yes, we've been friends for quite some time."

"Have you been a guest in her father's house?"

Turning back to face the inquisitive youngster, Cabot found himself looking at Davia in a different way. She definitely had beautiful eyes, large and expressive. Her nose was small, attractive, and her lips had a lovely, tempting shape to them. Her breasts were—Damn! he caught himself just in time. What was he doing appraising Samuel Lawrence's sister?

"Did you hear my question?" Davia asked.

Cabot cleared his throat rather loudly. "Yes, yes, of course, I've been a guest many times."

Davia's smile eased into genuine delight. "Then perhaps I'll see you when we go to Atlanta to visit Michaela's father?"

"I should like that."

"I'll ask that you be invited to dinner when we visit. Good day, Cabot."

She was flirting with him, Cabot realized with a start. What a charming girl! Girl? No, he didn't know her age, but she wasn't a girl. She was a lovely young lady. His guess put him at least ten to twelve years older than Davia. "God, help me," he swore to himself. The last thing he wanted right now was to have Samuel's little sister on his mind. She's just a child, he tried to convince himself. "A very beautiful child," he said aloud, and headed toward Michaela.

After a long good-bye to her wedding guests, Michaela found the front porch a place of escape from people. The day was warm and quiet except for the chirping of distant birds and the humming of an occasional bumblebee. She was tired of too many hugs, kisses, and farewells. What she wanted was to be left alone so she could remember her wedding night and think about tonight. A warm smile slid across her lips. She walked over and sat on the swing, letting her lilac dress fan out beside her. Closing her eyes, she breathed in the fresh smells of spring.

"Ah—there you are," Cabot said, climbing the steps to stand before her.

Michaela's eyes opened. "Oh, I'm sorry I haven't had

time to speak to you this morning, Cabot, but there are still so many people here."

"I know, my sweet. Ooops—" He chuckled humorlessly. "I must get out of the habit of calling you pet names."

Michaela smiled indulgently. "You will in time. I'm so glad you came. It meant a lot to me."

"So am I." He paused. "However, Michaela, before I go . . . I feel I must tell you some distressing news that I was only made aware of this day."

"Whatever are you talking about, Cabot?" The hesitancy she heard in his voice put her on the edge of her seat. Something was wrong.

Cabot put a finger to his lips and sighed. "No, perhaps it's best if I remain quiet. I'm not certain anything can be gained by my telling you."

"Cabot, you can't do this." Michaela rose from the swing, brushing at the folds of her skirt. "You can't tell me you have news, then not tell me what you're talking about. Please feel free to speak."

Making a clucking sound, Cabot took both Michaela's hands in his and sighed deeply. "I overheard something this morning that I'm afraid will destroy your happiness. That's why I'm reluctant."

Butterflies formed in the pit of Michaela's stomach. "What? Cabot, don't be so timid. If you have something to tell, then tell me. You're frightening me."

"I'm sorry to say you may have reason to be frightened."

Frustration trembled through her. "Cabot, enough of this! Tell me now," she insisted, her voice strong and firm.

"All right. A short while ago, I was on my way to the barn to get my horse when I overheard your father and Samuel talking. I was about to speak up and let my presence be known when I heard something that stopped me.''

Michaela pulled her hands away from Cabot. "What, for heavens sake! Tell me what you heard.''

Cabot stuck his hands in his pants pockets and said, "I heard your father say he was glad he had offered Samuel money to marry you, and should Samuel need more, all he has to do is ask.''

Michaela's stomach lurched, and she stopped breathing for a moment. Her lips parted, but no sound came out. Money to marry her? "No, you're wrong!'' she whispered, her throat constricting with fear.

"My dear Michaela, would I hurt you over a lie? Never!'' He grasped her hands again, offering comfort. "Give me the word and I'll challenge Samuel here and now.''

Everything was hazy. She couldn't breathe properly. She couldn't think straight. "No. No, of course I don't want you to challenge Samuel.'' A lump formed in her chest, growing larger with each breath. "There must be some mistake.'' She turned away from Cabot and rubbed the back of her neck, but that didn't seem to be where the pain was coming from.

"No. There was no mistaking what your father said, and regretfully I couldn't hear Samuel's replies. I decided to tell you on the basis that you have a right to know why your husband married you.''

Michaela turned on Cabot, angry that he would accuse her husband and father of such deceitfulness. "Samuel loves me! I know it. You're wrong.''

"Ask him, Michaela. Don't take my word for it. Your father offered him money and told him to ask if he needed more.'' Cabot remained calm. "I will look Samuel in the eyes and swear to God I heard it. If he's the man you think he is, he will answer you truthfully. Ask him.''

Michaela couldn't move or speak. Her pulse raced as silence lengthened between them. No, she couldn't believe Samuel had married her for money. He loved her. She was sure of that.

''I must go, Michaela. I don't want to be caught riding in the chill of the night. You know how easily I catch colds.''

Trying to shake off the searing effects of Cabot's news, Michaela willed her voice to be steady as she said, ''Yes, of course. You should go. I don't want you sick again.''

''May I have a kiss from the bride before I go?''

Without thinking or caring, she leaned toward him, and Cabot took her lips in a passionate kiss and reckless embrace. She was too stunned to care that Cabot's lips sought hers with hunger.

''Turn her loose. Right now.'' Samuel's voice was low and menacing.

Startled, Cabot let her go abruptly. Michaela's eyes met Samuel's. Silent, angry accusations immediately sprang between the young lovers.

''Thank you for inviting me to the wedding, Michaela, and for the good-bye kiss,'' Cabot announced with clarity. ''You know where to find me if you need me.''

Samuel stood on the porch steps staring at Michaela, wondering if he was going to bash Peabody's face in when he walked by. His right hand made a tight fist.

He didn't know why Michaela had let Peabody kiss her so boldly. If she hadn't been so passive in Peabody's arms, he would have attacked the man then and there, but she had calmly let her former beau's lips ravish hers and his hands explore her body. The problem was with Michaela, not Peabody, but that didn't make Samuel like him any better.

Samuel climbed the rest of the steps two at a time and stood before a confident Republican and an angry wife. He trained his eyes on Cabot and said, "Touch her again and I'll kill you."

A sneer formed on Cabot's lips. "You have enough to worry about without adding murder to your troubles." He turned back to Michaela. "Good-bye, Michaela."

The thud of Cabot's boots on the ground faded in the distance. A long moment of utter stillness punctuated the tension between the young couple while their eyes accused and blamed.

"Wasn't that kiss a little more than brotherly?" Samuel taunted dryly.

"What do you care?" Her response was abrupt and lined by rigid pride.

"A hell of a lot." Samuel grabbed her arm, and she flinched. Why was she angry? He wasn't the one caught kissing someone. The gut-wrenching stab of betrayal kept his voice low. "I don't want him touching you, let alone kissing you. You're my wife now, and I expect you to act like it."

Michaela twisted free of his hold. "How much did you get for me?" she demanded in a husky voice, her expression fierce.

"What?" Samuel tensed instantly.

"How much did my father pay you to marry me?"

Guilt raced across Samuel's face and settled in his eyes. A knot formed deep in the pit of his stomach. He watched Michaela tremble with emotion and started telling himself no before he spoke the word aloud.

"No."

"That's right." She lifted her chin and her shoulders. "Cabot overhead you and Papa talking this morning. Your dirty little secret is out." She wiped away a tear with her fist, letting her eyes accuse him. "Now that you've married me and taken me to bed, do you get more money?"

He reached for her, but she was too quick. "Michaela, don't say these things. Let me explain." His voice grew louder. "That idiot didn't tell you the whole truth. He has it all wrong."

"You said you loved me." Her words challenged him.

"I do, dammit. I do!"

"I don't believe you anymore."

The pain in her voice scorched and wounded him. He grabbed her arm and held tightly, his heart pumping. "Let me explain what happened, how it all came about."

With one quick jerk, Michaela freed her arm of Samuel's grasp. "Do you really think I want to hear how much you were paid to marry me or why?" She lifted her chin a little higher. Tears spilled from her eyes and down her cheeks, leaving sorrow in their wake. "Leave me some dignity, please." She turned away and hurried into the house.

For a brief moment Samuel was tempted to ride after Peabody and beat the devil out of him. He'd obviously overheard part of his conversation with Padraic and then told Michaela his own version of it. But right now Michaela was more important. He'd take care of Peabody later.

Damn that man for telling her! Damn him for breaking her heart, for kissing her. Now she'd walk around the rest of the day with Peabody's kiss on her lips. Samuel's fist opened and closed convulsively. Fury ate away at him.

He needed time to calm down before he approached

her again. She needed time, too. Tonight when they were alone, he'd make her listen to the truth.

"What's wrong with Michaela, Sam?" Davia asked as she joined him on the front porch.

Samuel massaged his forehead and grimaced. He wasn't in the mood for Davia. "Nothing," he muttered, and turned away, not wanting her to notice how tense he was.

"She looked like she'd been crying to me. Her eyes were wet and her nose was red."

Davia's words twisted like a knife in Samuel's stomach. He should have ridden after Peabody and beat the living daylights out of him for breaking Michaela's heart. Instead he faced Davia and asked, "Would you be concerned about her if she had been crying?"

Opening her mouth to speak quickly, Davia caught herself and thought about what she was going to say. "I guess I wouldn't want anyone to cry." She lowered her lashes. "I wouldn't want anyone to see me cry, either. I think that's the reason she ran when I called to her."

Samuel's heart constricted. He sure as hell didn't want Michaela crying. "She'll be fine." A dull ache formed in his throat. He had a feeling it would be there until he could talk to Michaela. "We just had our first argument."

"You shouldn't make your wife unhappy the first day you're married, Sam."

Her advice was well noted. A wisp of a smile showed on Samuel's lips. So his little sister was growing up. "You're right, Muffin. It was a damn fool thing to do. But I'm going to make it up to her. You wait and see."

Michaela avoided Samuel and her father for the rest of the day and into the evening. She spent the afternoon trying to keep from crying. She considered it a challenge to make sure no one realized her world had been destroyed. If her father had not been in on Samuel's deceitful act, she would have insisted they return to Atlanta immediately. She'd really believed Samuel loved her. That was a mistake, and she wouldn't be so foolish again.

There were fewer than five guests, including her father and Kate, remaining at Twin Willows after dinner that evening, so Michaela pleaded a headache and went upstairs early. Davia offered to help her undress, and even though she wanted to say no, Michaela agreed to let her.

"Your clothes are so beautiful," Davia said as she unbuttoned Michaela's topaz-colored dress. "When Samuel gets the plantation going again, I'm going to have dresses like this."

"I'm sure you will," Michaela answered automatically, rubbing her temples. She hadn't been faking the headache. The effort of keeping a smile on her face all day had been too much of a strain.

"Sam's a very smart man. You won't be sorry you married him."

Michaela squeezed her eyes shut, glad that Davia was behind her. Last night she would have agreed. Last night she had experienced the most glorious hours of her life. Last night she had loved her husband and thought he loved her. Tonight she didn't want him to touch her.

"There were a lot of women who wanted to marry Sam," Davia continued.

"I know," Michaela agreed, and stepped out of her dress. When she turned around she found herself looking into soft brown eyes.

"Sam didn't mean to make you cry this morning. He was really upset about it."

Touched by the caring in Davia's eyes and voice, Michaela wished she'd never heard of Samuel's deceit. Davia was trying hard to ease her pain, but she wasn't ready to be comforted.

"I'm sure he was. Now, if you'll unlace me, I think I can take care of everything else." Michaela turned her back to Davia once more.

"Do you know Cabot Peabody very well?" Davia asked as she pulled on the corset strings.

This new line of questioning took Michaela completely by surprise. She gasped, wondering what Samuel had told his sister about Cabot. "Well, yes, I suppose." Her voice sounded airy.

"He's simply divine. The most handsome man I've ever seen," Davia announced.

Michaela's breath came in gulps. Davia was interested in Cabot? "Yes, he is. Cabot is a very handsome man." Her voice trailed away on the last words. Why had Cabot told her about Samuel, knowing it would destroy her happiness?

A short time later Michaela shut the door behind Davia, thankful for the peace and quiet her absence created. She was tired. The whole affair of the wedding, Cabot's news, and the argument with Samuel had taken their toll on her strength. At some point she would have to talk to Samuel, but not tonight. The pain was too raw. Then there was her father to consider. Maybe she should speak to him first. After all, he'd offered Samuel the money. But why?

Earlier in the day Michaela had decided she would

have to sleep in Samuel's room until all the house guests had left, and at least for tonight, she'd have to sleep in his bed.

In her bedroom at her father's house, Michaela had a day bed as well, but Samuel's room only had a very uncomfortable slipper chair with no arms. It would be foolish to spend the night curled up on it. Still, that might be better than sleeping with a man who'd been paid to marry her.

Michaela crawled into the bed, feeling so drained she was sure she'd be asleep when Samuel came up for the night. Unfortunately he came in before her head touched the pillow.

The tautness of her body increased. She turned her back on him and crowded as close to the far edge of the bed as she could without falling off. She listened to all his sounds of undressing and feigned sleep when the bed sank beneath his weight.

"Michaela," he whispered.

She remained still and quiet, determined to fool him into thinking she was asleep.

"Michaela," he said in an aching voice, then touched her shoulder.

"Don't touch me," she muttered, and shrank away from him even though the warmth of his hand on her had a soothing effect.

"Let me explain exactly what happened. Peabody got the story all wrong. It's not as bad as you think."

Part of her wanted him to explain why he had accepted money in exchange for her hand in marriage. But his answer could make the hurt worse, and she couldn't bear any more. "I don't want to talk to you," she mumbled into the security of the quilt.

"Fine." His voice grew cold. "I'll talk and you listen."

"No. And take your hand off me. If you continue to touch me, I'll be forced to sleep on the floor."

Suddenly Samuel pulled her to him roughly and pounced on top of her, pinning her to the bed. Her eyes grew wide with fear, not knowing what he intended to do.

"All right, you stubborn little vixen. You can sleep on the floor if you want to, but I'm not going to let you go to sleep with Cabot Peabody's kiss on your lips. You're my wife, and I don't want anyone kissing you but me."

His lips came down on hers, hard and bruising. Michaela pushed at his shoulders, but they wouldn't budge. She wiggled and struggled beneath him, but his body was too hard to move. Memories of the night before seeped into her mind. His gentleness and caring. His warm hands on her flesh. She loved the feel of the weight of his body on hers. Gradually she stopped fighting and opened her mouth to her husband and accepted his tongue, wantonly. Her body arched to meet his. Their hands touched, clasped, gripped.

He whispered her name, achingly soft, against her lips as she yielded beneath his caresses. Michaela knew the pleasures his touch could bring, and she found it difficult to deny him. Her arms circled his back and drew him closer.

Samuel parted her nightgown and sought her breasts, kissing, sucking, caressing, teasing first one, then the other. His hand slipped lower to caress her abdomen and lower still, bunching the fine cotton of her nightgown.

Michaela tried to think even as her body cried no. She wasn't supposed to let him do this. Then why did it feel so good? He had deceived her, taken money to marry her.

"No!" she cried, and pushed at him.

Samuel raised his head and looked deeply into her eyes. "Michaela, I love you. I'm sorry I hurt you. Give me the chance to make it all right. Let me love you." His voice was rough with desire.

She was tempted, so very tempted. "I can't. You accepted money for my hand in marriage, and now you're trying to buy my love with lies."

"No, dammit, I didn't. I'm not." His fist pounded the side of the bed, and Michaela jumped, clutching the front of her nightgown together.

As if realizing he had frightened her, Samuel spun around and turned down the lantern, enveloping them in darkness. "Go to sleep, Michaela. I won't touch you again."

The bed creaked and bounced until Samuel settled down on the other side. Tears held at bay burned in Michaela's eyes. Her body was still on fire from his touch. She wanted him to finish what he'd started, but her pride clothed her like a garment. They could have been so happy together. They were so well suited to each other. She loved him. Was he lying about his love for her? If not, why had he accepted money? Why had her father offered it? Did he think he had to buy her a husband? She shivered. Suddenly she wanted the answers.

Eleven

"**M**R. Brennen, while we have a moment alone this morning, I should like to tell you that I've applied for another post." Kate was pleased that her voice sounded normal, even though her heart beat crazily in her chest. It was silly of her to be upset at the thought of leaving the Brennen household. Padraic was a difficult man at times, but she never minded that.

"What, so soon?" Padraic moved down the buffet line, adding two fluffy, golden-crested biscuits to his plate.

"As soon as Michaela was officially engaged, I started making inquiries. I'm expecting an answer by the time we return to Atlanta or shortly thereafter." She followed him down the side of the laden table, bypassing the eggs, bacon, and fried potatoes. "I realize I can't stay on in your house, so I'll look for a boarding room as soon as we return.'' Kate saw they were nearing the end of the table and she had nothing on her plate. She quickly added one of Velvet's pancakes to her plate. It wasn't like her to be as nervous as a young girl talking to her first beau.

"Nonsense. You'll stay with me.''

Startled, Kate whipped her head around to Padraic. "Oh, I'm afraid that wouldn't be proper.'' She felt a moment of light-headedness. She'd been hoping for some show that he didn't want her to leave. "I must go.''

"There are plenty of servants in the house to chaperone *you*, dear Kate, until you hear from your inquiries. I'm certainly not going to let you stay in some dreary boarding house.''

Kate smiled, breathing easier as they walked to the dining room table and sat down. "Well, perhaps an answer will be waiting for me, and I can leave immediately upon our return to Atlanta.''

Padraic unfolded his napkin and gave it a loud shake before placing it in his lap. "I don't think you should be in a hurry, Kate. You may not want to take the first position offered. You should take your time and be sure you go to the right family. There's no need for haste in leaving my employ, I assure you. For now you can continue to run my house and supervise the servants.''

Relief washed over her. At least she didn't have to think about leaving immediately. "Thank you, Mr. Brennen. That would be helpful, but I may have to leave on very short notice.''

Padraic sliced open a biscuit and spread butter on both halves. "Let's not worry about that until the time—''

"Papa, I'm sorry to interrupt, but may I speak with you?"

Glancing up from her plate, Kate took a long look at Michaela and didn't like what she saw. After the wedding Michaela had been very happy, deliriously so. Sometime late yesterday afternoon she'd changed. Not only was the smile gone from her lips, but the sparkle was missing from her eyes. Now, this morning, dark circles smudged her eyes, and her complexion and lips were pale. Kate didn't have a clue as to what had happened; but judging by the determination written on Michaela's face, her father was about to learn the details.

"Of course, sit down and join us," Padraic encouraged as he reached for his coffee.

Michaela looked at Kate and bit down on her bottom lip. "I'd like to speak to you alone, Papa. Let's take a walk."

Padraic looked at his untouched plate and then to Kate. She gave him a nod and a look that said, Go with your daughter, she needs you.

"Certainly, dear." He pushed back his chair. "You will excuse us, won't you, Kate?"

"Oh, yes, of course." Kate continued to watch Michaela. "I'll finish breakfast, then make sure our bags have been brought down."

The sky was a mass of gray over their heads as they walked through the flower garden at the back of the house. The darkening clouds matched Michaela's mood. Today she felt that she'd never be happy again. Her first night with Samuel was like an elusive dream that had escaped her, never to return.

"I suppose you'll be leaving soon. It looks like rain is on the way."

"I had hoped to be on my way in less than an hour. However, if you're not comfortable with that, I can stay a day longer."

"No, that's fine." Michaela cringed. She'd never lacked the courage to talk with her father. Now here she was stalling and stammering. For all her bravado, she really didn't want to know why he had paid Samuel to marry her.

"I haven't seen Samuel this morning," Padraic offered as an observation as they continued down the walkway, his hands firmly in the pockets of his brown pants.

"I don't know where he is." She refused to look at him, and her tone was icy.

Padraic stopped and touched her arm. "What is it, Michaela? We've been close too long for you to watch your words so carefully. What's bothering you? Have I done something to upset you? Has Samuel?"

Michaela moistened her lips, looked up to the heavens for strength, and said, "Papa, did you offer Samuel money to marry me?"

He didn't have to say a word. Michaela saw it in his eyes. She saw sorrow, too, but she pushed that aside and cried out in desperation, "Why? Didn't you think I could find a husband on my own?"

"Michaela, come, let's sit on this bench." He touched her arm and propelled her to the backless lawn seat.

"No!" Michaela covered her eyes with her hands, hoping to hold the threatening tears inside. "I don't want to sit down. I want you to tell me why you thought you had to buy me a husband."

"Give me the chance to explain, child."

"I'm not a child! Don't call me a child again." Her angry words were backed by eyes spitting fire.

"I did offer him money to court you. I'm sorry, Mich—"

"Why!"

Padraic looked away briefly. "Perhaps I don't always do what's right, but I always do my best. I could see you were becoming more interested in Cabot Peabody than any of your other suitors. I didn't think he would be the right man for you."

"Papa!"

"Wait, let me finish. The first time I met Samuel, I said to myself, There's a man who can make my daughter happy. And you weren't indifferent to him. I saw the way the two of you looked at each other in the bank that first day. Oh, there was something there. No doubt about it. I knew I felt the same way when I looked at your mother."

"You shouldn't have interfered, Papa."

"I know. I shouldn't have meddled in your life, but I saw that Cabot's main interest in life is politics and Samuel's is his home. I knew Samuel was the man who, in the years to come, would make you happy. I was thrilled when he refused to take the money."

Disbelief flooded her eyes. "Samuel didn't take the money?"

"Certainly not! He won your hand on his own, Michaela. You chose him. I didn't force you to marry him, and Samuel wasn't paid to marry you. He realized immediately what a bad idea it was. I swear on your dear mother's grave, he wouldn't take a penny. Now, he did accept a loan, but he's made it clear on a number of occasions that it's strictly a business loan that will be paid back, and I believe him. He wouldn't even accept a dowry.''

Michaela rubbed her temple, her forehead, her eyes, the back of her neck. Her chest hurt from holding herself so rigidly. Samuel had told her Cabot had the story wrong, and Cabot had said he hadn't heard everything. ''Papa, are you telling the truth?''

''What a thing to ask!'' His voice stern for the first time, he asked, ''Have I ever lied to you? I was merely trying to think of some way to get the two of you together. I knew nature would take care of the rest, and it did. I didn't think he'd take the money. He's a proud, honorable man. Do you really think he'd consider taking money from me? From anyone? No, he's a man who'll do everything on his own. The kind of man you need. He loves you. He told me so.''

''He did?'' A breeze blew a strand of hair across her face, and she brushed it away.

''Yes, of course. When a man truly loves a woman, he's not ashamed to admit it to anyone.'' He patted her hand. ''Michaela, Samuel didn't do wrong. If you must, be angry with me. Don't harbor ill feelings toward your husband. Go to him and talk. Let him explain in his own words what took place between us. Now, I must start back. We've a long trip to Atlanta. I only hope the rain holds off until we get home.''

''Papa, why didn't you just invite him to dinner? Why offer him money?''

''He was desperate. He'd been to every bank in town and others still. I was a last resort. He didn't want to do business with me because he considered me a carpetbagger. In offering him the money he'd asked for, I was merely giving him the opportunity he wouldn't seize on his own because he thought our kind beneath his social circle. In fact, I remember him telling me that he wouldn't court a Yankee.'' Padraic chuckled. ''Imagine calling us Yankees.''

Michaela needed time to sort out all her father had said. If it was true that Samuel hadn't taken money to marry her, then she had no reason to be angry with him. As for her father... She looked up into his green eyes and saw the love in his face. He'd just done what he thought was best for her.

''When will you be back to see me, Papa?'' she asked in a voice filled with emotion.

Padraic picked up his daughter in a big bear hug, lifting her feet off the ground. ''Soon. We'll come again soon.'' When he set her down again he asked, ''Tell me, can you forgive an old man for meddling in your life?''

Michaela smiled. ''You're not old. You're still a handsome man, and you have a lot to offer a woman. Have you thought about asking Kate to marry you, Papa?''

''Heavens, no!'' Padraic took her arm, and they started toward the house. ''Kate's applied for a new post. I'll be sorry to see her go, though. Like your mother, she can keep me on my toes.''

''Why don't you marry her?''

''Hush, Kayla. I'm too old and set in my ways. Besides, I'd never have a moment's peace with that woman around. You're trying to play the same kind of game that just got me in a world of trouble.''

"You're right. I didn't realize how easy it was to get involved in manipulating someone's life."

"It's very easy, Michaela, very easy."

Kate and Padraic left shortly after that. Michaela helped Velvet, Evelyn, and Davia put away the wedding presents while she waited for Samuel to return. She had taken Cabot's word as fact and accused Samuel unjustly. She wanted him to come home so they could talk.

"Davia?" Michaela asked as they folded a long, hand-stitched tablecloth, "do you know where Samuel went this morning? He left without awakening me."

"No," she answered, taking her time with the creases. "I asked him to take me riding before he left, but he said he didn't have time. He told me to tell Mama he wouldn't be home until dinner."

Dinner! Michaela's heart dropped. "Oh, I see." She walked to the window and looked out. If it rained, maybe he'd come home earlier. She'd been wrong, and she wanted the chance to explain. She almost laughed aloud. How many times had Samuel asked her to let him explain?

But it didn't rain, and Samuel didn't come home until just before dinner. His mood didn't seem any better than it had been the night before. Michaela could see that Velvet and his mother, as well as Davia, knew something was wrong. He washed his face and hands and joined them for a quiet, strained meal. As soon as it was over, Samuel ordered Henry to send the washtub up to the bedroom and fill it with hot water.

Michaela stayed in the parlor with Evelyn and Davia doing needlework while she waited for Samuel to finish his bath. After an hour she said her good-nights and went upstairs, hoping he'd be kinder to her than she'd been to him.

Squaring her shoulders, she opened the door and went inside. To her surprise, Samuel was still in the tub of water. He opened his eyes as she came inside but didn't speak.

"I'm sorry. I thought you'd be through with your bath by now."

"You thought wrong," he commented dryly.

Michaela moved closer to him, determined not to let him undermine her efforts to apologize. Only one lamp was lit, and the room was dim and shadowy. Samuel kept his gaze on her but didn't move.

"You should get out before the water gets too cold."

"After sleeping with you last night, I'm used to the cold."

His words stung and spurred her to anger. "I'm trying to be nice," she argued defensively. "I want to explain."

"Hell, no!" His hand hit the water with a splash, spilling it over the sides. "Who was the one begging to explain last night? Did you give me the chance to explain?"

She came closer still and stood before him. "I thought you'd been paid to marry me. I had a reason to be angry." She wasn't going to back down. She loved him, wanted him.

Samuel stood up in the water with the speed of lightning. He grabbed Michaela's shoulders and pulled her close to his wet body and held her tightly. "So what if I had accepted that money? There's not a man in the world who wouldn't do far worse to marry a woman like you."

His arms were wet but warm and strong, and she leaned into his embrace. She wanted to appease his anger. "You didn't take the money." She held his eyes with hers.

"How do you know? You wouldn't let me explain." His voice was low, his eyes peering intently into hers.

His wet body soaked her dress, but she didn't care. She was in his arms, feeling his strength, his power, his love, and it felt wonderful. Her feet were off the floor, the hem of her dress dangling dangerously close to the water.

"I talked to my father," she whispered, and moved her lips closer to his.

"Why wouldn't you talk to me?"

His words warmed her. She wanted to kiss him. She didn't want to fight anymore. She ran her hands up and down his back, feeling the slickness left by the water. The texture of his wet skin excited her. Her abdomen tightened, and she moved her lips closer.

"I was hurt and angry."

"Michaela, don't you know I would never do anything to hurt you? That pompous idiot hurt you by telling you half the truth." His arms tightened. "I could kill him for it."

She closed her eyes as her lips grazed his. "Don't say that," she whispered, and bit him gently.

He took her lips in a fierce, brief kiss. "I mean it. I won't have him hurting you, and I damn sure won't have him kissing you."

Samuel stepped out of the water and carried Michaela to the bed, placing her on top of the quilt. His wet body covered hers. Droplets from his hair fell to her face as his lips found hers again. His kiss was wet, urgent, and demanding.

He lifted his head and gave her a serious look. "This marriage is new to both of us. I don't want it to start out with you sleeping on the other side of the bed. I want what we had on our wedding night, every night." He wiped the water from her face and let his eyes move down to her breasts. The thin silk of her dress had soaked the moisture from his body and outlined the sheer garment she wore underneath.

"Don't ever let Peabody touch you again." His words were more of a groan, but Michaela understood him. He kissed her passionately, his tongue probing the warm recess of her mouth.

"Never again," she whispered as his lips slipped to her neck and down the front of her dress, kissing and biting her lovingly through the wet fabric. Michaela's body arched to meet his. She reached around his neck, slid her fingers into his damp hair, and tugged playfully at it.

"Look at how wet your clothes are," he said. "I'd better take them off before you catch cold." He straddled her hips and raised her to a sitting position, reached around to her back, and, as he slipped each button through its hole, allowed himself a congratulatory kiss. It seemed to Michaela that it took hours until she was completely undressed and forever until each pin had been pulled from her hair.

Finally, no barriers were left between their trembling, naked bodies. "In our bedroom I want to see you and feel you, not a corset with whalebone running through it." His hand traced the curve of her breast, then his lips followed and lingered, withdrawing only so that he could whisper, "I want to touch only you."

Michaela felt wild, reckless with desire. She moved her hand down between their bodies, and Samuel lifted himself so she could find what she sought. When her warm hand closed around him, he welcomed her caress, and she felt powerful, abandoned, and elated when she heard him gasp with pleasure.

Then his lips covered hers, and his tongue moved in and out of her mouth with slow, leisurely strokes, foretelling the rhythm of a deeper ecstasy yet to be enjoyed.

"Damn!" he swore in a raspy voice, his eyes glazed with passion. "You're so beautiful. Soft. All woman."

At his words of love her stomach tightened, her breasts ached for his warm mouth, and her body yearned to be filled. She was ready for him, and she wanted him to know it. "Now," she whispered. "Let me feel you inside me."

Samuel answered quickly with several long thrusts. She met him with equal strength until in one powerful explosion, they were satisfied.

"You take everything I have," Samuel said a short time later as they lay facing each other.

"What do you mean?" she asked, feeling gloriously content.

He chuckled and brushed at her hair. "I'll tell you sometime. I'm too tired tonight. I spent the day digging holes for fence posts, hoping to make myself so tired I wouldn't ride into town tonight and give Peabody the beating he has coming to him."

Michaela reached over and caressed his cheek. "Forget

about Cabot. He didn't do anything you wouldn't have done had your roles been reversed.''

"He hurt you, and I don't want anyone hurting you, including myself.''

She looked at him with all the adoration she was feeling. "I love you, Samuel Lawrence.''

His eyes crinkled with a smile. "Come here,'' he said, and pulled her to him, tucking her body solidly against his. He slipped his hand under her neck so that her head rested on his shoulder. With the tips of his fingers, he lifted her chin and tilted her head back so he could look into her eyes. "You, Michaela Lawrence, are one special woman, and I'm one damn lucky man.''

His lips closed over hers once again.

Twelve

"*D*AVIA , you must sit still if you are going to learn how to do this stitch," Evelyn admonished her daughter as they sat in the parlor late one afternoon.

"I'm not interested in learning how to sew. I don't want to make fancy little scarves for the dresser or samplers to hang on the wall. I want to go out and help Samuel build the fence for the new horse he's going to buy."

"Nonsense. A young girl can't help with those things. You'll be fourteen soon. You must learn how to cook and sew and manage a home. Tell her, Michaela."

"I agree with your mother, Davia. You should learn how to take care of a household. Your husband will expect you to know those things."

"I'd rather go out riding and learn how to shoot a gun."

Evelyn gasped, and Michaela laughed.

"Why on earth would you want to know how to shoot a gun?" her mother asked.

Davia jumped up defiantly, knocking her embroidery to the floor. Her hands splayed across her hips. "Because it's more fun than sticking a little needle through a piece of cloth. I don't care what husbands think."

"Davia, don't use that tone of voice—"

The sound of a horse approaching silenced mother and daughter. Michaela looked at Evelyn. Samuel wouldn't ride up to the front door. He'd go directly to the barn and put away his horse before coming to the house.

"We must have a guest," Davia said, and ran to the window and looked out. "I don't know who he is. I've never seen him before."

"Come away from the window and keep your voice down," Evelyn told her. "When he knocks, we'll answer the door and find out."

"Why should we wait for him to knock when we know he's here?" Davia yelled back over her shoulder as she rushed out of the room to confront the caller.

Davia was already introducing herself to the stranger when Michaela and Evelyn caught up with her.

"How do you do, Mrs. Lawrence." The tall, broad-shouldered man removed his wide-brimmed hat and smiled broadly. "I'm Rufus Tully, an old friend of Samuel's. I hope you don't mind that I stopped by, uh—unannounced?"

"Oh, not at all, Mr. Tully. Any friend of Samuel's is always welcome at Twin Willows. Please come in." Flustered with pleasure, Evelyn made the introductions. "Michaela, dear, this is Mr. Rufus Tully, a friend of

Samuel's. And this is Samuel's wife, Michaela. You've already met his sister, Davia.''

"Ah—Sam's wife.'' He inclined his head toward her, and Michaela felt a sinking in her stomach. She didn't like the way the man openly leered at her. He made her uncomfortable.

"Won't you come in and have some refreshment? Samuel won't be home for at least an hour.''

"That's mighty kind of you, Mrs. Lawrence. I don't mind if I do.''

"Were you in the army with Sam?'' Davia asked as they walked into the parlor.

"What a smart young girl you are,'' Tully remarked. "Yes, as a matter of fact, we were on a special assignment together during the war.''

"Another army friend of Sam's was here a few weeks ago. Isn't that right, Mama? His name was Mr. Riverson. Do you know him? Sit here, Mr. Tully.'' Davia didn't take a moment for a breath or give anyone else time to speak.

"Davia, please go ask Velvet to bring in some coffee.'' Evelyn issued the order firmly. "And if she's too busy with dinner, you prepare it for us.''

"But I want—''

"Davia.'' Evelyn spoke sharply, although her voice remained soft. "Mr. Tully is tired and thirsty from his journey, and it's unkind not to get him a drink immediately. Michaela and I will entertain him until you return.''

Michaela couldn't take her eyes off the stranger. He was the second army comrade to visit Samuel recently, and there might have been others that she didn't know about. It seemed a bit odd that both of the men she'd met had mentioned they had been on a special mission with Samuel. She felt as if her skin were crawling. Something was wrong. Mr. Tully, like Mr. Riverson before him, showed signs of being nervous and edgy. She wondered why.

At a glance, Michaela had thought Mr. Tully was a nice-enough-looking man. But now that she studied him while Evelyn had his attention, she didn't like what she saw. His mousy brown hair looked oily and dirty, and his bushy eyebrows emphasized the fact that he had eyes so small, they appeared closed when he smiled. Maybe she was just looking for reasons not to like this man, but every instinct warned her that he meant trouble.

Michaela cleared her throat and lowered her lashes when the man caught her staring. Manners dictated that she ask a question because Evelyn had fallen quiet. She lifted her eyes. "Where are you from, Mr. Tully?"

"Just Tully, ma'am. I was born in Kentucky, but I spent the last couple years, since the war, in Alabama."

"And you served the Confederacy, Mr. Tully." Evelyn's words were a statement.

"Oh, yes, ma'am. I wasn't ready to give up when Lee surrendered," he bragged. "That just about killed the rest of us."

Evelyn smiled contentedly. "We're so proud of all our men who served."

Michaela felt momentarily out of place. She didn't have the soft spot in her heart for all Confederate soldiers that Evelyn had. And for some reason she hadn't yet put her finger on, she especially disliked this one. She'd talk to Samuel tonight. She had to know what was going on. Why were his old army friends suddenly showing up to visit him? And why had both of them mentioned a special mission?

"Yes, ma'am." Tully picked up the banner. "We lost a lot of good men in the war. Folks can say what they want, but the South won't ever be the same again."

When Evelyn's eyes filled with tears, Michaela's protective instinct was aroused. She wouldn't have this stranger coming in and reminding her mother-in-law of a war that had taken her husband's life. It was one thing to tell funny stories, as Mr. Riverson had done on his visit, but this insensitive playing on a woman's emotions seemed callous and deliberate.

"I'll go see what's keeping Davia and ask Velvet to set another place," Michaela said. She rose and turned to Mr. Tully. "You will stay for dinner?"

"Oh, yes, ma'am. Thank you kindly. I'd be most obliged to have dinner with you."

"Splendid," she answered coolly. "Excuse me." Michaela felt his eyes on her back until she was well out of the room. On her way to the kitchen she stopped and rubbed her arms to ward off the chilling effect of Tully's gaze. She squeezed her eyes shut for a moment and shuddered, hoping Samuel would hurry home and that this man would leave as quickly as the other one.

Samuel wasn't happy about Rufus Tully's appearance, either. Michaela knew it the minute he walked into the parlor and saw the man lounging on the settee, filling Davia's head with more war stories. His expression was vastly different from the beaming smile he'd worn when he'd introduced Mr. Riverson.

"We invited Tully to stay for dinner," Davia announced to her brother.

"I'm glad you did. It's been a long time, Tully."

The two men shook hands, but there was no friendliness in either face. Suddenly Michaela felt sick. Her husband was obviously keeping something from her. They'd only been married a week, but she already knew his moods. Mr. Tully had put Samuel in a black one. Something was definitely wrong, and that frightened her.

"I've got to wash up. We'll talk after dinner."

"Looking forward to it, Sam. Don't be in any rush. I'm having myself a fine time visiting with your favorite ladies."

Samuel gave him a cold stare before turning away.

The next hour was the worst Samuel had spent in his life. He'd been scared many times during the war, and some since he'd been home, but nothing compared with the way he felt tonight. In the war Samuel had had only himself to worry about. Now there was Michaela, his mother, and Davia. Tully's appearance had confirmed Riverson's story. The look in Tully's eyes substantiated Samuel's belief that the man was capable of cold-blooded murder.

Samuel's military training was coming back to him. He must be the initiator, the aggressor, the one to take charge and put his opponent on the defensive. As soon as Tully's dessert spoon hit his empty dish, Samuel suggested they take a walk so Tully could have a smoke. He wanted this man out of the house and away from Twin Willows as quickly as possible. If what Riverson said was true, Samuel's family was in danger.

"Slow down there, Sam," Tully complained when

Samuel hurried him toward the barn. "You'd walk the horns off a billy goat."

Samuel stopped abruptly and turned on Tully, "All right then, what are you doing here?" His voice was low and menacing.

"I think you know why I'm here." Tully remained calm, his voice smooth. "I want the other half of that map you drew one cold day in Vermont." He sniffled and wiped his nose with the sleeve of his shirt. "Thomas and Shareton don't have it, so the only ones left are you and Riverson. Now the way I figure it, one of you has it, and I aim to get it." His voice was as pleasant as if he were talking to the preacher about Sunday morning services.

"What makes you so sure Thomas or Shareton don't have it?"

Tully sneered, letting Samuel see a hint of the man beneath his false smile. "I just know, and so do you. I spent a little time looking for Riverson but couldn't find him. Now, that pretty little sister of yours tells me he was here."

"Yes, he was here a few weeks ago. He and I burned the map."

Tully let loose a nervous giggle, for the first time showing a break in his control. "I don't believe you."

"It's true, damn you!" Samuel insisted. "That money doesn't belong to any of us. And it certainly isn't worth killing for." His hands curled into fists, and the muscles in his neck jerked. Tully was a plague on decent society, and he was itching to do away with him.

Tully took a step backward, still smiling. "Maybe you're right. Maybe it's not worth a killing." He took a deep breath, grabbed his pants by the belt, and pulled them up and over his spreading waistline. "Well, think I'll mosey on up to Vermont and try to find that Yankee gold with the half I have. Who knows, I might get lucky and go right to it." He laughed with ease. "Now, wouldn't that be something."

Samuel gritted his teeth and sneered at the older man. "Why didn't you try that before you paid your visit to Thomas and Shareton?"

Tully laughed, sniffled, and laughed again. "So you know about that, do you? Well, you won't do anything about it. You were always too weak in the knees, Sam. Never could stand the thought of killing, could you?" He laughed again. "That's a right nice woman you're married to. She's got fire in her eyes and her hair. I bet she has fire between her legs, too."

Fury raged inside Samuel. He grabbed the front of Tully's shirt, bringing his face so close he could see the crusted dirt in the lines around the man's mouth. "Get away from here, Tully, and don't come back. If I hear of you poking your nose around here again, I'll show you how weak in the knees I am when it comes to killing."

Their eyes locked together for one long moment. Samuel shook inside with fear for Michaela. Tully's last comment was meant as a warning. He knew that. His one hope was that Tully also meant what he'd said about heading to Vermont.

Tully pulled out of Samuel's grip and stepped back. The malice-filled smile on his lips let Samuel know this wasn't the last of it. Then he turned and swaggered toward the barn to get his horse.

Under his breath Samuel swore, using words that hadn't passed his lips since the war. He hadn't asked to be selected to rob those banks. He hadn't wanted to do it, damn it. Now, his sins were coming back to haunt him. He stood shaking under the soft covering of moonlight, cursing himself for his past.

Within a couple of minutes Tully rode out of the barn as if devils were after him. Samuel stood in the darkness, thinking, making plans. First thing tomorrow morning, he would take Michaela and Davia to Atlanta to spend a few days with Padraic. They would be safe there.

Thirteen

WHEN Samuel opened the bedroom door he saw Michaela at the dresser brushing the tangles from her hair. With her long-sleeved winter white gown buttoned all the way up to the base of her throat, she looked virginal and tempting.

"Has he gone?" she asked, laying aside her silver-handled brush. She turned away from the mirror and looked directly into Samuel's eyes.

He wasn't expecting her question. All he wanted to do was look at her. He had to repeat her words to himself before he comprehended. "Oh. Yes. He couldn't stay the night."

"Good."

Samuel's terror was intensified as he faced Michaela. She was so beautiful and in such danger. He should be taking her in his arms, kissing and loving her, but all he could think of was that he had to get her away from Twin

Willows. Tomorrow. Tully's mention of her name had been a subtle threat, one that demanded an immediate response. Michaela wouldn't leave easily, but her safety had to come first.

Samuel turned away from her as he unbuttoned his damp shirt and threw it over a chair. He poured water from the pitcher into the basin and splashed it on his face and neck several times, letting the droplets run down his chest. When had it gotten so hot?

"Samuel, we have to talk," Michaela said, touching his arm with a gentle hand.

He raised his head and looked at the dancing reflection of her beautiful green eyes in the mirror. It wouldn't do to let her see how vulnerable he was. If she did, he'd never get away with what he was about to do.

With reluctance he hardened his eyes. "All right, talk," he answered in a clipped tone. It was easy to sound angry. All he had to do was think about that viper Tully, and fury bubbled up inside him.

"I want to know what's going on. Why are men from your army regiment suddenly showing up?"

The concern in her eyes didn't escape him, but he couldn't let it sway him, either. He picked up a small towel and wiped his face and neck, wondering what he could tell her. Certainly not the truth.

"Yes, it was nice of them to stop by, wasn't it?" he mumbled. That wasn't even a good lie, and he knew it, so he deliberately avoided her eyes.

"Samuel, I knew the minute you walked into the parlor tonight that you didn't like Rufus Tully. You were extremely nervous all through dinner, and I think it's because of him. Why did he come here? Why did both men mention that they'd been on a special assignment with you?''

''Michaela, stop it.'' He took her by the shoulders and pulled her close to his chest. He had to hold her for a moment and reassure himself that what he was doing was right. She felt so good. When she laid her cool cheek on his bare, fevered chest, he wanted her desperately. He stroked the length of her silky hair, holding her tighter than he should have. He would worry enough for both of them.

''A lot of soldiers had special assignments during the war. There's nothing unusual about that.'' He realized he was trying to soothe her. Taking her in his arms was a mistake. He turned her loose and stepped away. ''However, you have no cause to question me about my friends or the war.''

Looking up at him, she asked him to be truthful. ''Samuel, I know something's wrong. Your heart's beating in your chest the way a madman beats against prison walls. Tell me what's going on.''

''Nothing!'' Dammit! He turned away so he wouldn't have to see the pain in her eyes. ''Nothing's wrong.''

Michaela grabbed his arm, and he spun back around to face her with a scowl on his lips. ''Don't lie to me, Samuel. I want to help.'' Her words were a forced whisper, and her eyes sparkled like heated emeralds, burning into his soul.

The love he saw in her face, heard in her voice, weakened him. He couldn't fight against her love. He had to make her angry—too angry to care that he was sending her away.

"This is none of your damn business, Michaela," he yelled, pointing a firm finger at her. "So stay out of it."

She flinched, clearly stunned by his abusive attack. He had told her he loved her. How could he be this cruel?

"How dare you speak to me that way!" she cried. "I am not a servant in this house. I'm your wife, and I demand a certain amount of respect."

Her voice was loud and shaky. For a moment, Samuel doubted he had the strength to go on, but this was the only way to get her away from Twin Willows and to the safety of her father's house. He must be hard, even though it was tearing him apart.

"You demand?" he sneered. "You have no right to demand anything. You have no rights except for the ones I choose to give you. And I haven't given you the right to poke your nose in my affairs. I thought Kate was supposed to teach you how to be a proper wife. It looks as if she forgot to teach you not to question your husband.

"I think you should go back to your papa's for a few days." His voice softened. "I'll arrange for Henry to take you tomorrow."

"I—I don't want to go. You can't use me for a few days, then send me back to my father's. You can't order me around. I'm not one of your slaves!"

At last she was getting angry. He could deal better with her anger than her hurt. "Twin Willows hasn't had slaves for years, Michaela. But the people who live here obey me." He struck his chest with his thumb. "What I say, you do."

Her hands curled into fists, and she struggled for control of her voice. "I won't go! You can't make me."

"Watch me!"

"Samuel, what's wrong?" There was a desperate plea for understanding in her voice. "You're not yourself, and I don't care what you say—I know this has something to do with those men. With that special group."

"No!" Samuel grabbed her shoulders and held her firmly. "You want the truth. It has to do with you. I'm tired of you. You don't please me, and I want you out of here!" The words flew fast and furiously from his trembling lips.

He saw the tears in her eyes. He didn't want to make her cry. He didn't want her to leave. He didn't want to spend one night without her. What the hell was he doing to her? She'd never forgive him for this. But she'd be safer in Atlanta until he was sure Tully wasn't going to show up again. When he knew Tully was indeed on his way to Vermont, he'd go after Michaela. It'd probably take a long time to persuade her he didn't mean any of the things he had said tonight. A damn long time.

Abruptly he let her go and turned away. He couldn't look at her or touch her again. If he did, he might change his mind. "Just be ready to leave first thing in the morning." If he stayed any longer, he'd break. He moved to the door with heavy feet.

"Samuel, I won't go!" she called to him.

"You don't have a choice."

He closed the door behind him with a bang. Hurting her was the hardest thing he'd ever done. As he walked down the stairs, he didn't think he'd ever stop shaking, stop hating himself.

He hurried across the hallway and into his office. From his desk drawer he took a silver-handled pistol and tucked it into his belt. From the gun rack he chose a rifle, then stuffed several shells in his pockets and walked out the door.

The night air was no longer sultry. A cool, crisp breeze chilled his bare chest as he ran toward the barn. He didn't have a minute to waste.

"Henry! Henry!" he called as he swung open the door and headed toward the old man's room. His loud voice stirred the horses. They snorted and stamped their hooves as he rushed by.

Buttoning his trousers, his shirtless, dark chest gleaming against the glare of a lantern he held in one hand, Henry rushed out of his room. "What's da mattah?"

"I've got trouble, Henry. Big trouble."

"Whatcha want me ta do?" Henry hung the lantern on a nail in one of the posts and finished fastening his trousers. The horses continued to stamp and snort, sensing the unease of the men in the barn.

Samuel's throat was dry. "Sleep with one eye open," he said. "The man who was here earlier tonight may be up to no good. I won't go into all the details." He took a deep breath and rubbed his forehead irritably. "I want you to take Michaela into Atlanta tomorrow to stay with her father. Take Davia, too. Ask one of the Jackson boys to go with you, and send the other one up here to keep an eye on the house until you get back from Atlanta. I want him to stay with Mama and Velvet. Tell him to make sure no one gets inside."

"Yessuh, but what you gonna do?"

"I hope I'm going to find tracks leading north." Samuel pulled the pistol from his belt. "Take this and keep it with you at all times. You'll find extra shells in my desk drawer." He gave Henry the gun.

Henry stared at it for a moment, then looked at Samuel. "I don't know nothin' 'bout guns, Mr. Lawrence." The whites of Henry's eyes shone brightly in the shadowy light of the lantern. Sweat had popped out on his upper lip, and his nostrils flared with each shallow breath.

"Take this, too." Samuel shoved the rifle into Henry's other hand and reached in his pocket for the shells. "This is for Jackson. Let him take a couple of practice shots if he hasn't ever fired one before. If you see the man who was here tonight, don't take time to ask questions. Start shooting. Do you understand, Henry?"

"Yessir, I shore do. That man's afta yore missus. Don't you worry, Mr. Lawrence. That man won't get yore woman. Not whiles I'z alive."

"Thanks, Henry. I'm counting on you." He gripped Henry's shoulder for a moment. "If I'm not back by nightfall tomorrow, I want you to stay near the house and keep that gun with you at all times."

"Don't you worry. I won't let nothin' happen to your mama. I took care of her whiles you in de war. I know how."

"Velvet may give you a hard time about spending so much time around the house, but don't pay her any mind. Just do what you have to do."

Nodding, he answered, "I'll take care of her, too."

"Good." Samuel pointed toward the gun. "Don't be afraid to use that if you have to."

Henry pursed his lips for a moment. "They'll hang me fa shore iff'n I kill a white man. You knows dat."

Samuel's chest swelled with gratitude. Fear hadn't prompted Henry's statement, and he appreciated the old man's loyalty. "It's my gun. If anybody asks, I'll swear I did it. You just make sure no one gets to any of the women."

"Yessuh, I shore will. You can depend on me." He wiped his upper lip with the back of his palm.

Samuel pressed his hand to his forehead, trying desperately to think of every possibility and plan accordingly. "I don't want to go back upstairs, and I forgot to grab my shirt. While I saddle my horse, see if you can find me a shirt. And look for a couple of Velvet's biscuits while you're at it."

"Yessir, I'll be right back." Henry hurried away.

Samuel felt like putting his fist through the aging barn wood. Damn! When did things get so crazy? When were the things that happened in that damned war going to stop haunting him?

Michaela refused to go down for lunch. She hadn't eaten much breakfast, either. In truth, she felt as if she'd never want to eat again. She stood at her bedroom window in her father's house, where she'd spent most of the last two days. The gray morning sky had brightened to blue. Flowers bloomed in the backyard, but they were few compared with the magnificent gardens at Twin Willows.

She'd been stupid to think Samuel loved her, to put her complete trust in him. If he really cared for her, he would never have shamed her by sending her back to her father. People would think she hadn't pleased him or worse, that she wasn't pure when they married. She squeezed her eyes shut, blotting out the brightness of the day. How could she ever hold her head up in society again?

"Am I intruding?"

Michaela turned away from the window and saw Kate standing in the doorway. She hadn't heard her knock. "I'm really not feeling well, Kate," she said. "I'd like to be alone."

Ignoring Michaela's protest, Kate moved into the room and shut the door behind her. "We haven't talked since you arrived, Michaela. I think it's time we did."

Michaela turned back to the window. "I don't want to talk."

"Oh, I can see that. You want to feel sorry for yourself, and you expect the rest of us to allow you to do it."

"I expect no such thing." Michaela whipped her head around and glared at Kate.

"Then why are you hiding up here in your room? All we can say is, 'Poor Michaela. What is wrong with her?' "

"I only want to be left alone. What's wrong with that?"

"I'll tell you. When you showed up on the doorstep, you said you'd come to bring Davia shopping for new dresses; but you haven't left this room, and poor Davia has been begging to see Atlanta."

Kate was right. She'd lied about the shopping so her father wouldn't know Samuel had thrown her out. She hadn't stopped to think that Davia would believe her or to question Henry when he'd said Samuel wanted Davia to go, too. At the time, she'd been too numb, too caught up in her own misery, to really consider why Samuel had sent his sister along. But now she realized there had to be a reason.

"Michaela?" Kate asked, laying a gentle hand on her shoulder. "You seem to be in another world. Talk to me. Tell me what's going on. I may be able to help."

Michaela looked into Kate's eyes. She saw concern and friendship. Maybe Kate's wisdom would help her understand what Samuel was doing. "It all started a couple of days ago when Mr. Tully, an old friend of Samuel's, came to Twin Willows for a visit."

They drifted over to the window seat and sat down while Michaela told the rest of the story, ending with Samuel's abusive verbal attack and his sending her back to her father.

"So Samuel didn't deny that Tully had been on a special assignment with him?" Kate asked, making sure she had the story straight in her mind.

"No. Just that many soldiers were assigned special missions during the war, and I'm sure that's true." Michaela rose from the velvet-printed cushion and walked across the room. "I'm sure of one other thing, too. Samuel changed the minute he walked through the door and saw that man sitting in the parlor."

"Mmm—I don't know. I remember that Samuel was happy to see that first man who visited while we were at Twin Willows. There could be a good reason he wasn't happy to see Mr. Tully." Kate sighed. "Are you certain nothing else has happened?"

"Well, there was the problem of my father offering Samuel money to marry me, but I'm certain this couldn't have anything to do with that."

"What?" Kate rose from the window seat and stood in front of the dresser. "What are you talking about?"

Michaela made a stab at laughing, trying to cover her

slip. "Never mind. I'm sure that's not the problem. I won't even go into it. Papa and Samuel cleared that up quickly enough when I asked about it."

"But—"

"No, really, Kate. I shouldn't have mentioned it. It's not important, and—"

There was a loud knock at the door. "May I come in?" Davia's muffled voice came from the other side.

"You're right. I have been neglecting Davia." Michaela headed for the door, her full green skirt billowing around her.

"I'll talk to you again after I mull this over, Michaela," Kate said as Davia burst inside.

"What are you talking about?" she asked the two older women.

"I was just asking Kate if you'd finished lunch. I'm feeling much better, so I thought we'd send for a carriage and go to the dressmaker's."

Davia's eyes lighted up with anticipation. "That would be wonderful. Shall I ask Bessie to get one?"

Kate spoke first. "Yes, please do that, and I think I just heard a knock on the front door. Find out who's calling before you return."

"Maybe it's Cabot Peabody. Did you tell him I was here?" Davia asked Kate.

"No, I most certainly did not. As I told you before, Mr. Peabody is much too old and you are much too young. Now go see who's at the door."

With a pout on her lips Davia turned away. Michaela smiled ruefully when she was gone. "She's so full of life. Everything is still so exciting for her. Wouldn't it be something if my first beau turned out to be hers, too?"

"Michaela, don't speak as though your happy times were all behind you. Let's try to sort things out."

"You're right, Kate. I need a friend who'll listen without making judgments. A friend who'll give advice when I ask for it. Thank you for being here."

Kate's smile was beautiful. She put her arms around Michaela, and they hugged tightly. "I don't want to see you unhappy. You and your fath—" She stopped and cleared her throat. "I'm very fond of you."

"And talking to you made me see everything much more clearly. I think the men Samuel rode with in the army have come to cause trouble, and he's worried. That's why he sent Davia and me away. The first thing tomorrow morning, I'm going back to Twin Willows. This time I'm going to stay and fight Samuel until he realizes we are on the same side."

"That's exactly what you should do. If he's in trouble, you should be by his side."

Out of breath and with a flushed face, Davia rushed back into Michaela's bedroom. "You'll never guess who it is. Mr. Tully, Samuel's friend."

Fourteen

"**K**ATE, I'm home." Padraic shut the door with a bang. "Michaela, I'm home." Hanging his hat and coat in the foyer, Padraic listened for sounds that didn't come.

"Hello," he called again as he walked into the parlor, where he expected to find the women waiting for him. He was late, but surely they wouldn't have gone in to dinner without him.

"Hmm..." He made the sound with pursed lips and walked toward the back of the too quiet house. When he found the dining room and kitchen empty, and no dinner prepared, his heart fluttered, and a chill ran up his spine. Something wasn't right. He turned from the kitchen and hurried toward the stairs, calling for the cook and the housekeeper as he went. With steps agile for a man so large, he took the stairs two at a time. At the top he was forced to stop for a deep breath. His ears rang and his heart hammered.

"Kate! Michaela!" he called breathlessly, and flung open the first door he came to. The room was empty. Quickly, he ran to the next one and the next.

"Heaven's gate! What in God's name has happened?" Padraic briefly took in the scene before him. Kate lay crumpled on the floor beside the fireplace, dried blood smeared across her forehead, her face ashen. Not far away Davia struggled on a chair, her hands and feet tied with rope and a scarf covering her mouth.

He ran first to Kate and knelt down to make sure she was alive. "Thank God," he whispered, and quickly made the sign of the cross. He grunted as he rose from the floor and rushed to Davia.

"What's happened? Where's Michaela? Who did this?" Frantically he worked with trembling fingers to untie the gag that kept Davia silent.

"He took Michaela!" Davia cried as soon as she could speak.

"Who took her, and where?" Padraic fumbled with the rope that tied her hands to the chair. "Keep still," he admonished harshly. "I can't untie the rope with you wiggling."

"Mr. Tully took her with him!" Her big brown eyes were angry, her face flushed.

"Who is Mr. Tully? Did he do this to Kate?" Padraic threw a glance back to Kate. She was too pale.

"He hit Mrs. Spencer and took Michaela with him."

Padraic thought his heart would beat out of his chest. Kate was at the point of death, and Michaela was missing. Fear for his daughter gripped him. *Hurry,* he told himself, and went back to the task of unknotting the rope.

"I'll get my feet," Davia said when her hands slipped free of the bindings. "You see about Mrs. Spencer. She hasn't moved since he hit her. She's not dead, is she?"

Padraic scrambled back to Kate. With quaking limbs, he went to his knees once again. Carefully he put one arm under her head and the other under her knees, then lifted her up into his arms. He was surprised at how little she weighed, how light she felt. With extreme care he laid her on the bed and turned her head so he could examine her wound. He wouldn't be able to tell anything until it was washed.

Davia crowded his arm and asked, "Is she alive?"

"Yes, but barely. How long has she been out? When was she hit?" He picked up her wrist and felt for a pulse. "Where are Bessie and the cook?" Padraic turned to Davia, his legs trembling so badly he could hardly stand. "What in heaven's name happened here today! Where's my daughter?"

Davia explained as she covered Kate with a blanket. "Mr. Tully told Mrs. Spencer she had to give the servants the night off, so they left."

"And what time was that? How long ago did all this happen?"

Davia scratched her head as if doing so would help her remember. "I don't know. Sometime after lunch."

"Was Michaela hurt at all when this man took her away?" Padraic questioned.

Davia shook her head.

Padraic was getting his breath back to normal, but his stomach was knotted with fear. "Good. We'll find them.

First we have to see to Kate. Davia, you must go quickly and get the doctor. I'm afraid she's in a bad way." He touched Kate's cold cheek, then tucked the blanket around her shoulders.

With a blank expression on her face, Davia looked up at Padraic. "I can run fast, but I don't know where to go."

He wiped his mouth. "Out the front door and to the left. Three blocks on the right. He has a big sign hanging on the front porch. Go quickly." His voice was husky with fear. "We'll talk about this man who has Michaela when you return. Quickly now."

Davia was out the door in a flash, and Padraic turned back to Kate. She looked so pale, so still. With a warm hand he brushed the strands of hair away from her soft cheek. "Don't die, dear Kate. Don't die," he whispered.

In less than ten minutes Davia was back, tugging the doctor into the room. Padraic had placed a cold wet cloth on Kate's forehead. He'd cleaned away some of the blood and revealed a slash on her head that was deep and about three inches long.

Leaving Kate in the doctor's care, he took Davia downstairs to get the details. He'd been trying to piece together the bits of the story she'd told. "I want you to tell me everything, Davia. Who is this Mr. Tully?" he asked, his chest tight with fear.

"He's Samuel's friend—or at least he fought in the war with him. He came to see Samuel at Twin Willows, and today after lunch he came here. He was very pleasant at first. Then, all of a sudden, he pulled a gun out of his pocket and told Kate—I mean, Mrs. Spencer—to go dismiss the servants. He said if she hinted to them about anything being wrong, he'd shoot us all." Davia took a breath. "I need some water."

"In a minute, lass. Go on. I must know where he's taken Michaela."

"I can tell you all this on the way back to my place," Davia said in a take-charge manner. "Samuel needs to know so he can go after Michaela. He's going to be madder than a wet hen if we don't go right away."

"Yes, yes, you're right. We can't wait to see about Kate. Michaela is in danger. I'll go next door and ask a neighbor to come stay with Kate. Perhaps you should stay here, too. I can go faster by horse. With you along, I'll have to hire a carriage, and we won't get to Twin Willows much before morning."

"Get me a horse! I've been riding since I was four. You'll have a devil of a time keeping up with me. You get that neighbor and the horses. I'll get something to drink and check on Mrs. Spencer. I'll meet you out front. Hurry!" she called back over her shoulder as he vanished from view.

Samuel sat in the kitchen with his feet propped on the table, drinking watered-down whiskey. He'd made it back to Twin Willows just before dinnertime. Henry had informed him that Michaela and Davia had been safely delivered to Atlanta and there had been no sign of Rufus Tully. That's what worried him.

He hadn't been able to pick up Tully's trail. He'd checked every stagecoach and livery stable leading in and out of Atlanta, and no one had seen Tully. If he was heading for Vermont, he hadn't stopped to eat, rest his horse, or take the train.

Samuel filled the shot glass with the weak amber liquid. It hadn't been easy fielding his mother's questions over dinner. He knew she was worried, concerned, but he couldn't tell her the truth. He was glad when she and Velvet chose to go to bed early. He had to do some thinking.

There was no use trying to sleep, even though he had Bo Jackson watching the house. He gulped down the cheap whiskey and started to pour another shot when he heard the sound of approaching horses. Someone was riding fast and hard. He picked up his rifle and headed for the front door at a solid run.

Hurrying down the front steps, he heard Davia calling, "Sam! Sam!" A heavy cloud of fear seized him. He swore under his breath and ran to meet her.

Davia reined her horse to a stop in front of him. "Mr. —Tul—Tully got Michaela." Her breathing was ragged, her words barely audible.

Padraic stopped his horse a few feet from Samuel and Davia. "We—must—hur-ry, Samuel. He's—got Michaela." His whole body heaved with each jerky breath.

Out of the corner of his eye, Samuel saw Jackson's gun pointed at Padraic's head, and he knew Henry would be sneaking up from the back. "It's okay, Bo," he yelled. "He's not the man we're looking for." He turned back to Davia, wrapped his arm around her, and lifted her off the horse. "Let's go inside and you can tell me everything."

Velvet and Evelyn met them in the foyer, voicing their own fears. "What's going on, Samuel?" Evelyn asked.

"He put a gun to her head and made her do it!" Davia clung to Samuel's arm.

"Whatcha want me ta do, Mr. Lawrence?" Henry stood, pistol in hand.

"I came home and found Kate on the floor in a pool of blood," Padraic said.

"What? Kate? Oh, my, no!" Evelyn cried.

"Stop it! Shut up, all of you," Samuel yelled above the frantic chatter around him. Quiet settled over the frenzied group. "Just be still and let me think," he said in a softer voice. "Let me ask a few questions, and we'll find out what happened." Samuel wet his lips and looked at the horror-stricken faces waiting for him to tell them what to do.

"Velvet, you go make coffee. Strong. Mama, you get Padraic and Davia water. Henry, you saddle my horse and have it waiting out front for me."

"You two"—he pointed to the still breathless Davia and Padraic—"come in here and sit down and tell me what the hell happened."

"Davia will have—to tell you," Padraic said between gulps. "I didn't take—the time to hear the whole story. We sent for the doctor, then came straight away."

Samuel looked at Davia. Her face was red, her hair a tangled, windblown mass. "Just the high points."

"Mr. Tully came in and pulled out his gun. He made Kate dismiss the servants, then forced us to go upstairs. Kate had to tie me to the chair and put a scarf around my mouth like this." She showed him what she meant. "It was tight, too."

"Where was Michaela?"

"Mr. Tully was holding her by the hair with the gun pointed at her head. He promised he'd shoot her if Kate didn't do as he said."

Samuel's heart jumped to his throat. He'd kill Tully. For the first time since the war, he felt he was going to be sick. He took a deep breath, trying to settle his stomach. "What happened next?" he asked hoarsely.

Davia took the glass of water from Evelyn and drank thirstily.

"Not so much. You'll make yourself sick," Evelyn cautioned as she smoothed the damp hair back from her daughter's face.

"What happened next?" Samuel asked again.

"He told Michaela to tie Kate to the other chair; but as soon as he let Michaela go, she grabbed for the gun. Mr. Tully did a lot of cussing and swearing and pushed Michaela to the floor. Kate lunged for him, and he hit her with the gun. She didn't move again after she fell."

"My God," Evelyn whispered. "Who is this man? What does he want, Samuel?"

"Mama, please," Samuel said. "Now think hard, Muffin. Did you hear him say where he was going?"

She nodded. "He told me to tell you he'd give you Michaela when you gave him the map. He said you'd know where to find them."

"What map?" Padraic and Evelyn said in unison.

A cold chill of fear went up Samuel's back. "It's nothing," he replied. He didn't have time to get into the story of the buried gold.

"Don't tell me 'nothing' when a madman has almost killed Kate and has my daughter in his clutches, pointing a gun at her head!" Padraic said angrily, rising from his chair. "Give him the map!"

"I don't have the damn map! I burned it," Samuel ground out between clenched teeth. His fierce anger was directed at himself, although he'd attack anyone at the moment.

Gasps came from everyone in the room, including Velvet, who stood holding a tray of steaming coffee. "I don't have the damn map," Samuel said again, not sure if he were trying to exonerate himself or remove the doubtful look from the faces that surrounded him.

"What kind of map was it? Can you get another?" Padraic asked.

"No."

"Sam, you have to do something. He's got Michaela!" Davia pressed against Samuel, and he hugged her tightly, wishing he'd done so many things differently.

"Don't worry, Muffin, I won't let him hurt her. Come on now. Give me a smile. You've been too brave tonight to start that." He wiped a tear from her cheek with his thumb, then set her aside. "Give me a cup of that coffee, Velvet. Mama, go upstairs and pack me a change of clothes."

"Where're you going?" Padraic asked.

"To get Michaela."

"I'm going with you," Padraic said.

"Me too," Davia added.

Samuel took the coffee from Velvet and sipped the scalding liquid. "No to both of you. Padraic, you have to go back to look after Kate, and you need to be home in case Michaela gets away and tries to get in touch with you." He rubbed Davia's head affectionately. "Sorry, Muffin. You're just too young. Besides, Mama's going to need you to take care of her."

"She's got Velvet. I can ride fast, Sam," she argued, determination in her voice.

"I know you can. You ride better than most men I know. But you can't come with me."

"Where's he taking her? Do you know?" Padraic asked.

"Vermont." Samuel saw Padraic pale at the distance Samuel was going to have to cover before his daughter was found. "Don't worry. I'll bring her back. But don't expect to see us for a while. I'll send a telegram when I've found her."

Samuel grabbed his clothes from Evelyn as she swept into the room. He took a moment to kiss his mother and Davia before rushing out the door.

He stopped in surprise at the front of the house; Henry had two horses saddled. "I'z going with you, Mr. Lawrence. I already spoke ta Bo. He'z going to look afta the women here."

Although Samuel's heart swelled with fondness, he said, "I have to go alone, Henry."

"That man got yore wife, and I don't like it. I'm gonna kill him for ya. Won't nobody ever know."

Samuel clamped a friendly hand on Henry's shoulder. "I appreciate you wanting to do that, Henry, but I need you for something else. If I don't come back, Mama's going to need you to help her get that corn to market. Let Davia help, too. She's smart. She'll need to know how to run this place if I don't come back. You show her for me, all right?"

"Yessir, Mr. Lawrence. I'll show her, but I'd rather kill that man gots the missus."

"Thanks, Henry. I knew I could count on you. Now I've got to go. I want to be on the first train in the morning heading north out of Atlanta. The way I figure it, Tully has a full day's start.'' Samuel swung up on his horse to ride out, but Henry grabbed the reins.

"Don't you worry, Mr. Lawrence. Iff'n you don't come back. I'll find that basterd for ya and kill him.''

Samuel grasped Henry's hand. He had no words. The only thing left to do was head for Vermont.

Fifteen

MICHAELA pressed close to the window of the train. The bumpy ride occasionally knocked her head against the pane, but she had no room to move. Tully was sprawled over most of the seat, sleeping peacefully except for an obnoxious snorting sound every now and then when a loud clatter erupted or the whistle was blown.

How confidently he slept, so sure she wouldn't try to escape or alert the authorities that she was being held against her will. He'd told her he was a murderer and laughed. "So's that dear husband of yours. If the police get me, I'll tell all about the men he killed right along with me. And if that don't fix him, I'll kill him. I'll get out of prison like I done before. I got paroled after two years in jail last time, and I'll be out again."

Michaela knew he must be lying when he said Samuel was a murderer. But she believed Tully was capable of anything. She thought about Kate lying still as death on the bedroom floor. If he could do that to a sweet woman like Kate, what would he do to Samuel? Maybe Kate was dead, Michaela thought. Maybe she soon would be, too. He could kill her when he got whatever he wanted and then come back and kill Samuel and Davia anyway. But she wouldn't let him do it without putting up a fight. For now, she'd stay quiet. When the right time came, she'd be ready.

Michaela had no idea what he wanted from her or Samuel. She didn't know where they were going, only that they were headed north. While Tully slept, she'd tried to put some of the events together.

Samuel had sent her to her father's to protect her from Tully. She was sure of that now. And he knew the only way to make her go was to pretend he didn't want her. Knowing that Samuel still loved her and would be coming for her lifted her sagging spirits.

Whatever Tully wanted from Samuel had something to do with their time together in the army. But what? That special mission he spoke of? She knew so little of Samuel's army life that she couldn't even make a good guess.

Out the train window, she watched the sun rising in the east. A glance around the railroad car showed everyone but her sleeping. That was the best thing to do. She had to try and sleep. She had to keep up her strength. When it came time to run or fight, whichever became necessary, she had to be ready.

They rode the train for three days. Michaela came to hate the sound of the train whistle blowing, signaling that they were either coming into or leaving another town, taking her farther away from Samuel. When the train stopped to pick up or let off passengers, they got out and walked. Tully never let her venture far from the platform. A couple of times she asked him to tell her where they were going. He always gave her an evil smile and told her not to worry about it: she'd know soon enough.

Their train ride ended in a small town in Vermont. Michaela had an eerie feeling about the place. She hadn't been to Vermont since she and her father had first come to the States early in the winter of '63. Her experiences there hadn't been good ones, and she had never wanted to return. Again she tried to question Tully as to their purpose, but he refused to tell her anything.

With the money he'd stolen from her father's house, Tully purchased two horses and enough supplies to last a week. He bought two shirts and a pair of riding britches for Michaela. He complained about having to spend extra money on jackets and gloves because it was much colder in Vermont than it had been in Atlanta. If only she knew what he'd planned, she could make some plans of her own.

Although he hadn't said anything to her directly, it was clear they were about to leave the town and ride into the hills. She hadn't been frightened of Tully while they rode the train and other people were close. But once they left town, it would be just the two of them. He could do anything he wanted to her without witnesses.

Tully walked the packed horses out of the livery stable and approached her. She took a deep breath and lifted the collar of her jacket to the chilling wind. She wasn't going anywhere with that man until she got some answers.

"Mount up," he said.

"No." She stood her ground and answered firmly.

Tully spit tobacco juice close to the toe of her shoe. Michaela's stomach turned a somersault. Maybe what she was doing was foolhardy, but she could no longer acquiesce to his demands without answers. Fear for Samuel's and Davia's lives was the only thing that had kept her passive for so long.

She stuck her hands in the pockets of the brown knee-length jacket, tilted back her head, and said, "I want to know where we're going and why."

"Up in those hills," he answered quietly, throwing his thumb over his shoulder.

Her eyes held steady. "Why?"

He studied her for a moment as if he were trying to decide whether or not he should say more. "I've said about all I'm going to for now." He looked around the quiet street where they stood. "Now, you can either get on that horse and ride out of here with your head high, or I'm going to have to give you a hard one to the head and knock you out."

Michaela bristled. "You're a fool. If you hit me, someone would see you. There are people all around."

"Doesn't matter. You'll be out cold, and I'll tell 'em you were giving me trouble about going to visit my ma and pa. There's not a man around here that'll get into an argument between a man and his woman."

"His woman!" she spit the words out with vehemence. Inside her pockets her hands made fists. "How dare you infer such a thing!"

Tully grinned, showing stained teeth. "They'd only know what I told them. Now get up on that horse like I told you. Don't you worry none. I'm going to tell you the whole story when we get where we're going." He grinned again. "That's a promise."

Less than an hour later, the biting edge of the wind had already chapped Michaela's cheeks and numbed her fingers and toes. The end of May was only a couple of days away, but with the chilling wind it was like a cold February day in Atlanta. Gray, threatening clouds added to the damp feeling of winter.

Michaela made the ride easier to bear by thinking of Twin Willows with its glorious spring flowers. She fought the stinging wind by remembering the feel of Samuel's warm body pressed close to hers.

They didn't ride hard, but Tully kept a steady pace, stopping only occasionally to decide which direction to take. Michaela knew how to stay on the horse, but not much more than that. The muscles in her arms tired first, followed quickly by the muscles in her thighs and back.

It was full dusk before he gave the sign to make camp. Michaela groaned audibly when she dismounted, and her knees nearly buckled under her. Every muscle in her body screamed for her to be still. Tully's laugh gave her the remaining strength she needed to hobble over to where he was starting a fire.

"You should have told me to take it a little easier," he said.

"Would you have stopped if I had?" she questioned sarcastically, taking off her gloves and rubbing her hands together.

"No, but I would've enjoyed hearing you ask."

Tully laughed, and Michaela wanted to slap him. If she hadn't been trembling from the cold and the pain in her thighs, she would have lunged at him. Instead she answered her body's demand and sat on the ground in front of the small bundle of twigs.

Fire caught among the straw and small pieces of wood he'd been nursing, and Michaela was drawn instantly to its warmth. She moved closer to it. With care she rubbed the knots out of her tightened leg muscles but didn't take her eyes off Tully.

She watched him pour water from the canteen into the coffeepot, then open a can of beans and set them at the edge of the fire. While he went in search of more firewood, Michaela did as instructed and kept a close eye on the coffee so it wouldn't bubble out of the pot.

She continued to massage her body and plan what she would do if Tully attacked her. She'd been fairly safe as long as other people were within hearing distance, but now she was on her own. She could kick and bite and scratch, but those things would be useless against a knife or gun. The fire was her only weapon. If Tully jumped her, she'd do her best to roll him into the flames.

It was pitch dark by the time they'd eaten and the plates were wiped clean and put back in the saddlebags. Michaela unfolded her bedroll, every movement a torment.

"I want to know what we're doing here," she said without preamble when Tully came back to the fire with his blanket.

"I guess I can tell you now. Won't nobody hear if you start screaming and acting like a crazy woman."

His cold words reminded her of the bleak chill in the air and the fact that she was in the hills of Vermont, a place she had never wanted to revisit. She became acutely aware of the night's sounds, the fire crackling and hissing, the crickets and night birds. The smell of smoke lingered heavily around them, and the taste of strong coffee lay bitterly on her tongue.

"You ever been to Vermont?"

Icy fingers of doom climbed up Michaela's back, and she realized how alone she was. She pulled her jacket tighter around her throat. "Once," she answered, then immediately regretted telling him when she saw his lips widen into a broad smile.

"Was it anywhere around here?"

"I don't know. I don't remember. I was too young, and we'd just come to the States from Ireland." She rubbed her arms, trying to shake the dreadful feeling of foreboding. His smile intensified her fear. Maybe he did intend to rape her. The fire burned between them, but it wasn't a big fire. Tully could easily step over it and never feel the heat.

"Why did you bring me here? What do you want with my husband?" she asked angrily. "I have a right to know why you're doing this to us."

"Gold."

"Gold?" she shot back quickly. "You're not making sense. Any money Samuel might have would be at Twin Willows, not here in these woods."

He laughed, and his shadowed teeth gleamed in the darkness. "No, you're wrong. There's gold buried somewhere in these hills, and Sam knows exactly where it is. I intend to see that he finds it for me."

"Why would Samuel know where gold is buried? Besides, he may not even come for me. He was angry with me and sent me back to my father's." Desperation gripped her, and she fought hard to ward it off.

"He was only trying to protect you from me. He didn't

know I found out all about you before I went to Twin Willows. I spent a couple days in Atlanta, watching your pa's house, getting to know his schedule. Just in case.''

Tully had obviously planned this well and was pleased with himself. It made him feel secure. Maybe she could take advantage of his overconfidence. Michaela looked around the campsite. Darkness surrounded her. If she had to run, it could become her protector and shield her until morning.

"You see, I know something you don't know, or don't remember," Tully continued.

"It seems to me you know a lot of things I don't." Her voice was edged with a healthy hint of fear.

He laughed heartily. "How would you like for me to fill you in on what I know? I think it's about time."

He took his handkerchief out of his pocket and placed it over the bridge of his nose and tied it at the back of his head. Then he stood up and loomed over the fire and peered into Michaela's eyes. She shrank back, terror filling her throat.

"Still don't recognize me, do you?" he said from underneath the makeshift mask. "Well, see if you remember this. 'That locket belonged to Mama, Papa. I won't let him have it.' "

Michaela screamed and tried to scramble to her feet, but Tully jumped over the fire and landed on top of her, pinning her to the ground. She pushed at his chest. "Let me go!" she screamed into his face.

She kicked and hit, but with the full weight of his body on top of her she was almost powerless. Still she kept kicking, struggling. Suddenly his fist came down on her cheek, and a sharp pain struck her eyes. Michaela was stunned into stillness, the pain so intense she almost lost consciousness. Her eyes blinked rapidly. She'd never been struck in her life.

Breathing heavily from the weight of Tully's large body, she tried to focus on what her next move should be. She feared if she moved her head again, the piercing pain would return. Perhaps the best thing was to remain still and let him think he'd knocked her out.

She felt stale breath upon her face and tried to breathe shallowly so that she wouldn't inhale his scent too deeply. She wanted to scratch out the eyes of this horrible man who'd taken her mother's locket and filled her nightmares for years. How had he found her? Where was Samuel?

"Samuel," she murmured.

"That's right. Call for your husband. Call for the man who robbed you and your pa in the bank that day."

Michaela's eyes flew open, and she stared at the man who sat on her stomach peering down at her. "Wh— what did you say?" she asked, panting.

Tully yanked the kerchief off his face. "Yep, Sam was in the bank with me that day, Riverson, too. We robbed the bank, then everyone in it. We were chased by some damn Yankees, so we hid the money in these hills. Sam's the one that buried it."

"No!" she screamed as loud as her lungs would allow. With the last of her strength she heaved Tully off her.

Her action had caught him off guard, and she was able to run a couple of steps on her aching legs before he dragged her to the ground with him. In an effort to keep him from pinning her down again, she tried to keep them rolling across the low-lying bushes, but with his superior strength he soon straddled her waist and held her hands above her head. She had managed to wriggle them closer to the fire, but she was the one lying so close the flames heated her cheeks.

"You might as well hear it all, little girl," he taunted when she had no more strength to fight.

"That's right. Settle down now and I'll tell you the whole story. You wanted to know what I want with your husband, and I'm going to tell you. Me and Sam are old army buddies all right. We were regular Robin Hoods, taking from the Union bastards and giving to the Confederacy."

His evil laugh chilled her to the bone. "No, you're lying," she whimpered, trembling as much out of fear he might be telling the truth as from the pain in her head and overworked muscles. She couldn't give up. She bucked beneath him.

"Easy now, easy. Let me tell it, and you'll know I'm not lying. Since ol' Sam was the youngest of our group, we let him keep watch at the door for us. We were afraid he might go soft on us. And he would have. He didn't like us stealing from Yankees like you. The only reason President Davis wanted him to go along was 'cause he could shoot straighter than the rest of us, and I guess the president figured Sam would be a big help if we got in a tight spot."

Tully chuckled as if he were truly enjoying story time by the campfire. Michaela groaned and tried to pull her arms out of his hands, but her struggles only made him hold her tighter.

"I didn't recognize you at first. But when you opened your mouth and I heard that same pretty accent, I knew you were the girl in the bank that day. Sam must have recognized you, too. Guess he never said anything, though. I don't blame him. If I had a woman as pretty as you, I wouldn't want her to know I had robbed banks, either.''

''I don't—want to hear any—more of your lies.'' She couldn't take any more. Exhausted and out of breath, she heaved once again, trying to shove him off her. She made little groaning sounds as she tried in vain to wrestle away from the wicked man who held her to the ground. She didn't know where her strength came from, but she was making headway. At last one arm broke free, and she struck out, hitting him hard with a tight fist. She heard him grunt, and she smiled just before a fierce blow jerked her head and another sharp pain raced across her eyes and everything went dark. She tried to open her eyes, but they wouldn't focus properly. Suddenly she wanted to go to sleep. Yes, sleep.

''Wake up!'' A hard slap to her cheek made her wince, and her eyes popped open. ''I'm not through telling you about that husband of yours.''

She tried to answer, but all she could do was make garbled sounds. If she went to sleep again, the pain would leave her head and she could rest. After she rested, she could fight him again.

''All right, I'll let you sleep a couple of hours.''

His words were distorted, but she understood. ''Yees—sleeep,'' she whispered, and let the darkness take her away from the stabbing pain in her head.

It was raining on her. She had to get shelter, but where? It was too dark for her to see. ''Papa!'' she called. ''It's raining—raining.''

The cold wetness hit her face again, and slowly she opened her eyes. Two Tullys stood above her dropping water on her face. The images swayed back and forth in front of her, laughing. "No," she groaned, lifting up her arms to shield her face from the offending droplets, moaning from the pain above her eyes and the ache in her muscles.

"Come on, girl. Time to wake up. I expect Samuel to be paying us a visit in a couple of hours."

"Samuel?" she managed to whisper.

"Yep, I figure right now he's riding as hard as we did that day the Union soldiers were after us. The bastards didn't catch us, though."

"No." She didn't want Samuel to come. He'd deceived her. He was a bank robber. She couldn't move. She ached all over, and a wave of nausea swept over her.

Tully grabbed her under the arms and started to lift her. Michaela raised her hand and caught him across the face with a hard blow that snapped his head around. He grabbed the front of her shirt and hit her across the mouth with an open palm.

Michaela screamed and fell back against the ground as blood trickled into her mouth. Tully swore viciously and snatched her under the arms again. She kicked and swung at him, but he managed to drag her over to a tree and prop her against it. She couldn't fight any longer. Her strength was gone, and the whole world spun out of control. She grabbed her stomach and forced down the eruption inside her.

"I wanted you to look real purty for your man. I'm sorry I had to hit you so hard, but when you reached up and took that swing at me, it was a natural reaction. You didn't hurt me, though.''

He rubbed the cheek Michaela hit, and she knew he was lying. She wanted to smile but realized her lips were too swollen and her throat too dry. All she wanted was sleep. She closed her eyes once again.

When she awoke she realized she was sitting on the cold ground, tied to the trunk of a small tree. Her hands were positioned behind her and the rope wrapped twice around her chest and waist. After she had blinked several times, her vision cleared.

''So you're finally awake.''

Tully watched her from the warmth of the fire. She suddenly realized she was cold. In his hand he held a pistol. She didn't remember seeing it last night. She started shaking and didn't know if it was caused by the gun or the cold air.

''I'll get you some coffee. It's a mite nippy this morning. Downright cold. But it'll warm up today. The sun's shining.'' He shuffled over to her. ''Here, drink this.''

She had it in her mind to refuse the coffee, but it smelled so good, and the warmth tempted her to obey immediately. Fighting the urge to be sick, she drank when he put the cup to her cold lips. The warm liquid went down easily. After a few sips he set the cup aside and took the front of her plaid shirt and ripped it open, exposing one of her breasts.

''No!'' she screamed. She strained against the ropes, but her arms wouldn't move. Her legs were free, so she kicked at Tully, striking him once before he subdued her by sitting on top of her legs.

''Don't get so excited.'' He laughed. ''There'll be plenty of time for us once Sam finds that gold.''

The rough rope dug into the sensitive skin beneath her breast. The cold air made her nipple as taut as an early rosebud. ''Don't do this, please,'' she begged for the first time since he had kidnapped her. She didn't want Samuel to see her like this.

Surprisingly, Tully turned gentle and brushed her hair away from her injured cheek. ''Don't worry. I'm not going to rape you. I only want Samuel to think I have. That will give me a bigger thrill than feeling myself inside you.''

Michaela winced and turned away from his crude comment. He continued to be gentle as he pulled and tugged at her shirt and jacket until he had them positioned just the way he wanted it. ''We can't have you getting pneumonia,'' he said in a voice that sounded as though he were trying to reassure her.

She felt his warm, rough hands against her bare breast and squeezed her eyes shut. ''Stop! Please!'' She couldn't tolerate his touch. She couldn't stand the thought of Samuel seeing her like this, to have him think she'd been with Tully. ''Samuel,'' she whispered as the first tear rolled down her cheek.

''That's right. You sleep, honey. 'Cause when Sam gets here I want you wide awake.'' He touched her cheek once again before walking back to the fire.

Michaela tried to move her shoulders back and forth enough to shift her jacket around to cover her breast, but her movements only made the rope cut into her skin and burn like liquid fire. Maybe if she just laid her head back against the tree and rested for a moment, she'd get enough strength back to loosen the ropes.

As she lay resting, her thoughts skittered wildly. Was Tully telling the truth about the bank robbery? His story sounded so credible. Would he kill Samuel after he got the gold? Was Kate alive? What had the shock of all that had happened that day done to Davia? How would she and Samuel live together now that she knew he was an outlaw?

Sixteen

*T*HE trail of smoke in the early twilight of the morning sky gave Samuel his first indication that he'd found Michaela. His heartbeat quickened. His hand clutched the reins. The thought of Tully touching her fed his rage.

He estimated he was still four or five miles behind them—a distance he could cover quickly enough if he didn't have to be so wary. He didn't know what kinds of traps Tully might have set for him along the way. Maybe none. Tully was sure enough of himself just to sit quietly and let him ride into the camp.

In fact, that was probably exactly what Tully wanted. He'd left Samuel a very easy trail to follow. Obviously he wanted to be found so he could get his hands on that gold. Getting a day ahead of him on the train was a smart move on Tully's part. Samuel had no choice but to bide his time until the train could get him close enough to travel on horseback. That train journey had been nerve-rackingly slow.

His horse snorted and jerked on the reins that held him. He was rested and ready to go. Samuel patted his neck affectionately. "You're right, ol' boy. It's time to go. I think our best bet is to ride into camp and hope Michaela can get away when the action starts." He urged the horse forward with his knees. He was kidding himself. He knew Tully would never give up his ace.

Half an hour later Samuel was close enough to smell the smoke. He'd moved cautiously the last few miles, alert for any sign of an ambush. He felt pretty sure there wouldn't be one but decided not to take any chances.

As the horse picked his way closer to the fire, Samuel saw Tully sitting in front of it. His gaze followed the length of his arm to where his gun was pointed directly at Michaela's head. Dammit! He swore several more times under his breath. A swift appraisal of her face and torn clothes told him that at the very least she'd been beaten. Desire for revenge kindled inside him and took control. He fought his natural instinct to rush Tully and kill him with his bare hands. Common sense told him Tully could get off enough shots to kill both of them.

"That's far enough. Stop right there or she's dead where she sits." Tully cocked the hammer of the pistol, and Samuel stopped a few feet from his enemy.

Samuel couldn't take his eyes off Michaela. She was either sleeping, or she was out cold. Or worse. Her torn clothing had left her breast exposed to the chilling air. Samuel bit his lower lip so hard that he tasted blood. Even if it meant he'd lose his own life in the process, he'd kill Rufus Tully.

''She ain't dead yet, so you can take that look off your face. I don't want to kill her, but I will if I have to.''

''What do you want?'' Samuel asked hoarsely. Burning rage kept his lips tight and his teeth clenched. If he didn't get control of himself, he could make a costly error. He took several deep breaths.

''First things first. Throw that piece you're wearing in the bushes. The rifle, too. And any others you might be hiding in your clothes.''

Quaking with eagerness to get to Michaela, Samuel did as he was told.

''Now get off that horse nice and easy like. I'm sure you've been riding all night to catch up with us. I always liked you, Sam, so I'm going to let you have a cup of coffee to warm your bones. And while you're at it, wake your little woman over there and try to get her to take some. She got a nasty blow to the head when she fell off her horse.''

''You bastard,'' Samuel growled. ''She didn't fall off any goddamned horse. You beat her.''

''Careful now. You wouldn't want to make me mad. I might accidentally pull the trigger.'' His eyes glittered coldly.

''I'll kill you,'' Samuel muttered.

''Maybe. But not before I get off a shot to her head. Now while I'm feeling kindly toward you, pour some coffee and see if you can wake her. She's got something she wants to tell you.''

Tully started laughing, and Samuel's stomach muscles constricted so fast he could hardly breathe. The bastard had something up his sleeve, and it worried hell out of him. He picked up a cup, poured the coffee, and hurried over to Michaela.

He pulled her jacket together and buttoned it as best he could. Then he gently cupped her chin and raised her head so he could get a better look at her injuries. Tully had beaten her badly. Her face was swollen, and blood had dried around her mouth and across her forehead. An ugly bruise marred one of her pale cheeks. He didn't like the color of her complexion or her lips.

"How long has she been tied to this goddamned tree?" Samuel barked over his shoulder as he patted her injured cheeks to wake her. She needed warmth. She needed to get her circulation going again. His only response from Tully was more laughter.

"Michaela, love, wake up." He tried to soothe her with comforting words while he patted her face. "Can you hear me, Michaela? It's Samuel. Wake up."

She groaned. "No, go away," she mumbled.

Although she didn't open her eyes, her words were coherent. That was a good sign. "Michaela, wake up. You've got to move around." He rubbed her neck and shoulders and down her arms, talking to her all the time.

"I need to untie her. She's suffering from exposure." He looked back at Tully. For an answer a bullet whammed into the tree trunk just above Michaela's head.

Samuel ducked. "Dammit, Tully—you fool! You could have missed and hit her." He shook with fear for Michaela.

"I wasn't aiming for her. I was after you. You untie her and the next bullet will be in your back."

The shot or the shouting woke Michaela. She was looking at him when he turned back to her. He expected to see love or at least relief in her eyes, but all he got was a blank stare.

"Do you recognize me, love?" he asked tenderly. He wanted to gather her in his arms and hold her.

"Samuel . . ."

He smiled. Relief was sweet. "Yes. Everything's going to be all right now. Here, drink some of this. You've got to warm up." He put the coffee to her lips, and she sipped slowly. When she tried to turn her head away, he forced her to drink more until the cup was half-empty. Then he set the cup aside and started rubbing her arms and shoulders again. She cried out for him to stop, but he knew he had to do it. She quieted down when he moved to her legs and massaged the tender muscles there. At last she started to shiver, and Samuel knew her body was waking up. He went for a blanket and more coffee.

"Where're you going?" Tully asked.

"A blanket. Another couple of hours and she would've been dead." Samuel wished he had the time to dwell on all the ways he wanted to kill this man.

When he got back to Michaela he took off his jacket and placed it over her chest, tucking it around her shoulders and over her neck. "I'll kill him, Michaela. I swear to God I'm going to kill him." He put the coffee to her lips again, and she drank the lukewarm liquid thirstily. It worried him because she continued to look as if she weren't really seeing him.

"Easy, love, not too much at one time."

When she'd had enough she moved her head to the side and took a deep breath before saying, "Bank robber."

Samuel froze for an instant. "Shh—don't try to talk right now." He brushed a hand across her tangled hair.

She moved away from his touch but kept her eyes on his face. "Did you rob a—a bank?" she asked in a raspy voice.

No use to deny it. Tully had obviously told her the whole sordid story. His only recourse was to admit it and promise to tell her the whole story when they were back home.

"I'll explain all that to you when I get you away from here. Don't worry about it right now. Save your strength."

"Did you help...rob...a bank here in this part of—Vermont?"

"Michaela..." He brushed at her cheek.

"Don't touch me—just answer—me."

Her words were broken from emotion, not from exposure, and that ate little pieces away from his heart. Her eyes shone with anger.

He sighed and whispered, "Yes. Tully and I were in a band of Confederate soldiers that robbed several banks here in Vermont." He lowered his lashes. "I'm not proud of it, Michaela, and I swear I'll explain it all when we get away from here." He looked back at her, hoping he'd calmed her fears.

"I—I was in one of those banks."

"What!"

Tully laughed, and Samuel started shaking. "What are you talking about?" He shifted to his knees.

"I can't believe I was the only one who recognized her," Tully said, coming up behind him.

"You stay out of this!" Samuel yelled.

"It was the last job we pulled, Sam. Remember the little girl who wouldn't let go of her locket and you told me to let her have it? Remember now?"

Memories hit him like a shock of cold water in his face. "No!" He whipped his head back around to Michaela. Tears gathered in her eyes.

He was stunned into silence, but Tully continued talking. "It's understandable you didn't recognize her. Seeing as how you stood at the door the whole time. I guess this little darling was too frightened to remember, and we did have our handkerchiefs over our faces."

"Is this true?" Samuel asked, tenderness coating each word. "Were you in that bank? Were you the girl who lost her locket?"

"Yes," she whispered. "And you knew it."

Samuel started to touch her, then thought better of it. "I swear to God, Michaela, I didn't recognize you. I tried not to remember any of those people. I didn't want to know any of those faces."

"Look at mine," she mumbled in a trembling voice.

"We robbed five banks. It was four damn years ago. How in the hell was I supposed to recognize you?"

"Just—stay away from me. You're no better than he is."

Michaela leaned her head back against the tree and closed her eyes. Samuel watched the tears trickle down. Rest was the best thing for her. He took the blanket and covered her, tucking it around her legs. He needed some time to think about the past, about that last bank robbery. What had happened that day?

"This is a holdup! Don't anybody move!" Samuel barked loudly as the five men burst into the sparsely filled bank, their long wool overcoats doing little to conceal the dirty Confederate uniforms they wore. A woman was knocked to the floor in their haste to subdue the patrons as quickly as possible.

"Everyone keep quiet and stay still. No one will be hurt. We only want the money."

Samuel sized up the situation as each of the gray-clad men pointed a gun at the terrified people in the bank. One man stood beside the woman on the floor. Another man and a girl stood on the other side of the room. He knew the pattern well. Tully and Shareton were responsible for getting whatever gold or paper money was in the safe, while Thomas and Riverson kept their guns pointed at the customers. Samuel's job was to watch the door to see that no one entered.

For weeks now he had traveled over the hills of Vermont with this unsavory group of rough riders who had plagued Union banks. This was their third robbery in twice as many days. And for Samuel it wasn't any easier than the first. He was as loyal to the Confederacy as any soldier who ever drew a breath, but he hated this dirty operation. He wasn't after any glory for himself from this war, yet he couldn't help but think that there was more honor in charging a troop of Union soldiers from the front line than in robbing defenseless citizens of their hard-earned money.

He'd only been told the Confederacy needed money. He'd been selected because he had a good aim with a rifle. That skill would come in handy if the bluecoats started chasing them. So far he hadn't fired his rifle.

A scuffle in the corner of the room caught his attention, and he glanced over at the stricken white face of a young girl, barely in her teens. She was partially hidden behind a tall, broad-shouldered man who appeared as frightened as his charge. Even though they were in the middle of a bank robbery, he couldn't help noticing that the girl would one day be a beautiful woman.

Remembering his duty, Samuel once again gazed out the cloudy window pane to each side of the street. If anyone approached the door, it was his job to see that they entered quietly, not suspecting anything until the door was closed behind them. Only once had anyone bolted, sensing something was wrong, and Samuel had quickly grabbed the man's arm and swung him inside before he could yell for help.

Their grain sacks bulging with gold and silver coins and what paper money they could stuff inside, Tully and Shareton hurried back into the room to demand money and jewelry from the bank's patrons. This was the part Samuel detested. He could cope with robbing faceless banks, but every time Tully stripped a wedding band from a woman's finger or stole an old man's pocket watch, he hated him more and more.

Neglecting his post, he watched Tully go for the big man and the young girl.

"Believe me, sir, I have nothing to donate to your cause."

With the back of the hand that held his gun, Tully hit the man squarely across the face. The dark-haired girl bit her bottom lip to hold in her scream.

"You wouldn't be in a bank if you didn't have money," Tully yelled into the trembling man's face.

Fumbling in his pockets, he brought out two bills and shoved them at Tully. "Here. This is all we have."

Tully laughed without humor and gathered the front of the man's shirt in one hand and stuck his gun under his chin with the other. "Now you don't expect me to believe that, do you? Not with that gold watch chain showing from underneath your waistband."

"No, sir, I beg you to let it be. It's not a watch, only a locket with my dear wife's picture in it."

"Sure, and it's gold." Tully said, mocking the man's Irish accent as he jerked the chain free.

In an instant the girl lunged for the locket and caught hold of it before it fell into Tully's bag. Samuel saw something sparkling in her eyes that was lacking in many soldiers, Confederate and Union alike—courage that came from indignation at a wrong being committed.

"What do we have here?"

"Give it to him, Michaela," the man said.

"No, Papa. It belonged to Mama. I won't give it to him."

"Let her have it," Samuel shouted from the doorway.

Tully gave him a quick glance, then turned his attention back to the girl. "You little—"

"Leave her alone and let's get the hell out of here while the streets are clear."

"I can't let you keep the locket, honey." With a swift jerk Tully tore the chain through her hands and dropped it into his bag.

The girl screamed, and Samuel threw open the door. Shareton and Thomas ran out, then Riverson.

"I won't forget this, Sam," Tully mumbled as he ran past Samuel and out the door.

Slowly Samuel came back to the present and turned to look at Tully, who stood with his gun pointing at him.

Samuel had a lot of debts to settle with that man. A lot of debts to settle.

"Over there in my saddlebag, you'll find some paper and a pen. Now I suggest you start reconstructing that map. Looks to me like that pretty woman of yours needs a doctor. The sooner we find the gold, the sooner you can get her help."

Samuel rose to his feet, a deadly calm coming over him. "I don't need the map. I know where the gold is buried."

Seventeen

"**M**R. Brennen, I simply can't put on this bed jacket. It's not proper for me to accept a gift of such a personal nature from you. You shouldn't even come into my room without Bessie being present. You've taken too many liberties since I've been in sickbed."

"And I intend to take more," Padraic stated firmly, brushing at the front of his brown plaid waistcoat and smoothing his thinning hair with his hand. "Now, either put on the jacket or I'll put it on you. You don't want Father McCleary to see you in your nightgown, do you?"

"What? What on earth are you going on about, Mr. Brennen?" Kate rose up from her pillows and fixed wide hazel eyes on her employer.

"I've decided to marry you, Kate. I've sent for the priest, and he should be here within minutes to perform the ceremony."

"Oh—what? You haven't asked me to marry you. This is an outrage! Leave my room this instant," she ordered. She brushed at him as if to sweep him away, then fell back against the fluffy pillows arranged neatly behind her back.

Padraic had no qualms about ignoring her instructions. He should have been a little more romantic, but this way he would get the job done. On a number of occasions since Kate had been hurt, he'd tried to let her know he had deep feelings for her and that he didn't want her to leave his house. Yesterday when she'd started talking about applying for another position as chaperone, he'd decided drastic measures had to be taken. He didn't have time to court her, so he'd simply marry her.

Bessie appeared in the doorway and announced, "Father McCleary is here. Should I send him up?"

"By all means, and then you must remain as a witness to the ceremony, Bessie."

"I should be happy to, Mr. Brennen."

"You can't do this!" Kate protested again, pounding a soft fist on the eyelet bedcovers. "I won't agree to marry you. This is madness."

She was such a fussy woman, Padraic didn't know why he was even bothering with her, other than the fact that he didn't want her to leave him. Somehow she had wormed her way into his life, and he was determined that she wasn't going to walk out of it. "Come now, we must hurry. Put your arms through here."

"I can't marry you, Mr. Brennen," she said, but she allowed him to help with the beautifully stitched bed jacket. "I don't know what's come over you."

Padraic pulled at his dark brown cravat and straightened the knot while he watched her button the short silk-and-satin robe. She was a lovely woman: soft but firm, sweet but stern. Yes, she was definitely the kind of woman he needed in his life. For a long time he'd thought no one could replace his first wife. He'd loved her so much. But now he had Kate, and although he didn't feel the burning urgency of young love he'd felt with his first wife, he was sure of his feelings.

Belatedly he remembered that a bride was supposed to have flowers. He glanced around the room. On the nightstand sat a bouquet of pink and yellow flowers. Exactly what he needed. He reached over and pulled the flowers out of the vase of water and thrust them at Kate. "Here, hold these."

"Oh, they're dripping! Do be careful. I need a towel. Quickly, Mr. Brennen." Kate held the flowers over the edge of the bed, away from the expensive coverlet, so the water droplets wouldn't stain the beautiful cotton fabric.

"Ah—Father McCleary," Padraic said as he handed a small white cloth to Kate, a big smile rounding his chubby cheeks and making the edges of his eyes crinkle. "So glad you could come on such short notice. As you can see, we're all ready for you."

"Father, I'm not marrying this man," Kate protested as she carefully wrapped the flower stems in the towel. "I don't know what possessed him to—"

"Go ahead, Father. Don't worry about what she says. Since that bump on the head, she has a tendency to forget about the most important things. Like agreeing to marry me," he added in a soft voice especially for Kate.

"I understand." The priest cleared his throat, resettled his glasses on the bridge of his nose, and opened his book. "Shall we begin? Kate Spencer, do you take this man for your lawful wedded husband, to have and to hold from this day forward?"

"Indeed not," she said firmly, lifting her chin and staring into Padraic's eyes, daring him to find a way out of her blunt reply.

He did. "Do you want me to leave this room?" Padraic asked her.

Smiling with the grace of a feline, she said, "Yes, I most certainly do."

"There, she said yes. Go on to the next question, Father."

Unperturbed by Padraic's unusual tactics, the priest looked back at his book. "Padraic Brennen, do you take this woman for your lawful wedded wife, to have and to hold from this day forward?"

"I do."

"I object!" Kate butted in urgently. "Father, this is a farce. This man never asked me to marry him." She turned furious eyes on Padraic. "And I wouldn't marry you even if you asked me on bended knee!"

Father McCleary gave Padraic a questioning look, but Padraic waved it away and nodded at him to continue.

He cleared his throat and looked at Kate. "Kate Spencer, do you promise to love, trust, and obey Padraic Brennen as long as you both shall live?"

"Certainly not." Kate dropped the flowers onto the bed and folded her arms across her chest in a rare act of defiance. "Furthermore, I insist the two of you leave my room immediately. This absurdity has gone on long enough."

"You want us to leave?" Padraic asked innocently.

"Yes!"

Padraic smiled. "She said yes. Continue, Father."

"This is *insupportable*!" Kate cried out, and placed her hands over her ears.

"Padraic Brennen, do you promise to love, trust, and cherish Kate Spencer as long as you both shall live?"

"I do."

Father McCleary snapped his book shut and with a satisfied smile said, "I pronounce you man and wife."

Bessie laughed and clapped her hands. Kate beat on the bed with an open palm. "No, Father, I did *not* marry this man! I insist that you listen to me."

Father McCleary patted Kate's shoulder. "I was so sorry to hear about your accident. I'll be back when you're feeling better." He turned to Padraic. "Should I leave the papers downstairs so Mrs. Brennen can sign them when she's more herself?"

"Excellent idea," Padraic agreed. "Bessie, would you make sure Father McCleary gets some refreshment before he leaves? Also, there's an envelope for him on my desk. See that he gets it."

Kate's face was red with anger as the priest and Bessie left the room. Padraic knew he had to assuage her injured pride but wasn't sure how to accomplish that. Soft words and tender moments didn't come to him easily.

"You don't look well, Kate. Should I have the cook bring you some hot tea?"

"I cannot believe what you just did." Her voice shook with emotion.

Padraic felt a pull on his heart, and pushing the flowers to the foot of the bed, he sat down beside Kate. "Kate, my sweet woman. I know I'm rough and callous and forget my manners some of the time, but I do want you to be my wife. I didn't want you to leave, yet I couldn't bring myself to ask you to stay. I felt that you should have known how much I needed you without my having to tell you. When I heard you were applying for another post, I knew something had to be done. I couldn't keep giving you bad references— eventually you'd have found out."

"What! You gave me bad references? Is that the reason I've been denied every position?"

She looked so shocked, Padraic experienced a moment of guilt. "Yes. I'm sorry, Kate." He sighed, and his whole chest heaved. "I wanted you to stay after Michaela left. That's why I asked you to run the house. You seemed quite happy and content except for worrying what others would think."

Kate shook her head. "You deliberately spoiled my attempts at other employment. Mr. Brennen, how could you?"

"It was horrible of me. I admit I was wrong. Do forgive me, Kate. I couldn't bear the thought of you leaving me." He took her hand in his.

Kate lowered her lashes and sighed.

Padraic pressed his point. "When I came home that afternoon and found you at death's door, I was beside myself with worry. I prayed to all the saints in heaven for your complete recovery. Then the minute you were better, you started complaining about how improper it was for you to live here." He took a deep breath and squeezed her hand with very little pressure. "Will you forgive me? I was only trying to make you happy. You certainly can't say it's improper to live here now."

Her eyes looked deeply into his, and she placed her small hand over his. In a soft voice she said, "Mr. Brennen, all you had to do was ask."

Padraic's eyes widened. "Ask? That's all I had to do?"

Kate smiled. "Yes, and I would have agreed to marry you. I didn't want to leave, either. One of the reasons I felt I had to go was because this house was beginning to feel too much like home, and I was afraid you would one day find out how much I wanted to be more than your employee."

Padraic gave her a relieved sigh and reached over and kissed her cheek. "So you forgive me, you'll marry me?"

"I do believe we're already married, Mr. Brennen." Kate smiled and lightly brushed her new bed jacket, her wedding gown. "Why don't you ask the cook to prepare two trays tonight and we'll celebrate our wedding dinner together right here in my room."

A beaming smile swept across Padraic's face and lighted his eyes. He rose from the bed. "I'll tell her right away."

"Oh, and, Mr. Brennen..." She paused and gave Padraic her first official request as Mrs. Brennen. "You can bring those papers I need to sign when you return."

Even though the night and early morning had been cold, the sun had come up as a fiery ball, bearing down on them with unrelenting heat. Samuel estimated that they'd been riding for about four hours. His muscles were sore from two days in the saddle, but he tried to think only of Michaela and how he could make things easier for her. With all the bruises from Tully's beating and the fact that she wasn't used to riding, she surprised him with her ability to stay on the horse. She was indeed a remarkable woman.

As the horses picked their way over the stone- and brush-covered terrain, he tried to formulate a plan. He had to find a way to kill Tully before Tully killed him. Samuel hadn't been fooled for a moment. Tully wouldn't let either of them live after that gold was found. Rufus Tully was a ruthless man, and unfortunately Samuel would have to be every bit as unscrupulous to save Michaela's life.

Michaela. How could he think clearly knowing she was so angry and disappointed with him about his past? Some way, he had to make her understand that when he was in the army he was a Confederate soldier and had to do what he was told. He didn't have a choice. He had to make her understand why he'd robbed those banks. And the fact that she'd been in one of them and lost her locket added to his guilt.

Michaela's quiet acceptance of what was going on around her worried him. Maybe he should have lied to her about the robberies, at least until they got home and he could explain. He could have made her believe that Tully didn't know what he was talking about. Apparently silence was her way of dealing with the current situation.

A few minutes later Samuel reined in his horse and stared at the large rock that faintly resembled the face of a man with a pointed beard. His hunch had been right. Four years hadn't made that much difference in the landscape; he should be able to find the gold without any trouble. His problem lay in what to do about Tully once the gold was uncovered.

"We have to walk from here." He jumped off his horse and hurried over to help Michaela dismount. The swelling in her face looked worse, and once again he had the urge to pound Tully with his fists.

"How are you feeling?" He tried to touch her cheek with his gloved hand, but she turned away, letting him know she wanted no part of him. Her rejection hurt, but Samuel brushed it off quickly.

"Let Michaela stay here and rest," he said as he tied the horses' reins to the limb of a small tree.

"She goes with us!" Tully ordered. He pulled a shovel out of the supply pack and threw it on the ground in front of Samuel. "Stay five paces ahead and bring the rope that's on your saddle horn."

"Dammit, Tully, you're not going to tie her up again. She can hardly stand up. She's not a threat to you. Leave her alone."

Remaining calm and even-voiced, Tully responded, "The way I see it, you got two choices. You can tie her or I can shoot her." He aimed his pistol at Michaela and pulled back the hammer.

Samuel froze. He trembled with the need to take that gun and ram it down Tully's throat. He couldn't remember a time when he'd felt so defenseless. But he was so proud of Michaela. She looked down the barrel of Tully's six-shooter and never flinched. Maybe she was numb, or too disillusioned with him to care but he refused to see it that way and credited her with amazing strength.

"Walk behind him," Tully told Michaela. "If he decides to swing that shovel, I want to make sure you're between us." He laughed and pushed her shoulder to get her started.

If Samuel remembered right, it wouldn't be a long walk, then Michaela could sit in the shade of a tree. He needed the extra time to plan exactly how he was going to get that gun away from Tully. At least he had a shovel, a weapon, and he didn't intend to let it go. If Tully lost his composure for even one moment and got close enough, Samuel could hit him. He'd make sure he didn't have to hit him a second time.

Samuel stopped and looked around. There were more shrubs and bushes now, since the rough riders had been here in early spring. Unless he missed his guess, the loot was buried seven paces to the east of the swaybacked birch. One pace for each of the original seven bank robbers. Samuel took off his hat and wiped sweat out of his eyes. The sun hung in the sky at about two hours past noon, plenty of daylight left. Enough time to dig up the gold before darkness surrounded them.

"Wait here," he said, and walked over to the trunk of the tree and positioned his back against it. He took his time trying to remember how he'd walked that day. Was it toe to heel or striding steps? In his mind he went back to that day and felt the wind sting his cheeks and the danger fill his chest.

Striding steps, he concluded after a minute, and started his paces. He stepped over some low-lying bushes and stamped on top of others, trying to get an accurate distance from the tree. Since he was elected to do the digging, he didn't want to use up extra strength digging several inches away from the gold.

He stopped. "It should be somewhere in this vicinity."

He made a sweeping motion with his hands, drawing an imaginary circle around himself.

"Tie her to that tree and start digging," Tully ordered.

Samuel looked at Michaela, standing quietly with her shoulders high and her bruised chin lifted. Without a word she walked over to the tree and sat down. Damn, he wished he knew what she was thinking. He wished she'd look at him, talk to him.

"She can't hurt you, Tully," Samuel tried again, unable to bear the thought of putting rope around her already bruised and battered skin.

Tully laughed and wiped his forehead with the hand that held his gun. "Good try, Sam, but I'm getting tired of you worrying so much about your woman. Now tie her."

Samuel dug his heel into the hard earth, leaving a mark he could come back to, and strode over to Michaela. He bent down close to her and whispered, "I'm going to make the knots as loose as I can. Try to undo them. Run through those trees behind us when he's not looking and don't come out unless you hear me call."

"No talking," Tully yelled at them. "And the ropes better be tight when I check 'em."

Michaela didn't say a word. She didn't even acknowledge she'd heard him. Samuel wrapped the rope around her waist once and then pulled her arms around the trunk. He saw Michaela wince as her sore muscles were stretched, but she didn't complain. He made the knot as close to the palm of her hands as he could. If she worked at it, she could get them loose. Now he had to keep Tully talking so he wouldn't pay too much attention to the knots.

"What are you going to do if someone's already come for the money?" he yelled over his shoulder to Tully.

"I know Thomas and Shareton didn't get it. That just leaves you and Riverson. I expect if you or Riverson had it, you'd have given it back to the Union. Being the honest, law-abiding citizens that you are. If that'd happened, the whole South would've heard about it."

"Hell, anybody could've come here and found that gold." Moving closer to Michaela's ear, he whispered, "It's a simple square knot. Push a finger through the hole and you can loosen the knot enough to slip your hand out."

"You better hope they haven't," Tully responded.

Samuel rose. "How many times did you have a few too many and tell about how we stole that Yankee gold and hid it in these hills?"

"Hell, I didn't tell anybody. I don't go shooting off my mouth when I've had a little whiskey."

Samuel made it back to the spot he'd marked. So far Tully hadn't made a move to check the ropes. It was working. He had to keep him talking. He made his first stab with the shovel at the hard earth. "What about Shareton? He was a talker. I remember he could tell a convincing story when he had a few drinks in his belly."

"Naw, he couldn't have told anyone where to look. You were the only one that really knew where we buried that gold, and that was because you drew the map. Besides, I think he'd have told me if he thought he could have found the money."

Tully seemed to be too engrossed in the conversation to think about Michaela. Samuel took that as a sign that if he played his cards right, he could manipulate Tully into the right position when the time came.

"What about Riverson? He told me he was on his way to California. He must've gotten some money from somewhere." California was a lie. Riverson was headed for Texas, but there was no way he'd tell Tully that. When the gold was found, Tully wouldn't let anyone live who knew about it.

"California?" Tully walked a little closer to Samuel. "Did he say where? I hear it's a mighty big place."

Samuel continued to dig. It wasn't an easy task because the ground was hard and dry. "Nope, he didn't say. I hear it's big, but not too much of it's settled. You could probably find a man if you looked hard enough." Out of the corner of his eye he saw Tully smile and knew he had the man's undivided attention. He jabbed the shovel into the ground.

Keeping up the conversation with Tully and digging the packed earth took its toll on Samuel's strength. He stopped once for water and a quick glance at Michaela. She appeared to be sleeping. Damn, he'd wanted her to untie those ropes and get away. He knew she was hurt and exhausted, but this was a life-and-death situation. If she made a run for it, he could jump Tully.

By the time he hit the rotting saddlebag with the shovel, Samuel had his plan worked out. As they'd talked, Tully had moved closer, but not close enough to knock the gun out of his hand. He had to bring him closer.

It was risky. Tully could easily get off a shot by the time he saw Samuel lunging. If that happened, he had to hope he'd be left with enough strength to make a swing at Tully's head. Samuel shivered. He wouldn't think about what might happen to Michaela if he didn't succeed.

"Whew! Damn it to hell, I've never seen anything like it." Samuel laughed heartily and took off his hat and wiped his forehead, careful not to lose his grip on the shovel.

"What is it?" Tully asked. "Is it there? Did you find the gold?" He took a couple of steps closer, trying to see into the three-foot hole Samuel had dug.

Samuel laughed again and jumped up and down like a kid getting a candy stick. "I don't believe it. I've never seen such a beautiful sight."

After the third jump Tully was close enough. In an instant, Samuel's attitude changed, and he swung the shovel with all his might. The gun went off just as it was stripped from Tully's hand, and Samuel grunted as the bullet tore through the meaty part of his arm. Tully fell backward onto the dry earth, and Samuel dove on top of him.

Michaela screamed as the horrible scene unfolded before her. The bullet had caught Samuel in his upper arm, and his shirtsleeve was immediately soaked with blood. Fear gathered in her throat and constricted her chest.

She'd been working furiously to untie the knots at her wrists while at the same time trying to appear as if she were sleeping so Tully wouldn't bother her. Her plan was to get free and catch Tully off guard long enough for Samuel to do something. Now Samuel was shot and wrestling in the dirt with Tully, and she still hadn't untied the ropes. It may have been a simple square knot to Samuel, but she was having a difficult time with it.

She screamed again when she saw Tully's hand reaching for the gun. Samuel swung and hit Tully in the chin and knocked him away. Michaela sent a prayer to the saints in heaven as the knot began to loosen under the constant pressure of her fingers.

Terror gripped her when Tully managed to get on top of Samuel and put his hands around his throat. Samuel held Tully's wrist, but Michaela feared he didn't have enough strength left to pull free. His shirtsleeve was nearly dripping now with blood. His face lost all color. Oh, God, he was dying!

"No! No!" Michaela repeated in a frantic monotone as she watched this wicked man killing her husband. In a show of uncommon strength, she pulled one hand through the small opening she'd created in the knot. The other came with ease, and then she was on her feet running for the gun. All the demons in hell couldn't have stopped her.

Tully was too intent on strangling the last ounce of breath out of Samuel to see her pick up the firearm. With trembling, sweaty hands she placed her finger on the trigger. Samuel had stopped fighting and appeared to be unconscious, completely at Tully's mercy. She had to act quickly.

Pointing the gun at Tully's chest, she yelled, "Stop or I'll shoot!" Tully didn't even look up. Maybe her voice wasn't as loud as she thought it was.

Without giving it a second thought, she squeezed the small metal trigger and fired a shot over Tully's head. His head jerked up, his body frozen momentarily by the shock of the gunfire. "Get up, or I'll shoot." Her voice was stronger this time, firm and commanding, although her hands trembled.

Tully eased back on Samuel's stomach and laughed at her. "You don't have what it takes to pull that trigger." Slowly he rose to his feet. Michaela didn't take her eyes off him, but her peripheral vision told her Samuel didn't move when he got up. She was filled with the fear that Samuel might be dead. No, he had to be alive. He had to be.

Tully continued to move slowly toward her. What was she going to do? She had the gun, but by the look on his face she knew he wasn't afraid of her.

"Don't come any closer. I swear I'll shoot." Her voice was shaky but loud. She stood holding the gun with both hands, both index fingers on the trigger. Tully kept coming. She knew he'd kill her if she let him wrestle the gun away from her. There still hadn't been a move from Samuel. Tully moved closer . . . closer . . .

Instinctively she sucked in her breath and held it. Then without blinking an eye, she pulled the trigger. Tully jerked backward. The smile ebbed from his face, and his eyes widened with shock. A red stain appeared on the front of his shirt.

"No!" she whispered vehemently as a remnant of the past invaded her consciousness. Suddenly it wasn't Tully before her, but her mother. There was blood on her mother's white blouse. Her face was still, pale. She was all in white except for the blood staining her blouse. Her mother reached out for help.

"Do it again, you bitch. Pull the trigger."

The growling words brought Michaela back to the present. Tully stood before her, an eerie grin on his face.

She shuddered with revulsion. With glassy eyes and an unsteady arm, he reached for her. She screamed and pulled the trigger again. Tully fell on her, knocking her to the ground.

Screaming, she pushed his body off her and scrambled away on her knees. Her throat hurt and her eyes burned as she tried to calm herself. She heard a groan and a cough. Fearful Tully still wasn't dead, she spun around and looked at him. He wasn't moving. She heard the noise again and jerked her head around. Samuel was spitting and sputtering, trying to sit up.

She started shaking when she realized he was alive. Somehow she got to her feet and ran to him and helped him sit up. Her eyes were so full of tears, she couldn't see his face clearly. He wasn't dead! Thank God!

"I—had to—kill him . . ." Her chest started heaving in spasms of choking, gulping sobs as she cradled Samuel's head to her breasts. "I—had to—kill—him!"

Eighteen

S *AMUEL* stepped inside the bedroom and shut the door quietly. Michaela looked at him and he at her. He was so handsome, so appealing. Knowing about his past hadn't erased her love or the attraction that always passed between them whenever their eyes met. Part of her wanted to rush into his arms and let him love away all the hurt, disappointment, and disillusionment. The other half cautioned her, *You really don't know this man. He will hurt you again.*

By the time Michaela and Samuel made it back to Twin Willows, her excruciating headaches were gone and numbness had set in again. Samuel had been extremely considerate on the three-day train ride, but now it was time to make some decisions as to what she was going to do.

Both had come back with scars from the trip to Vermont. Samuel's arm was mending and Michaela's bruises were fading—but she also carried emotional scars. She'd killed a man. She knew she hadn't yet come to terms with that fact, and it would probably be years before she did. She didn't take killing lightly, but she had known that it had to be done. Tully would have killed both of them. Still, it hadn't been easy for her to pull the trigger.

Samuel had wanted to stop in Atlanta and see Padraic and Kate, but Michaela had insisted on coming straight to Twin Willows. If Kate wasn't alive, she didn't want to know it—not yet. She also had the fear that if she saw her father, she would break down completely. She was a married woman now, and she had to deal with all her problems herself. Her father couldn't help her. In order to start the healing process, she had to come home.

There was yet another emotional upheaval she had to deal with. She'd found out that Samuel was not the man she thought she'd married. He'd obviously led two lives: as a bank robber and as a gentleman. That day in Vermont when she'd lost her mother's locket had been one of the most frightening of her life, and Samuel had been part of it.

Michaela had spent many hours thinking about all that had happened since Rufus Tully first appeared at Twin Willows, and now it seemed there was only one thing to do. She'd asked Velvet to move her belongings into one of the guest bedrooms. Now the time had come to tell Samuel about her decision.

Samuel leaned against the closed door and watched her with dark, intense eyes. "I just got back from seeing your father. Did Mama tell you where I'd gone?"

"Yes. I'm—ah, sorry I haven't done anything but

sleep since we returned.'' She squeezed her eyes shut for
a moment, then looked back at Samuel. "Kate?''

"She's up and about, feeling just fine. You're the one
who needs rest.''

Michaela sighed with relief. "Thank God. I've been
so worried about her. I'm very pleased to hear she's
doing so well,'' she answered softly.

"I've other news for you. Kate and your father were
married while we were away. They're both very happy
and want you to come for a visit.''

Michaela gasped in surprise. "That's wonderful news!
Yes, yes, I'll visit them soon. I'm glad Papa finally
realized that he and Kate were meant for each other.''
She turned away from Samuel and walked to the window.
At one time she had thought she and Samuel were meant
for each other, too. Now, she wasn't so sure.

She wished he weren't so nice. She wished he didn't
look so appealing leaning against the door with one foot
propped behind him. She wished she didn't have to have
this conversation with him.

How was he going to take her news? Would he
understand that she needed time to come to terms with
the fact that he was not the man she thought she'd
married?

"I was hoping you'd be more excited about this. I
knew you wanted them to marry.''

"I'm very happy for them,'' she said, refusing to
glance back at him. Whenever she looked at him she
wanted to throw reality to the wind and forget all that had
happened. She missed his embraces, his kisses, his
loving. If there were some way to turn back the clock so
she'd never have to find out about his dual life, she

would do it. She hadn't wanted things to change between them.

"Don't turn away from me, Michaela. Look at me. It's time we talked about what happened. I know we've been back only two days, but I can't go on not knowing how you feel or what you're thinking."

Taking a steady breath, she faced him and said, "I've been waiting for you to come up so I could tell you that I had Velvet move my things into another room today. I need some time alone."

He didn't move, but she saw his hands clench at his sides. His brown eyes intent on her face, he asked, "Why, Michaela?"

She turned away from him and, parting the drapes, looked out the window. Dusk was giving way to twilight, the most beautiful time of day. A flower-scented breeze from the open window whisked across her face and ruffled her hair. She knew he was still watching her—that he didn't, couldn't, understand what was going on inside her.

"You don't have to ask that," she said at last. "Too much has happened for me to just walk gently back into your arms."

"It won't ever get any better if we start sleeping in separate rooms." He walked closer. "I love you. I want to help you get over all the horrible things that have happened. I want to hold you and love you."

"Stop it!" she cried, and whirled around to confront him. "You can't help me. Every time I look at you I remember that day in the bank when I was so frightened I could hardly stand. Every time I look at you I see Tully. I feel his hands and hear his words." She stopped abruptly when she saw his face go white and his eyes light with fire. She took a deep breath and forced her shoulders to relax. "I need some time to myself," she repeated as she clutched at the folds of her heavy cotton skirt.

"Michaela, look at me. Listen to me," he pleaded, and took her by the shoulders, his strong fingers digging into her flesh. "You're not going to forget Tully until you put him out of your mind and hear my words of love and feel my loving hands on you. Michaela, I love you. Let me hold you and love you. Let me make you forget."

She pulled away from him. "I can't forget! I don't want you to touch me. I don't want to remember your touch or hear your lies."

His face darkened with anger. "Lies! When have I ever lied to you?"

"You passed yourself off as a gentleman, but you're a bank robber. You hurt innocent people, and I don't know if I can forgive you for that. You're not the man I married."

"Yes, I am!" Fury made his face red. "Dammit, Michaela, listen to me. I was a Confederate soldier. I had to do what I was told. I wasn't like Tully. I didn't enjoy it, and I never stole from the people in the bank." He reached into the pocket of his pants and pulled out something. "Here's the locket you were trying so hard to keep that day." He threw the chain and locket onto the bed with such force that it slid across the covers and fell to the floor with a clank.

Michaela gasped. "You had my mother's locket?" She trembled with anger. "All this time you had my mother's locket!" Swiftly her hand sliced through the air, Samuel's face her target.

"Hell, no!" He caught her wrist and with a gentle push sent her up against the wall. He pressed his body against hers as she struggled to break free. "Dammit, Michaela, be still before I hurt you!"

Rage glowed in his eyes as she glared at him. His breathing was deep, heavy, allowing his chest to press hers. A tremor shook his hands as he held her wrists against the wall. She felt his breath, his warmth.

He swallowed hard. "The bank you were in was the last one we robbed. I knew that necklace had to be in one of those bags, so I dug it out before I buried Tully with the gold."

She believed him. Her body relaxed, but her eyes remained hard and accusing.

"Michaela, will you think about what you're saying? I'm not like Tully. I never was." He let her go and stepped away. "Dammit, I did far worse in the army when I pulled the trigger and killed good men just because they didn't think the way I do. If you're going to blame me for doing something wrong, that's where the blame should be. Not because I stole money from Union banks."

She placed her hands over her ears. "Stop it! I don't want to hear any more. Just go away and leave me alone."

"Does the truth hurt?" he continued harshly. "I robbed banks and killed men in the name of the Confederacy. I didn't have a choice. You were in the same position when you killed Tully. You didn't have a choice."

"I did!" she screamed at him. "I could have let him kill you. I wish I'd let him kill me, then I wouldn't be living every day seeing the blood on his shirt, or that twisted grin on his face, or hearing his last gasping breath as he fell against me and died. I feel dirty, and I can't get clean!''

''Michaela—''

She whirled away from him and covered her face with her trembling hands. She wouldn't listen to any more. It was Samuel's fault—the fear, the nightmares, the self-loathing. All of it was his fault.

''Don't turn away. Don't shut me out. I want to help you.''

Samuel touched her shoulder, and she cringed away from him. ''Just leave me alone. Please,'' she whispered.

She was filled with so much tension, she could hardly breathe; a roaring filled her ears, but she heard the door open and close. She coughed, choking on the tears that had lodged in her throat.

On trembling legs and gasping for breath, she ran to the foot of the bed and picked up the locket she hadn't seen in years, the locket she thought had been lost to her forever. The gold chain was broken from where Tully had jerked it from her hands, but the locket hadn't been damaged. Carefully she pressed the clasp, and it popped open. Her mother's smiling face stared back at her.

The longer she looked at the picture, the softer she felt inside. Samuel had given her back her treasure. She didn't want to hurt Samuel. She didn't want to push him away, but she didn't trust him. She needed to feel his arms around her, hear his loving words, but . . . because of him she had killed a man.

A few days later Michaela decided it would be best if she went to visit her father and Kate. She had to talk to someone, and it couldn't be Evelyn or Davia. She'd remained in her room for almost a week, and the constant strain was telling on her. Worse still, the exaggerated politeness that had developed between her and Samuel since she'd moved out of his bedroom had begun to wear on her nerves. She was at the breaking point.

Just after lunch Velvet came up to tell her that Cabot Peabody was downstairs asking for her. At first she didn't want him to see her because her face was still puffy and discolored from her bruises, but her need to talk to someone prompted her to agree. Before going down she thought up a convincing story to tell Cabot.

"Cabot, I was surprised when Velvet told me you'd stopped by to see me," she said, sweeping into the parlor with a brief smile and outstretched hand. "Davia and her mother will be so sorry to have missed your visit. They're away for a couple of hours."

"Michaela, what happened to you? My God! You look like you've been beaten by the devil himself." He took her hand and kissed it, but his eyes never left her face.

"Samuel was teaching me to ride, and I fell off the horse," she said, touched by the concern she saw in his eyes. "Yes, it was a nasty fall. I was in a bad way for several days. I thought that was the reason you came to visit. I thought Papa must have told you about my accident."

"Indeed not. I only came by because I was visiting the O'Dell family not far from here." He scrutinized her face. "How did it come about that you have so much damage to your face?"

She knew Cabot would be quite inquisitive about her injuries. He wasn't an easy man to fool. "I simply went over the horse's head and landed on my face. Now, let's not talk about it anymore. Sit down. I'm so glad you came by. It's good to see an old friend.''

Cabot perched on the settee beside her. ''It's not my intention to belabor the subject, Michaela, but I've known you almost a year. There is more wrong with your face than a fall from a horse could cause.''

She appreciated his concern and sincerity, and her throat burned with the silence she had to maintain. ''No, really, I'm fine. The bruises make the injuries appear worse than they are.''

''It's what's missing in your face that worries me. Where is the sparkle in your eyes and the gaiety in your step? No, something is wrong. You can't hide it from me. I'm sure of it.''

''Oh, Cabot,'' she said, fighting the bout of weakness that washed over her. ''Don't delve too deeply.''

''Michaela, my dear friend, talk to me. You can trust me to understand and to help.''

''There is something else. But I can't discuss it with you.'' She was beginning to realize that it had been a mistake to see Cabot. She needed to talk, and he wanted to listen.

Cabot took her hand and folded it between both of his. ''I think I know what the problem is. We've already discussed it once. Remember, I'm the one who told you that Samuel was paid to marry you. Is that what happened? Did he find out you knew about this? Did he get upset and take his anger out on you?''

Almost amused by Cabot's questions, Michaela laughed lightly. So much had happened since that incident, she'd completely forgotten about Cabot's discovery the day after her wedding.

"Heavens, no!" She pulled her hand away from his. "No, no, that was settled long ago." In fact, that seemed like years ago, now. "That's all cleared away." She rubbed the back of her neck where tension had settled. "Believe me, Cabot. Samuel has never laid an unkind hand on me. Never."

Cabot appeared to be thinking about it. Then, as if convincing himself she was telling the truth, he said, "All right, if that isn't the problem, what is? I'm certain I can help."

He smiled at her compassionately, giving her a warm, secure feeling. She knew he couldn't help, but it might make her feel better to talk about it. If she talked it through, maybe she'd understand everything better.

She sighed and leaned back in the sofa. "It has to do with Samuel's past. I've found out some things that upset me terribly. When he . . ."

"Go on," he prompted.

"When Samuel was in the Confederate Army he was commissioned by President Davis to . . ." She stopped again. Maybe she shouldn't tell him.

Cabot slipped closer and took her hand, urging her to continue. "Yes, go on. You must tell me all of it."

"He robbed Union banks. The Confederacy needed money, so President Davis commissioned some soldiers and sent them up north to bring back money. Samuel was one of those men."

"Yes, yes, I heard about that group. Vermont's where it happened. St. Albans was one of the towns, I believe.

Interesting. And you say Samuel was one of them? Very interesting.''

She watched Cabot's eyes closely for accusations, for judgments, but all she saw was exactly what he voiced. He was clearly interested in what she was saying. It surprised her that he wasn't as horrified as she'd been.

"Are you sure about this? How did you find out about it?" he asked.

The tension in Michaela's neck eased when she saw that Cabot was taking it so easily. "I really can't go into all the details, but believe me, I'm sure it's true." She rubbed the sore spot above her eye where Tully had hit her and winced. Would the tenderness ever go away? Occasionally she still had headaches that hurt so much, she had to go to bed. Sometimes when she awakened in the mornings, she'd be dizzy.

"Michaela, you can't tell me so little and expect me to help."

She looked back at Cabot. "There's nothing you can do," she answered. "I know a lot of horrible things happened in that war. Things that are difficult to understand. I just didn't realize that Samuel was a part of them. I wish I'd never found out," she whispered.

"Surely things happened that should never have happened. The war itself."

"I know." She smoothed her hair with a shaky hand. "I have to come to terms with the fact that Samuel's not the man I married. He's led two lives."

"Does anyone else know about this?"

"Oh, no." She rose from the sofa and looked down at him. "You're not going to tell anyone, are you? I only told you because I needed to talk to someone."

"What? No, no, certainly not. Your confidence in me is not misplaced." He stood up and smiled at her.

"Thank you. I knew I could count on you."

"You can. I have bits and pieces of an idea that may help."

"What? How can you help, Cabot?" she asked eagerly. "You can't change the past."

"No, but you can manipulate the future."

Michaela frowned. "What are you talking about?"

"I can't discuss it, but I shall get to work on it right away. I really must be going now." He took her hands for the third time. "Michaela, dear, don't worry about this. There are ways to handle these dirty little details."

"What are you doing here?" Samuel asked in a growling voice as he met Cabot Peabody coming out of the barn. His temper had been explosive the last few days, and seeing Peabody at Twin Willows was reason enough to set it off.

Cabot jumped off his horse and stood before Samuel, who'd been on his way to the barn. "You're just the person I want to see. I need a moment of your time."

"I don't have any to spare. Now get back on that horse and ride before I find out what you were doing here and decide to rearrange your face." Samuel started to walk away.

"The same way you did Michaela's?"

In an instant Samuel grabbed Cabot by the throat and slammed him against the side of the barn with enough force to knock the breath out of his lungs and rattle the old boards. He was itching to put his fist in Peabody's stomach. "You go near her again and I'll kill you. You stay away from my wife!"

"Mr. Lawrence, be civil. Let go of me. I shouldn't have said that. Michaela told me she was thrown from a horse."

Samuel relaxed a little. Michaela had lied to protect him. That proved she was still loyal to him, even if she'd moved out of their bedroom. He softened, and his heart quickened. Maybe she was finally coming around.

"What are you doing here? What do you want?" Samuel didn't bother to turn him loose, even though Cabot's face was colorless.

"I can't talk. You're holding me too tight," Cabot said in a squeaky voice. Sweat beaded his upper lip and forehead.

Samuel eased his hands away from Cabot's throat but remained perilously close. "What do you want?" he asked again.

Cabot rubbed his neck as if to make certain no damage was done. While clearing his throat he straightened his shirt and tie. "Michaela told me about your past, Samuel, and I—"

"Dammit!" he swore, but felt like putting his fist through the wall.

"Wait! Don't get angry. I have an idea that will help you." Cabot's Adam's apple bobbed continuously. "May I call you Samuel?" he asked hesitantly.

"What the hell do you want? How do you think you can help me? What do you mean by coming here and upsetting my wife?" Samuel took a menacing step toward Cabot and backed him up against the side of the barn.

"I only stopped by to see Michaela because I'd been visiting the O'Dells," Cabot explained quickly. "I had no idea Michaela had fallen from a horse or that she was extremely upset about your past. She needed someone to talk to, so she told me about the bank robberies during the war. She wouldn't give me specific details, but I think I got enough information." He rubbed his neck again. "I have an idea that might help. That's all," he finished quickly.

"What are you talking about? How can you help?" Skepticism laced Samuel's every word.

"Just listen for a moment." Cabot pulled on his jacket and drew a relieved breath when Samuel took a step backward. "You were not covered in President Johnson's general amnesty plan because of your high-ranking military status during the war and because Twin Willows would be valued at more than twenty thousand dollars. Perhaps there are other reasons, too?"

"Could be," Samuel answered.

"What I don't know is, did you apply to the president for a pardon? Did you take the oath of allegiance to the Union and receive amnesty for your war crimes and acts of treason?"

"Hell, no!" He wasn't going to go into all the reasons he'd never asked for a pardon. The fine hairs on the back of his neck raised. "I don't intend to. I'm not interested in voting or running for *political* office." His sneer on the word *political* did not go unnoticed by Cabot, who flinched.

"A pardon can do more for you than give you back your voting rights." Cabot's face turned serious. "Think, Samuel. If you turn yourself in to the authorities and admit to your crimes and ask for a full pardon, you will be completely exonerated.''

''You've got to be out of your goddamned mind.'' There was a cold, deadly edge to Samuel's voice.

''No, listen.'' Cabot held up his hands to make Samuel stay. ''You've got to do it for Michaela. She is the one who's most concerned about your past, your war crimes. Think about her. She believes you've done wrong. You are guilty in her eyes, and you have not been acquitted. Once the president pardons you, so will Michaela. At first, Johnson handed out pardons sparingly. Now he doesn't turn away anyone the provisional governors recommend.''

Cabot's words hit Samuel hard. For once the fool was actually beginning to make sense. Michaela was a victim of one of his crimes. It sounded good, but would it work? Would Michaela forgive him if the president pardoned him?

He ran both hands through his hair. His neck was damp from the heat of the sun blazing on his back. He looked at Peabody's face and knew he was serious. It made him angry to think that this man might be right. ''Get out of here. You're wearing my patience thin.''

Cabot hoisted himself back onto his horse. ''Think about what I said. You can't expect Michaela to forgive you when you refuse to acknowledge you did wrong by rejecting the very act that will absolve you.''

''Did she tell you this?'' Samuel asked calmly, looking up at him.

''No. I didn't mention it to her. That's up to you.''

''You'd like to see me behind bars, wouldn't you? That would leave you wide open to comfort my wife.''

"I don't want Michaela now. If I married a divorced woman, I'd be throwing my political career out the window. Think about what I've said. It's your life. Your decision." For the first time that afternoon, Cabot smiled. He dug his heels into the flanks of his horse and galloped away.

Later that night Samuel hoped to talk to Michaela, but, giving the excuse of a headache, she went to bed right after dinner. He went to his office, where he'd spent most of his nights for the past week. The stand-off with Michaela couldn't go on forever. He was trying to understand her feelings, but it was getting harder. He wondered if it would do any good if he forced her to talk about it again.

He looked at the papers before him. If the weather held, the corn would be ready to pull in another month. He could then make his first payment to Padraic and still have money in the bank. He'd have everything, except Michaela back in his arms, in his bed.

There was a soft knock on the door, and it opened.

"May I come in, Sam?"

"Sure, Muffin." Samuel got up from his desk and poured himself a snifter of brandy. "What do you have on your mind?"

Davia dropped to the gold-covered brocade armchair and sighed. "You want the truth?"

"Of course. What's bothering you?" He took the first sip and let it go down quickly. The brandy definitely had a bite to it.

"Why isn't Michaela sleeping in your bedroom?"

Samuel coughed as much from the brandy as his

sister's question. "I don't think that's any of your business." He pointed a stern finger in her direction and coughed again. "Now, if that's what you want to discuss, I think you'd better turn around and march your little self out of here."

"I'm not little anymore. I turned fourteen while you were gone. I'm a woman now. And I know that a woman is supposed to sleep with her husband."

He softened. Davia was growing up, and she was right. A woman was supposed to sleep with her husband, but he couldn't force Michaela to sleep with him. He walked back to his desk and sat down. "Michaela had a bad shock. Rufus Tully wasn't very kind to her."

"Did he rape her?"

Samuel almost spilled his drink as he placed it on the desk. "Where the devil did you hear that word?"

"Maybella," they said in unison.

"Do you know what it means?"

She nodded. "It means a man has hurt a woman really bad."

"Yes, it does." He took another drink. "Did you tell Maybella we had separate rooms when you saw her today?"

"No! I wouldn't do that, Sam. I'm smart enough to just listen and let Maybella do all the talking. That's the way to learn what you want to know. We didn't even mention you or Michaela today. I've known what rape means for years."

Samuel rubbed his eyes. "What made you think Michaela had been raped?"

"Her face and arms are black and blue. It's obvious he beat her. I just wondered if he did anything else."

"No, thank God, he didn't rape her." Samuel gave her a brief smile. "Mama would faint if she knew we were talking like this."

"Why is she mad with you, Sam? You didn't hurt her."

Samuel held his glass in front of him and swished the amber liquid around. Davia was wrong. He had hurt her, deeply.

"In a lot of ways I did, Muffin. A lot happened to her when she left Padraic's house that day. She's got a lot of forgetting to do."

"What about you? You were hurt, too. You still can't use your arm very well."

Samuel worked the muscle of the arm that had taken Tully's bullet. Whenever it hurt, all he had to do was think of the pain Michaela had gone through and his seemed to fade away.

He'd never forget that afternoon when he'd come to, gasping for breath, and seen Michaela running wildly toward him. Blood had covered the front of her shirt and stained her hands. Between broken sobs she'd told him that she'd killed Tully. He winced. He wanted to hold her. Damn, he wanted to hold her!

"Michaela will be okay, Muffin. It's just going to take a little more time. In fact, I've been thinking about something I can do to speed up her recovery." He took a big swallow of the brandy. "I'll be going into town tomorrow for a few days. I want you to look after Michaela and Mama while I'm gone. Will you do that for me?"

"I guess so, Sam. But I'd rather go with you."

"Not this time, Muffin."

Nineteen

"**K**ATE, this is a surprise," Michaela said as she led her into the parlor at Twin Willows and helped her onto the sofa. "You don't look well."

"I don't feel well, Michaela. I'm afraid I have had news for all of you."

Michaela tensed. She'd known something was wrong the minute she'd opened the door and seen Kate alone. She turned to Velvet. "Would you please bring some tea for Kate? Davia, get those pillows off the window seat and bring them here." There was concern in her voice as she continued to talk. "Kate, what's the matter? Is it Papa? I must know."

"Please, Michaela. Let me catch my breath," Kate said, placing a hand on her chest and taking deep breaths. "I asked the driver not to take a rest stop. We've been traveling quite a long time."

"Yes, of course. Here, put your feet up. You're still not well from that nasty bump on your head."

"What's all the noise?" Evelyn asked, hurrying into the room.

"Kate has bad news," Davia answered as she rushed over with the pillows and started stuffing them behind Kate's back. "Michaela thinks it's about her father."

"No, no," Kate insisted while Davia fussed with the pillows. "It's Samuel."

Everyone in the room went still. All eyes were on Kate.

"Samuel is in jail."

"What?" Michaela's stomach lurched as fear lodged in her chest. "What do you mean?"

"Oh, no. You must be mistaken," Evelyn assured Kate in a calm voice, although her eyes belied her steadiness.

"What'd he do?" Davia asked, stepping in front of Michaela in order to get Kate's full attention.

"Let me tell what I know, and I think it will answer many of your questions." She looked over Davia's shoulder to Michaela. "Apparently Samuel has some crazy notion that he has to be pardoned for his participation in the war."

Michaela squeezed her eyes shut as a spasm of guilt stabbed her.

"I don't understand," Evelyn whispered.

"I had coffee already hot in the pot, so I brought it," Velvet announced. "I hope you don't mind, Kate."

"No, not at all. Thank you, Velvet." Kate looked at Michaela. "I don't know all the details. Mr. Brennen should be on his way here by now. He closed the bank and went directly to speak to Samuel. I knew a carriage ride would take longer, so I left without him. He's coming by horse, so he should be here soon."

Michaela pushed Davia and Velvet aside and knelt in front of Kate. "What else do you know?" she demanded.

Kate looked at Evelyn, Davia, and Velvet before she returned her gaze to Michaela. "Apparently Samuel feels that if the president pardons him for his war crimes, so will you." She touched Michaela's hand. "He's doing this for you, dear. He feels he's lost your respect and love, and he wants it back."

Michaela sucked in her breath. Suddenly her head was spinning with thoughts. Samuel was in jail? To regain her respect? What had she done to him? Why did he feel he had to turn himself in to the authorities?

Evelyn gasped. In a weak voice she asked, "What war crimes?"

Michaela heard the terror in her voice and rose. Her mother-in-law's face was pale, and she looked as if she were going to faint.

"I must lie down," Evelyn managed to say in an agonizing tone of voice. Velvet grabbed her shoulders.

"Help her upstairs to bed," Michaela told Velvet, and walked with the two of them to the stairs before returning to the parlor.

"This is all your fault," Davia said tautly. Her hands rested on her thin hips, and her accusing eyes looked fiercely into Michaela's.

"Stay out of this. It has nothing to do with you," Michaela answered Davia in a clipped tone.

"He's my brother." Davia's eyes were cold and ruthless. She didn't back down an inch.

Neither did Michaela. "He's my husband, so you stay out of it."

Davia lunged at Michaela, forcing her to lose her balance and fall back against the sofa. Kate shrieked and rolled out of their way. Davia's hard open hand struck Michaela's cheek before she could grab her wrist. Davia was kicking and trying to bite as Michaela tried to subdue her.

In the midst of the scuffle, Michaela heard Kate scream, "Davia! Stop this immediately. Stop this at once!"

Michaela tried to bring the younger girl under control by pinning her arms to her side, but Davia was strong. The ensuing struggle reminded her that her body hadn't completely healed from her trip to Vermont. Her only hope was to get on top of Davia.

Michaela rolled to her left, and they fell off the sofa and onto the hard floor. Michaela grunted when her head struck the leg of a small table, but she didn't stop until she had pinned Davia to the floor by straddling her stomach and holding her hands above her head, a trick she'd learned from Rufus Tully.

"Let me up, you damn Yankee! Let me up!" Davia spit the words into Michaela's face.

Heaving from expended energy she didn't have to spare, Michaela ground out, "Not—until you promise to—behave."

"I'm not going to promise you anything, you Yankee bitch. I'm going to scratch your eyes out!"

"Your mama needs to—teach you how to be—a lady instead of a hellion. I'm going to stay here on top of you—all night if I have to," Michaela insisted.

"Get off me. I've got to help Sam." She brought her

legs up and tried to kick Michaela in the back, but Michaela didn't budge.

"Michaela, Davia, please stop this instant!" Kate bent over the two of them.

"I'll take care of Samuel—he's my husband."

"You don't love him, and I do!" she screamed. Davia bucked and almost succeeded in knocking Michaela off her.

"What's all the noise? Mrs. Lawrence sent me down here to find out what's—My heavens!

"Oh, Velvet, do help Michaela with Davia. She's overwrought."

"Let her up, Michaela." Velvet touched Michaela's shoulder.

Michaela shrugged off the helpful hand and moved her face closer to Davia's. "I do love Samuel. Don't *ever* think otherwise. I'll fight anyone for Samuel—including you." Her voice had a deadly ring to it.

Davia went still. "Then why did you move out of his bedroom?"

"That is none of your business. Now I'm telling you for the last time to stay out of it." She said each word slowly and with emphasis.

"Come on, missy. Your mama needs your help. No more fighting. We can't help Samuel by tearing into one another."

Neither Michaela nor Davia looked at Velvet, but her words seemed to sink in. Slowly Michaela let go of Davia's wrists and stood up. Davia scrambled to her feet, and Velvet caught her by the shoulders.

"It's your fault Sam's in jail. And I'll never forgive

you.'' Davia spun around and ran out of the parlor and up the stairs.

Michaela pushed her hair out of her eyes, took a deep breath, and coughed. Her ribs were sore, and the side of her face burned from Davia's stinging slap. But the truth of Davia's words hurt far worse than her cheek. Samuel was in jail because of her.

The amazing thing about this whole affair was that Michaela felt better than she had in weeks. It was as if she'd just awakened, or stepped out of a haze into the sunshine.

"Samuel," she whispered, then turned to Velvet. "I must go to him. Velvet, pack a small case for me. Kate," she said, turning to her friend. "Is your driver waiting?"

"Yes, but I think you should wait for Padraic. He should be here soon. I think I hear him riding in now. Go let him in. If he had the opportunity to talk to Samuel, we'll have news."

Michaela ran to the door and threw herself into her father's arms. "Oh, Papa, what did I do? How can I get Samuel out of jail?"

"Come—Michaela, we need to talk," Padraic said breathlessly. "Kate, dear, would you forgive us—and give us time alone?"

"Of course. I'll go check on Mrs. Lawrence."

"Let's go into Samuel's office. I have some things to tell you that can't be put off another minute." With his arm around Michaela, they walked into the private room and he closed the door.

Michaela was so tense, her stomach felt as though it were tied in knots. She didn't want to hear what her father had to say. She wanted to get to Samuel as quickly as possible and tell him that she loved him. She didn't care that he'd robbed the banks. She didn't care about anything at the moment except to tell him how she loved him and how much she needed him.

Padraic took the top off of a crystal decanter and poured a small amount of brandy into a glass. "Michaela, I must tell you something I hoped we'd never have to mention to each other again."

"Oh, Papa, I want to go to Samuel. I need to talk to him. I need to explain some things to him. Can't we talk about this later?"

"No." His firm voice surprised her. "We have to talk first. We have to talk about the dead man down by the river."

Chilling memories washed over Michaela. She saw the man as clearly as if it had only been yesterday. How could she ever forget? Suddenly she shivered. She didn't like the serious expression on her father's face. A lump formed in her throat, but she managed to say, "No. No, I don't want to talk about that."

"We have to. It's time you knew the whole story." Padraic handed her the brandy. "Take a sip of this. You're going to need it."

With a shaky hand Michaela took the glass and put it to her lips as Padraic started his story. "I left you in the cave that morning and ran down to the river myself. Do you remember?"

Padraic's bulk didn't slow him as he ran toward the river. His hands were cold, so he balled them into fists, hoping to keep them warm. As he neared the river he slowed his pace considerably and walked cautiously to the edge of the clearing. From behind a small tree he looked at the man Michaela had described. He lay face up, arms outstretched. His long, open coat revealed a white shirt and gray pants. A horse grazed nearby, but no one else was visible.

With fear in his heart Padraic drew closer. Just as Michaela had thought, the man was dead.

"Oh, holy Mary," Padraic prayed, and made the sign of the cross. The cold weather had stopped the decaying process, so it was hard to tell how long the man had been dead. He'd been shot in the upper part of his belly just above the belt buckle. Padraic shook his head. A man seldom lived if he took lead in the stomach.

The horse snorted, and Padraic almost jumped in the river. "By the saints in heaven," he swore as his heart beat rapidly in his chest. He couldn't help the man, and he didn't want to be caught hanging around the body.

Cautiously he knelt beside the dead man and felt in his pockets for papers to identify him. He could notify the authorities in the next town. There was nothing in his pockets. The next step was to check the saddlebags on the horse. If he could find something, maybe the poor man's family would give him a reward or at least a job.

Padraic talked gently and quietly as he approached the horse so he wouldn't scare him away. He took a few moments to pat and rub the horse's head, soothing him. When he was confident the horse wouldn't buck and run, he checked the left pouch. It was filled with gold coins and paper money. "The Lord God Almighty be with me and bless me." He quickly made the sign of the cross again and whistled lightly through his teeth.

With cold, trembling hands, he searched the other side

of the saddlebag and found a brown piece of parchment. He skimmed the neatly written paper, and fear mounted inside him.

"Here it is, Michaela. This is the note I found that day. I kept it all these years." He handed her the wrinkled piece of paper.

She took it. Her voice was husky as she said, "I remember you told me you didn't find anything to identify him."

"I lied to you at that time—not because I wanted to, but because you were so young I didn't know how to explain everything to you." Padraic paced across the room.

"After reading that"—he pointed to the paper—"I knew the dead man was a Confederate soldier and that he was supposed to deliver the money to someone in the South named Davis." He shrugged. "I didn't know what to do. Can you imagine what the authorities would have said had I taken that money and piece of paper to them and said, 'Send this to the Confederacy'? And at the time we needed that money more than the Confederates. We had no loyalty to the North or South, Michaela. We didn't have a shilling left between us, so I considered the money a gift from the heavens. I always have. I used it wisely and have made back many times what I found."

"Why are you telling me all this now? What good can it possibly do to tell me all this now?"

Padraic stopped pacing, poured himself a drink, and sipped it. "Because there's more to the story. As I talked with Samuel about the bank robberies, we were able to put the whole story together. The money I found was stolen money, Michaela." He paused and looked in her eyes. "The man we found by the river was one of Samuel's cohorts."

The room was dimly lit, the house was quiet. Michaela sipped the brandy, and it sent heat down her throat and a flush up her cheeks. She was certain he'd made a mistake. The money her father had found couldn't be what Samuel's band had stolen. Samuel had found that gold and buried it with Rufus Tully.

She looked up at her father. "I don't understand. We encountered the Confederate raiders in the bank after we found the dead man."

"In the beginning there were seven soldiers." Padraic sat down on the chair beside his daughter. "When they'd robbed three banks, two of the men were given the stolen money and sent back to the Confederate Capitol in Montgomery. Samuel and I have no idea if the two men quarreled between themselves or if they were spotted by the Union. In either case, the man with the money was shot and died on that riverbank."

"Oh, Papa, this is terrible." Michaela rose from the chair. If what her father said was true, they had been living off part of the money Samuel stole. "No," she whispered. "It can't be."

"I'm afraid it is, Kayla."

Filled with anguish, Michaela turned on her father. "Don't you see the problem, Papa? We're guilty of what I've been blaming Samuel for. I was feeling so self-righteous, and now I find out that we were just as guilty as he was. We've been living off stolen money. Oh, Papa, how could you? You knew it was stolen. How could you do this to me?" Tears threatened her eyes.

Padraic rose to comfort her. "Michaela, you were only a child. You had no reason to question where that man got the money. You had no reason to believe it was anything other than a gift from the saints. Try to remember that time. We were roaming streets in freezing weather, stopping at houses to beg for a bite of food, living in caves. We were starving. That money saved our lives. It *was* a gift from heaven."

"No. No, it's not true. That money was stolen from people like you and me." She laughed bitterly as the tears took over. "All this time I thought I was better than Samuel. I thought because of the bank robberies and Tully, he'd dragged me down to his level; and now I find out I was there all the time and didn't know it."

"Michaela, try to understand—sometimes we don't have a choice." Padraic said in a tired voice.

"You *did* have a choice!"

"What? Ride up to the Union soldiers and tell them I'd found this money? They'd have put me in jail. And if I'd told the Confederacy? They would have gladly taken the money, and then taken my life. I'm sure of it. I had to think about you and me."

His words hit Michaela with enough force to snatch the breath from her lungs. He didn't have a choice. Samuel had said the same thing. He robbed banks; he didn't have a choice. She killed Tully; she didn't have a choice. They were starving; her father didn't have a choice.

Michaela whirled around. "I've got to go see Samuel. I must go tonight."

"I won't hear of it."

"I've got to, Papa. I've got to let him know I under-stand. I've got to tell him I'm sorry and that I love him."

"Nonsense. You can go back to Atlanta with Kate tomorrow and stay with us until we get Samuel out of that jail."

"Can we get him out, Papa?"

"If I have to use every penny I have. We'll get Samuel that pardon."

A little past noon the next day, Michaela walked into the sheriff's office in downtown Atlanta. The room was bigger than she expected and busy with people milling around, talking and laughing. One man in a corner shouted at another.

Summoning her strength, she straightened her shoulders and walked over to a police officer who sat quietly behind a desk.

"Excuse me, sir, but could you possibly help me? I'd like to see my husband."

The man looked up at her and wrinkled his upper lip, causing his full mustache to wiggle like a caterpillar. "That depends. What's he in for?" he drawled as he looked her over carefully.

"Ah . . ." Michaela had to think quickly. She wasn't sure exactly what the charge was. "I believe he seeks a pardon from the president. His name is Samuel Lawrence."

A silly grin appeared on the man's face. "Oh, that one." He laughed under his breath, which annoyed Michaela. "Yep, you can see him. It's not every day we have a man walk in off the streets and say he's turning himself in for his war crimes." Still laughing, he pushed back his chair and stood up. "War crimes, hell. So he killed a few Yankees. No harm done as far as I can see, but the sheriff said to lock him up.'' He walked from behind the desk. ''You'll have to leave your purse in here, ma'am. I'll take care of it for you.''

She lifted her chin a little higher, more piously. ''Certainly,'' she said in a tight voice, and handed him her velvet drawstring bag. She didn't like this man's condescending manner. And since when was there no harm done in killing a man, be he Yankee or Rebel?

Her lips tight, she followed the officer to the back of the large room and through another door. The passageway was narrow and dark. Each small window they passed was open, but there was no sign of a breeze to cleanse the hot, musky-smelling air of the jail.

''He's in here,'' the officer called over his shoulder with a smirk on his face as they stood in front of a locked door. ''We had to put him in the back cell where we keep the real dangerous killers.'' He chuckled.

Michaela would have liked to slap that silly grin off the man's face, but she knew she'd never get to see Samuel if she did that. Instead, she smiled falsely and said in an unusually thick accent, ''I'd like to see my husband alone, if you don't mind.''

He rubbed his chin, then moved his hand up to smooth his overgrown mustache. ''It's not our policy.''

''I'm sure it isn't. And I understand why.'' She smiled sweetly once again and held up her hands. ''But as you can see, I have no weapon to give him.''

''I guess I can do it. Since he turned himself in and all. But don't you tell a soul.''

She placed a finger over her lips. ''Not a one.''

He unlocked the heavy wooden door and opened it.

Michaela stepped inside a large room containing three separate cells. Samuel stood in one of the barred cells, with his foot propped on the cot, looking out the window. He didn't turn around, although she was sure he must have heard the loud squeaking when the door opened.

For a moment she stood, looking at him through the bars that separated them, drinking in the sight of him. She loved him more at this moment than she ever had. He had turned himself in because of her. He didn't really care whether or not the government pardoned him. She knew he wanted her to forgive him. She walked up to the bars and grasped them. The iron was hard, cold.

"Samuel."

He spun around, disbelief registering in his eyes, annoyance on his lips. "You shouldn't have come here," he said.

"I wanted to see you," she answered in the same quiet tone he'd used. She wanted to touch him, too. All those times she'd pushed him away came back to haunt her. Right now she'd give anything to be held in his arms. "I have many things to tell you."

"Go away, Michaela." He turned back to the window. "You shouldn't be here."

She pressed her forehead against the cold bars, trying to get closer. "I love you, Samuel."

In an instant Samuel flattened his body against the bars and wrapped his hands around her fingers. "Dammit, Michaela. Why didn't you tell me that two days ago?" His eyes were intense, his lips wet and desirable.

His touch warmed her fingers. "I don't have an easy answer. I want you to get out of here and come home to me. I've been childish and foolish. Why didn't you come to me before you did this?''

"I've been coming to you since I buried Tully." His voice was husky with emotion, his eyes caressed her face.

Michaela lowered her lashes. She'd been such a fool. "I know. I'm sorry. Ever since we buried Tully, I've felt so compromised. I felt you were a criminal and you'd turned me into a murderer."

"Don't say that. You're not a killer." He squeezed her hands, agony on his face.

"I know that now. I know I didn't really have a choice. I'd do it again."

"Oh, God." Samuel let go of her hands and slipped his arms through the bars and around her back. Michaela did the same. It was torture to be so close yet not be able to feel his warm body next to hers. The iron bars pressed into her breasts as she tried to get closer.

"Papa told me the story of the gold. I can't believe I was putting all the blame on you when all the time we were living off stolen money."

"Don't think about that anymore. Padraic told me you were starving. He did the right thing. He wouldn't have received a warm reception from the North or the South if he'd shown up with a bag full of gold."

She looked up at him. "Thank you for finding my mother's locket." Her eyes clouded. "I thought it was lost forever."

"It should never have been taken away from you."

Even though his hands felt good on her back, she pulled away from him. "Samuel, can you get out of here? Now?"

He brushed her cheek with the back of his hand. "Sorry, love. I'll be here until the president signs that pardon."

"But that's not right!" she pleaded. "Many other Confederates have received amnesty without spending time in jail."

He moistened his lips. His eyes traveled lovingly over her face. "I have to do this, Michaela. I never felt right about the things I did during the war. I hate like hell to think that you or anyone else will associate me with the likes of Rufus Tully."

"Samuel, you don't have to get a pardon for me—"

"Shh, let me finish. It's true when I first turned myself in I was hoping that if the government pardoned me for the robberies, you would, too. Now I realize it's more than that. Once I get that pardon and have the indictments of treason against me disposed of, I'll be free of that damned war."

Michaela's heart swelled with love for her husband. He was a gentleman in every sense of the word. She had come too close to losing him. "I love you, Samuel," she whispered, her eyes glistening with tears of happiness.

"I love you, Michaela," he echoed as the door opened and the guard stepped inside.

"Time's up!"

Twenty

"**M**ICHAELA, how wonderful to see you again," Cabot said as Bessie showed him into the parlor of the Brennen house where Michaela was waiting. "Your bruises are healing nicely."

"Yes, they are. Thank you for coming so quickly, Cabot." Michaela extended her hand, and he gave it a perfunctory kiss.

"I wasn't surprised to hear you're staying at your father's. The news of Samuel is about. If every Confederate could be as noble as your husband and turn himself in and pay his debt to society, we would truly be on our way to reform."

Refusing to be upset by Cabot's pomposity, Michaela cleared her throat loudly. She could be making a big mistake in talking about this with Cabot. "Yes, that's why I wanted to see you today. Please sit down. Would you care for a cup of tea or coffee?'' she asked.

''Mmm . . . I don't think so.''

Michaela moved her dress so Cabot could join her on the small sofa. ''I asked you over, Cabot, because I need your help.''

Cabot smiled, and Michaela knew why she was once attracted to him. He was handsome, intelligent, and quite entertaining when he wanted to be. But Samuel was the only man she wanted.

''You know I'd do most anything for you. You said this had something to do with Samuel. What's on your mind?''

Michaela brushed her skirt, taking time to choose her words carefully. ''You know, of course, that Samuel has asked the president for a pardon.''

''Indeed. I'm aware of it.''

''Unfortunately the request has to come from the governor, and he is out of town at the moment. I know this because Papa went directly to meet with him and was told as much. Papa asked the governor's aide if he would send the appeal on to the president, but the man remembered that he had asked Papa for a donation to the governor's campaign and that Papa had refused. The aide refused to help. I want Samuel pardoned and released as soon as possible.'' She looked directly into his eyes. ''Is there any way you can help?''

''Are you forgetting that Samuel is a Democrat and that I'm a Republican?''

''No.'' Michaela's voice was strong and sure. ''That's the very reason I came to you. President Johnson is

Republican. Can you make the appeal for Samuel to him?''

Cabot rose from the sofa and turned his back on her. Michaela jumped up and grabbed his arm, forcing him to look at her once again. ''If anyone can speed up this ridiculously slow process, you can. Please help me, Cabot.''

He studied her face. ''That's asking a lot, Michaela.''

''I know. I don't have anyone else to turn to.'' Her eyes didn't waver.

''All right, I'll do it, but I need your promise of a favor in return?''

''A favor? What kind?'' she asked, suddenly not sure she could trust him. His doubt had turned to confidence too quickly.

''A favor to be named at a later date.''

''But it isn't right for you not to tell me what I'm promising,'' she argued, feeling a stab of unease at his request.

''That's the way it has to be. All in good time. Once I have your promise, I'll go to work immediately to secure Samuel's pardon for treason and war crimes.''

Michaela watched Cabot's blue eyes. He was serious. She had to give her word first. Her shoulders sagged a little. She suspected he would ask her to be unfaithful to Samuel. He was obviously still angry that she had chosen Samuel over him. Cringing inside, she took a deep breath. Did she have a choice?

''You have my promise. You'll get your favor when Samuel is free.''

Cabot gave her a sugar-coated smile. ''Splendid.''

* * *

Samuel slowed his horse to a walk as the lights of Twin Willows came into view. Shifting the reins into one hand, he touched the pocket of his vest with the other. The piece of paper was still there. Clemency had been granted; he'd taken the oath. He glanced up at his bedroom window and saw that a light still burned. Michaela hadn't gone to sleep yet. His heart swelled with love, and he spurred his horse into a gallop.

He'd sent Michaela home earlier in the day, thinking it could be weeks before he heard from the president. For a week she'd been running back and forth from the jail to her father's house, and he knew she needed to rest. The only way he'd convinced her to leave was to say he was worried about his mother and wanted Michaela to check on her. Now he was glad he'd done that. Coming home to Michaela and Twin Willows was a dream come true.

When he neared the barn, Samuel walked the horse once again. He didn't want to ride in and disturb the household. He hoped everyone else was asleep. He wanted to slip inside and upstairs to Michaela. He could wait until morning to see his mother and Davia.

Quietly he dismounted and reached to open the barn door.

"Hold it! Or I'll pump you full of dis buckshot." Samuel heard Henry but couldn't see him. He smiled. Henry had obviously heard him ride up and was ready to accost anyone who approached.

"You going to shoot me, Henry, or help me get this horse rubbed down?"

"Mr. Lawrence! I didn't knows it was you. It's too dark out here. Did you break outta de jailhouse or they let you go?'' Henry came from the side of the barn and helped Samuel open the door.

Samuel chuckled. ''They let me go, Henry.''

''I'm shore glad you'z here. That corn's goin' to be ready to pull next week.'' Henry struck a match and lit the wick of the lantern. ''Yessir, I'z shore glad to seez you.''

''Did Michaela get home all right?'' he asked as he loosened the saddle cinch and buckle.

''Yessir. She got home befo' supper, and she patched everything up with Miss Davia. They ain't gonna fight no more.''

Samuel's hands went still, and he looked at Henry. ''What do you mean?''

Henry's eyes widened and whitened. ''I suppose I'z best not tell no more iff'n you ain't heared about it.''

''I suppose you'd best tell me everything,'' Samuel answered as he heaved the saddle off his horse and threw it across the stall gate. It seemed Michaela had forgotten to tell him about this incident.

''No, sir. I ain't gettin' in no business ain't mine.'' He shook his head vigorously.

Samuel's voice remained low but firm. ''What happened?''

Rubbing his gray-whiskered chin, Henry capitulated with a sigh. ''Well, Miss Davia and yore missus had a big fight when they heared you done got yoreself in de jailhouse. They wuz kickin', bitin', scratchin', and rollin' all over de floor.''

''Damn.'' Samuel took a deep breath. It would be difficult to get the whole story out of Davia or Michaela, and Henry wasn't much help.

"They'z all right now. Like I'z said. They ain't gonna fight no mo'."

Samuel pushed his hair back over his head with both hands. This wasn't good news. If he had to guess, he'd bet Davia was the one who'd started it. The little spitfire. She was going to be a handful for any man who had the guts to court her. On the other hand, he didn't like the idea of Davia fighting Michaela. He didn't want anyone hurting his wife, including his sister.

"Who won?" Samuel had to ask.

"The missus." Henry looked at Samuel and broke into a wide grin that showed gleaming white teeth.

"Good." Samuel grinned, too. "Do you have any soap around here, Henry? I want to go down to the pond and wash the stench of that jail off before I go upstairs."

Still grinning, Henry said, "I'll beez right back. And don't you worry 'bout yore missus. She can handle yore sistah."

Samuel spent more time in the water than he intended. He scrubbed his scalp until it tingled. The water felt so good after being shut up in jail for more than a week. That was a place he never wanted to see the inside of again. A man could go crazy being shut up in a cell day and night.

Thoughts of Michaela lured him out of the cool water. Not bothering with his shirt, he stepped back into his pants for the walk to the house. If he were lucky, he could sneak upstairs and into bed with Michaela before she awakened. The image of her lying soft and warm in bed made him grow hard, and he picked up his pace.

It was easier than he'd expected to enter the house, but he was startled to find his bedroom door locked. He cursed silently when he remembered Michaela always locked her bedroom door, something she'd learned to do as a child. Samuel ran a hand through his wet hair and down his bare chest.

He knocked lightly on the door and watched the crack for the light to come on. Holding his breath, he knocked again, a little louder this time. He let out a trembling sigh of relief when the light sprang out of the darkness.

"Who is it?" she asked.

To his surprise, Samuel found he was shaking. On the other side of that door was the woman he loved above all others, and she was his. He put his lips to the opening and whispered, "Samuel. Let me in."

The door flew open and Michaela threw herself into his arms. He immediately silenced her cries of happiness with a hard, demanding kiss. With his foot he shut the door as quietly as possible, then carried her to the bed and lay down beside her.

"I don't want anyone to know I'm here tonight," he whispered. "Tonight is for us."

"Samuel, how did you get here?" she asked as her hands ran up and down his chest.

She was so lovely with her dark hair spread across the white pillow, shining in the dim light of the lamp. Her green eyes sparkled with love and happiness.

"The telegram came late this afternoon. I took the oath and received the pardon."

"Oh, Samuel." She hugged him close to her warm body. "I love you. I'm so glad you're home."

They kissed passionately, and hunger rose inside Samuel. Damn, he loved her so much. "I've missed you," he whispered between deep kisses. "Let me look at you."

He raised his head, letting his gaze caress her face while his hand smoothed her hair away from her face. "The bruises are almost gone," he said huskily, and she answered with a nod.

With skilled hands he untied the three ribbons that held the front of her cotton gown together and pushed the panels away from her breasts. Below the swell of the soft mounds he saw a faint scar from the rope burns when Tully had tied her to the tree. He felt a lump in his throat and wished again he'd been the one to kill the bastard.

He looked back to her eyes, and she was loving him with them. He was on fire with wanting her.

"Michaela," he whispered, every muscle in his body trembling. "I've got to know if you've truly forgiven me for being a part of those robberies. I have a pardon from the president, but what about yours?"

She reached up and caressed his cheek. "I was the one in the wrong, Samuel. I was judging you instead of trying to understand what you were going through at the time. You can't forgive a crime that was never committed."

Samuel smiled and kissed her lips tenderly. "I think we've both learned a lot about pardons. I love you, Michaela."

"And I love you."

Samuel shook off his clothes, then helped Michaela discard her gown. He slipped beneath the sheet and into her arms.

The pinkish brown tips of her breasts were hard and thrusting toward him. He wet his lips and bent his head to taste her. Groaning with desire, he cupped her breast with his hand and pulled more of it into his mouth. God had given Michaela back to him, and he felt like the luckiest damn man in the world.

"Sam, why didn't you wake me last night?" Davia rushed into the room without knocking and halted beside the bed.

Michaela pulled the sheet up around her neck, hoping Davia wouldn't know she was naked beneath the covers.

Samuel rubbed his eyes and sat up. "Haven't I told you never to enter my room without knocking?" he said with annoyance.

Davia looked from Samuel to Michaela. It was clear she was suppressing a giggle, and Michaela knew it was because she'd caught her in a state of undress.

"It's well past noon, Sam, and Cabot Peabody is downstairs waiting for you. He told Mama and me everything. He's so smart and so handsome." Davia rolled her eyes and lifted her head.

Michaela recognized the very words she'd used to describe Cabot. But suddenly she didn't think of him as handsome. He'd obviously come for the favor she'd promised. She hadn't expected him to ask for it so soon. And for him to come all the way to Twin Willows had her more than a little worried. What could he possibly want? What was she going to do? How could she tell Samuel she'd promised to return a favor?

"I don't give a damn about who's here. Don't open that door until you get permission." Samuel remained firm.

"I'm sorry, Sam. I won't do it again." Davia clasped her hands in front of her, not the least bit worried about his harsh tone. "Now will you get dressed and come downstairs? Cabot says he must get back to Atlanta soon.''

''What the hell is he doing here, anyway?''

Samuel looked at Michaela, and she felt as if guilt were written all over her face. How was she going to explain to Samuel that she'd promised Cabot anything he wanted if he could secure the pardon as quickly as possible? Should she tell him now or wait and see what Cabot was going to say? Suddenly she didn't feel very well.

''You don't look well,'' Samuel said, and reached over and brushed her long hair away from her shoulders. ''You stay in bed. I'll go down and see what he wants. He probably has more papers for me to sign. Go tell him I'll be right down, Muffin. And close the door behind you.''

Michaela threw the covers aside as soon as Davia was gone. ''No. No, I'll come with you. I'm fine.''

''Are you sure?'' He smiled. ''You look a little pale.''

''I'm fine. Really.'' But she wasn't. Her stomach was jumping and her head was pounding. She had no idea what Cabot wanted. She had to be there.

A few minutes later Samuel and Michaela walked into the parlor to greet Cabot. Evelyn rushed to her son and hugged and kissed him, tears in her eyes.

While Samuel assured his mother that he'd eaten well, Michaela watched Cabot trying to fend off Davia. His face gave no hint as to what he had in mind as his reward for helping Samuel. Well, Samuel was home. She'd given her word. Whatever she had to do, she would.

Evelyn excused herself to go for coffee and insisted a reluctant Davia go with her. As soon as the three of them were alone, Michaela cleared her throat and announced,

"Samuel, I promised Cabot a favor in exchange for his help in obtaining your pardon. I assume you're here because of that, Cabot?"

"Oh, indeed I am," he said with a smile.

"What kind of favor?" Samuel asked, his brown eyes darting from Michaela to Cabot and back again.

Michaela cleared her throat. "I'm not sure. He didn't tell me what he wanted."

"What? You mean you made a promise and you don't know what it is?" Anger hardened Samuel's words and glinted in his eyes.

She looked up at him with love shining in her eyes. "It didn't matter to me. I wanted you out of that jail."

"It matters to me. I—"

"Samuel, Michaela, please just listen to what I have to say, then you can go on with your argument," Cabot interrupted.

Samuel glowered at him. "All right. Talk fast."

"The favor I want is your full political support."

Michaela gasped with relief. A smile lit her face. How stupid of her to ever think Cabot would demand anything else. Politics had always been the most important thing in his life.

"Are you out of your mind?" Samuel took a few menacing steps toward Cabot, but Cabot stood his ground.

"No. I could use your support to win the election. By helping you, I have proven that I want to help facilitate the restoration of the South into the Union and promote goodwill among Republicans and Democrats."

Samuel inched closer, a scowl on his face. "Get out of here."

"No, Samuel!" Michaela took his arm and forced him

to look at her. She loved him and wanted him to see it in
her eyes. "I gave my word."

He softened. "Why?"

"At the time, I didn't have a choice."

Samuel opened his mouth to speak, but those words
were an irrefutable argument. He reached down and
kissed his wife instead.

"If Michaela gave her word, Cabot, I'll stand by it."
He extended his hand. "You have my support."

Cabot shook Samuel's hand with generous enthusiasm.
"Excellent. I'll be back in touch soon. Now I must hurry.
I've been here too long as it is." He headed for the door,
then turned back and said, "Do say good-bye to your
mother and . . . to Davia for me."

Samuel took a step forward, but Michaela slipped into
his arms and asked, "You're not angry with me, are
you?"

He looked lovingly into her eyes, rocking her gently.
"I should be. I'm going to have a hell of a time
explaining why I'm campaigning for a carpetbagger."

Michaela laughed and kissed her husband's neck, breathing his scent deeply into her lungs. She'd never get
enough of him. "Why don't we go back upstairs to
bed . . . and just stay there."

"Mmm . . . That's exactly what I was thinking." Samuel
pressed close to her. "By the way, what's this I hear
about you and Davia fighting?"

"Oh, it's not worth telling about. There are no hard
feelings between us. We both love you very much."

"Is she old enough to get married?" Samuel asked
with a grin on his face.

"Not yet," she answered with a smile. "Besides, by

the time she's married and gone we should have our own little ones running around the house worrying us.''

"You're not—"

"No, not yet." She laughed lightly and hugged him. "But when we do have a son, I think we'll name him Samuel Cabot Lawrence."

A frown crossed his face. "Over my dead body. No son of mine will ever carry *his* name." He growled and lifted her into his arms.

"Have you no appreciation for the man who got you out of jail?" she asked in a teasing voice as she combed her fingers through his hair.

"None whatsoever," he declared, and started up the stairs. "As far as I'm concerned, you're the one who got me out of jail." He stopped halfway up and gave her a kiss. "And now I'm going to say thank you in a way you'll never forget."

Michaela laid her head on his shoulder and whispered, "I love you, Samuel."

Author's Note

History records that a band of twenty-two Confederate raiders robbed three banks in St. Albans, Vermont, in 1864. Fourteen of the men were later captured in Canada and had most of the money with them, but $114,522 was missing. It is believed they buried it somewhere near the Canadian border.

After his first amnesty proposal in May 1865, President Andrew Johnson subsequently issued two general amnesty statements before issuing his final universal amnesty on December 25, 1868. This gave clemency to all who remained unpardoned, including those who were under indictment on the charge of treason.

GET
LOVESTRUCK!
AND GET STRIKING ROMANCES FROM POPULAR LIBRARY'S BELOVED AUTHORS

Watch for these exciting romances in the months to come:

October 1990
PASSION'S CHOICE by Gloria Dale Skinner

November 1990
EMERALD FIRE by Laurie Grant

December 1990
AND HEAVEN TOO by Julie Tetel

January 1991
INTIMATE CONNECTIONS by Joanna Z. Adams

POPULAR LIBRARY